# GREEN TO RED

# GREEN TO RED
## *Dennis Sheehan*

TATE PUBLISHING
AND ENTERPRISES, LLC

*Green to Red*
Copyright © 2016 by Dennis Sheehan. All rights reserved.

No part of this publication may be reproduced, stored in a retrieval system or transmitted in any way by any means, electronic, mechanical, photocopy, recording or otherwise without the prior permission of the author except as provided by USA copyright law.

This novel is a work of fiction. Names, descriptions, entities, and incidents included in the story are products of the author's imagination. Any resemblance to actual persons, events, and entities is entirely coincidental.

The opinions expressed by the author are not necessarily those of Tate Publishing, LLC.

Published by Tate Publishing & Enterprises, LLC
127 E. Trade Center Terrace | Mustang, Oklahoma 73064 USA
1.888.361.9473 | www.tatepublishing.com

Tate Publishing is committed to excellence in the publishing industry. The company reflects the philosophy established by the founders, based on Psalm 68:11,
*"The Lord gave the word and great was the company of those who published it."*

Book design copyright © 2016 by Tate Publishing, LLC. All rights reserved.
*Cover design by Bill Francis Peralta*
*Interior design by Jomar Ouano*

Published in the United States of America

ISBN: 978-1-68301-294-8
Fiction / Action & Adventure
16.03.10

# Foreword

Most people in developed societies take freedom for granted.

They are born with it, accept it, and live with it every day of their lives but occasionally have scant regard for its true origins. The harsh reality is that freedom is often fought for and too easily given away. It is a concept misunderstood here and there.

Often, one finds an immediately recognizable connection between a country's armed services fighting in a war zone for a freedom of some kind or other. In some places, there is a constant battle to preserve such freedom in ways and means that the general population is usually unaware of.

Until it is too late.

Indeed, freedom can be won on the split-second turn of events on a battlefield, but lost over the years by a denial of its true importance.

When I was asked to write a foreword for this book, my first image of Dennis Sheehan came to mind. He, craggy-faced, dressed in a casual leather blouson with an open-necked shirt, and she, in the background, representing freedom and standing proud on Liberty Island in New York Harbor.

The Statue of Liberty, a gift to the United States from the people of France, is of a robed female figure representing the Roman goddess of freedom, who bears a torch and a *tabula ansata* (a tablet evoking the law) upon which is inscribed the date of the American Declaration of Independence, July 4, 1776. A broken chain lies at her feet. The statue has become an icon of freedom representing the United States.

And so, from my home one full mile, and not a step more, from the remnants of Hadrian's Wall, in Cumbria, England, I acknowledge a quiet understanding for the reasons countries are separated by walls, disconnected by religion, and divided by culture. I can wholeheartedly live with the issues raised by the author, Dennis Sheehan, and his coconspirator, the Roman goddess of freedom, despite the separation of our lands by only a huge pond.

Many good authors might deal with freedom at the microeconomic level and try to dissect its meaning in an acceptable work of fiction centered around a couple of page-turning heroes attempting to be part of a fast-moving tale of pointless murder and limited plot.

Sadly, Dennis Sheehan is not a good author; he is a great author.

Dennis does not explode a bomb on the first page. Rather, he plants a slow fuse on the first page and allows it to burn throughout the work as he pulls the reader into the deep and meaningful conspiracy in play as he takes them on the journey he intends.

There are few fiction writers who would score well on global economic politics and the conflicts that seek to undermine our social order. Dennis Sheehan does so admirably as he uses his lifelong experience in the world of international trade. We capture the voyage from his early days on the shipping docks of Brooklyn—through Libya, South America, and Russia—to the People's Republic of China.

In China, Dennis wrote the basis for what is now the "Joint Venture Rules and Regulations of the People's Republic." In his time overseas, he became an expert in international finance and the privatization of communist countries. In 1987, Dennis went to Russia to help develop a plan for the privatization of the cooperatives and collectives. He has worked with government officials from Russia, Finland, Holland, France, Italy, Germany, the United Kingdom, and the United States. It is little wonder that his novel *Green to Red* penetrates behind the scenes of a fictitious global society where the Green Party is in the process of usurping the very core of independent societies across the globe. His cleverly constructed characters all have a part to play in this masterpiece of a socioeconomic political spy thriller.

We witness elements of the Green Party seeking by clever—but often corrupt—means, global media manipulation matched only by a long enduring attack on the money and energy markets that anchor so many democratic systems in the world.

In the world that Dennis has lived and worked, he has rubbed shoulders with the good, the bad, and the ugly at all levels of society. His gritty account of a global contest involving a communist party that has infiltrated the Green Party at every level of humanity will shock you to the very core with its truly realistic possibilities and technically astute plot.

A taste of Dennis Sheehan's macabre: "Where a man sells his soul to the devil, where congressmen, senators, and lobbyists end up on Satan's payroll." "The political climate in the States is not good. The most powerful man on the globe has been elected by a conspiracy of money, media, and muscle; and there's an unholy alliance in place." "The Democrats have been handed over to very liberal socialists, and the population is fighting back. But they could lose all."

Impeachment is a short step from a new world order when world domination of the Green Party by the Communist Party is mooted in this exciting and intriguing work of fiction. But I'll let you into a secret; some of these true-to-life characters live and work in the yachting industry.

And it's not all plain sailing.

This is a commendable piece of literary fiction with a clear and concise message written by a globe-trotting master craftsman at the top of his game.

Tony Scougal, Special Branch, England NW, Retired

# Prologue

John and Rebecca were seated in a small room in the Great Hall of the People located in Tiananmen Square, the center of Beijing. A long-awaited press conference would start in less than twenty minutes, hopefully ending their year-long struggle to survive. Both expected that the information Rebecca had uncovered would guarantee their safety once it was shared with the world.

Feeling content, John turned toward Rebecca. Just as he was about to say something, a nearby window shattered, and a red mist filled the room. Rebecca's head flew back as her body was thrown to the floor. Seconds later, Chinese security people ran into the room. John was on his knees, holding her lifeless body in his arms. They could see that his face was contorted, as a silent scream erupted from the core of his being. Within moments, John was rushed to Capital Hospital, catatonic with grief.

A Chinese minister held the press conference shortly thereafter. The implications of the information sent devastating shockwaves around the world. The world populace requested the resignations and the arrests of several world leaders, politicians, high-level police officials, and multinational corporate CEOs. Sadly, the intensity of the outcry would diminish with every twelve-hour news cycle. It would probably be forgotten within a few weeks.

John was still under sedation when his close friend and employee, Chong, arrived to take him back to Hong Kong. After speaking to the doctors, Chong thought it best to take care of the funeral arrangements for Rebecca first. John was still numb with shock, unable to embrace the loss of the love of his life.

# 1

YK escorted Ascot Chen out of the soundproof atrium, through the garden, avoiding the staff. Chen's car was waiting just inside the gate.

"Ascot, your flight leaves in two hours. I am delighted with the success of the Zurich project. I am sure Manheim will be pleased with the information you have for him."

Ascot began to speak, but YK put up his hand. "You don't have much time, make sure Manheim gets the details before his meeting with Saris."

Chen sat in the backseat as he rode down L Street in the heart of Jakarta's red-light district. He looked out the window. The hookers were as plentiful as leaves on a tree, all hoping to meet a mark, a man that would take them from this place. It had happened to a lucky few. That thought gave hope to all the rest.

Once inside the first-class lounge, at the airport, he handed his ticket, along with a hundred-dollar bill inside the envelope, to the attractive young woman behind the counter. "I am in seat 2A. Please try to arrange it so that the seat next to mine is vacant."

"Yes, sir, I'll try. May I get you a drink? You have half an hour before boarding."

"Thank you, I'll have a Cognac, Hennessey five-star, please."

He walked to the gate and arrived just as first-class seating was called.

Chen was sitting comfortably in his seat as the stewardess delivered another Cognac to him. The plane taxied toward the runway.

He began thinking of the last year and how those events led him to the current situation.

*Such a shame, I had to have that young woman killed. I had no alternative, what a pity.* He shrugged. *But it was only business. It had cost a lot, too much, I had underestimated her protector. What was his name? Ah yes, John Moore.*

Ascot smiled to himself. *Moore was a worthy opponent, and I allowed him to live. It might have been a mistake, but I still think he might have some future value.* He shifted in his seat. *Enough of that, I have to come to terms with the situation at hand. YK and Manheim have made a serious mistake joining forces with this messianic psychopath, Aristotle Saris. It's not my place to tell them, I'm only an employee, but they're making a catastrophic error. I would like to get out now, but they'll never let me go, I know too much. Even though YK is my cousin, he'd have me killed in a heartbeat, and if he didn't, Michael Manheim would.*

The Cognac made him drowsy. He nodded off and was awakened when the captain announced they were landing.

The car arrived at the Steigenberger Hotel Herrenhof at Herrengasse 10 Vienna, Austria, Michael Manheim's European office and residence. Manheim was the CEO of the Liddo Group in the United States.

Chen took a private elevator that led directly to Manheim's office.

"Ascot, I'm delighted to see you. I hope all is well?"

"Yes, Michael, everything is fine, but I'm a bit tired. I flew from Zurich to Jakarta yesterday, and I'm back in Austria today.

*This bastard knows I don't like to be called Michael.*

"Michael, everything went well in Zurich. Peter Tsillman is our exclusive account manager at the bank. He will set up the transaction so that it will not actually run through the bank, nor will it be traceable to Liddo when completed. We will acquire all the credits, the total value will be ten billion dollars."

"Ascot, this is great news, that's the last piece I needed to make this work. I have a meeting with the Saris people in twenty minutes. I'd better leave now, but would you like to have dinner with me later this evening?"

"I'd love to, Michael, but I can't, I'm already booked on a flight, it's leaving in two hours."

Manheim knew Chen would refuse the dinner invitation, so he said nothing more. Putting on his coat, he said, "That's too bad. I have a car waiting. You can drop me off at the meeting, my driver will take you to the airport."

"That is very kind of you, Michael."

They got in, and Chen gave Manheim some of the subtleties of the transaction while they drove to Saris's office.

....................

The meeting was just about to start when Manheim arrived. Saris loved drama; the room was dark with lights shining only at the podium and at the high desk where Saris positioned himself. As soon as he saw Manheim, he brought the meeting to order.

"Gentlemen, we have all traveled here to report on the successes that are bringing us closer to our ultimate goal. We will have total control—there will be no more superpowers, no more democracy. It is not as if we wish to govern or take over any governments. We will simply control the money supply, a global currency controlled by strong successful bankers and industrialists. Baron Rothschild said something apropos many years ago: 'I don't care who writes the laws, give me control of the money supply and I will control the country.'

"Our small group will define the realities of life for everyone—there will be no more war, no more power struggles. Everyone will have the same decent life, and they will never know that they are working to serve us. We have almost everything in place. We've accomplished this without turmoil or bloodshed.

"Under the guise of environmental protection and global warming, we've brought the world together to fight an imaginary enemy: climate change.

"In the past, our only obstacle has been the United States. Too much wealth and too many markets are held in the hands of individuals in the USA. We need a truly socialist-regulated society for our plan to work there. You have all seen our successes in Europe. It has taken time, but we are closer to our goals in the US as well. With that said, let me introduce you to Michael Manheim from the United States."

"Thank you, Aristotle. As you all know, we control the US media. I think we have done an outstanding job using it to make the 'green' issue all important and to install several presidents and vice presidents to push the agenda further. We have vilified the oil companies and the energy companies. We are now working on a strategy to do the same with the banks and the communication companies. Government regulation and the unions have put the automotive industry under our control. The money center banks have been weakened by low interest rates and regulations. I believe we are almost ready on our end."

After a small round of applause, Saris introduced the next speaker.

"Let me now introduce you to Simon Atutu of South Africa."

"Our TV and radio stations have been promoting civil unrest and blaming BP for all of the pollution in South Africa. The issue of blood diamonds has been the center of our plan to show that the exploitation of our resources has led our people to the brink of starvation. My uncle, working for the UN, has helped foster these issues and has given us worldwide credibility. I believe we are ready."

"Excellent," Saris interrupted, "we will now hear from our European delegate, Ian Brady of the UK."

"Good morning, everyone, I have used the newspapers, as well as British and American cable TV, to spread the word. The Green

Party in Britain is now stronger than the Labor Party and the Tories combined. The Green Party has convinced our growing Muslim population that voting for the Green candidate will enable them to live in Britain under their own Sharia Law. The Iraq and Afghan wars have worked in our favor—the exploitation of oil, and all that. The next election is in six months, and the Green Party is a certain winner. I think we have done our part."

The rest of the group—representatives from Indonesia, Mexico, Brazil, Chile, and Venezuela—had similar reports.

Aristotle thought about his plan for a moment before continuing; after all, he had just cornered the world platinum market and made one of the largest fortunes ever amassed by one man. *I am almost there. I am going to take over the world.*

"Mike, have you been able to set up the mechanism to trade the emission credits?"

The response was affirmative. He felt compelled to go over the plan once more while he had his group assembled.

"The UN, the US, and the EU have issued ten billion dollars' worth of emission credits. Every country in the Western world has forced their energy producers to reduce the amount of greenhouse gases emitted from their plants by fifty percent over the next five years. These credits allow the holders to release more than the fifty percent of allotted greenhouse gases from their stacks, but they must use credits for any amount above fifty percent. The credits will only cover them for the five-year period, and then they will have to pay fines, which would be cost prohibitive.

"Almost all of the coal-fired-generation plants in the Western world have been closed down. The cleaner, natural gas is about forty US dollars more per megawatt of production than burning coal. This, in conjunction with the fact that the existing producers have shut down their coal plants and have had to further reduce their output to reach the fifty percent threshold, has driven energy prices to historic highs. We have been buying the emission credits issued by our respective governments and are now in control of most of them. We would like to thank the British Labor Party and the American Democratic Party for their cooperation in this effort. We will now commit to purchasing all of the ten billion dollars' worth of credits, which are now being issued by the United Nations, the US, and the EU. When all of the credits are ours, the Liddo Group and their network of subsidiaries will begin to purchase all of the coal-fired power generation plants for pennies on the dollar. We will use the emission credits to burn coal in our plants and drive energy prices down, which will put all of the existing energy companies either out of business or under our control.

"If we control a major stake in global energy, we can hold entire countries ransom.

"As a precautionary measure, we have also funded supremacy groups around the world. In the US, we have arranged it so that the government funds community groups and activists. This will allow us to have standing armies in place internally in every country to take care of dissenters and opposing political organizations. We already control the media and the unions in most countries. Gentlemen, this 'green' movement will truly save the world—for us!"

After thunderous applause, Manheim left the meeting. *This guy is a certifiable lunatic, but if we pull this off, we'll be wealthier and more powerful than ever. YK is right. We help him achieve his goal, and then I kill him. The world will go back to normal, and we'll reap the profits.*

# 2

## Hong Kong

John finished shaving; he cleaned the shaving cream from his face and looked into the mirror. *Shit, I look ten years older than I did a year ago.* He could see the rage in his own eyes. *I'll get those bastards. I don't care what it takes, I'm going to get them.* At that moment, he realized his life had changed forever. He went into the bedroom, picked up the phone, and called Chong.

"I'm home. Can you get here in half an hour?"

..........................................

He had just poured himself a cup of coffee when the doorbell rang.

"Chong, thanks for coming over on such short notice."

Chong Li smiled. "No problem, boss, I wasn't doing anything anyway."

Chong followed John into the living room.

"Chong, sit down. I have something to tell you."

"You're not going to fire me, boss, are you?"

John sighed. "No, I'm not going to fire you, but I'm leaving Hong Kong. Rebecca was killed over four months ago. I can't take it anymore. The Hong Kong I once loved is gone for me. I'm finding it more difficult to get through the day. I've just got to get out of here. I'm leaving you in charge. You are now CEO of Sailcraft–Asia."

John handed Chong a manila envelope.

"Here's a bonus, your new business cards, and a letter of authority. Go to Woo & Woo solicitors tomorrow and have the paperwork authenticated. I've already given them instructions. Use your bonus money to buy some new suits. I want you looking good since you'll be representing the company."

"Boss, are you sure about this? Why don't you just go home for a while and think about it? You're just depressed, maybe a little time at home and you'll snap out of it."

John looked at his friend. "No, Chong, I can't stay. It's just too hard for me. I loved Rebecca…too many bad memories about this last year. My bags are packed, and I leave for home in three hours. I was hoping you'd drive me to the airport. I'll fill you in on the way."

Chong drove John to Kai Tak Airport. Chong was visibly upset as John walked into the departure lounge after saying goodbye. While walking through the terminal, John felt overwhelmed. *I'm going to miss Chong. We've been through a lot together. I've only known him for a year, but it feels like a lifetime.* John couldn't believe how bad he felt. Trying to rid himself of this feeling, he thought of Peter, his partner and lifelong friend. He hadn't seen him in almost eight months, and he was looking forward to their reunion.

# 3

### Coming Home

The flight was long and uneventful. When he arrived in San Francisco, it took about forty-five minutes for John to clear customs, collect his luggage, and get out of the terminal. He spotted Peter and started to shake. A feeling he had never experienced came over him as the past year's events flashed before his eyes.

Peter ran up to him, then stepped back. "John, are you all right?"

"Yeah, I'm fine, just a little tired. Man, is it good to see you!"

Peter hoisted John's bag as they headed to his car. "I'm really sorry for your loss. I know what she meant to you."

John smiled, even as that stake was driven through his heart once again.

"Thanks, Pete. Tell me what's going on. I can't wait to see the place."

Since John had left Sausalito, Peter had acquired the adjoining property and built a new dry dock, allowing him to double the office and design space.

Peter started to fill him in on the additions to Sailcraft. He also talked about the condo he rented for him on the bay.

"I rented it with the option to buy it at a fixed price, about twenty percent below market."

John listened to Peter, but his mind kept drifting back to that horrible day when Rebecca was murdered. He was about to tell Peter something when the car stopped.

"Here it is."

Peter pointed to a nice-looking two-story condo; the front was stuccoed with plenty of windows and a three-car garage. It was right on the bay, complete with a wood deck leading straight down to a boat dock. A boat, "John's Back" painted on the stern, was tied to the dock.

John smiled. "It's great."

"I'm glad you like it. I looked at about ten places before taking this one."

John was impressed, cathedral ceilings and windows everywhere with a fireplace that opened to the living room and the kitchen, bedrooms upstairs. The bedroom had a glass wall looking out over the bay, a skylight that took up half of the ceiling. *I'll be able to study the night sky.*

"Thanks, buddy. This is a lot more than I expected. I love the place."

"I'll let you get settled in. I'll pick you up in the morning and bring you to work. Be ready at eight sharp."

He unpacked, familiarized himself with the place, and spent the rest of the night sitting out on the deck, enjoying the view and the summer breeze.

••••••••••••••••••••••••••••••••••••••

Peter arrived at eight o'clock on the dot. John got into the car. "Hello, Peter, I'm anxious to see what you've done with the expansion."

"We'll be there in a few minutes."

Upon arrival, John was blown away. "Holy shit, you got all this done in a year?"

"Brains and money—plenty of money."

"I'm definitely impressed. I can't believe it. The yard used to be impressive, but now it's beyond imagination."

"Come on in. Let me show you around the place."

Walking through the administration complex and up to the observation tower, which was the prominent structure in the center of the yard, they took the elevator up five stories and entered a comfortable sitting room.

"John, I can't take credit for this, it's all Brad's idea."

"Who's Brad?"

"The young designer I hired. We bring potential clients up here. It's worked great for sales."

From this vantage point, they could see every aspect of production. The original two sheds were still there. Next to them were two new four-hundred-foot-long sheds and a dry dock for repairs with two floating dry docks adjacent. One could accommodate boats up to eighty-seven feet long and the other could take boats up to two hundred feet.

Peter went over the entire layout.

"With the yard and the showroom across the road, we now cover about one hundred and fifty-seven acres. Your retirement is guaranteed. I just received the appraisal last week, the land alone is worth $570 million. We've got a fifty-million-dollar mortgage on the new property, which means we have equity of about $520 million. Not bad for a couple of old tuna fishermen, right?"

John just stared at him.

"Snap out of it. We've been very lucky. If you remember, we had a fifteen-million-dollar mortgage on the original property. I was able to buy the adjoining piece for a song when old man Collins died. I didn't realize that when we picked up that property, it gave us a total of forty-six hundred feet of shoreline. It made the whole parcel worth almost four times what the two parcels were worth separately."

"Holy crap!" was John's only reply.

The elevator door opened, and a young man walked toward them.

"John, this is Brad Bond, our chief designer."

The kid didn't look like he was more than twenty, with a shaved head and an earring, his right arm tattooed from his wrist to his shoulder, wearing a tee shirt and cargo shorts. John was going to say something about his appearance but decided against it, for now.

"I really like your design ideas. You're a talented guy. I'm glad you're working for us and not the competition."

Brad beamed like a schoolkid who had just gotten a gold star.

"I'd like to meet with you in my office as soon as I find out where it is."

Taking John to his office, as Brad followed behind, Peter said, "You get settled in and I'll see you for lunch. I have a few things I've got to get done this morning."

As John looked around his office, he noticed Brad staring at him.

"What you are thinking, Brad?"

"How do you like it? I designed it specifically for you, per Peter's instructions. He told me that efficiency and comfort were imperative for you."

"I couldn't have done better myself. Now, tell me about yourself."

Several hours went by before Peter came in.

"How do you like it?"

"What's not to like? I've been going over everything with Brad. I didn't realize how out of the loop I was. Peter, let's go to lunch. Brad, if it's okay with you, I'd like to have production meetings here in my office every morning for at least a week or so until I catch up."

"That will be my pleasure, sir."

"It's John."

"I'm sorry, sir, I mean, John,"

Over lunch, they discussed the business. It took four hours for Peter to explain everything to John. Peter looked down at his watch; then he jumped up.

"Sorry, John, I got to go, I'm meeting a client in fifteen minutes."

"You go ahead, I'll grab the bill."

John paid the bill and took a cab back to the office.

He sat at his new desk, looked down, and saw car keys with a note: "Hope you like it. It's the black Mercedes convertible in parking slot 1 just outside the building."

John went down to the parking lot and smiled as he looked at a black Mercedes convertible with saddle leather interior. He thought back to the days when he and Peter were working on that tuna boat many years ago. It had earned them the money they needed to build their first boat. He remembered lying on deck at night, exhausted, telling Peter, "When we make it big, I want a Mercedes convertible, black with saddle leather interior." John stood there with a bigger smile on his face. *This is another one I have to thank Peter for.*

In the days that followed, John immersed himself in his work, but the nights were tough. He couldn't sleep, so he'd get dressed and go back to the office in the middle of the night, but that didn't help much. He tried to work, but he was constantly distracted. Thoughts of Rebecca kept coming to mind. *I did everything right, so how did my life get so screwed up?* He finally realized there was no answer to that question.

Peter came into the office early one morning about a month after John had returned and found him deep into a project.

"Hey! It's six a.m. What time did you get here?"

John looked up from his work. "About two."

"What are you trying to do, kill yourself?"

John looked up; his answer actually frightened Peter, "Maybe I am."

Peter studied his old friend with care. "Look, buddy, you've had a bad time, but take a look at everything you've got going for you. Put that stuff down. We're taking the day off."

John knew, at that moment, that he had to leave—perhaps he'd start traveling to see if he could outrun his own thoughts.

They played a round of golf, had a couple of drinks, and went back to John's house to talk. John had set up a makeshift bar on the deck. He started to tell Peter every detail of the events that led up to Rebecca's death. It wasn't until about three in the morning that Peter first spoke.

"Shit, John, I had no idea you went through all of that."

John looked at his friend, staring directly into his eyes.

"The men who are responsible for this are animals. They're the people you and I have elected or supported, and we're the ones who gave them their power. Peter, it's eating me alive. I feel helpless. There's a worldwide network of really bad people who feed on the weaknesses of officials. They've gained the power to do anything, even kill the innocent, and get away with it."

At that moment, Peter realized the torment his friend was going through, but there was nothing he could say to lessen the burden.

Neither of them knew that the same people they were discussing were the people responsible for Sailcraft's recent business growth. They sat quietly for a while, and then Peter got up.

"I'll see you in the office some time tomorrow."

Peter went home, but he couldn't sleep. The story John had told him was so unbelievable, but he knew his friend was not subject to exaggeration. He spent the remainder of the early morning hours developing a plan to help his buddy—if, in fact, he could be helped.

·····················

John was at his desk when Peter stuck his head in the door.

"John, can I speak to you in my office?"

"What's up?"

"I was up all night thinking about what you told me."

John interrupted, "I'm sorry I unloaded on you like that."

"No, that's what friends are for. I'm glad you still consider me a close friend.

"Crap, are you going to start playing the violin now?"

"Don't break my balls. I can still kick your ass."

John just smiled.

"This place is too mundane for you right now. It might be better for you to get over to Zurich and visit Tsillman. He's been selling some boats, but I believe we could do much better in that market."

"I had the same thought about getting out of here. I have some ideas about streamlining the production schedule, reducing production time, and making the overall system more efficient. It should make Brad's work even better."

"Great, how long do you think it'll take?"

"I don't know, maybe a month or two."

John felt better knowing he was going to be leaving soon. He worked almost round the clock for the next month. He was going over some changes with Brad a few days before leaving.

"Brad, your design is pure genius."

"Thanks, John."

"Brad, we're both lucky that I wasn't here when Peter hired you."

"Why?"

"I wouldn't have hired you. Peter is a lot more tolerant than I am."

"What do you mean?"

"You're a true genius, but that Oakland grunge thing you've got going doesn't cut it. I wouldn't have taken you seriously, and we both would've lost. I would've lost a great designer, and you would've lost the opportunity to show off how good you really are. If you want to be taken seriously, you have to look the part."

"Where are you coming from, the sixties?"

"As a matter of fact, yes, but the world is a strange place, and I've learned that people regard you differently when you not only show respect but demand it. It would be hard for you, on a first meeting, to demand respect when you have an earring in your ear and your boxer shorts are hanging out of your pants."

Brad laughed out loud.

"I'll buy you some new clothes if you let your hair grow to a decent length, at least long enough to get a proper haircut. I want you to have more input with the customers, and I need you to look the part. Are you up for it?"

Brad wasn't sure if he was embarrassed or angry, but he agreed.

After buying clothing for Brad in a nearby mall, they went to dinner. John explained why he wanted Brad to have more interaction with the clients.

"Brad, I think that your enthusiasm and design genius will be a great help to Peter in the sales department. The more interaction you have with the clients, the more you will understand their wants and needs, which will enhance what you already do. I'm going to ask Peter to give your raise, one that is appropriate to your new position."

"My new position?"

"Yes, senior design engineer and sales manager."

"Thank you, John, I won't let you down."

"Okay, but no more grunge and lose the earring."

They both laughed and toasted to Brad's new position.

The next morning, John was in Peter's office as a well-dressed young man walked by. "Excuse me, may I help you?"

The young man stopped. "Excuse me, Peter, I didn't catch that."

"Brad?"

"Brad, come on in. Peter and I were just discussing your new position."

The three of them sat down and went over some of Brad's new responsibilities. Brad was grinning from ear to ear when he left the meeting.

Peter turned to John. "Are you sure you have to leave? You're a magician. I could never handle people the way you do. You're already doing a great job with Brad."

"Yeah, you're right, but I would've never hired him. That's why we work so well together."

The night, before John was scheduled to leave, Peter joined him for dinner. They talked about John's goals in Europe and a plan for future production. Hours later, John suggested they head back to his place.

John poured drinks, a Famous Grouse for himself and a full snifter of Five Star Crescent, an Armenian Cognac, for Peter.

They sat and sipped their drinks for almost an hour, in silence. John finally spoke.

"Pete, you've been my friend almost all my life, thanks for that. Your help over the last year and a half, first with Lucy and then the horror with Rebecca went above and beyond. I'll never be able to repay you."

Peter put his head down and shook it, trying to compose himself.

"Pete, please don't say anything and don't go sissy on me."

"Hey, buddy, don't break my chops. You might have learned all that kung fu shit, but I can still kick your ass, don't forget it."

John just laughed with him and said, "Pete, you have made me a bloody fortune and your friendship has made me a truly rich man."

With that, Peter stood up, moved toward John, and put his hand on John's shoulder.

"Have a safe flight tomorrow. Give me a call when you get settled in over there." John started to get up to see him out, but Peter pushed him back into his chair and walked out.

# 4

Within thirty minutes, John had gotten his luggage, cleared customs, and was seated in a cab heading for the St. Gotthard Hotel in Zürich. Twenty minutes later, they pulled up to the curb in front of the hotel. As John paid the driver, a porter opened the door and took his luggage. The manager was waiting for him as he greeted him with the standard.

"Herr Moore, it is so good to have you back at the St. Gotthard." The manager handed John a key and said, "Your regular room has been prepared. I have engaged a driver and an assistant as you requested, available to you at all times."

John said, "Thank you. Is Frederic available?"

Frowning, the manager replied, "I am sorry to say no, he is not. He is in Luzerne at the Hospitality School. Franz will be your driver, and I think he will be to your liking. Your assistant is Iris. She is fluent in several languages and a graduate of the American University in Brussels."

John palmed a hundred-dollar bill and shook the manager's hand.

"Thank you again. I am sure everything will be perfect."

John went to his room and unpacked. He was still wide awake but thought it would be wise to get some rest. He slept for about three hours when awakened by the phone.

"Herr Moore," the exuberant voice on the other end shouted, "this is Peter Tsillman. Welcome to Zurich."

*I never told Tsillman I was coming. How he always knows when I get here and where I can be contacted is beyond me.* John smiled at the thought.

"Peter, how good of you to call! I was going to call you tomorrow, but I am glad you beat me to it. Are you available for dinner this evening?"

"Herr Moore, I am always available for you. Would like to meet me at the Dolder Grand at nine?"

"That would be fine, see you then."

*How the hell does he always know when I get here?*

John left about five and walked across the street to the Vodka Bar, once known as the Bird Watchers Club, before the Russians took it over. It hadn't changed at all, still dark and loud, a typical European club. John ordered a drink, sat by himself, and observed the standard eclectic group of characters that frequented the establishment. He noticed two German businessmen discussing the poor quality of Swiss beer. He saw a Finn sitting a few stools farther down, wearing the typical plaid sports jacket that always seemed too short. On the other side of the bar, there were a couple of young local girls hustling drinks from an Arab; he was trying to look aloof, but obviously he had had too much to drink. John was looking for her, the beautiful but sad Russian woman sitting alone, a fixture in European clubs.

Just as John was about to leave, he heard a melodic voice over his shoulder.

"I have met you before, some time ago. It's me, Utsie."

John turned and looked into her young strikingly pretty face. "Yes, I remember you, my name is—"

"John, I remember. You are the American living in Hong Kong."

John, appearing a little flustered, replied, "Well, not anymore, but you have a good memory. May I buy you a drink?"

Utsie smiled and sat down. "I'll have a Kouplee."

"Crystal or Berringers?"

"House, they are too expensive, especially in this place."

They talked for about an hour and then John excused himself for a dinner appointment. As he was leaving, he asked her if she was free for dinner the following evening. Utsie nodded. John recommended they meet at the Storchen Hotel Restaurant at eight.

"Okay then, it's a date, I'll see you tomorrow."

The Dolder was only a few blocks away, so he decided to walk.

As he approached the front door, he noticed that Peter Tsillman was already waiting for him.

"John, it is so good to see you. Our table is ready, so why don't we go in?"

Pleasantries exchanged, Tsillman said in English, "So let's get down to brass nails."

John looked at him incredulously and started to smile. "I said something wrong?"

"Not at all, but I think you meant tacks, brass tacks, never mind, I'm here because of the success you've had. I believe this is a better market than we first thought. I've come to work closely with you to see if we can increase sales even more."

"You are going to be here full-time? That is wonderful! With my contacts and your knowledge, we will make a fortune. Yes, let's toast to that."

After several hours of discussion, John said good-night and told Tsillman he would be in touch with him the following week to get organized.

"Please, my staff and I are at your disposal. Anything you need, just call me."

John thanked him and said good-night again.

It was a nice night, so John decided to stroll back to his hotel. When he got back to his room, about three in the morning, sleep came easily.

The phone rang at seven.

"Herr Moore, your coffee and croissants are on the way up. Your driver and assistant will be here by eight-thirty. Is there anything else I can do for you?"

He got up and showered quickly. Coming out of the steamy bathroom, he was delighted to see coffee and croissants already on the terrace table, the french doors open, and an English newspaper folded and placed on the end table.

Just as he finished his third cup of coffee and two croissants with crème fraiche and strawberry jam, there was a knock on the door. He opened it to find his new assistant and driver standing there.

"Please come in, you must be Iris and Franz."

The young woman spoke first. "Yes, sir, but my name is pronounced Ear-ris." Franz was quiet. Iris was about thirty, wearing stylish glasses. Her face looked more Slavic than Germanic. John estimated she was about five foot eight. She had dark hair and a very nice figure. Franz was large, almost brutish, with kind eyes and the look of a man who could handle himself. As John continued his assessment, he noticed they seemed to be sizing him up as well.

He suggested that they go shopping and pick up three phones and two laptops to be used only for work.

"Do either of you know where we might purchase these right away?"

John was pleased with Franz's knowledge of the city and impressed with the negotiations Iris had with the shopkeepers. They went back to the hotel, and John asked Iris to load all the phones and laptops with their contact numbers, along with his personal contact list. He also instructed her to add the numbers of all the hotels and restaurants in and around Zurich. He asked Franz to bring the car around. "I'll be down in a minute."

Finally, he asked Iris to rent a sailboat on Zurichsee for a week, starting the next day.

John got in the car and asked Franz if he knew any realtors in Winterthur, Eck, or Tremmlie. Franz explained that property was usually handled by attorneys or notaries in Zürich; he knew several, the best being Wilhelm S. Von Hertzen, notary.

Within an hour, John had found a house that he liked for rent at a fair price, built on the side of the mountain in Eck overlooking the city of Zurich. The view was magnificent. You could see the entire city all the way to the lake.

Although the house was owned by an Arab sheik, it was decorated in a tasteful, almost subdued manner. The notary told him he could have all the paperwork done in two days. John called Peter Tsillman, and the payment was arranged that afternoon. John told the notary he would move in the following Monday. Von Hertzen agreed to leave the keys with the hotel manager, and the deal was done.

John took Franz and Von Hertzen to lunch at the top of Tremmlie, and they had Goulash with Weiner Schnitzel and Pommes Frites.

As they were leaving the restaurant, John called Iris to tell her to order lunch for herself from room service. He was surprised, she seemed delighted.

They took Von Hertzen to his office. John asked Franz if he was married while they drove back to the hotel.

"No, why?"

"Are you free to travel?"

"Yes, I can travel at a moment's notice"

"Good, we will be leaving Zurich tomorrow to sail Zürichsee for a few days, so pack appropriately."

Handing Franz some cash, he said, "Would you buy a good digital camera with a telescopic lens for the trip?"

Franz told John he would have the camera with him in the morning. Arriving at the hotel, John said good-bye to Franz and asked him to be back by nine the following day.

"Herr Moore, this is Herr Froogle and Herr Schmidt, the yacht brokers," Iris said as she went to the desk and showed him a group of pictures. "These are the best boats available."

John studied the pictures and asked the two men if one had separate sleeping accommodations for three.

"Actually the *Princess* has four separate staterooms," Herr Froogle offered.

"How much for a week-long charter without crew?"

The price was agreed upon after a short discussion. John called Tsillman and arranged payment.

"Thank you, gentlemen, we are going to take her out for the week, at ten tomorrow morning. Have the charter ready for me to sign at the boat at nine thirty."

Both men thanked him and left the room promptly.

*This man is exciting. I'm going to like this job.*

"Iris, are you married?"

She began to flush, and John quickly qualified his question.

"I meant to say, are you free to travel without advance notice?"

"Yes, I mean no, I'm not married, and yes, I'm free to travel."

"Good, pack tonight, mostly casual clothes, but bring a dress or two along as well."

Iris looked at him quizzically.

"May I ask where we're going?"

"Oh! Yes, I'm sorry. We are going to sail Zürichsee so that I can get an idea of the yacht trade on that section of the lake."

Iris showed John how she had set up their phones and computers. John was pleased with her work and told her so. Iris went home to pack, leaving John with enough time to shower, change, and get over to the Storchen to have dinner with Utsie. He was going to call Tsillman on his new cell phone, but decided it could wait until morning.

Utsie was already there when he arrived. She was a vision of beauty with her hair up, showing off her long shapely neck. She wore a short fitted dress that accentuated her fantastic figure.

John thought back to the first time he'd met her. He recalled that Utsie's parents had left her a farm within the Zurich city limits. She still worked it as a dairy farm, but the real estate value was astronomical. She was a dichotomy—a beautiful, ridiculously wealthy, hardworking farm girl.

John asked her if she would like to have a drink at the bar before dinner. When they had finished their drink, John offered his arm to escort her into the dining room. She was so stunning, even the women turned to glance at her. It made John a little uncomfortable to be that noticed.

The meal was great. John liked this girl, not only was she beautiful, she was intelligent and naturally funny. During dinner, they discussed world politics, music, art, and business. Utsie was also a Swiss wine connoisseur. She explained that Swiss wines were very good and that the label over the cork always had a symbol that designated which canton it came from. She chose a white wine, Eagle, which, oddly enough, had a lizard on the label. It was from a canton north of Zurich and was a favorite of hers.

Utsie gave John a history of the cantons and the origins of their logos, most dated back to Hellenic times.

On the ride home, John pondered. This girl is not only beautiful, she's also a good resource for local knowledge.

Utsie's farm was surprisingly close to John's hotel, only about a five-minute drive. Before they said good-night, John told Utsie he would be out of town for a week. He asked her if she would like to have dinner when he got back. She agreed, leaned over, and gave him a long sensuous kiss. John said good-night, a little overwhelmed. *I really like her.*

# 5

Iris and Franz showed up early, and both had packed light.

"Franz, please park the car and we'll take a taxi to the boat. Iris, organize the computers and load the camera software. Thank you."

John took this opportunity to call Tsillman.

"Peter, this is John, we're leaving for a week. Do me a favor, would you have everything in my hotel room moved to the new house on Monday and settle the bill with the hotel? The three new boats will arrive in Amsterdam on the ICL ship, *Morning Glory*, on Friday. Arrange to have two of them put into storage and the third put in a slip on Zürichsee, preferably near the George Clinic, and thanks."

"John, it's already done."

"Thank you. When I get back, I would like to have a meeting with you, allow several hours. Maybe we can meet on Friday evening at the new house. I'll be back on Wednesday, it will give me a little time to settle in."

John hung up the phone and looked at his watch.

"It's quarter after nine, time to go."

·····················

Herr Froogle was waiting at the boat. They did an inspection, and he pointed out some of the finer points of the yacht. John signed the paperwork and went on board, followed by Iris and Franz. Once on deck, he turned to them.

"I'm sorry that I didn't ask before. Do either of you get seasick?"

Iris shook her head and Franz just smiled, ran to the bow, cast off the lines as soon as John started the engine, then immediately loosened the cleats and made the sails ready. *This is a bonus, the man knows how to sail.*

Once they were farther out, they raised the sails and were underway. John studied the navigation charts and worked out a plan to cover as much of the lake as possible in five days. John realized that he would only be able to cover a small portion; he hadn't been aware that Zürichsee is only part of the Lake Luzerne region. He was trying to come up with a plan, so he asked Franz if he knew these waters.

"Yes, I know them very well. Zürichsee is part of the lake system which covers several cantons including Zug, Interlaken, Luzerne, and Zurich, covering almost all of Central Switzerland.

"Lake Geneva or Lake Lamanche, which is its real name, covers a good portion of western Switzerland, and Lake Lugano covers the southern part."

John realized why this was going to be a great market.

"Franz, can you read a chart?"

"Yes, very well."

"Great, please map out a course to hit the more affluent towns and cities which we would see in a week's sailing?"

The old town of Zurich was well behind them, and John took in the views while Franz was busy. After sailing for about five hours, John turned the helm over to Franz.

"Put in at the next available town, we need supplies."

John went forward and saw Iris sunning herself on the bow. She reminded him of Rebecca. He turned and went below to get that image out of his mind.

He began organizing the galley. Later, he went back up on deck, feeling better. Iris was at the helm, and Franz was lowering the sails. John jumped in to help; in minutes, they were back under power, pulling into a quaint little village.

John and his crew walked into town. They were back on the boat in under an hour. John was surprised when Iris asked the two men to get out of her kitchen while she prepared lunch.

*This is another bonus.*

They ate a well-prepared lunch of air-dried beef, a cheese platter, bread, and a fine local wine. John was gaining small insights about his new staff, enjoying a pleasant conversation. He was thinking about hiring them full-time; they were more than competent, and he liked them both.

After lunch, they set sail. Franz took the helm. John took in the scenery and had a long discussion with Iris about his intentions, growing the business in Europe. The conversation was interesting and time passed quickly.

"It's ten o'clock and it's still light."

Iris said, "I'll go below and start dinner."

John walked back to the cockpit and found Franz with a pleasant smile on his face.

"What are you thinking about, Franz?"

"Nothing really, I just enjoy being out on the water. This is the nicest boat I've ever sailed on."

"Wait until you see the boats we've just sent over here from the States."

They were coming up to a small town where they could anchor for the night. John began to lower the sails and make ready for the stop. They found a beautiful anchorage with a view of the city on one side and the mountains on the other. Iris called out that dinner was almost ready. Franz went below and came back with a folding table. While Franz prepared the table, John went forward to straighten out the lines. When he returned, he couldn't believe his eyes; there was a beautifully set table with a linen tablecloth, china, and silverware and a nicely presented dinner consisting of five courses. John grinned from ear to ear.

"Bravo, let's eat."

The next day, they stopped at almost every marina, taking boat counts and pictures, occasionally getting off to speak to some of the local marina managers.

By 9:00 p.m., they were tired. Iris took charge of getting dinner while Franz and John took care of the boat. After a great dinner, they decided to turn in. John slept for about three hours, got up, and went up on deck. He sat quietly and studied the night sky, one of his favorite pastimes. John did not hear Iris approach, and he was startled when she spoke.

"You couldn't sleep either?"

Iris sat down next to John.

"I slept a little, but truthfully I love this time of night. It is so peaceful."

Iris told John some of her hopes and dreams for the future and a little about her life. They talked for several hours as dawn approached.

"Iris, I enjoyed our conversation, but maybe you should go down below and get some sleep. We have a long day ahead of us."

Iris agreed and left John alone. His thoughts returned to Rebecca.

Franz was up around seven. He found John sleeping in his deck chair. He decided to make coffee before he woke him.

John thanked Franz for the coffee and went over the plans for the day. Iris came on deck carrying a tray of food. They were busy for the rest of the day. It ended with another fantastic meal.

John was in his cabin preparing a report for Peter and Brad when there was a knock on his door. He opened it, and Iris was standing there.

"I put together a slide presentation from the pictures we've taken so far. I thought you might want it to go along with your report."

Iris opened her laptop.

"I have separated the pictures first by boat size, then design, and I have listed locations and registrations for each."

"Well done, Iris."

She pushed herself into the cabin and started to organize his report while collating it with her slideshow. They were finished about 5:00 a.m. Iris said good-night. John went up on deck, sat in his chair, and began formulating a plan to hire Iris and Franz full-time.

Franz came up on deck about seven and handed John a cup of coffee. John went to his cabin.

Iris called them for a late breakfast. John handed each of them an envelope with an offer for full employment. He asked them not to answer him just yet. He would meet with them individually at eleven and twelve o'clock, Iris first.

When John finished his meeting with Iris, he asked Franz to anchor the boat and come to his cabin while Iris made lunch.

The three of them sat down for a leisurely lunch. John had another surprise for them.

"Since both of you have decided to join my team, I have another proposal for you. You both live alone, assuming rent is expensive in Zurich. I'm proposing that you come to live with me in Eck. The house is built on four levels. The top level will be my quarters. The next can be our office and dining area, leaving the other two levels for you. I thought Franz would take the lower, and Iris could have the second level. Each level has at least one bedroom, a sitting room, and all have private access by way of the terraces. Perhaps you could sublet your flats and make some additional income? If this is agreeable, I'll hire a cook and a housekeeper."

Franz and Iris looked at each other and simultaneously said, "Great!"

"Alright then, when we get back, please finish the tasks I've given you and take the rest of the week off. Sublet your flats, and get moved in. We'll start fresh on Monday."

They were quiet on the trip back. John wondered what was going through their minds. Just before they came to Zurich Old Town, John lowered the sails and Franz turned on the engines.

Working together, they had the boat stowed and tied up in short order. John left them at the pier and took a cab to his new home.

Upon arrival, his clothes were hung in the closets, the kitchen was fully stocked, and there were English language magazines in the bathroom. John shook his head. *Tsillman is very good.*

After stowing his gear, John picked up the phone and called Utsie.

"Are you free for dinner this evening?"

"Yes, how about going to the Restaurant in the Church with 1776 on the steeple?"

"Yeah, I know the place, Restaurant Im Stock, sounds great, good choice."

Utsie roared with laughter.

"What's so funny?"

"*Im Stock* means 'first floor.'"

"I thought that was the name of the restaurant. I'll see you there at nine." *I guess I'm not the international bon vivant I thought I was.*

*Why am I so intrigued with this girl?* She was beautiful and smart, but there was something else, he couldn't put his finger on it.

It was about eight-thirty when John realized he had no transportation. He was about to panic, then he saw it. Tsillman had left a notebook for him with emergency numbers prominently displayed. *Tsillman really is good.*

The taxi pulled up to the restaurant just before nine. Utsie was standing just outside the door. They kissed in European fashion and went inside. The restaurant was on the first floor.

"My mother died when I was ten, my father passed when I was sixteen. My extended family has tried desperately to take the farm, as did some major corporations and a few suitors. I sold a few small nonproductive parcels to get the money to attend university, and I have degrees in business and law. I never practiced law. I had to know how to fight legally, the farm was mine, it belonged to me, no one else."

"Have you ever been to Asia?"

She paled momentarily. John didn't know what he said to make her react like this. She noticed the look on his face and quickly recovered.

"I'm sorry, John, this is an emotional issue for me, but I have not been to Asia." She hesitated. "John, last year when you were here, I was going through a bad time. An Asian business group wanted my property, and they tried to kill me three times. I was saved by the bodyguards I hired after the first attempt on my life. The head of the security company told me that they had been contacted, and assurances were made that I was no longer in danger. The Asian group lost interest. It was horrible, I actually saw people die."

He saw the same look in her eyes that he saw every day in the mirror, the look of someone who has been close to the brink and survived. They were drawn to each other, two people who have shared what few others have. Suddenly he wanted to get off this subject.

"Utsie, how would you like to get out of here and go to a club?"

She hugged him. "Fantastic idea, John!"

They went to several clubs in the district off the Limmat. While dancing, Utsie came very close to John and purred, "Take me home and make love to me."

Without a word, John took her hand, and they left.

The next morning, John prepared breakfast on the patio. He glanced at her sitting in his robe. *She is so beautiful.*

John was sipping his coffee, enjoying their time together, when Utsie told him she had to leave. He really didn't want her to go. Dressing quickly, she kissed him passionately. John watched her as she walked down the path leading to the street. She turned suddenly. "Call me later."

・・・・・・・・・・・・・・・・・・・・・・・・・・・・・・

John had to make a conscious effort to get to work. His mind kept going back to Utsie's story. He could feel rage engulfing him. *Who the hell are these people? The powerful can do as they please without regard for anyone. Money buys them power, and they use it to do whatever they want, even murder.* After he calmed down, he called Tsillman and asked him to bring all the completed sales contracts and copies of his accounts and portfolios with him to tomorrow night's meeting.

John spent the rest of the day looking over the house, trying to figure out if any modifications were needed to accommodate Iris and Franz. By late afternoon, he was finished, so he mixed himself a drink, satisfied with his assessment.

"Do you want to have dinner tonight?"

"Yes, at your house. I'm bringing fresh meat and vegetables from my farm, and I want to cook for you."

He reveled in a forgotten emotion, anticipation, a big smile on his face.

Utsie arrived, and she noticed a look on John's face.

"I look different in jeans and a tee shirt, yes? This is why the locals call me the Pleasant Peasant. I am one of two farmers in Zurich."

John laughed and took the packages from her, putting them in the kitchen. Utsie went right to work. John watched, impressed.

"Get out of here. I don't like people watching me work."

John laughed again and obediently went out to the deck. Sitting there, sipping a drink, he lost himself in the view and last year's tragic events.

"Dinner is ready."

A formal table was set with silver trays of game and fancifully prepared vegetables with a flowered centerpiece and an oversized candelabra.

"I am more than impressed."

Utsie blushed at the compliment.

"You should be. Now sit."

The meal was well above his expectations, and the conversation was sublime. Utsie told John about the history of Zurich and the surrounding areas. John marveled at her knowledge and appreciated her sense of humor. He hadn't felt this good in a long time.

She left early in the morning. John said good-bye and made a pot of coffee. He was on his third cup when he started to think about Utsie. She was tender and passionate and ferocious all at the same time. He was still thinking about her when the phone rang.

"Hello, John? It's Peter Tsillman. Everything is ready for tonight's meeting."

# 6

After meeting with the bank's most important customer, Ascot Chen of the Liddo Group, Tsillman asked him if he would join him for a cup of tea.

"That would be delightful."

Peter ordered the standard four tea assortment to be brought to the private dining room with instructions to clear the room.

Chen selected Indian black tea, and Tsillman poured it for him.

"Mr. Chen, do you like to sail?"

"Why do you ask?"

"I represent an American yacht builder, and a man of your stature should have a superior yacht."

"What is the name of the American company?"

"Sailcraft Yachts."

Chen smiled. This coincidence was some sort of sign. He did not believe he owed anything to John Moore for killing his girlfriend. As a matter of fact, he did not believe he owed anything to anyone. He admired John Moore's fortitude, courage, and cunning. The boat business in China had been very profitable. If he were going to do business with anyone, why not someone he was familiar with?

"I am not interested myself, but we have several associates in that business. I'm sure you stand to make a hefty commission."

"Peter, I will make some calls. I want nothing from this, but please remember the favor if I need something from you later."

"Thank you, Mr. Chen. I will not forget."

"You will receive a call from Mr. Wolfgang Putz, the managing director of our affiliate who handles the sales of boats and planes. Never bring up my name with this business, agreed?"

"Mr. Chen, I am Swiss. Secrecy is my stock in trade."

Chen left the bank and called Putz from his car.

"I want you to purchase thirty Sailcraft yachts through Peter Tsillman at Wertshaft und Privat Bank. Expect to pay about twenty-five million USD. Ship them to our dealer in Latvia."

Chen hung up the phone and told the driver to take him to the airport.

Tsillman arrived at John's house with the requested files in one hand and a bottle of Crystal in the other.

"What's the champagne for?"

"An order of"—Tsillman gleamed—"thirty boats at a price of over eight hundred thousand dollars each to be delivered to Latvia as soon as possible."

"Well done, Peter."

It did not go unnoticed that John called him Peter. He usually called him Tsillman.

"I'll have an anticipated delivery date for you by tomorrow with a firm date within thirty days."

After the details were ironed out, John excused himself and left the room, returning a few minutes later.

"Before we get into this other business, I want to give you this."

He handed him a check for $50,000.

Tsillman made a gesture of putting the check on the table, but it never left his hand.

"No, take it as a token of my appreciation for your efforts to date."

"Well, the fact that you are showing your appreciation alone makes me feel good," he said as the check disappeared into his pocket.

John smiled. *This guy is slick as shit.* The rest of the evening went by quickly. When John was satisfied, he said good-night, made himself a drink, and called Peter in San Francisco.

"Peter, hold on to your hat. I need thirty-eight seventy footers fully geared, ASAP. Tsillman just gave me the order, $807,000 each. Have Brad call me, I'll go over specifics and work up a modified production schedule with him."

"Holy shit, you're only there two weeks and you've sold more than we did all last year!"

"It's a coincidence, my friend, pure coincidence. Tsillman came up with this on his own."

Peter got Brad on the phone with them, and within two hours, they had a temporary production schedule in place.

After wrapping up the details, John walked over to the bar to pour himself a drink. He was just about to sit down when the phone rang again.

"Hello, Peter?"

"No, it's Utsie. John, I can't sleep. Can I come over?"

"Of course."

A few minutes later, the doorbell chimed. When he opened the door, Utsie was standing there.

During breakfast, John asked Utsie if she could take a couple of days off. John and Utsie laid out a plan to go to Lugano, Geneva, and Devone.

"I'm going to be very busy for the next month, and I need a few days to unwind before it gets too hectic."

"Is this a real holiday? I haven't taken a break in quite a while, it will be fun."

For the next few days, they went on excursions, played at the casinos, and sampled fantastic French, Italian, and German foods.

Sunday morning, John announced, "I have to be back in Eck tonight to get ready for the morning."

"John, promise me we will do this again soon. I don't remember the last time I enjoyed myself so much."

"I promise."

The ride back was interesting as Utsie pointed out some landmarks, giving John a complete history of each. He dropped Utsie at her house and went straight to work.

Iris and Franz showed up at about 8:00 a.m. John told them to go into his office. He brought in a pot of coffee and handed each of them an envelope.

"Take a look inside."

In each of the envelopes, there was a set of keys for the house, an alarm code, and a set of car keys. John took them both by the arm and walked side by side to the garage. They both gasped at the same time, and John laughed out loud.

"Franz, the Mercedes AMG is yours. I was told it's the fastest car in Europe. The red Mercedes convertible is for you, Iris."

They were speechless, so John broke the silence, "Take them for a spin and then get your living spaces squared away. I'll see you both back in the office this afternoon at two sharp."

They looked like kids at Christmas. John was generous and also understood the value of grateful employees.

Over the next few weeks, they worked hard on production scheduling, setting up and streamlining administration and communications. John also had long conversations with Franz about European design subtleties. The group worked well together and seemed to genuinely like each other. When Utsie was around, Iris developed a proprietary attitude, but John wrote it off; Iris was just being protective of her boss.

Four weeks later, John decided to call Peter in Sausalito.

"John, it's great to hear from you, everything's on schedule here. How's the office coming along?"

"Peter, it's working like a Swiss clock. Franz and Iris have turned out to be fantastic. I really enjoy working with them. I need a favor."

"Anything, John, what do you need?"

"I need Brad's personal input. I have been studying the market, and I think we have to make some adjustments to design. I want Brad to work it out with Franz before we go any further."

"John, isn't Franz your driver? What the hell does he know about design?"

"Peter, Franz has a lot to offer, he's more than a driver. He has sailed these waters for a long time. I respect his knowledge and have confidence in what he says."

"Brad will be on a flight to Zürich tomorrow."

"Thanks, buddy, call me later with the flight information."

•••••••••••••••••••••••••••••••

Franz picked Brad up at the airport and drove him to a small hotel in Winterthur, about three kilometers from the house.

"Get some rest. I'll pick you up at six and take you to dinner."

John took Brad to dinner and then on a quick tour of Zurich. John brought him back to the hotel around eleven.

"Franz will pick you at eight sharp."

•••••••••••••••••••••••••••••••

When he got home, Utsie was waiting for him on the terrace.

"Utsie, this is a pleasant surprise! How did you get in?"

"That girl, Iris, let me in. I don't think she likes me."

John laughed, but it confirmed his feelings on the subject. They sat on the terrace and talked well into the night. Utsie left just before sunrise.

He was just finished dressing after three hours of refreshing sleep when he heard Franz come in with Brad. They were already discussing the subtle differences in European and American boat design.

"Brad, how are you? How's the hotel? Did you get some rest?"

"The hotel is great, and I slept well."

"Good, let's get to work."

John took both men to the terrace and had coffee brought out.

"Brad, I believe we have to change our design for this market. Our boats are designed for the ocean. Most people here are sailing the lakes. Franz has been sailing for years, and I wanted you to get his input on the matter."

They discussed various designs and differences in utilization. They came to the conclusion that the real problem was draft. Although the lakes in the area were deep, the canals and connecting tributaries were not. European boats seemed to have more beam and shorter centerboards.

Brad came up with some initial ideas. Franz, with his knowledge of the area's waters, was able to give him input along with some of his own ideas. John liked one idea, a modified V hull with a semiretractable centerboard. He told them to concentrate on that.

"I have to run into town. I'll be back around six."

# 7

John returned about five-thirty. He went directly to the office and sat with Iris to go over the day's communications. When they were done, Iris asked if he was going out for the evening. John told her he was going to meet with Franz and Brad. Iris asked if she could cook dinner for them. "Iris, that's not necessary, but I do love your cooking." Iris assured him it was her pleasure and went off to the kitchen. John went out to the patio and found Brad and Franz arguing over design points. There were drawings everywhere. John could see they hadn't taken a break since he had left. "Hey, guys, have you been at it since I left?"

Brad looked at John. "I think I have something here, but Colonel Klink keeps shooting me down."

Franz looked puzzled. "Who's Colonel Klink?"

John laughed and explained it was a character from an American TV show.

Franz looked down and simply said, "Call me Franz, please."

They worked on the basic design for about two hours before Iris announced, "Dinner is ready." When they got to the dining room, John was not disappointed. Iris had put together one of her impeccable dinners.

Brad was amazed. "Do you guys eat like this all the time?"

Iris answered, "Yes, when John is home."

John had that feeling again that he was being chastised for Utsie, but he shrugged it off. The meal was too good to think about anything else.

After dinner, Brad and Franz wanted to get back to work, but John stopped them.

"You guys have been at it all day. Take a break. Why don't you take Iris out on the town? Iris, I'm sure you know some night spots you could show these two workaholics."

Again, Franz questioned, "Workaholics?"

John and Brad laughed.

"No, seriously, what is workaholic?"

John answered, "People who work too much. Now go out and enjoy yourselves."

"I'll have to change, but I'll just be a minute."

She returned quickly. John smiled at the look on Brad's face. "Easy, boy," and he began to laugh.

John picked up the phone and called Utsie. He asked her politely not to come over that evening; he explained that he had to reconcile all of the accounts that Tsillman had dropped off last week. He wanted to take advantage of the fact that he was alone.

John turned on some music and dove into the figures, finding small discrepancies in each of the accounts, all under $1,000. The dates coincided with his dinners with Tsillman. "That son of a bitch." Tsillman had charged his accounts every time he invited John to dinner. He laughed but made a mental note to confront Tsillman about it. John was still working when the group returned. It was about 2:00 a.m.; he was not surprised when he saw Brad heading toward Iris's apartment.

The next morning, they were all up before John. Looking at the small group, he realized that his plan had worked. Iris was preparing breakfast, and Brad and Franz were joking and laughing, like old friends. They were fast becoming a team. During breakfast, John told them they were going on a trip.

"I thought we'd go to Lugano. There's a lot of money in that area, and I want to show Brad the boats on the lake. Franz, have you ever sailed there?"

"Yes, often. I know those waters well."

Brad said, "I assume most of the boats there are of Italian design?"

"One side of the lake is actually in Italy, so it makes sense that a good portion of the boats are Italian."

After breakfast, John asked Iris to make hotel reservations for them and then pack, meeting back in the office in one hour.

Franz drove. Brad asked if he could sit up front to continue his conversation with Franz. John climbed in the back with Iris. The four-hour ride passed quickly. John decided not to get in between Brad and Franz, so he and Iris worked on production scheduling and a marketing plan. The more he worked with Iris, the more he liked her. Iris was intelligent and imaginative. Some of her marketing ideas were the best he had ever heard.

They checked into the hotel, and John suggested they drive to some of the marinas close to the city. They spent the afternoon surveying at least five marinas. John and Brad got a good idea the local market. When they got back to the hotel, John told them to rest, get cleaned up, and he would take them all to the casino for dinner.

"It's six o'clock now. Let's meet back here in the lobby at eight." They all agreed and went their separate ways, at least Franz and John did.

The casino was European decadent. Brad had never seen anything like it.

"I've been to Vegas, but this is really classy."

The dining room was small and comfortable; the food was superb. After dinner, John excused himself and told the others to stay and have fun. He took a cab back to the hotel and was happy to see Utsie waiting for him. They went right to his room.

After morning coffee, John told Utsie that he wished she could spend the day with him.

"You go and play with your friends. I want to go shopping. We'll have dinner together tonight."

John agreed and left Utsie with a playful pout on her face. *Crap, I'm falling in love again.*

Iris refined her cataloging program, and now, as soon as a picture was taken, it was cataloged, sorted by size, country of origin, and approximate cost. On the ride back, John reflected, *Now that Iris has gotten involved with Brad, her mind seems to be off Utsie and me, but it's still better to keep my life as private as possible.*

They got back to the hotel; as soon as they were in the lobby, Franz said that he was going to the casino. Brad asked Iris to have dinner with him and looked at John. "Well, that's a good idea because I feel like staying in this evening."

John and Utsie found an intimate little restaurant about twenty kilometers from the hotel. The restaurant was just off the lake, an old stone building, with a few steps off the street at the entrance. He and Utsie were shown to their table on a private little terrace overlooking the lake with an arched cobblestone portico above them. The menu was simple; food was fresh, light, and well prepared. John could not remember when he had had such a pleasant evening. Just as they were about to leave, John's phone rang. It was Peter Tsillman.

"John, can I see you?"

"Peter, I'm in Lugano. I won't be back until Friday. Is it important?"

"Yes, but not urgent. Can we meet Saturday morning?"

"Okay," John answered, "I also want to talk to you about charging my accounts for our dinners."

"John, that's bank policy, but if it bothers you, I will reimburse you from my own pocket." John laughed and told him to forget it, thinking, *He really is some operator.* "I'll see you Saturday at my house at ten a.m." John hung up the phone.

The next morning as they were sitting in bed having coffee, Utsie told him she had to get back for work but she would see him Saturday evening.

While Utsie was showering, John called Franz.

"We'll meet in the lobby in one hour."

John glanced up as Utsie came out of the bathroom, naked, propping her arm high against the door, posing for him. *I should've told Franz two hours.*

They met in the lobby. John told them they were going to take the excursion boat and be gone all day, returning at eleven that night. Once aboard, they found a table on deck that would accommodate them and their work papers. Brad and Franz were excited and couldn't wait to show John a design that could be way ahead of the curve.

Brad began the presentation while Franz asked Iris to call up specific boats that they had pictured and cataloged to illustrate how Brad's design was better. The design was brilliant—a modified V hull with two retractable boards, one on either side of the V, which would give them a shallow draft and superb stability without making her boxy. Brad thought he would be able to computerize a hydraulic system, which could use sonar to raise and lower the boards automatically while under sail and would fully retract under power.

John loved the design, so he asked Iris to make flight arrangements for Brad and Franz to fly back to Sausalito on Monday.

"I'll call a Visa service and arrange to have a Visa waiting for Franz on our return Friday."

"I want you guys to work on this together, and when it's ready for water trials, I want Franz to captain the boat. Brad, you stick with him as the tech. This is important, it may enable us to take over the market here. I think we should go with the fifty to seventy foot with all the bells and whistles. I'll call Peter to see if we can locate another manufacturing facility. We'll need at least six molds to start. I want Volvo engines. The parts are readily available here. Rig it, 220 50 cycle with European outlets. Franz, make sure you have your Visa. Guys, take the weekend off. Brad, may I see you privately for a minute?"

Franz got up and left.

Brad asked, "What is it, John?"

"Here," John gave Brad a couple of thousand euros. "It's a little bonus. Take Iris away for the weekend and have some fun. You're not going to see her for a while. When you get back, I expect you to work your ass off."

"John, this isn't necessary. I get paid well and I love my job."

"I'm aware of that. I just want to show my appreciation. You're doing a great job."

Brad was red-faced. "Okay, what can I say, thank you?"

"It's nothing, and on your way out, find Iris and ask her to come here."

When John saw Iris, he told her he had given them all off until Monday but needed her to do a few things before they got back to Zurich. The entire list was taken care of before they got off the boat that evening. John was amazed.

# 8

Tsillman arrived at the house at 10:00 a.m. on Saturday. John led him out to the terrace and offered him coffee.

"Peter, what can I do for you?"

"John, I want to make you a very wealthy man."

"I'm already a wealthy man."

"What you now have is nothing compared to what I am about to propose to you. I wish to share in this wealth, if you decide to do it. Something has been put into my hands by another client that I cannot put through the bank. It is totally legal and aboveboard, but by charter, the bank is not allowed to do this kind of business."

John asked, "Well, what is it?"

"I have a large client who wishes to purchase ten billion dollars of United Nation's emission credits in ten-million-dollar increments. They wish to remain anonymous. They're willing to pay one US dollar per share. I can buy them from the UN at ten cents per share. You'll make a thousand percent return on your money, and all you will have to put up is the original ten million. After that, I will submit the orders so they continually roll until we buy all of the ten billion dollars' worth. You will receive nine billion dollars. My fee will be three percent, or two hundred seventy million. The only downside would be if they backed out upfront. You'll have ten million dollars of worthless emission credits. If they take the first buy, they will take it all, and we will both be very wealthy men."

## GREEN TO RED

"I don't know, Tsillman. I don't know anything about these instruments. Why would someone pay ten times their value at issuance? It sounds like trouble. If something sounds too good to be true, it usually is."

"John, I am not a frivolous man, nor am I a fool. I know this client, and if they are willing to pay this amount, it simply means it has more value to them if no one knows they are involved. Secrecy sometimes comes at a high price."

"Why me?"

"That's simple, John. I could have brought this to several different brokers, but my clients' anonymity would not be safe and it would have been more difficult for me to profit from this as well."

John was interested, but he told Tsillman he would get back to him Monday. When Tsillman left, John picked up his phone and called Peter in Sausalito.

"Peter, John here, hop on a plane tomorrow morning, get over here. It's important."

He spent the entire night on the Web investigating emissions credits. He found the UN offer dated almost a month ago, and there did not seem to be any takers. The next morning, he decided that with the money he and Peter had made on the property, he could afford to risk ten million for a return like this. John was not a gambling man, but the look in Tillman's face made him believe this could be worth it. He still had to talk it over with Peter, but Peter normally went along with him.

That night, Utsie came over around seven. John told her he had some good news: his partner and lifelong friend, Peter, would be arriving tomorrow. "Utsie, he's like a brother to me, and I want you to meet him." Utsie listened to John for hours as he told stories about him and Peter. She didn't stay over that night; she wanted to give John some time to prepare for his meeting with Peter. After listening to John's stories, she was anxious to meet Peter.

John met Peter the next day at the airport. When they got back to the house, Peter was impressed with the layout.

John filled Peter in on everything that was going on, and he was more than happy.

"John, in two months, you've organized a team, come up with a dynamite business strategy, and a design that could revolutionize sailing in this area."

"No, the design credit goes to Brad and Franz. You'll meet Franz and Iris tonight. Franz will be going back with you to work with Brad until the first boat is built. Peter, why don't you take a shower and change? I'll get us some lunch. I want to tell you about a new financial offering. That's the reason I asked you to come over here so quickly."

John led him out to the terrace after he refreshed himself.

"John, this is breathtaking,"

They sat down to a nice lunch, and John laid out the proposal.

"It sounds a little odd, but if you think it's a good investment, I'm in."

"Ten million dollars is a lot of money, Peter. Do you want to think about it?"

"John, we're partners. I have all the faith in your business acumen. If you think it's a good deal, let's go for it."

John hedged a bit, "Peter, I think the return is outrageous. I have never seen an investment with such a large quick return. I don't really understand why Tillman picked us, but it's worth a shot."

"John, as I see it, the worst that can happen is that we would get stuck with ten million dollars' worth of these emission credits, and if that did happen, we could use them as a tax write-off for the next five years."

"Peter, you're right. I'll tell Tsillman we're in. He can withdraw the money from our private accounts on Monday. If this works, we will be very, very rich men. I also wanted to tell you that business here will be extremely profitable, so I instructed Tsillman to put all sales through the Hong Kong Company. Sailcraft will sell to the company at a small margin. This way we capture all of the profit and Sailcraft will show enough in sales to cover overhead and a small profit. The money will flow through the company and be split equally into our private accounts."

"John, that's genius, great job."

"We'll see."

"John, where will you be taking me for dinner? I'm starved."

"A very nice place right on the lake, and I've invited a guest, someone I want you to meet."

Peter beamed. "I knew it. You found a girlfriend. That's why you look so happy."

"Yeah, and I think I am in love with her."

"In love or in lust?"

"Seriously, this one is special."

•••••••••••••••••••••••••••••••••

"Peter, this is Utsie."

"John told me you were beautiful, but as you might know, he's a master of understatement."

"John has told me all about you also. I am so happy to meet such a good friend of his. If half of what he's told me is true, I already like you."

Dinner was excellent, and they enjoyed each other's company. They laughed, joked, and shared a feeling of camaraderie that is seldom found in the human experience.

Utsie said good-night. Peter told her what a pleasure it was to meet her. He gave her his contact information.

"If you ever need anything, please do not hesitate to call. You have made my friend very happy, and I won't forget that."

John and Peter got back to the house just as Brad and Iris were pulling into the drive. They all went up to the terrace and were soon joined by Franz. They spent the rest of the night and into breakfast going over the strategy for the European market. John interrupted the meeting, looking at his watch.

"Hey! Start getting ready, your flight leaves in three hours."

John was left alone as they ran out. He began to think how lucky he was to have Peter as a friend and how well his new "family" was getting along.

It was time to leave for the airport, but Brad and Iris were nowhere to be found. John heard a racket coming from Iris's room.

"Brad, we're leaving for the airport!" John yelled. Within seconds, Brad came running out of the room, dressing as he ran. John could hear Iris say, "I'll post your things this afternoon." Brad, red-faced and sweating, didn't make eye contact with John as he ran straight to the car.

John returned from the airport and found Iris in the office, working. John looked at her sternly.

"Call FedEx and have them pick up Brad's luggage and have it sent to the office. It'll be there before he is."

They spent the afternoon putting final touches on the business plan and designing some brochures for the Italian, Swiss, German, and Austrian markets.

That evening, Utsie stopped by for a quiet dinner. They talked for a while and went to bed early. John woke at about one and went out on the terrace. He heard something and looked down to see Iris on her terrace. John walked down and found her sitting alone, weeping. She looked at him, tears flowing down her face.

"I'm going to miss him. Brad is the only person I have been within three years. I feel so alone already."

John took her in his arms and held her as she cried. Iris settled down, and John released her. She looked up at him the way he imagined a daughter looked at her father in this type of circumstance.

Iris said, "I've only had one boyfriend in my life. We met at university, and I was truly in love with him. He was Dutch, Hagar. We moved in together, but after two years, I found out he was seeing someone else the entire time. I've never been with anyone since."

"I know what you're feeling. My wife of many years did the same thing."

John reached out and hugged the girl once more. Iris began to weep quietly.

John pushed her away a little.

"I'll make sure you and Brad have ample time to see each other. Stop crying, go in, and get some sleep. I need you fresh tomorrow."

Iris rose and kissed John on the cheek.

"Thank you, John. Why are you so kind to us?"

John smiled. "I see something in you guys that's hard to find: you are driven to always excel. I believe, given the proper guidance and experience, that Brad, you, and Franz will become the best team in the industry. Iris, you're an extremely talented young lady, and I know you'll play a significant role in the success of our company."

"John, you are the kindest man I've ever met. I will do everything I can to make you pleased that you've hired me."

John leaned over and gave her a kiss on the forehead.

"Now get some rest and don't worry about Brad. You'll see him soon."

John went back up to his apartment and walked into the bedroom to find that Utsie was gone. He walked to the terrace and found her sitting there.

"John, she is right. You are the kindest man in the world."

"Only when I want to be."

They sat on the terrace and talked, watching the sunrise. Utsie told John she had to go home. Before she left, she told him she was going to be out of town for a few days, that she would see him Thursday evening. They kissed, and Utsie left. John felt tired and went back to bed.

John couldn't believe it, it was eleven o'clock. He took a quick shower and ran down to the office. Iris told him that Tsillman had called twice.

John called Tsillman and told him that he would go forward with the deal.

"Take five million from my personal account and five from Peter's."

"I will do it immediately. I'll bring the paperwork over this afternoon for your signature."

Tsillman was ecstatic because he knew he was going to be a ridiculously wealthy man.

The next morning, Tsillman called John and told him he had made the buy. He would roll the ten million over, depositing the residuals in their respective accounts.

"What about your commission?"

"I will only take it when the entire transaction is complete."

The truth was he had not set up a mechanism to hide it yet. He could not let the bank know he was doing this.

John called Peter in Sausalito immediately.

"Peter, it worked. Tsillman just called, and the first transaction is done. Check your records, it should have shown up already. I think you and I should celebrate when the process is complete."

John hung up. He didn't want to say too much over the phone.

It took almost three months, but when it was done, John and Peter had four billion five hundred million dollars each in their private accounts. John called Peter and asked him to fly to Zurich; he would pick him up at the airport.

Peter got off the plane and told John he hadn't been able to stop smiling since he left. When they got back to the house, Tsillman was already waiting for them. Tsillman explained that the emission credits were bearer instruments. They had only to sign them over to the bank to hold in escrow for the persons who are holding the trade contracts. Tsillman had taken the liberty to have one buy-and-sell agreement made up for the entire ten billion dollars' worth. After signing the agreement, John and Peter toasted each other with the bottle of Crystal Special that Tsillman had brought. Tsillman stood, made a toast, and said,

"Now, gentlemen, I only have one more thing for you to sign. It is a transfer demand for one hundred fifty million from each of your accounts."

John signed the document.

"Tsillman, does this mean we're going to lose you as our banker?"

"Good heavens, no, this is for my retirement. If a man who has been a banker in Zurich gets three hundred million dollars in one day, that would raise too many questions. I will use it to quietly supplement my lifestyle, without changing it too much, and go on some wonderful vacations. I will probably retire a little early, move somewhere warm, and live the rest of my life in luxury."

Peter said, "That is sound thinking, John. It might be best for us to do the same."

John agreed. Tsillman continued, almost as an afterthought, "I can get you the three percent you have paid me quickly if you allow me to put your funds in a currency portfolio account."

John said, "Not right now. We want to come to grips with this whole thing before we start anything else."

"That is probably wise."

After Tsillman left, John and Peter sat quietly for a while.

"John, I was just getting comfortable with the fact that we are millionaires, now we are billionaires."

"Peter, this won't change anything other than the fact that we will never have to worry again. I suggest we don't even think about this, at least for a while. We both have a pretty good life the way things are, and I can only foresee this kind of ridiculous wealth screwing us up. If we're prudent and don't get crazy, it will allow us to have a nice life and possibly help some folks along the way."

"John, that's why I respect you so much, you always know when to put the brakes on."

"Let's take Utsie and Iris out on the town tonight."

John hadn't been this happy in a long time. At dinner, he was surrounded by people he loved and admired. The dinner was great, and Utsie was funny; she's on top of her game. Iris asked Peter about Brad repeatedly. She wanted to know every detail of what he had been doing. After dinner, Iris suggested that they all go to a club; at first, John said no, but Utsie prodded him. Peter thought it was a great idea.

They went to the Joker, the best dance club in Zurich. As soon as they were inside, Iris grabbed Peter's hand and dragged him to the dance floor. Utsie commented on the fact that as large as Peter was, he was very graceful on the dance floor. John simply agreed, took her hand, and walked to the least crowded place on the floor. John had never danced with Utsie before, and he was startled when she began to dance. Her movements were extremely sensuous. John found himself getting aroused. Her movements were strong, but fluid, and the more he studied her, the more aroused he became. John decided it was best for him to sit this one out. He arranged for a table and ordered a bottle of Crystal. Utsie never ceased to amaze him. Every time he thought he was starting to know her, she came up with something new.

John and Utsie were talking when a strange little man with a horrible voice interrupted them.

"Utsie, my darling," he said as he grabbed her hand and kissed it.

"John Moore, this is Helmut Fragge."

John stood and shook the man's hand. "It's a pleasure."

Helmut clicked his heels. "Likewise."

He didn't know why, but his gut was telling him that this guy was bad news. Before John could seat himself, the little man sat down. John was a bit perturbed, but kept the smile on his face. Utsie told him that John was the owner of a yacht company, and Helmut's response seemed odd to John.

"This is wonderful. I need you to join our organization, and I won't take no for an answer."

The man reached into his pocket and produced an envelope. "Here is an application. Just fill it out and post it back to me with your check."

John took the envelope and put it in his pocket. The man got up, excused himself, and left.

"What the hell was that all about?"

Utsie started to roar with laughter. The more she saw the look on John's face, the more she laughed.

"Sure, just make a joke at my expense." Utsie started to laugh again.

Peter and Iris came to the table.

"You guys look like you're enjoying yourselves."

Utsie, still laughing, told them what had just transpired.

Iris said excitedly, "Helmut Fragge was here?"

"Yes, a reprehensible little man who wanted me to join his club."

Iris excitedly told John that Fragge was a very important man and joining would be good for them.

John was puzzled. "In what respect?"

"He's likely to be the next prime minister of Switzerland."

"That guy is going to be the next prime minister?"

"Yes, he's the head of the Green Party here, and he's very popular."

Utsie said, "She's right. He helped me keep my farm. He's a powerful man. The fact that you have sailboats instead of power boats might be good for you too."

"Okay. I'll join the club, but that guy gives me the creeps."

The next morning, while John was putting his clothes away, he took the envelope out of his pocket and decided to give it to Iris to fill out.

Later that morning, Iris brought him a stack of papers to sign, including the application for membership in the Swiss Green Alliance, with a check attached for $12,500. John was amazed at the price of entry into this club. He put it to the side and signed everything else. Iris took the signed papers away but returned a few minutes later and asked if he had the application.

John asked Iris to sit down and tell him what she knew about this man and his organization. After the explanation, John signed the check. He realized that membership in this prestigious club might do them some good.

Brad and Franz returned after a few weeks. They were excited about the results of the water trials and the performance of the newly designed boat. Franz told John that he had never sailed such a boat. Not only was it the fastest boat he had ever sailed, it was the most responsive.

"We did the trials using the seventy-four footer. It was easier to maneuver than the thirty-seven footer, the one we sailed on Zurichsee."

John was delighted with the news. Brad showed John the differences from a typical design. The retractable stabilization boards were hidden inside of cabinets with shelving and plenty of storage. The salon was comfortable. Brad had used Franz's knowledge of European styling. John knew right away that it had been a good idea to send Franz to the States. Brad explained every feature of the boat and the possibilities of future improvements. They worked for several more hours. John told them he was taking them out to dinner. He took Brad aside and told him to take the next day off and spend it with Iris.

"Franz, I have something to discuss with you in the morning, privately."

Dinner was good, almost festive. They were exuberant over the success of the new design.

Franz came up to John's apartment about eight in the morning. John was already on his fourth cup of coffee.

"Franz," John greeted him with a smile, "would you like a cup of coffee? I just made a new pot."

"Franz, you have done exemplary work on the design, and I believe I am totally underutilizing you. I've made a decision to make you general manager—Europe."

Franz couldn't believe it. "John, are you sure? You hired me as a driver."

"You're not a driver anymore."

John told Franz that he took orders well, but that didn't stop him from taking the initiative when necessary. Secondly, John told him he appreciated the way he jumped right in on the design and was not afraid to stand his ground when he thought he was right; finally, John said he just liked him. John then asked Franz to talk about his background.

Franz, feeling a bit awkward, started to tell John his life story: born in a valley near Zug, he went to university, but was unable to complete his studies because his father became ill. He had returned to the farm to help his mother. His father died; shortly after that, his mother passed on. He sold the farm and completed his studies. Shortly after graduation, he decided to fulfill his obligation to serve in the Swiss Army. Franz liked the army and wanted to make it a full-time career.

With most of the money left from the sale of the farm, he invested it wisely so he could retire comfortably. He had excelled in the military and was put into Special Forces, and ultimately the secret service.

"Yes, I was a spy, but my career fell apart when I came up against a powerful private company involved in some things that were against our national security. I almost discovered who they were, but I was set up by someone in my own government. Not only was I thrown out of the service but left with several legal problems. I came out all right, but legal fees ate up all of my money. Broke and dishonored, a friend of mine helped me get into driving for some of the major hotels, and that's where I met you. If this information prompts you to change your mind about giving me this position, I totally understand."

"Franz, I appreciate your honesty. I knew you were working below your ability. In fact, the skills you have may come in handy sometime. I believe you'll be a considerable asset to us, and I'm happier with my decision after hearing this. Your salary has just been doubled, and you will receive a bonus based on sales at the end of each year." With that, John handed Franz an envelope. "Here's a bonus, a small token of my thanks for doing such a good job on the design. You will be leaving for Hong Kong tomorrow to train with Chong Lee, our managing director—Asia. I've already called him and told him you'd be coming. While you're there, ask Chong to introduce you to our clothing consultant. Have her help you pick out a new wardrobe, one befitting a general manager."

Franz was shaking. "John, I'll do my very best, and if that is not enough, just tell me and I'll do better."

"Franz, remember two rules: never be afraid to make a decision and never make the same mistake twice."

Franz thanked John again; John's only reply was, "That brings us to lunch."

The next morning at breakfast, John told everyone the news, and after a round of congratulations, John stood.

"Brad, why don't you and Iris drive Franz to the airport? His flight is leaving at noon. Iris has the itinerary."

They worked until seven, going over the new design, making arrangements for the three newly completed models to be delivered by the end of the month. When the meeting ended, John told the two of them he wanted them to go to Geneva, then over to Boden See in Austria to set up slips to use as showrooms for the new boats. He would do the same in Zurich.

"Leave in the morning, take a week."

They both left; Iris returned a minute later and kissed him. "Thank you so much."

"This isn't a pleasure trip. I expect you to work. Now get out of here."

Iris smiled and actually curtsied as she left. John sat back, a nice warm feeling came over him. He had not felt like that in a very long time.

John spent most of the next week with Utsie. He enjoyed every minute of it. They took a boat out on the lake for a day. They stopped in a small town, found a nice café, and spent the rest of the afternoon sipping coffee and taking in the sun. It was still light when they got back to the house. John asked Utsie if she wanted a drink and told her he wanted to go over the mail before they went out to dinner. John was astounded when he found an invoice for $25,000 for a table at the monthly fundraiser from the Green Alliance. The envelope included ten tickets. Utsie walked into the room and looked at John's face.

"John, is anything wrong?"

"Your creepy little friend at Green Peace, or whatever the hell it is, just billed me twenty-five grand for ten tickets to his monthly dinner."

Utsie sat across from John. "Darling, don't underestimate the importance of this man. These dinners are for all the most powerful people in Europe, and I think that is your market. Did you join the organization?"

"Yeah, I joined."

"Then I think this is your—how do you say it in English? Oh yes—monthly dues."

John went red. "The dues for this thing are three hundred thousand dollars a year?"

Utsie smiled. "That is why it is exclusive, membership offered only to the most powerful people, and you are one of those, aren't you?"

John looked at her. "Okay, will you come?"

"I'll consider it."

The phone rang.

"Chong, how's it going?"

"John, I think you have found a very good man. This Franz is knowledgeable and has completely reorganized the office here. And I thought I was supposed to be training him." Chong let out a long laugh.

"Have you brought him to China yet?"

"No, we're leaving tomorrow. We were delayed, Visa issues, but it's all settled."

"Good."

Chong continued, "John, the reason I am calling—would Franz be able to spend an additional week with me?"

"Yes, but he must be back here by the twenty-seventh. I've just reserved a table at a very expensive dinner, and I want him to attend. By the way, have business cards made up for him. Chong, one last thing, did you introduce him to that stylist?"

"Yes, his new threads will be ready this afternoon. I'll call you when we get back."

"Thanks, Chong. Say hi to the family for me."

He then took Utsie by the hand. "Let's work up an appetite."

The next several weeks were uneventful, everyone was back at work. On the twenty-sixth, Iris walked into John's office to remind him that the Green Dinner was the following evening.

John looked up. "Yeah, I know, have the guests all confirmed?"

"Yes, all but one: Utsie."

Brad had gone home two weeks ago, so it would only be John, Franz, and Iris representing the company. John called Utsie and asked whether or not she'd be coming over that night and whether she would be going to the dinner on the twenty-seventh. She answered yes to both questions.

The evening of the dinner arrived. John's group assembled in the office. Franz was wearing a silk and wool double-breasted suit, impeccably tailored, and then Iris made her entrance. John lit up and remarked, "Iris, you look stunning."

Iris smiled and did a spin to show off her new Oleg Cassini gown. Franz even raised an eyebrow.

"Iris, I have never seen you look more beautiful."

"Thank you," she said in an excited voice.

Just then the door opened and Utsie walked in. Everyone stopped and stared, time seemed to stand still, even Iris gasped. John walked over to greet her.

"Utsie, you are a vision. I've seen you look stunning, but never like this." They all seemed to hover closer to her.

"Well, we are all here. Let's go. I don't have to tell you that this is an important event. You all have your business cards? Iris, take notes on the attendees. I want you all to enjoy the evening, but this is a working dinner."

They reached the front door of the Baur au Lac hotel. The sign read Private Party. John thought, *God, they've taken over the entire hotel for the evening. That must have cost a bundle. Maybe this wasn't such a bad idea.*

Helmut Fragge almost knocked John down, running up to them and grabbing Utsie by the hand.

"I am so glad you could all come. John, I hope you will join me in the library immediately after dinner. There are some people I want to introduce you to." He started to lead Utsie away as he continued, "I am going to steal Utsie for a while. She is the urban farm girl that the world has to know about. Don't worry, I will deliver her back to you before the dinner is served."

*I really don't like this guy.*

John asked Franz and Iris to stay close for a while to help him identify some of these people. The guest list was like the European truly rich and famous. At one point, Iris said dreamily, "I never thought I would be this close to so many of these people."

John introduced himself to so many people. *I'll never be able to remember all of these people.*

Franz disappeared for a while and returned with a young man who didn't look like he fit in with this group.

"John, this is Francois Jole. He's a reporter with the *Gazette*, a widely published newspaper in Central Europe."

"It is an honor, sir. I've heard a lot about you and your company. We don't see many Americans in the leisure industry, and the fact that you are a Green Alliance member shows me that you are like-minded. May I ask you a few questions?"

"Please do."

"Are you a sailboat manufacturer because you believe in the Green Movement?"

John answered very carefully, "I love sailing, and my thinking is that boating, under power, pollutes and it doesn't give one the feeling of man against the elements in a way that sailing does."

"I know you are not a Swiss citizen, but are you supporting Herr Fragge in the upcoming election?"

"You are correct. I am an American, and as such, I don't think it appropriate to offer an opinion."

"Do you think Herr Fragge's work is valid?"

"I believe it is everyone's responsibility to take care of the planet we live on. It's the only one we have."

John was rescued by Utsie. "John, they are about to serve diner, we must go to the table."

John said good-bye to the reporter, took Utsie by the arm, and made his way to the table.

The speeches were long and boring. John felt his eyes closing when he heard, "The next speaker is an American. Please let me introduce you to John Moore of Sailcraft Yachts."

John was not prepared for this, but Utsie pinched him under the table, and he went to the lectern.

"Good evening, everyone," John began, "I am a new arrival to Zurich and am greatly honored to be speaking here this evening. I would like tell you a little bit about Sailcraft Yachts. My partner, Peter Fraus, and I started Sailcraft over thirty years ago. We both worked as tuna fisherman and earned enough money to build our first sailing yacht. That year, we sold five. To date, we sell approximately two thousand luxury yachts a year, worldwide. We believe that sailing is the most environmentally friendly leisure sport in the world. Even though skiing is a wonderful healthy sport, it does modify the terrain. You don't have to build stadiums or tracks to sail. As long as the sailor is prudent, he can sail any waters and leave no impact whatsoever. The earth is a place for us to live and enjoy ourselves. As long as we respect it and protect it, we can continue enjoying it. Thank you."

John returned to his seat amidst a loud round of applause.

Helmut Fragge grabbed John directly after dinner. "John, your speech was wonderful. Now come and meet some people."

He didn't know what to say, so he just followed the creepy little man. As they entered the library, John noticed some of the people that Franz and Iris had pointed out to him. Helmut made the rounds with John in tow. While speaking to a group of men from Akzol Nobel, he was approached by a Chinese man who introduced himself as Ascot Chen. John asked if they had ever met. There was something familiar about this man.

John said, "Your voice is familiar. Have we spoken on the phone, perhaps?"

"No, I don't believe I have had the pleasure. Although I am sure my voice sounds like many Chinese my age who were educated in Britain."

"Possibly, I lived in Hong Kong for a time."

"That must be it. I just wanted to tell you that I enjoyed your speech, but I think you upset the people from K2 and Rossignol. It has been a pleasure meeting you." With that said, Chen left.

John had an eerie feeling down deep in his gut.

At breakfast, the following morning, Franz told John that he had made a lot of connections at the dinner and several showed real promise for sales.

Iris beamed with excitement. "I made a sale last night. A man approached me and showed serious interest in our new line. I explained that our new design would revolutionize the industry, and I filled him in on some of the important design changes that Brad told me about. The man asked me about pricing. I told him from a million to one million four hundred thousand US. I told him they come in lengths from sixty-eight, seventy-four, seventy-six feet and as big as eighty-two footers starting at $2 million. The man smiled and asked how long it would take to deliver ten of each size to Rotterdam. I told him four to five months, he said that's acceptable and gave me this order."

She handed the paper to John. He studied it and frowned. It was signed by Ascot Chen. Iris asked if there was anything wrong.

"Not at all, great job, Iris. It just surprised me a bit. Well, I guess we covered the cost of the dinner."

Later that afternoon, John called Iris to his office and handed her a check.

"Fifty thousand dollars!" she screamed. "No, John, I can't accept this. You've taken such good care of me. I was just doing my job."

"You're going to take that and start an investment portfolio. I've set up a meeting for you tomorrow with Peter Tsillman."

"John, I can't thank you enough."

He truly felt affection for this girl, and he loved her enthusiasm and warmth.

"You're doing a great job, and it's me who owes you."

Once again, John thought about how happy he was with the group he had put together. He was pleased that his idea of having them live together had drawn them closer, like a family.

# 9

### Jakarta, Indonesia

Mike Manheim sat across the desk from Y. K. Chen, the unopposed head of the Liddo Group.

"Mike, you've done a great job for us. You have gained control of the American media, installed two presidents, and now you have put into motion a takeover of all the world's energy producers."

"YK, it's not done yet."

"Mike, you have never failed, so why the hesitation?"

Manheim explained that he had control over the union heads and enough people in the government to make it happen, but he believed Aristotle Saris was the weak link.

"Aristotle has used his own monies to fund the community groups and has a little too much control over them. We don't need civil unrest when we get this in place. It's in our best interest to do this quietly, and if done properly, we can use our hold on energy production as a lever to get what we want when we want it. If it all goes public, we will lose our wedge."

"When you have control of the power companies, kill him. In the meantime, use your media connections to instigate trouble with these so-called community groups. Push for arrests and get the FBI to keep a close eye on them. Tie a couple of politicians to them. Get that guy Michael something, whatever his name is, and the ex-VP to make a movie about it—something like 'Are there internal armies in place in America?' That should bring public focus on that and away from our endeavor."

"Good idea, YK. I'll get to work on that as soon as I get back."

"Mike, how's your new president doing?"

Mike looked at him, realizing that he was being tested.

"He's doing exactly what we expected," Mike lied.

Manheim made a mental note to set up a meeting with the politicos upon his return. He would tell them to start getting some serious Republican clout to slow this guy down until he could figure out a better way to control him. Mike knew that YK never liked the idea of throwing so much money at the DNC and the progressives. But he didn't fully understand US politics, where money talks and bullshit only goes so far.

After Manheim left, Chen put a call into Manheim's mistress; she was on his payroll.

"Paula, my dear, I haven't heard from you in a while, are you all right?"

"Yes, I'm fine, but I haven't been able to get the time alone to call you. Please ask Mike to send me to Jakarta so I can discuss some items with you."

YK realized that Mike must be suspicious if he was keeping her on such a short leash. *It's time to get her out of there.* YK picked up his sterile phone and dialed Manheim.

"Mike, sorry to bother you, but I just had a thought. I think you might be getting too close with Paula."

"Don't you think I can run my own shop? Do you believe for a minute that I would let a broad get me into trouble?"

"Not at all, Mike," YK said calmly. "I just think that neither of us needs any diversions at the moment. Please send her back here."

"Maybe you're right. I'll send her there the day after I get back."

Manheim had known from the start that she was spying for YK, but misinformation was his strong suit. *It's probably better I send her back now. If I had caught her, I would have had to kill her, and I'm fond of Paula.*

# 10

## Zurich, Switzerland

John was sitting with Iris and Franz when Utsie arrived. Iris put together some hors d'oeuvres and made drinks while John started the meeting.

"Utsie, I've asked you here to help us. We've developed a list of the people who are involved with Helmut's Green Party. As we go through the list, I would like to know any information you know about them."

"This sounds a bit like a police interrogation. Are you going to shine a light in my face?"

"I apologize. I didn't mean to sound like that, but I don't know these people at all. I believe you know many of them personally. I only want to work up a marketing plan geared specifically toward each person or group."

"I'm only fooling with you, John. Don't be so serious."

Iris broke in, "Let's start with Helmut Fragge."

"Helmut is an extremely powerful man. No one seems to know where he got his power other than that he started the Green Movement in Switzerland. As far as I know, he's a lawyer, and he was never really political. Everyone seemed surprised when he started the Swiss Green Movement. A short time later, he merged with the European Green Alliance about the same time that the last of the Eastern European countries was admitted to the EU. Everyone presumes he got a large amount of money from the Alliance, but I don't think so. Later that year, he donated fifty million euros to the Alliance. Why would the Alliance give him money and take it right back?"

Franz jumped in with, "John, that's what I was working on when I got into trouble."

John thought for a while and told them to go to the next person on the list.

They worked for hours before John suggested that they break for dinner. Utsie suggested a small restaurant near Bellevueplatz, just down the street from the Eden au Lac. After dinner, they all agreed the restaurant had been a great choice. The food was excellent, and the ambiance was wonderful. It was quiet, comfortable, and cozy.

When they got home, they all went their separate ways. John and Utsie, now alone, began an intimate interlude that lasted almost until morning. When they were spent, Utsie fell asleep, and John just looked at her in amazement for quite some time. Just before he dozed off, a thought occurred to him. *Franz has never been on a date, at least since I have known him.* Eventually, sleep took him as well. When he awoke, Utsie was lying awake next to him. When she realized he was awake, she rolled toward him and said, "I thought I would never say this to anyone again. I love you."

John surprised himself saying, "I feel the same way about you."

They embraced, held each other for a long time, letting the loneliness and heartache they each felt, for different reasons, drain from their bodies and their minds.

After breakfast, John told Iris that he was going to town to meet with Peter Tsillman and that he needed to borrow her car. Franz had taken his to the shop for servicing. Iris threw him the keys. "Don't get any scratches on it. My boss would be angry." John laughed and hurried out.

The drive into Zurich from Eck was pleasant, until you got to the town center where five trams converged into a large roundabout. He thought, *These people are supposed to be such good engineers. They must have been drunk when they designed this.*

Unperturbed, he got through the maze of traffic and reached the private garage of Wertshaft und Privat.

Before he could get out of the car, he heard Tsillman's voice. "John, I have made a reservation at the St. Gotthard for lunch. The chef called me and told me the crawfish were fresh this morning."

They walked the few blocks to the hotel. As soon as they arrived, John saw Helmut Fragge. Helmut came over and said hello to them. John was relieved when Helmut told them he couldn't stay for lunch since he had another appointment. They were seated at the table next to the crawfish pond. Tsillman seemed to take great joy in scooping out his own lunch. John had the fillet mignon with Béarnaise. The conversation went to the events of the last Green dinner. John told Tsillman that he was due a commission on the forty boats, as the area agent. Surprisingly, Tsillman refused and told John he had nothing to do with that sale, so the commission was not due him. *I guess the three hundred million he made is making him frivolous.*

"Peter, do you know Ascot Chen?"

Tsillman's face went ashen. He looked as if he were caught with his hand in the cookie jar. John was very suspicious at the man's initial response.

"Why do you ask?"

"Well, I thought you knew everyone."

Tsillman was now visibly shaking.

"Peter, what's wrong? I just met the guy at that dinner, and he's the one who ordered the forty boats."

Peter, now trying to compose himself, said, "If he's the one who ordered the boats, you will not have to worry about payment. Mr. Chen is one of the bank's best clients."

John had a bad feeling about Chen, and Tsillman's reaction confirmed it. John thought it prudent to change the subject.

"Peter, how is Iris's portfolio doing?"

"Fine," Peter replied, calming himself. "She's already doubled her money, and with exponential growth, I should have it up to a million in a matter of months."

"Peter, you're amazing."

It was three o'clock when he drove out of the bank's parking garage. John decided to visit Utsie on the farm. He drove up to the house and found the door open. He called Utsie's name and heard her crying in the next room.

"Utsie, what's wrong?"

"John, they're back. A man just came here and offered me a hundred million US for the property. I told him I was not interested, and he made a veiled threat. It's them. I just know it."

"Utsie, pack a few things. You're coming to my house."

When they got to the house, John told her to get some rest. He poured himself a drink and went out to sit on the terrace. It was about two in the morning when Utsie came out.

"Utsie, I think I have a plan."

John outlined the plan and told her he was still trying to work out a few kinks, but if she agreed, he would begin immediately.

"John, I don't want you involved. These people are very dangerous."

"If the plan works, they'll be totally defused. I couldn't take losing you."

Utsie threw her arms around him and said in a low voice, "I am yours forever."

John told her that he was going to fly to London the following day. He would work from there until everything was in place.

# 11

The plane landed in London. John went through customs within half an hour and was in a cab headed for the Grosvenor Hotel. He asked the driver to stop at a shop where he purchased a prepaid phone, thinking that would be difficult to trace. Once in his room, he called Chong.

"Chong, this is John. I'm wiring two hundred and twelve million dollars to you. I want you to leave it in our account. I also want you to hold a press conference and inform them that we are going to expand into the Asian market and we're looking for sites to build a new manufacturing facility. Loo & Loo has already been instructed to set up a new company. At their instruction, I want you to transfer one hundred and fifty million to the account they designate."

Chong interrupted, "Boss, are you in trouble again?"

"Just listen, I want you to go to China and buy a piece of property on the coast, probably near Nanjing. After you do that, tell the press that the property has been acquired for one hundred and fifty million US and construction will start on the new facility as soon as we have permission from the government."

Chong interrupted, "It's a woman, isn't it?"

"Damn it, just listen. Let me know if anyone is nosing around. Call me at this number only."

Chong said, "Okay, boss, I've got it. If you need any more help, just call me."

Then John called Peter Tsillman.

"Peter, hello, it's John. Could you put me through to the transfer desk? I'm transferring a rather substantial sum of money to Sailcraft's Hong Kong account. We've decided to build a manufacturing facility in China."

"Splendid idea, John. The property value alone makes it a sound investment."

John made the transfer and waited until he received word from Loo & Loo Solicitors that the company was ready.

As soon as Tsillman hung up from John's call, he called Ascot Chen and told him that John had just moved a substantial amount of money to Hong Kong to buy a piece of property in China for a new manufacturing facility.

"Well done, Peter, there will be a little something left in your mailbox this evening."

Tsillman immediately made arrangements for a short holiday in the Caribbean. Chen phoned his contact in China and told them to lock up some property on the coast. "The Sailcraft group is in the market. Add forty percent to the price we can buy it for. I am certain they'll come to you as you are their distributor in China."

John hung around his hotel room for two days before the call came in; it was Janet Loo.

"Is everything ready?"

"Yes, John, I'll walk over and tell Chong Lee personally. I'll have him transfer the funds. The account has been set up with the Royal Bank of Scotland."

"Thank you, Janet. I'll have the deed and the survey forwarded to you by hand. When you receive the documents, draw up a purchase agreement between the new company and the bearer of the documents. Have them sign a deed of trust and all other necessary papers."

"John, consider it done."

John called Utsie and explained everything in detail.

"Get all necessary papers ready, I want you and Franz to fly to Hong Kong. Let me talk to Franz."

John gave him his instructions and told him that Chong would pick them up at the airport.

"Franz, follow Chong's instructions to the letter."

John's next call was to Iris.

"Iris, I want you to make up a press release stating that Utsie has sold her farm to an Asian Group for an undisclosed amount, rumored in excess of one hundred million euros. Utsie will stay on to manage the property. Do not let anyone see it and do not do anything with it until I tell you. After that's done, I want you to hand deliver a thank-you note from me to Helmut Fragge for allowing me to join the Green Alliance. While you are in the Green Alliance office, I need you to find a way to send the press release from there."

Iris told John that it would not be a problem.

"Good, just make sure no one can trace it back to us."

"Okay, John. I'll change the date on the fax machine before I send it and readjust it when I'm done."

John decided to buy a new prepaid phone. He destroyed the old one. He walked through St. James Park and took a seat with a view of the London Hilton. He called Chong and apologized for waking him but he wanted to go over every detail.

"This has to be done with precision. I don't want anyone to be able to trace any facet of this deal. Use Franz as much as possible, but I don't want him to know all of the details."

Two days later, John checked out of the hotel. He had received good news from Chong. The transaction was done.

Before John walked through the entrance of Gatwick, he stepped on the phone, crushing it. He put part of it in the waste receptacle near there and threw the rest of it in a receptacle well within the terminal. He walked over to the ticket counter and bought a ticket for San Francisco. John wanted to tell Peter this one face-to-face.

# 12

The man that had initially made the offer to Utsie sat uncomfortably in front of Ascot Chen. Chen sat quietly, making the man squirm.

"Our principals will not be pleased with your results, Wolfgang."

Wolfgang Schmidt was the managing director of the Liddo Group's largest trucking company in Europe.

"How did you let this get past us for a measly forty-seven million? Have you lost your negotiating finesse?"

"How do you know she only got forty-seven million more?"

"I am surprised you have to ask. I know it the same way that I know you have recently deposited two hundred thousand euros, which you stole from the company."

Wolfgang paled as he started to protest and then decided that it was useless.

"Are you going to kill me?"

"My dear fellow, how could you even think that? I am not planning on telling the principals about your little indiscretion. I'll have to keep an eye on you, but I think that will remain between the two of us, for now. I want you to do something else. If you are successful, perhaps all will be forgiven."

"What do you want me to do?" he asked, visibly shaken.

"You are friends with the head of the German Transportation Union?"

Wolfgang, nearly vomiting, replied, "Yes."

"He has been very difficult lately, preventing us from going forward with a very large deal. I need you to make him disappear."

"No, I won't do it," Wolfgang yelled frantically.

Chen looked at him with a strange frightening grin.

"Well then, my friend, all of this is out of my hands." Chen got up.

"Wait," Wolfgang said, anguish on his face, "I'll do it."

"Now that's a good chap, I'll call you after I read about it in the newspapers."

As Chen walked out of the door, Wolfgang leered at him with unadulterated hate. Wolfgang finally understood the price he had paid for his wealth, his soul.

Chen made his report to YK, who concluded that since they also used Loo & Loo, they were better off not approaching them to find out who the buyer was.

"That little farm has been too much trouble since we started to go after it. Let's write that one off. We have more important issues pending."

Chen then told YK the transportation union business was almost taken care of and perhaps Wolfgang Schmidt might be a good person to put in that position.

"He will be extremely pliable."

YK, pleased, told Ascot he wanted him to go to America and visit Washington.

"Visit some of our White House contacts and give me a full report on the current political climate. Also, find out if Manheim is losing control as well."

Chen had reservations about getting in between YK and Manheim. He would have to think about how to pull this off without any repercussions. Once he was in Washington, Manheim would know he was there. He wouldn't like the fact that Ascot was meddling with his people on his turf.

The next morning, Chen made arrangements for his trip to Washington. He would call Manheim the day after he left, apologizing for not calling while he was there. He would tell him that there was an urgent matter in Europe, that he needed Washington's assistance and thought it best to keep him out of it.

Chen spent the next week in Washington, seeing congressmen, senators, and a few lobbyists who were on the payroll. On his last day there, his phone rang.

"Ascot, I'm hurt, you came to the States and didn't even call me."

"Michael, my dear fellow, I was going to call before I left. I had a problem in Europe with some trade unions, so I came here to solicit the assistance of some of your team. It did not concern you, so I thought it best not to involve you."

"Give me a call the next time you're in town. We'll have lunch. Okay, partner?"

Manheim thought, *Shit, YK is checking up on me. I'd better pull something off quick.*

Chen decided it was best for him to cut his trip short, so he made arrangements to fly out of DC that night.

He arrived in Jakarta two days later. He went directly from the airport to YK's office.

"Ascot, come in. How was your trip?"

YK is most dangerous when he was affable.

"My trip was fine, and I have much to report. The political climate in the States is not good. The democrats have been handed over to very liberal socialists and the population is fighting back. We could lose all of the senators and congressmen we've invested in. Manheim hasn't lost total control. However, the problem seems to lie with a small group surrounding the president. I believe that the new president is promising favors to several different groups. His heart is with Aristotle Saris, or at least most of the people around him have their allegiances there. I have been told by several of our people that Manheim is still the force behind the curtain. Saris is still the largest contributor to the DNC, and no one seems to know if it goes beyond that.

Manheim is using the media to keep the situation ambiguous, in the meantime. While I was there, the media featured several exposés on community groups and the new czars, which were less than flattering. The good news is that the administration has most of the population buying into the 'Green' thing. I would suggest that Manheim continues to push media focus on the community groups, which should cause at least some investigations, reducing the fire before it all boils over. I suggest you do whatever you are going to do before the next elections."

"Thank you, Ascot. I will take all of this into consideration."

"YK, one more thing. Michael knew I was there. He called me. If he thinks I am watching him or questioning him, I will lose my effectiveness. I told him there was a problem in Europe that I had to handle quickly and I was just there to get some help from our friends."

"Ascot, as usual, you are correct."

With that, YK picked up the phone.

"Hello, Michael, don't be angry at Ascot for not reporting to you when he came there a few days ago. I told him to keep you out of this one. It was a European matter and it did not concern you. I apologize. I should have informed you before the fact." YK listened to his response.

"Yes, Paula arrived safely last week. I will tell her to call you. Good-bye."

*That piece-of-shit Chen is scared out of his mind. YK is not happy. I better watch my ass.*

Ascot thanked YK for clearing that up and left. He grabbed the next flight out of the airport just to get away.

# 13

### Washington DC

The chief of staff was meeting with the president, going over the day's alerts.

"Ascot Chen was in town for a few days. He was asking about the stability of the administration. Like it or not, we owe those people. They contributed a lot of money during the election, their control of the media is enormous. If you piss them off, you could lose media backing. The three main groups that funded us were all like-minded before the election, but there is trouble in paradise, and that can't be good for us. Mr. President, we promised them a lot. We need them: Chen's group for their control of the media, the Saris group for their money, the Middle East group to calm the problems there."

"Look, we made them promises based on their promises to us. If they're having problems amongst themselves, it has nothing to do with us. What are we going to do about these people fighting us on the Health Care Bill?"

The chief of staff replied, "But, Mr. President, these are powerful people!"

"Powerful, my ass, I'm the president of the United States."

The chief of staff stormed down the hallway and slammed the door to his office as he went in.

"Get Wiley Pritchard on the horn now!"

"Hello, Wiley. It's Rob. Can you come to Washington today?"

"Gee, Rob, I'm playing golf with some of the boys today."

"Wiley, this is important. I'll send a plane for you."

"Well, that's nice of you, Rob, but I can't disappoint the boys, especially in this climate."

The chief of staff's face turned purple.

"All right, then I'll come down to Arkansas. We can have dinner this evening."

Wiley smiled. He knew he had Rob on the ropes as he mustered up his best country boy accent. "Well, I look forward to seeing you at my house around eight."

Wiley got on the phone to Manheim as soon as he hung up.

"Mike, the president's chief of staff is coming to see me this evening. I'd like to meet with you before he gets here."

"Wiley, that's great. Can you get over here now?"

When Wiley arrived, he found the "inner circle" already assembled: Mike Manheim, two ex-governors, the heads of three trade unions, and the CEO of the largest media group in the United States.

"Wiley, good to see you," Manheim began. "We were just discussing the situation. This is becoming a train wreck. We backed social change and the Green movement because it would help us. The government would get control of the people and we would get control of the government. We're set up to take over the automobile business, financial institutions, and the health care industry."

He was careful not to mention the energy producers.

"We've invested fortunes in these yahoos, and they're screwing it up. They've screwed up worse than any other administration. With all of the help we've given them through the media, they're still down in the polls. There's a groundswell of public opinion, and it's getting stronger every day—against them. If the republicans control the senate and congress in the next elections, we're screwed. This is a disaster, and the chief of staff, that asshole, promised he could control this guy."

Tom Grey, the media CEO, joined in.

"We have done everything we can to try to cover up some of this shit, but now we are losing credibility. For God's sake, when they're telling people that Grandma is not going to get her medicine, but they'll give her a check-out counselor, I mean, how do you put a positive spin on that one?"

With that said, one of the union leaders chimed in.

"Our unions have lost three hundred thousand jobs, and the ones who have kept their jobs are willing to make deals directly with management. We're losing control over our own people."

Wiley sat there watching this unlikely group. The labor boss was wearing a silk shirt with a gold necklace and bracelet, both about an inch in diameter. He was sitting next to the corporate exec wearing an Armani suit, who was sitting across from the other labor leader dressed in a sweat suit. Wiley thought, *What am I doing here? This little group is controlling the United States and all anyone of them cares about is what's in his pockets.* He realized then that he was in the same boat. He had amassed a fortune with these people, even though after he met them, all he wanted to do was take a shower. But he had made this choice a long time ago, so he figured he had better give them some input.

"Gentlemen, it seems to me that the biggest problem we face is to keep these people in office through the elections. Mike, can you dump five hundred million into the market?"

Manheim answered, "Yes."

"Good, put the money in companies that will give the strongest short-term gains that will drive the market up substantially. Tom, see that your headlines read, 'THE END OF THE RECESSION IS NEAR' and have as many TV commentators as you can report huge gains in the market. We'll find some companies with cash flow problems and promise them low-cost financing if they allow the unions in. Then we play with the unemployment figures and report that the unemployment rate is dropping at a Herculean pace. I'll tell Rob to get the administration to back off health care until after the elections, and we'll help them push it through later, no matter what. This way we'll get what we want and the country will appear to be back to normal."

"Great plan," Manheim said. "You all know what you have to do. Let's get to it."

They started to leave; Manheim asked Wiley to stay.

"Sit down, Wiley," Manheim began, "I need you to ride hard on this one. Pull out all the stops. I have to stabilize the situation fast or we are going to lose our backing. If we do, you and I are up the river without the proverbial paddle."

"Don't worry, Mike. I've never let you down."

"Well, this time it means our world as you and I know it."

Wiley left. *I have never seen Manheim like this before. He seems scared. What the hell is he up to now, and why did I ever get involved?*

# 14

### Zurich, Switzerland

Three weeks had passed since the transfer of Utsie's property. John and Utsie were sitting on the terrace.

"John, it looks as though your plan worked. I can't thank you enough. I went to my attorney, and you are now my sole beneficiary, just in case something happens to me. That money is yours, and it was the only way I could protect it for you without returning it."

"Utsie, you should never have done that. It raises too many questions. How do you know you can trust your lawyer?"

"He's been my family's lawyer for years, and he has protected me many times before. I told him I was worried that my family members might do me harm if they thought they would end up with the money. I told him that we were engaged, we planned to marry soon, and that you were much wealthier than I."

"You told him we were engaged? Is that what you want, Utsie?"

"No."

John didn't believe her. He asked her again, and again she declined. John decided to drop it for the moment.

"Utsie, it was kind of you to think of a way to protect me."

"John, after all you have done for me—you saved my family home, my fortune, and possibly my life. It was the only thing to do. I still can't think of a way to repay you."

"Utsie, there is no payment required. You're a good friend, and I love you."

Utsie walked over and sat on John's lap. She put her arms around his neck and just stared into his eyes for a long time. Finally, she said, "I love you too," as she laid her head on his shoulder. They stayed in that position for over an hour until Iris walked in. Utsie got up slowly and returned to her chair.

"Sorry to disturb you both, but I just got a call from Brad. Twenty of the new boats have been built and tested. The water trials went well, and they're ready to be shipped."

"Good, tell Brad to ship sixteen against the order and have one of each size with the company logo on the sails shipped here. We can't sell from an empty store."

"I'll get right back to him. He told me they were being packed as we spoke, so I'll stop him before they're all labeled for shipment."

"Wait! Have the following names painted on the four coming here: Utsie's Love, Iris' Escape, Franz's Dream, and Hole in the Water. I'm going to ask Franz to teach the two of you how to sail, and I expect you to be out on the water as much as possible. It'll be great visibility for us."

"The next Green dinner is scheduled for the week after they arrive. Why not ask Helmut if we could present the new design at the dinner? It will get plenty of attention."

"Iris, that's a great idea!"

Iris smiled and told him she would call Helmut right after she rang Brad.

"You really like her, don't you?" Utsie asked.

"Yes, I do. She's like the daughter I never had."

John surprised himself with that comment, but it was true.

"Let's get dressed and go out for dinner. We can go to that nice restaurant down by the Eden au Lac."

Utsie readily agreed and was already heading for the bedroom to change.

# 15

### Little Rock, Arkansas

The chief of staff arrived in Little Rock at seven on his way to the home of Wiley Pritchard.

The house befitted an ex-governor, while the location showed he was still just a good old boy.

The chief of staff was about to knock when the door opened. Wiley stood there with a big smile on his face.

"Rob, it's great to see you, boy."

Rob knew this "good old boy" shit was an act, but he would never call him on it. Wiley was still a very powerful man.

"It's good to see you too, Wiley."

"Well, come in and sit down. Can I get you a drink?"

"Rob, we're having some problems with your boy in Washington. It appears that you're losing control, and the boys here are upset."

"Wiley, we have everything under control. You don't have to worry about a thing."

"Well, powder my ass and call me a biscuit! You come to my house and talk to me like I'm some fucking party delegate that just gave you a thousand dollars."

Wiley slammed his hand down on the table; Rob jumped.

"I want answers, and I want them now! Have you lost control of that fool we put into office?"

"Things haven't gone a hundred percent our way. The media hasn't covered us properly."

"Are you shitting me, boy? The media has made a gosh darn god out of this guy, and it has covered your butts every which way but loose."

Rob, squirming in his chair, started to say something, but Wiley cut him off.

"You're going to pull back on the Health Care Bill and concentrate on the Green issue. As long as you do that, we will take care of everything else to make your boy look good. If you don't, we will withdraw all of our support—money, media, and muscle. That's right, the three *M*s, the ones that keep you where you are. We might even arrange a recall or an impeachment, and you know I don't make idle threats."

Rob knew Wiley meant every word. This guy is powerful and dangerous.

Suddenly, Wiley changed his tone.

"Now, Rob, we're on the same side here. Just get your boy to play ball, and we'll guarantee that he gets his Health Care Bill passed right after the elections. We've invested a lot to get you where you are. Don't be stupid, let it go. Cut your cords with these activist groups. Fire a couple of those so-called czars for not performing and rethink the whole health care issue. The republicans won't have anything to fight you on. After the elections, we'll go full force on health care, getting you and your boy whatever the hell you want."

With that, Wiley stood, putting his arm around Rob.

"Rob, it was so nice of you to drop by. I'll be in Washington in two weeks, and I expect to hear that everything is back on track."

Rob said good-bye and headed for the airport.

As soon as he was on the plane, Rob got on the phone to the president.

"Mr. President, I'll be landing at Dulles at twelve fifteen a.m. I have to see you tonight. I'll meet you in the oval office at one a.m."

Before the president had a chance to answer, Rob hung up. Rob was in panic mode. They made us and they can break us. I knew this guy didn't have the experience. He just doesn't get it. He knows how to play the game, but he doesn't understand the consequences. He can't not take care of the power base and think he can still survive. I really think this guy believes the hype we contrived.

He walked into the oval office at ten minutes to one. He was pacing when the president arrived.

"What's this all about, Rob?"

"Please, sit down, Mr. President. As you know, sir, we get a lot of support from the group in Arkansas, monetarily and politically. They're not happy with the way things are going, and they want us to do a few things to rectify the situation."

"What do they want?"

"First, we have to stop pushing the Health Care Bill."

"Absolutely not, that was the center of my campaign, and I'm not going to give it up."

Rob stared at him for a minute and then blew up.

"Sir, your campaign was funded, designed, organized, and choreographed by these people. You'd have said the sky was green if they told you to. Do you remember what you said when I approached you? Your exact words, sir, were 'I'll do anything you want.' You believe your own hype."

"Rob, you can't speak to me that way. I'm the president."

"Yes, sir, you are. But if you don't play ball, you won't be president for long. These are very powerful people, and if they want to, they can ruin you just as fast as they had you elected. Mr. President, think about this. Right now, as we speak, they are digging into your past, and if they can't find anything, they'll fabricate it. They own the media, all of the media. They have the power to make a choirboy look like a murderer. Please reconsider your stance. They've promised to give you whatever you want right after the elections. They also want you to fire some of the czars. In return, they will make the economy look better, skew the unemployment figures to show a dramatic drop, and make you look like a hero. Please, sir, consider it."

The next morning, the president announced that he was rethinking the Health Care Bill. He went on to say that after serious careful deliberation, he had decided not to accept any of the current proposals made by the house and the senate. He would ask them to put more time into the proposals, to better address the concerns of the American people.

Over the next month, three of the czars were fired; one had violated his parole after being released from prison, another was abusing his position, and the third was fired due to sheer incompetence.

# 16

**Bonn, Germany**

Helmut Fragge sat in a room with Aristotle Saris and four other men. Saris took charge of the meeting.

"Gentlemen, thank you all for coming. We are about to embark on a journey toward a new world order. There are only a few minor obstacles in our path, which is why I have summoned you here. We've made great strides, gaining power in most of the EU countries, but we've lost ground in some of the Eastern European countries, as well as Greece and Portugal. I want the Green Alliance to merge with the National Socialist Parties in each of these areas. We will focus on the poor and the unemployed. The new Green Socialist Party will fund programs and put pressure on businesses to hire more people. We need as much publicity as possible. We'll blame the business community for the poverty and unhealthy conditions in these countries. We'll organize marches and demonstrations across Europe. If we can't defeat the existing political parties, we will, at least, have them on the run. Our fight against oppression will be persistent, and when the smoke clears, we will be in power and have control of everything."

Helmut Fragge interrupted, "Herr Saris, how do you propose we do this? The economy is very stable in most countries now, and we have made great strides in ecology."

"My dear Helmut, if there is no problem, cause one. We must win at all costs."

Over the next few months, as planned, there would be a nuclear disaster in a French power plant, and the city of Florence would discover that its main sewer treatment plant had been dumping waste into the river for several months. There would be several executives arrested in Bonn, Germany, for dumping hazardous waste into the Rhine, two major food producers would be closed down just outside of Amsterdam, and the city of Montrose on the French/Swiss border would discover that the material used for paving their roads had caused cancer in thousands of people. Saris congratulated everyone and asked Helmut to remain.

"My dear Helmut, you've done well. I've made you a wealthy man. I need a favor."

"Anything,"

"I need you to step down and not run for prime minister. The head of the Swiss National Socialist Party is the man I want in office."

Helmut looked crushed. "But why, haven't I done a good job?"

"On the contrary, you have done an exemplary job, and that is why I need you to stay behind the scenes, so to speak. I want you to be the power behind the power. At this moment, you are almost assured of becoming the next PM, but if you are put under that scrutiny, it will be difficult for you to do what is necessary. You know most liberals are just that until it affects them directly, and then those nasty conservative notions raise their ugly heads. Let the Socialist Party deal with the socialists. We have bigger fish to fry."

"If that is what you want, then I am all for it," Helmut stated with false bravado.

"Good, you will be well compensated for your loyalty to our effort."

Helmut thanked Saris and left. Saris picked up the phone.

"Everything is in place. Europe should be ready in six months. One more thing—if the Socialist Party wins the election in two months, I need an accident to happen to Helmut Fragge. At that point, he'll be too expensive for what he's worth."

On the way back, Helmut smiled to himself, *The power behind the power. I've finally made it.*

Over the next few months, the Green and the Socialist parties merged. There were marches and demonstrations all over Europe. Television and newspapers were condemning businesses throughout the EU, and people were calling for the resignation of four of Europe's top leaders. Then the unimaginable happened, trade unions called for strikes and several countries shut down; there was rioting in the streets and martial law was ordered in France, Spain, and Germany.

Saris called an emergency meeting with his key people.

"The situation is serious, but salvageable. We started it, now we will stop it. The Green Socialist Party must start to condemn this behavior. They must call for the end of the strikes and announce plausible solutions for the inequities in these countries. I have already notified our media and union contacts, they'll work with us. If handled properly, the Green Socialist Party will be lauded as knights in shining armor, the saviors of Europe, and our power will be guaranteed."

It worked, and by the end of the month, all of Europe was praising the efforts of the Green Socialists to restore order to all the countries involved.

Saris sat alone, rejoicing in his brilliance. The visions of a world under his control, which he dreamed of as a boy, were coming into his grasp.

# 17

## Zurich

All of the boats had been delivered, and the presentation at the Green dinner was a great success, producing orders for ninety-two more boats. John and his team worked hard for several weeks after organizing the production and delivery schedules. After eleven straight hours at his desk, John took a break and went out on the terrace for a drink. A little later, Iris came out to join him. She plopped into his lap and rested her head on his shoulder.

"I'm exhausted. Do you mind if I sit here for a minute?"

John didn't say a word as he just rubbed her back until she went to sleep.

He lifted Iris up, carried her into her room, and placed her gently on her bed. He bent down and kissed her on the forehead. As he straightened up, he sensed someone; then he heard her voice.

"You're starting to care too much for her."

He put his finger to his lips and pushed Utsie from the room.

"Maybe you're right, but Brad, Franz, Iris, you, and Peter are the only family I have."

Utsie smiled playfully. "Then what are we waiting for? Let's try to make a baby."

John laughed and followed Utsie to his room, where they stayed for the entire evening.

The next morning, John was hard at work when the phone rang.

"John, Peter here. You're a miracle worker. I've been watching the news. They make it look like Europe is blowing up, and you get orders for ninety-two boats. You're incredible."

"You're not doing badly either. We've had sales last month of one hundred thirty-seven boats, and you've been able to build them all on schedule."

"John, that wasn't all me. Brad's a genius. He took the additional production space I acquired and modified the production line. We're getting twice the output than before the modification. That kid is great."

"Talking about that kid, can you let him go for two weeks?"

"Sure, everything is in place, and if there are any problems, I can jump in, sure. Why do you want him?"

"You don't want to know. You'd be pissed if I told you."

"Say no more. Iris is lonely."

"Peter, you're a good man."

"Take care of yourself and don't get into any trouble. See ya, John."

"Bye, Peter."

# 18

### Memphis, Tennessee

Mike Manheim preferred to be alone. It had been that way since his time in Special Forces. The amazing thing was that with all the psychological exams the government had put him through, they had never picked up on the fact that he was a malicious psychopath, or maybe they had. That could have been the reason he had been selected to work alone, as an assassin. He had worked on the Laos and Cambodian borders during the Viet Nam conflict. That was where he met Y. K. Chen. YK had been in control of the Golden Triangle and introduced Manheim to the profitability of the drug trade.

Manheim, the US head of the Liddo Group, was wealthy beyond his wildest dreams. It wasn't all about the money. He enjoyed the game. He was happy being alone in his twenty-two-bedroom house outside of Memphis. Today was a special day. Not only was it his birthday, but he had just received the results of his manipulation of the president. The findings were better than expected.

He poured himself a bourbon and branch water and went into the solarium. The solarium was made of special glass, impregnated with fine copper wire in a certain pattern that rendered even the most sophisticated bugging and listening devices useless. He called YK and told him that the political situation had been stabilized and that he was able to have the Green Automotive Bill pushed through the senate and congress. The bill outlined regulations on the gas mileage of every car before they were produced.

"Have our battery plants in Singapore geared up to start producing the required batteries for GM and Chrysler? I already had the contracts signed as sole supplier. We're now the largest tier-two company in Detroit. They pushed through the bill restricting credit card companies, so I have transferred ten billion dollars through normal channels to our secondary lenders who are beyond restriction. I'm putting a two-billion-dollar ceiling on each company. When they reach that, they have been instructed to buy out as many of the smaller banks as possible. They will transfer as much of their liability as they can into the newly acquired banks. That way, if the shit hits the fan, the FDIC covers us up to two hundred and fifty grand per account."

"Good work, Mike. Truthfully, I thought you were failing, but you pulled it off."

"YK, I have never failed you, but I'm a bit upset that you sent Ascot to check up on me."

"Mike, business is business, and right now there is too much at stake to take chances."

"You're right, YK. You're a wise man, and I still have a lot to learn from you."

"I couldn't have a better student. What about the Green Party in America?"

Manheim told Chen that the Green Party had been established, but they had no chance politically. He was using them as a conduit to supply money and favors to the liberal democrats. Manheim also told him that some of his media outlets had helped the ex-vice president set up his own Green media stations on radio and TV and that he was producing more movies with that lunatic who made those other successful documentaries. He informed YK that the brilliance of this was that the VP still had a bit of a power base in the DNC and that he used his media companies to feed the Green stations with misinformation and bogus scientific reports.

"Since the ex-VP started, I now control four Green cable stations."

"Excellent, now, Mike, I have to say good-bye, great work."

Manheim left the solarium and started to walk up the large staircase to the room where the three girls he had ordered were waiting for him.

# 19

### Zurich, Switzerland

Franz was instructing Utsie and Iris on the finer points of sailing. Franz told them that until they knew every sail, line, cleat, bolt, and rigging, they weren't going to leave the slip. Franz wasn't surprised that they were such quick learners.

On the third day of training, they cast off for a run on the lake. Mistakes were made, but Franz could see it wouldn't be long before the women were considered knowledgeable crew. Iris appeared to be more agile and sportive while Utsie was strong and didn't tire easily. They seemed to be enjoying the sail. Franz gave each one of them a turn in the cockpit and asked them to tack back and forth at his command, irrespective of the wind.

After six days of training, they were getting tired. They tied up that evening and Franz told them to take a few days off.

John was happy to see all of them. He asked if they were up to going out to dinner to celebrate their success. He walked Utsie to his room and told her how much he missed her.

"John, I feel like I'm rocking."

John laughed, and he assured her that the feeling would pass. She seemed relieved as she took a long hot shower.

While Utsie was showering, John walked down and asked Franz how they did.

"They'll be ready to solo in a week."

Franz started to tell John more about the training when he was interrupted by a phone call.

"Hello, this is John Moore. Oh, hello, Helmut, what can I do for you?"

"No, John, it's what I can do for you. We would be honored if you, as an American, joined our advisory board. The heads of the top companies in Europe sit on that board, and I believe it would benefit us both for you to become a member."

"I'm flattered, Helmut, but I'm kind of apolitical. I don't think I would be very good for you."

"John, I won't take no for an answer."

"Helmut, I'll think about it and give you an answer next week, if that's all right?"

"Fine, John, remember, I will not take no for an answer. I'll see you next week."

"I just don't like that guy. I don't know why. He's been very good to us, but I have a bad feeling about him."

Iris walked into the office. John asked how she liked the sailing lessons. She told him she loved sailing and had learned a lot from Franz.

"I love it, but I'm having some problems understanding navigation."

John was thrilled to work with Iris for several hours, and he marveled at how fast she picked up the finer points of navigation. All of a sudden, it clicked. She not only understood it, but she appeared to be proficient. Iris begged off dinner, saying that she wanted to get caught up on some work. He protested but soon realized she had made up her mind.

John took the rest of the team to his favorite restaurant. When they returned, John went up to his terrace and made himself a drink. He was relaxing, watching the sunset, when Iris appeared with her laptop.

"John, would you look at this and tell me what you think?"

John looked at the screen, he couldn't believe it.

"Iris, how the hell did you do this in two hours?"

"I set up a triangulation program and downloaded all existing charts from the Web," Iris explained. "You only have to enter the chart name or number, the latitude and longitude of your start point, the same for your destination. It will chart the course, give you approximate travel times, list any obstructions, or shallows, and, this is really cool—it will list all of the gas docks, restaurants, and hotels accessible on your route. I've input some language filters so you will be able to retrieve the information in English, German, Italian, Spanish, and Farsi."

"Iris, did you use any existing programs to do this?"

"No, I didn't."

"Iris, call Brad and tell him to do a patent search on this. You'll have to do a write-up on it. I want you to tell Brad to pick the best equipment and install this software in all future electronic packages if this works out. I want you and Brad to refine this so we can sell it as a standalone item. This will revolutionize the industry. We'll call it the Electronic Sextant. As soon as Brad has the program copyrighted and has applied for the patent in every possible variation, we'll manufacture it. Now, call our attorneys and have them draw up a royalty agreement for you to receive a five percent royalty on all future sales. We'll put the ownership in the name of the Hong Kong Company. Tomorrow you'll receive a wire transfer in the amount of two hundred and fifty thousand dollars into your investment account for the sale of the rights to this. Is that acceptable?"

She ran to him, throwing her arms around him.

"Oh, John, I can never thank you enough."

"Well, I'm going to have to watch myself now. You're becoming a wealthy young lady, and I might lose you."

"Never, I'm with you for life."

*I really love this kid.*

Utsie came up about ten o'clock, and John told her about Iris.

"Ah, the proud father."

"Utsie, don't give me a hard time. This is an incredible thing she's done. It'll allow you to plot a course in seconds without any calculations. By the way, did you enjoy your sailing lesson?"

"Yes, Franz is a good teacher. I liked crewing with Iris. She's a nice girl and a hard worker, a woman as strong as I am."

"Utsie, did you have your dessert?"

"Yes, thank you. I grabbed something on the way over here."

"Would you like a drink?" He offered her a glass of champagne. "What do you know about Helmut Fragge?"

She told him that he was an unsuccessful lawyer—and for many years, but somehow he took on a large client, and within a year or two, he expanded to became the largest law firm in Switzerland.

"As far as I know, he is still the senior partner in the firm, but he has not been practicing since he became the head of the Green Party."

"How do you know him so well?"

"When my parents died, the farm was left to me, but two of my uncles and an aunt contested my legacy in court. They contended that because of my age, I wouldn't be capable of running the farm. My relatives hired three of the top four attorneys in Zurich. I showed up in court alone, and the judge, who had known my father, told me I needed a lawyer, and he introduced me to Helmut. He worked very hard for me, and we won the case. He's been a friend ever since. In fact, he was responsible for me going to law school. I still remember his words, 'When you are weak, you need the law to fight for you, but when you know the law, you are never weak.' While I was going to law school, he was my mentor. He was very conservative, and I could not believe it when he took over the Green movement. When I questioned him about it, he simply said it was business, and he changed the subject."

Suddenly she drifted off; a few minutes later, Utsie snapped out of it.

"Excuse me, John, but I hadn't thought about those times for a while."

John told her that Helmut had asked him to be on the Green Party advisory board.

"John, that's wonderful! The heads of almost every major company in Europe sit on that board!"

"Why?"

"I think some feel it's a necessity to show that they are socially and environmentally astute. The others are there to watch the ones who really are. Helmut is in it for the power, not the money. He's not as bright or as good as most of his contemporaries, but he has a tremendous ego. Anyway, it would definitely be good for you and your company."

## 20

The Green Party dinner was held in a castle situated between Zurich and Bern. Helmut was anxiously waiting for them. He greeted each of them separately and gave Utsie a kiss on the cheek.

"John, my dear friend, have you made a decision?"

"Helmut, yes, I have. I would be delighted to become a member of your advisory board."

"John, you will not regret this. As a matter of fact, I think you will find this experience quite beneficial. I counted on your affirmation, and I have persuaded all of the board members' companies to each buy one of your boats. They must each be equipped with green sails and the logo of the Green Party. I convinced them that this will be a visible sign of their dedication to the movement. We'll have a fleet of one hundred and twelve Green Party boats."

"Helmut, are you telling me that you're ordering one hundred and twelve boats?"

"No, John, I'm not ordering anything. Your fellow board members are ordering them. Tonight I will announce that you have joined the board and that we are in the process of acquiring the fleet. Green sails will be seen all over Europe."

John thanked Helmut and went to join the rest of his party. He filled them in. Franz started to thank each member as he set up appointments to finalize the details. Iris opened her laptop and began e-mailing Brad, and then she called Peter and handed the phone to John.

"Peter, don't plan any vacations. We just got an order for another 112 boats. I'll call you tomorrow with the details."

Utsie was gone. John suspected she was with Helmut, but then he saw Helmut on stage.

"I would like to introduce you to the newest member of the advisory board, Herr John Moore."

John walked to the microphone and made his acceptance speech as Helmut handed him a plaque which read,

> The National Green Party of Switzerland
> The World Is Ours
> John Moore, Advisory Board Member

John quickly made his way back to his seat, looking for Utsie. Helmut grabbed his arm intrusively.

"John, please, we have to attend the advisory board meeting in the next room."

John had just become the 113th member of the board. Helmut began to introduce him to each member individually. John was impressed with his fellow members. He wondered why he was asked to join this elite group. His company paled to the likes of the companies represented here. *Why am I here? What do I possibly have to offer this group? These people are all heads of large multinational companies.*

"It's an honor that you have joined our humble ranks."

"Mr. Chen, isn't it?"

Ascot Chen smiled. "You have a good memory, Mr. Moore."

*Not good enough to remember where I met you before, Chen.*

Helmut got to the microphone and started to call the meeting to order. Chen politely left to go to his table. John found his chair in front of a small table with his name card on it.

He was impressed. There was simultaneous translation through the headphones at his seat.

"The Green Party has just merged with the National Socialist Party."

He went on to say that he was withdrawing from the prime ministerial race and going to support Herr Gregory Gruber, the head of the National Socialist Party for same. He further explained that he had, according to the polls, over forty percent of the popular vote and Herr Gruber had thirty-five percent, giving them seventy-five percent of the vote, locking in the office of prime minister for Gruber. Amidst cries of criticism, Helmut explained that he would endorse Gruber. In addition, Helmut explained, to being the head of the National Socialist Party, Gruber ran the European Transportation Union, as such, he could be much more of an asset for the Green movement than himself. Helmut asked everyone to join him in this endorsement. At first, there seemed to be a strong motion against this. The majority of the members started to shout their disapproval.

Ascot Chen stood and yelled, "Gentlemen, please."

The members all quieted down, and Chen began to speak.

"It is, in fact, disappointing that after all his efforts, Helmut is stepping down, but it is the only assurance we have for success. Neither the socialists nor we have enough votes, at the moment, to win the election. The merger is the only way. Herr Gruber is the head of Europe's largest union. He is the only logical choice. I say, well done, Helmut. You are a genius for coming up with this idea and you're a great man for putting the party before yourself."

After the applause died down, Helmut began to speak.

"Thank you, Ascot, I wholeheartedly give my support to Herr Gruber. May I see a show of hands from those who agree?"

Although John never raised his hand, Helmut continued.

"Excellent, the vote is unanimous. We are now the Swiss Socialist Green Party, and the next prime minister of Switzerland will be Herr Gregory Grubber."

During the applause, John realized, *I've just joined the Communist Party in a foreign country. What the hell am I doing here?* At that moment, John looked up and saw Utsie talking to a man that he recognized from photos in the newspaper, Gregory

Gruber. His mind was now reeling. *How does Utsie know this guy? Where was she all night? What does she have to do with all of this? I have got to get out of here and figure this out.*

John was outside the building waiting for his car when Utsie showed up.

"Where were you all evening? Did you see or hear what went on?"

"I had some business to attend to."

John said nothing. This wasn't the time; he was upset and confused. He would deal with her tomorrow.

John said, "I'm going to drop you off at your house. I have a lot of work to do tonight, it would be better if you went home."

Utsie gave him a good-night kiss. She sensed that something was wrong.

"What is it, darling? Are you angry at me?"

"No, I'm just tired and have to go over these orders tonight."

But he was angry and confused. *How does Utsie fit in to all of this? It is reasonable to think she had worked with Helmut before, but what is her connection to Gruber?* He did, in fact, have a lot of work to do that night. He had to process over a hundred million dollars' worth of orders. *I'll worry about Utsie tomorrow.*

He finished just before five in the morning, about 8:00 p.m. in San Francisco. He called Peter.

"I just e-mailed 112 orders, about 108 million dollars. There are some special requirements from a few of the customers, and I expect to get some more add-on requests over the next few days. I'll stay in touch. Transfer me to Brad. I have a few things to go over with him."

"Brad, I just sent orders for one hundred and twelve boats. How long will it take you to come up with a production schedule?"

After only a moment came the reply, "As long as there's nothing hairy, I should have it done in a week. Things are going smooth here since we opened the new facility."

"Brad, I need you to get me that production schedule as soon as possible, and then get over here immediately. I want you to go on sales calls with Franz, all top-of-the-line clients. I'm expecting a lot of additional business from these orders. I want you to talk to the customers, come up with some of your great ideas, and sell additional items, shoot for twenty-five percent in add-ons."

"John, that shouldn't be too hard. Franz and I have already discussed some possibilities."

John said good-bye, made himself a drink, and spent the rest of the morning deep in thought. *Why have I been pulled into the Green Socialist Party? What does Utsie have to do with that communist Gruber?* The thought that she might be involved in something nefarious was getting to him. He decided to take a break and asked Franz to go sailing with him.

He and Franz spent the weekend sailing. He enjoyed spending time with Franz, and they worked well together as a crew.

On Sunday, Franz told John to tie up in a small village, Tibol, on the eastern shore of Zurichsee. It was a scenic village for this part of the valley, and Franz assured John that he would like it. After they tied up and secured the boat, Franz took John to a small café.

"John, they make the best crepes in Switzerland here."

The waitress started to bring trays of crepes: blueberry, strawberry, fig, cherry, and chocolate.

"Franz, these really are the best crepes I have ever tasted, but I feel like I just gained ten pounds."

They left the café. While walking back to the boat, John felt bloated and out of shape.

"Franz, do you know any martial arts teachers in Zurich? I haven't worked out in months, and I'm getting out of shape."

Franz told him he knew a very good teacher, a Russian, an ex-KGB instructor.

"I'll call him tomorrow and make the introduction."

On Tuesday morning, Franz drove John to a small town, a suburb several kilometers north of Zurich. They pulled up to a house with a barn in the backyard. When they walked into the barn, a man jumped out and attacked Franz. Franz quickly moved to the side and gave the man a roundhouse kick, but it was blocked and parried. They both stopped, started to laugh, and then hugged each other.

"Ivan, let me introduce John Moore."

"Nice to meet you."

"My name is Ivan Romanovitch, it is good to meet you. You are Americanski. I have never trained one before. I have killed a few, but never trained one."

"That's funny, I've killed a few Russians, but have never trained with one either."

Ivan looked serious and glared at John. He turned to Franz.

"I think I like this American. I'll train him."

Ivan asked if he ever had formal training.

"I've had some training, informally, with a friend in Hong Kong."

"Did you bring clothes?"

"Yes." John held up a small duffel bag.

"Change in there."

John came out of the small room, and Ivan pulled a rug off the center of the floor. There were five concentric circles painted on the floor. Ivan told John that, for now, they would stay inside the outer circle to fight. "If you go outside the circle, you lose." He further explained that if you were hurt, you could step out of the circle and the opponent had to stop.

"Is this acceptable?"

"Yes."

"Then let us begin."

Ivan and John stood opposite each other and bowed; then Ivan leaped into the air and kicked John in the forehead. John fell outside of the ring and landed on his back.

"Mr. Moore, the idea is to stay on your feet and stay in the ring." He laughed.

Besides the pain in his head, the only thing that hurt was his pride. John faced the man again, but this time he was prepared. The man ran at him swinging. John was able to block everything he threw at him. John showed him a trick of his own. He dove at the floor, kicked Ivan in the face, grabbed Ivan's neck with his legs, and flipped him, letting him go before his neck snapped. Next, John kneed Ivan in the stomach while punching him in the throat and then threw him from the ring.

It took Ivan by surprise. Ivan composed himself, looking John in the eye.

"Well done. You are good. I am going to enjoy working with you."

Ivan gave John a hardy handshake.

"Let's go drink some vodka. I made some myself, saving it for a special occasion."

"Nastrovia!"

They drank, he poured another. Ivan asked John what he wanted to accomplish in his training. John told him he just wanted to stay in shape.

"I learned in Hong Kong, so I don't know the differences between that and Russian martial arts."

"There are a few differences. You will learn them as you go along."

They decided to work out four days a week. John went home and had lunch. The vodka had gotten to him, and he really felt out of shape, so he decided to take a nap.

He woke suddenly. Someone was next to him. Utsie told him to be quiet, to lay back and enjoy. She started to kiss him softly all over.

"John, you're hurt. You're covered with bruises!"

"No, I was just training for the first time in months. I have to get back in shape."

Utsie looked at him sympathetically and continued.

"I will kiss it and make it better."

After a very pleasant afternoon, they showered and got ready for dinner.

"I brought some vegetables from the farm. Iris told me she wanted to cook. I hope you don't mind."

"No, I love Iris's cooking."

John, Utsie, Franz, and Iris sat down for dinner. They joked, discussed business, and during dessert, Iris excused herself and came back with her trusty laptop.

"John, I have something to show you. I hope you won't get mad with me for doing this without your permission. Brad and I came up with a marketing research idea, and I hope you like it."

Iris opened her laptop; there was a map of central Europe visible with several lights blinking.

"These lights are boats that we've already sold. Brad has installed a small transmitter in the guidance system of each boat. It digitally sends us the location, start point and end point of a trip. By tracking this, we are able to compute the concentrations of boats, popular sailing destinations, and see what parts of the market we are not reaching. Each signal has been assigned a specific tracking number, so we know what boat it is and where it's been, where it's going, and where it is now. What do you think of it?"

"I think you're a computer genius, but isn't this a breach of privacy? If our clients find out we're tracking them, they might be upset. I know I would be."

"They can't find out. The signal is sent to a satellite via the GPS onboard, and we don't separate it until it bounces back. If you were checking to see if you were being monitored, you could only pick it up during the send phase, not on the return."

John argued, "Why take the risk of being found out?"

"We've informed all of our clients. They were told it was a waterborne On Star system, and they all seemed pleased. In fact, we came up with the idea as a safety device. There's a button on the GPS, with a remote button in the cockpit, which will send a mayday signal as well as exact position and heading. We didn't come up with the idea to use it as a marketing tool until it was operational."

"You guys amaze me."

After coffee, John said good-night to Iris and Franz and asked Utsie to join him on the terrace.

"Utsie, I have a few questions that have been bothering me since the Green dinner."

"I knew you were angry with me for some reason that night."

John continued, "First of all, did you know you were getting me involved in a communist organization?"

"Darling, these are not communists. European socialism is simply the method that is being used to solidify the EU. Look at the companies that are involved. They're all capitalists."

"Utsie, all of these people joined the Green movement because it was good for business. They didn't look too happy when it was announced that they were being merged with the socialists and that Gruber was going to be the next prime minister. Another question, how do you know Gruber?"

She stopped smiling and looked away from him for a moment. When she turned back to face him, she looked ill.

"John, Gruber and I grew up together. After we graduated from secondary school, he became very involved in the Socialist movement. In fact, he is a Marxist. He went to Russia and attended Leningrad University. When he returned, he started the National Socialist Party.

"After several years, the party gained some momentum, but it stayed relatively small. Then he made a deal with some unknown people, and the money started to roll in. Over the next few years, he and his movement became very powerful throughout Europe.

"We stayed in touch, but I did not see him often. As soon as I had the problem with the farm, I went to him and asked for help.

He arranged for the security and talked to the people who were trying to kill me. I don't know what he did, but he assured me the problem was taken care of."

John looked at her; he believed she was being totally honest with him.

"Utsie, that's some story. Why didn't you tell me this before?"

"John, I should have, but I get so upset just thinking about it. I think you Americans say, 'In chaos, there is profit.' No one really knows who the funding sources are, and there are vast fortunes being dumped into the Green and Socialist movements. Now that they have joined forces, there is no telling what they can do. They are very powerful, John."

"I know what powerful people can do."

He was so deep in thought that Utsie became a bit frightened.

"John, I didn't mean to upset you."

"I'm sorry, I was thinking of someone else, a different time and a different place."

Utsie saw the pain in his eyes, leaned over, and held him tightly. They sat quietly, embracing for a long while.

The next morning, John felt better and asked Iris to show him the tracking system again. Satisfied that the new technology would work as a safety device, he told Iris to have Brad put it in every boat and market it as state-of-the-art technology.

"Make sure you get the patents on it right away."

John went to his training appointment and was surprised to meet Franz coming out of the barn.

"What are you doing here?"

"Ivan's been my instructor for years, and today was my regular workout day."

John walked into the barn. Ivan gave him a big hello.

"John, today we are going to work on balance and stability."

Ivan took two cement blocks, spacing them about four feet apart. He then put a broom handle across them.

"I want you to stand on the broom handle with your toes pointed in the same direction as the handle. Here, I will demonstrate."

He was able to roll the handle from one side of the block to the other, while keeping his balance.

"That doesn't look too hard."

Trying to stand on the stick, it shot out from under him, and he fell on his ass.

"Sometimes appearances are deceiving. Try again."

John, embarrassed, tried again. By the end of the session, he had it mastered.

Later, John asked Franz where he could get two cement blocks and a broom handle. Franz showed up about an hour later and placed them on the terrace. John worked on his balance for hours.

When they got up the next morning, Utsie heard John cry out.

"What's wrong, John?"

He told her every bone and muscle in his body hurt. She could see he was having a hard time getting out of bed. She went over to him and offered to help him up.

"You're crying like a baby."

After a long hot shower and some stretching exercises, he felt better but was still sore.

Utsie left, John ate breakfast alone. He was looking over a production schedule when the phone rang.

"John, I have exciting news. I've received a total of 176 orders from various companies since you joined the advisory board of the Green Party. They all want the Green sails with their company logos on them. Can you handle this large order?"

"Yes, Peter, we can have them finished within 120 days, and that includes those already ordered."

"Fantastic, John, I knew you were going to make me a rich man."

"Okay, Peter, send the orders over, we'll get back to you before the end of the week with the preliminary schedule."

After Tsillman's call, John sat back down thinking. *Where is all this money coming from?*

He picked up the phone and dialed his friend Peter in Sausalito.

"Peter, hold on to your hat, we just got another 176 orders."

"How the hell did you do that?"

"I became a communist."

He told Peter he would explain it to him in person next week.

"I'd love to see you, but why are you coming back? You're doing great over there."

"Truthfully, Peter, I want to see you, but I'll also be going over production schedules with Brad while I'm there."

"Great, I'll see you next week."

*Well, that was a good day's work. Let me work on my balance exercises.* He spent the rest of the day practicing. That evening, he asked Utsie to give him a massage; he couldn't believe the pain he was in. The next morning, he went back to Ivan's.

"I've never been in this much pain."

Ivan began to laugh hysterically.

"I know, it doesn't do anything for you. It just hurts." He laughed so hard he almost went into a convulsion.

"Are you kidding me? I'll kill you."

Ivan only laughed harder. John didn't know how to take this, and he was getting pissed. Ivan saw John's face and calmed down.

"I'm only fooling with you, my friend. You can tell by the pain that you've not used all those muscles in a long time. We'll continue this until it doesn't hurt."

John wasn't happy with that prospect.

After walking the stick for about an hour, John thought his muscles were going to rip right out of his skin. Ivan told him to stop and lay on the floor on his stomach. Ivan gave him a hard chop to the back of his thigh; John saw stars.

"Are you crazy?" he screamed and then realized the pain was gone.

"Stay on your belly."

John received a crushing blow to his other thigh, same result, no pain.

"I am going to show you several exercises. You'll do these before and again five minutes after you've walked the stick. Also, take only cold showers after exercising."

"How cold?"

"No hot water at all. Okay, come. We will have vodka."

John realized it wasn't even ten o'clock.

After the vodka, John was pain-free. Ivan told him to come early next time so he could introduce him to some new exercises.

"Great," John answered. Ivan just laughed.

"You're not bad for an old man, especially an old American man." He laughed loudly.

*This guy is some character.*

The next few days, John was busy; time flew by. He didn't ask Utsie if she would like to go with him until the morning he was leaving.

"I would love to see San Francisco, but I can't. I've made several appointments that I can't reschedule."

John told her he would plan better next time. She seemed satisfied with that, wished him a safe trip, and kissed him good-bye.

Franz drove him to the airport.

# 21

### Memphis

Manheim sat at his desk going over the numbers again. If correct, the Liddo Group would become the first company to gross over five trillion dollars in one year. Satisfied, he picked up the phone and called Wiley.

"Wiley, would it be possible for you to come over about eight?"

Wiley started to beg off and then thought better of it. "Sure, Mike, I'll be happy to."

"All right, then I'll see you tonight."

Next, he called Chen on a secure line.

"YK, Mike. Everything is almost in place. We got world patent rights on the new refrigerant, Freenox. We are the sole source. Legislation passed both houses. On October first, Freon will be illegal and Freenox will be the only acceptable substitute. We've already got a twenty-year waiver against any antitrust problems.

"We've signed contracts with every auto manufacturer for the supply of batteries for both hybrid and electric cars. Building codes have been federalized and will be changed to meet California codes, so we've bought up as many paint manufacturers as we could. They're all being 'Green Certified' as we speak. We also took control of the accepted certification companies. This will give us the power to deny our competitor's certification. I've asked Wiley to come over tonight. He'll update me on his progress. I have given him five other patent applications to push through. If he is successful, they will be the only environmentally approved products which can be sold in the US. Our people in Germany, Italy, France, Great Britain, and Switzerland are all working on the same thing. I'll send you the projections on a secure line. I think you'll be pleased. Also, once we have a lock on the energy suppliers, these numbers could double. I have to hand it to you, YK, this Green Party was a brilliant idea."

"Thank you, Mike. It would still be an idea if you hadn't been able to implement it. Please keep me apprised."

"Wiley, I drew up a list of everything we need. Let's go over them item by item."

"Mike, I'm having a few problems."

Mike's face darkened, and Wiley appeared uncomfortable.

"What problems? You told me everything was in place."

"Well, Mike, that senator from Connecticut is backing out. He pledged his support, but now he's saying his constituency is angry. He was the one fighting against this Green crap during the election."

"Okay, we'll place an article in all the Connecticut papers and a report on the news that this is a trade-off so he can get his gay rights bill through. What else?"

"There are two Democratic congressmen and four senators that have pulled their support."

"Who are they?"

"The senior senator from Nebraska—"

"Wait, isn't that the guy who took the bribe for the construction of that mall and the office contract? He screwed up the zoning laws for the whole state to get that done. We know where he deposited that money. We did it for him. Give him one chance to reconsider. If he doesn't play ball, we will bring him down."

"Next one."

"That crazy congresswoman from California backed out."

"She's easy. We have pictures of her fooling around with her secretary, Mary. Even though she's a big gay rights activist, I don't think her husband would like this to go public."

They went through the rest of the list, and Mike seemed to have something on each one.

"Mike, what about the president? He's out of control."

"The chief of staff controls him, and we own the chief of staff. If he doesn't do what we ask, he won't last a day. I can have the media make him look so bad, his career won't be the only thing he loses, and he knows it. Wiley, this might be a good time to get him back out here and read him the Riot Act."

They went over their plans for strong-arming the group of dissenters. Wiley gave Mike a rundown on every bill that had been pushed through. Wiley showed Mike how the inane amendments tied into others, so that if you read one bill, it seemed like nothing; but when joined with items in other bills, these amendments were powerful, and they fit their agenda.

"Wiley, you're a genius. Golf next week?"

Wiley agreed and knew it was his cue to leave.

"Mike, call me if you need anything."

On his way home, Wiley thought about how he wanted to do good for people when he first went into politics. Now he was destroying people, selling his country down the river, and in bed with the same people he wanted to prosecute when he'd started out. He thought of committing suicide but knew he was a coward; instead, he'd get drunk, his usual mind-numbing aperitif.

# 22

### San Francisco

John arrived in San Francisco an hour late; Peter was waiting for him.

"Well, how in the hell are you, Peter?"

"I'm great. How's the man who's sold more yachts in one year than anyone in history?"

"I'm good, everything's going well, and I like Zurich."

"Come on, the car's over here."

"You are not going to recognize the yard with all of the changes Brad's made. We're going to have over two hundred boats in production at the same time. The new system you and Brad came up with is working well."

"That kid is something else. I never asked you, but where did you find him?"

Peter laughed. "It was kismet. One day, the kid came in and asked if he could rent some space to build a boat. We weren't using the old shed, and I figured he wouldn't be too much trouble, so I agreed to rent him space on a month-to-month basis. He moved into the old shed and began working by himself. I stopped in to see what he was up to about a week later, and he had a keel table built with all the ribs already angled. I asked him why he was building a wooden boat. He told me he couldn't afford a fiberglass hull. I looked around and found an old thirty-seven-foot mold, so I went back and told him he could have it. I guess it brought back memories. That kid took the mold, modified it, in three days, he had a hull totally different than anything we ever produced. He built that boat in two months, and it was better than anything I had seen in a long time. I asked him if he'd be interested in coming to work for us, and he jumped at it. The rest is history."

"Do you have any background on him?"

"Yeah, he's real good at what he does."

"I'm sorry, you're right."

They pulled into John's driveway. Peter told him that he had one of the girls stock the bar and refrigerator that morning so everything should be fresh.

"Come in for a drink."

John grabbed his arm and dragged him out of the car. They went through the house and out to the deck.

"Peter, the real reason I came home was to see you. You're the only family I have."

"Are you really all right? I think of you as a brother, but I know you well enough to know that you aren't normally this touchy-feely."

"Yes, I'm all right. No, it's…" He paused. "I think it's working with these kids. It has made me realize that I have wasted that part of my life. I've grown close to Iris, sometimes when I look at her, I can imagine the joy of having a kid. Maybe it's all the shit I've been through that's made me believe there's more to life than business and making money. I'm rich beyond my wildest dreams, and I'm lucky enough to have you as a friend, but I feel like I've missed something, I just don't know."

"You can't change the past, and I think you're doing well. You have us as family, and from what I've seen and heard, you have a beautiful girlfriend." Peter then smiled a mischievous smile. "You poor old bastard, all alone in the world and nobody loves you. What color panties are you wearing?"

John's head snapped up, and he started to laugh. "You're right. I'm just feeling sorry for myself."

"I'm going home and grab an hour or two of sleep."
John said he'd meet him at the office later.

·····································

"Brad, it's good to see you. The last design modifications were outrageous."

"Thanks, I want to show you the production changes I've made. I think you'll be impressed."

Brad showed John the production changes, the mold modifications, and the new spray system.

"The new molds are inverted, and the gel coat is sprayed on first. Then we spray in the glass and lay sheeting by hand. After that, we give the entire mold a positive charge. The fibers are charged so that when we spray them, they go on evenly. It's totally automated at this point, so we don't have highs and lows like you would have had before. After it goes to the ovens, we have a hammer shaped like the mold which pneumatically hits the entire mold at once. The hull is then grabbed. As soon as contact is made, it sets off a magnet that pulls the mold from the hull or top section. The mold is lifted out, set on a dolly, and pulled back through the oven for a final drying. Because everything is automated, we have fewer discrepancies in the gel coat, less hand finishing. We're pumping out a hull in one-third of the time it took before, with one-tenth of the personnel."

"You're right, I am impressed."

Brad gave him a big smile and told John that they had a patent on every part of this system.

"Brad, between your designs and Iris's software, you're going to take over this industry."

He told Brad he would meet him for lunch later, but he had a few things to do first. John walked into Peter's office and closed the door.

"Peter, I've been thinking."

"Oh no, my god!"

"Get serious for a minute. I've been thinking, you and I have a lot of money and we've built this into a huge company. Why don't we make the kids business partners? It'll give them more incentive, and when the time comes, you and I can semiretire and leave the company in good hands."

"How much do you want to give them?"

"I don't know. What if we gave them five percent each now, and two percent each year for another five years? That would give them a forty-five percent interest, fifteen percent each—for Brad, Iris, and Franz. They'd have to sign an agreement. If they wanted to get rid of their interest, they would have to offer it to the others, or it would revert back to the company at book value. What do you think?"

Peter thought for a moment and smiled at John.

"It'll be a good incentive, and it's only fair. It looks like we're going to clear over fifty million this year on that electronic sextant program alone. John, you're good."

"Why not join Brad and me for lunch, we can tell him then."

"Good idea. I just have some things to tidy up here, and I'll join you a little later."

John and Brad got to the restaurant a few minutes before Peter. Brad was telling John about his latest ideas and developments, almost hyperventilating with excitement. John was impressed and glad that he and Peter had agreed to give this kid a piece of the pie.

"Brad, we have something serious to discuss with you."

"No, please don't fire me. I know I should have told you before I incorporated Iris's program. I never gave any thought to the privacy issues, but please don't fire me. I'll never do it again."

The boy was near tears.

"Brad, that's not the issue."

"Have I done something else wrong? I got a haircut, and I'm wearing the clothes. What did I do wrong?"

They burst into laughter, and the kid looked like he was going to pass out.

"Brad, you haven't done anything wrong, although it would be advisable to talk to either Peter or myself before you do anything like that again. We want to make you a partner."

Brad looked totally confused.

John said, "We want to give you, Iris, and Franz each a five percent equity share in the business. You will receive an additional two percent per year for the next five years, or as long as you wish to stay with us."

He started to say something and then bolted for the men's room.

"I think he's going to hurl," they both said at the same time.

When Brad returned, he assured them that he would do everything possible to make a great product even better.

John said, "Brad, we have a lot of faith in you. Don't let us down."

They hadn't been served, but Brad excused himself and told them he had work to do. John asked him not to spill the news to the others.

John got back to the office later and saw a message from Utsie:

> John, call me at once, upon receipt.

He had a bad feeling as he dialed the phone.

"Utsie, John here…anything wrong?"

"I can't talk over the phone. When are you coming back?"

He told her he would be back at the end of next week. She asked if he could come sooner.

"I'll be back tomorrow."

"Thank you, John."

"Peter, I have to leave. Something's come up that needs my attention. Nothing to do with the business, it's Utsie."

"I'll have Janet arrange for your ticket. If there's anything I can do, let me know."

*What could be so bad that it couldn't wait a week?* He thought about that over and over during the return trip.

# 23

### Back in Zurich

Franz was waiting for him at the airport. He told John it was good to see him. John called Utsie from the car and told her to meet him at the house. She cryptically told him she couldn't be there until ten. He asked Franz to have dinner with him about seven-thirty along with Iris.

John saw them in the office just before seven and told them they would be going to his favorite restaurant, the one by Bellevueplatz. Franz drove, Iris got in the back with John.

"It's so good to have you back," she said with a big smile, grabbing his arm, squeezing it.

She held on to him until they arrived at the restaurant. *She's great.*

During dinner, John told them they would both get an equity share in the company if they agreed. He explained the deal. John was delighted with their reactions.

Iris blurted out, "I'll work hard and do everything I can do to make the company better."

"I know you will, Iris." He leaned over and gave her a kiss on the head.

Franz was quiet and emotional. "I can never repay this kindness, John."

"Nonsense, you have earned it and my trust, Franz."

"Thank you, I'll try to live up to it."

They drove back to the house without saying much, thinking of the future.

Utsie finally showed up. It was after eleven. She ran to him on the terrace, hugged him, and started to sob.

"What's wrong, Utsie? What the hell happened to you?" noticing facial bruises.

Utsie told him the story. John felt sick.

"So Gruber was your boyfriend? You overheard him talking to someone on the phone, and he beat you up. Utsie, start from the beginning. Calm down." He got up and made her a drink, handing it to her. Looking up at him, she felt safe.

"Gregory was my boyfriend through secondary school and university. We lived together for about a year. He was involved in politics, the National Socialist Party, but the Party was weak in those days. One day, he received a visit from Ascot Chen. After that, he had all the money he needed. I knew something was wrong, so I left him after I confronted him, and I didn't speak with him for years, until I had the problem with the farm. He told me he would take care of everything, and he did. Gregory told me that if I could convince Helmut to merge the Green Party with the Socialist Party, I would never have another problem with the farm.

"I talked to Helmut, but he balked at the idea. I reported to Gregory, and next day, a man showed up and threatened me. Helmut went and spoke to Gregory on my behalf, that did nothing, and then you helped me. Gregory called me again after that and asked to meet him during the dinner. He told me that Helmut had finally agreed. He said he would need me to help the cause from time to time. I didn't like the people he was associating with, so I refused adamantly. The night of the dinner, I told him I didn't want to hear from him again, and we had a fight. He called me the same day you left for San Francisco and asked if we could get together. I said no. He wanted to apologize for the incident at the dinner.

"He told me that he had a suite at the Bauer Lac Hotel and had a free hour from seven to eight. I agreed to meet with him.

"He met me at the door, held my hand, and told me he was so sorry that he had upset me. He explained that politics was a hard road to take, then the phone rang and he asked me to wait in the next room.

"I thought he was finished and started to come back in the room when I heard him say, 'We have to kill him. This could be bad. Helmut is well-liked.' I ran for the door, but he dropped the phone and caught me. He punched me in the face and knocked me to the ground. I looked up at him, kicked him in the groin, and he fell next to me. I grabbed a nearby vase and hit him in the head. Then I got up and ran for the door.

"When I got to the street, I hailed a cab and went to a friend's house. She lent me her car, I drove to Interlaken and stayed at a youth hostel. I've been there ever since. I had to bring my friend's car back to her and wait for her to get off work so she could drive me here. I'm sorry, John, that's all I know."

"I'm sending you to Peter back in the States until I get this sorted out. Get some sleep. I'm going to the airport right now to buy your ticket." *This can't be happening again.*

# 24

**Jakarta, Indonesia**

Y. K. Chen was in his office when his assistant told him that Aristotle Saris was on the phone.

"Aristotle, what a pleasant surprise. How are you?"

"I have a problem and need your assistance. Gregory Gruber was overheard talking about killing Helmut Fragge."

"Helmut is dead?" YK asked.

"No, Gregory was getting instructions to kill him."

"That is unfortunate. Who would have ordered such a thing, and why?"

Saris did not like the way this was going.

"YK, I might have been in error, but the fact is that it was done and the conversation was overheard."

YK hesitated. "Did the person who overheard the conversation know it was you on the other end of the line?"

"No, but this could slow things down immeasurably, we are so close. What do you suggest?"

"Do nothing. If that person goes to the press with an accusation, we will deny it since we own the press. We simply discredit the accuser, it will go away."

Saris felt relieved, the burden lifted.

"Thank you, I knew I could count on you."

YK sat and contemplated the conversation with Saris, reached over, picked up the phone, and called Mike Manheim.

"Mike, call me back from the solarium. Thank you."

"Mike, how much longer before we take over the energy companies?"

"Why?"

"We have a slight problem in Europe, and I'm trying to figure out when we can get rid of our friend Aristotle permanently."

"We're about nine months from total control of the energy plants, and we're making headway on oil as well. Wiley just got the Department of Transportation to give two billion dollars to Saris's company in Venezuela for exploration. It will be the biggest oil find of the century. Saris will give us sole rights to all of the production."

"That does complicate matters if we get rid of him. We'll lose that and some of his European and American political contacts as well."

"YK, what exactly is the problem?"

"Saris gave Gregory Gruber an order to kill Helmut Fragge, and he was overheard."

"That's bad. Do you want me to take care of this?"

"Thank you, Mike, not right now. I told Saris to do nothing. There's a possibility that the person who overheard this will be too frightened to do anything, and then nothing will happen, but if you do hear anything, call me."

"Okay, will do. Good-bye."

# 25

## Zurich

John took Utsie to the airport and told her that Peter would pick her up on the other side.

"Only get in the car if Peter is alone, not if he is with anyone else, no matter who it is."

"John, I'm so sorry for all this."

"Utsie, sometimes we're just drawn into situations beyond our control. Don't worry about a thing. I'll take care of you."

She kissed him and went to the departure gate.

John got on the phone immediately.

"Peter, we have a major problem. It's Rebecca all over again."

"John, what the hell are you talking about?"

John told him the story and gave him the flight information.

"Peter, pick her up by yourself and bring her to my place. Don't even tell Brad she's there, tell no one."

"I understand. I'll be there to pick her up."

"Thanks, buddy, give her some money, cash only. I don't want her using credit cards. As a matter of fact, take her ID and credit cards away from her, put them in your safe. I can't take any chances."

"Okay, John, whatever you want."

"Peter, wait, do you still have friends on Fire Island?"

"Well, yes, but it's off-season, and they live in Greenwich Village for the winter."

"Great, see if they'll lend you the house for a month or so. This way there will be no connection made between Utsie and us."

"I'll call my friends when we hang up. I'll bring her to New York myself and get her set up."

"Thanks, Peter. One more thing—buy a two of those prepaid phones. Give one to Utsie, you keep the other. Tell her to contact you via phone only. If she needs to talk to me, tell her to call you and I'll get back to her. Tell her not to contact me directly. You can bet I will be tailed and my phones will be tapped very soon."

"John, you're experienced with this stuff, aren't you?"

"Yes, Peter, but let's hope it doesn't end like the last time."

John hung up and went back to the house. He sensed something was wrong as he walked up the drive. He bent down to tie his shoe, looked behind and to both sides. There was nothing. When he keyed the door lock, it swung open; he lunged forward and delivered a ferocious blow. Franz hit the floor, knocked out cold.

Iris screamed, "John, surprise!"

He told Iris to calm down and bent over Franz. He slapped his face gently until he regained consciousness.

"Franz, I'm so sorry,"

Franz stood up. "John, excellent punch."

"Franz, I really apologize."

Rubbing his jaw, Franz replied, "It's my own fault for allowing you to train with Ivan. Let's forget it and have a party."

"Yes, John, you've been so kind to us, so we wanted to show our appreciation. Franz and I prepared a feast in your honor."

"This isn't necessary, but thank you both," John replied, a big smile on his face.

Iris's presentation was unbelievable.

"They couldn't prepare a better meal in the finest restaurants in the world," John complimented them.

"It's not over yet," Iris said. She went into the kitchen and came out carrying the highest soufflé John had ever seen. Franz took out a bottle of Cognac and poured it over the top. Franz lit it, and the blue flame turned the soufflé a beautiful dark brown.

"Franz, I must apologize again for hitting you, I really—"

"No apology necessary. If I can help you in any way, let me know." He shook John's hand, and Iris kissed him on the cheek.

They went to their rooms, and John sat in his usual place on the terrace. *Does Franz know something is wrong, or am I being paranoid?*

The next morning, John went to see Ivan.

"John, it's good to see you. You will hate me more after today. I have something new to show you."

John looked past him and saw two steel rings about seven feet in diameter, held together by four poles welded to each of them.

"Get inside, stand on that bar. Hold this one with your left hand. Okay, are you holding tight?"

Ivan pushed the contraption down a hill behind his house.

"What the hell are you doing?" John screamed.

Ivan laughed. "That's right. Hold on with your left hand only. If you fall out, you might get hurt." He laughed again.

As the cylinder rolled downhill, it gained momentum; John was getting dizzy and nauseous. The deathtrap rolled down the hill, halfway up the next and then back down, finally coming to rest. John tumbled out and vomited.

Ivan walked down to where John had stopped and roared with laughter.

"Please do not mess up my yard," Ivan said once he caught his breath.

"Are you a lunatic? What the hell was that all about?"

"To answer your first question, yes, I am a lunatic. In reply to your second question"—he hesitated for a moment to get the wording right in English—"you are old, your balance is poor, and you got sick, I guess your equilibrium is bad. The loops are a tool used by the KGB. You must learn to focus your eyes on the horizon, no matter what position your body is in. When you get the hang of it, I will give you a weapon. You will target practice doing this."

"Do you really think I would do this again?"

"Now, roll this back up the hill and try again."

John couldn't believe it, but he decided to try again.

"Now hold with your left hand and focus on something faraway. Forget that you are rolling, just keep your eyes fixed on that point."

He rolled down the hill again as instructed. Eventually, he was able to ignore the rolling sensation and fix on a point on the horizon. After several more attempts, John had the hang of it.

"Now, I want you to fix your eyes on a spot ten feet away."

John tried, but he became so dizzy that he fell.

"Are you all right?" Ivan yelled.

John got up. "I'm all right."

"Good, do it again."

*I am too old for this shit.* He told Ivan he had enough after two more attempts.

"You did well. This is difficult. You're training your body to do what it does not do naturally. Someday, it may save your life. It has saved mine."

"If it doesn't kill me first."

Ivan laughed. "Come, it's time to drink vodka."

*Time to drink vodka? It's nine in the morning.* John excused himself after two. He left deep in thought. *I can't drink like this in the morning.*

John got to the Dolder Grand Hotel on time, even though he had stopped to buy breath mints to cover the smell of the vodka and the vomit on his breath. Tsillman was already there. They sat at a small table in the lobby.

"John, I must get your account divested. Your portfolio is much too profitable this last quarter. You have over two billion dollars in the currency account, and it's causing ripples in the market. If I pull it out now, the dollar will drop. If I leave it in, you'll start to lose by next week."

"What do you suggest?"

"I want to pull out fifteen percent per day until it is all out."

"Where are you going to put it in?"

"Energy stocks, we know someone is making a play with all those emission credits and the market is going to skyrocket. With a two-billion-dollar influx, it will drive it even higher."

"No, Peter, I want to stay out of the market with that money. Put a half a billion in euro bonds, two hundred million in US treasuries, three hundred million in Japanese commercial paper, and the rest in CDs."

"Over a billion in CDs? John, that's wrong. You'll only get two percent on the money."

"Peter, you didn't let me finish. Do you know of a solid bank for sale? I want something small but solid, a good boutique bank."

"John, what do you know about banking?"

"Nothing, but you do, Peter. I want you to find a solid bank that you'd be comfortable running."

"John, you are fooling with me, yes?"

John told him he wasn't. Tsillman stared into space.

"Excuse me, John, but I am overwhelmed with your confidence in me. I'll search for the best possible bank and get back to you as soon as I can."

John arrived at his house; Iris was just pouring herself a cup of coffee and asked if he would like one. "Yes, thank you."

Iris told him that he had a pile of papers to sign and another pile to review and initial before they started the next production run. After several hours, he was bleary-eyed. Iris had prepared one of her signature meals.

John sat down. Franz came in to join them.

"He really rolled you down a hill?" Iris asked.

"Yes, it made me sick."

Franz looked at John. "This is very important. If you can master this, you will be able to find your center, and that is very important in combat."

John considered the validity of his advice. They ate and talked for over an hour. Iris excused herself; she was meeting some friends at a club downtown.

"That's great, Iris. You work too hard. You need to have fun at your age."

As she said good-night to John, she leaned over and kissed him on the cheek. She waved good-bye to Franz and left.

"Franz, what do you know about Gregory Gruber?"

John noticed Franz turn red and seem uncomfortable with the question.

"Why?"

"I want to meet with him on a personal matter."

"Who told you? Did someone say something about me?"

Franz appeared to be in a rage.

"Franz, I was just asking. No one said anything, calm down."

"I apologize."

"John, this is the man that I was investigating when I had my problem."

"Franz, I have a problem with this man. Utsie is hiding in the States. She overheard Gruber making plans to kill Helmut Fragge, and he attacked her. I don't know what is going on yet, but I thought it best not to take any chances. Can you give me some insight into this guy and his organization?"

Franz stopped for a minute to collect his thoughts.

"John, what I am about to tell you is classified, I am not only putting you in danger, but I am breaking the laws of my country. Even though I was discharged from the intelligence service, laws still apply."

"Understood, go on."

"We have never made a distinction between internal and external security, so we do not have a CIA or FBI. The SIA is the only Swiss Intelligence Agency. The SIA works for all the government bureaucratic agencies, so secrecy is difficult. I worked in the core group. It operated autonomously and answered to a committee formed within the SIA, thus avoiding direct contact with government officials.

"The people in my group usually worked alone, without backup. I was gathering information about the infiltration of communist and socialist organizations into Swiss politics when I was set up and disgraced. The committee disavowed any knowledge of the work I was doing. Several politicians got together and had me arrested on charges ranging from criminal mischief to espionage.

"The head of the SIA was a close friend. He was my mentor during my training. He managed to have me exonerated, but the best he could do was to have the charges reduced. I had to sign an affidavit of guilt. I can never work in intelligence again. He arranged for me to get the chauffeur job, and that is how I met you. Thank you again. Your confidence in me has restored my life."

"Franz, I appreciate that, but what was going on with Gruber that got you into so much trouble?"

"Europe was changing. Most countries had already joined the EU. Eastern Europe had just opened its borders. Eastern Europeans and Russians were scattered. When the Eastern European countries accepted the euro as their currency, their economies went bad. The people could not afford to live from day to day. One member of every Eastern European household had to go into Western Europe to work. That was the only way they could then earn enough euros to send to their families back home.

"The problems began when businesses hired Eastern Europeans at cheap rates. Their work ethics were poor. Years under the Socialist regime had drained their spirit. If you paid them half normal pay, they only produced a tenth of what a Western European would have produced at regular scale. Hiring cheaper labor led to higher unemployment in the West. The unions began to fight. When the unions started to gain momentum, they became stronger. Out of nowhere, the National Socialist Party began to gain power, and it was well-funded. They were using Western European unions and Eastern Europeans for muscle.

"They started to become political threats in several European countries. At first, we thought the Russians were behind this movement, trying to regain what they had lost. It didn't take long for us to realize that the Russians couldn't afford the kind of money backing these groups.

"That's when I met Ivan. He was working for the Russians, trying to find out who was behind this National Socialist Party. Ivan and I decided to join forces. We became friends as a result.

"So we followed the money, and it led us to Gregory Gruber. Then Ivan was told to back off because Gregory Gruber was a Russian asset and on their payroll. Later, Ivan called me and said he was back on the case. Evidently, Gruber had a new master, and the Russians didn't like it. During that time, Gruber's group was getting stronger and no one could figure out who funded them or how they were becoming so widely publicized.

"One day, we caught a break. An old friend of Ivan's, an ex-KGB man, ran into him and told him to take it easy on Gruber, that a large financial group was backing him and they didn't want Ivan to upset the applecart. Ivan was told his retirement would be taken care of if he dropped the investigation.

"He told me the whole story, and I told him to comply. He made arrangements to meet with them, and they gave him more money than he ever imagined. After they paid him off, they asked Ivan to work for them. He agreed, and within a few weeks, he found out that the money was coming from Aristotle Saris, several European multinational companies, and the Liddo Group."

When John heard this, he went pale.

"John, are you all right?"

"Franz, they're the same people who killed Rebecca, when I lived in Hong Kong, I thought they were an Asian group."

"John, are you absolutely sure?"

"Yes, I am, go on."

"At first, it didn't make any sense. Why would the most renowned capitalists in Europe want to back socialist organizations using communist money? In order to make an airtight case against them, we had to find out their true purpose.

Then we found out they were also funding the Green movement. When the American vice president started to push his global warming theory, we found out that huge amounts of money were going to environmental groups all over the world.

"I used some contacts I had in the banking community. They told me there had been billions of dollars transferred to these groups, but the transfers disappeared. Only small amounts were retained in the Socialist and Green parties' accounts. The rest was drained immediately with no deposits on record anywhere. One day, I was tracing a large transfer of funds from UBS to the Green Party, and I pulled up a screen that allowed me to see all the transfers from the bank. Luckily, the Green Party had all of its accounts in UBS. I traced the funds. They went to the American DNC. A few days later, money was transferred from the DNC to Helmut Fragge's law firm and then moved to one of his personal accounts. At this point, I needed to know how it all tied together, so I asked Ivan to look into it from his end. The man who hired him caught Ivan in the act, so he had to be eliminated. So he retired quietly, not before giving me all of the information he had taken from his employer. It seems that there is a global group of financiers, headed by Saris and a man in Asia, known to me only as Chen, that are forming a new world order, one government controlled by a few men. This new world government will control all other governments by direct control or financial force and coercion. It's happening now, right in front of everyone, without anyone realizing it. I have copies of all the documents. I can show you right now."

"They use financial coercion, and they buy politicians and law enforcement people at the highest levels. They have organized the National Socialist Parties to control the unions, the Green Party to control the population, and now they've merged."

"Franz, this is a nightmare, but I will fight them. Are you with me?"

"John, these are extremely powerful people. You never know who is in league with them. It's impossible to fight them."

"Franz, nothing is impossible. We'll find a way. These bastards killed one woman I loved, and now they're trying to kill another—Utsie. They have ruined your life, and now they want to kill Helmut. Perhaps if he believes that they're going to kill him and that we could save him, we'll have an ally on the inside. We have to be careful, but even if we can't beat them, we can cause them some serious damage."

"John, you gave me back my life, and I know you're a good man…I'm in."

"Great, Franz, let's get some sleep. We'll start to work on a plan tomorrow."

John sat up most of the night. *I can't believe this is happening worldwide and no one has noticed.* He finally fell asleep.

Franz was at breakfast early the next morning. Iris came down next, had a cup of coffee, and told Franz she was going to make croissants.

John walked into the dining room last; he had smelled the croissants, just like Pavlov's dog (Franz smiled thinking about that).

"Iris, you're the best cook in the world. No one can make these things as good as you. I'm going to miss you terribly."

"John, are you going somewhere?"

"No, you are."

"Am I going to America? Will I see Brad?"

"No, my dear, you're going to Hong Kong. Chong is having some organizational problems there, and he asked me if you could help him run the office for a while. He might have to come here to discuss building some new plants in Asia, and I need you to run things there. I'll have Brad join you in Hong Kong just as soon as the last orders have cleared production, but he can't stay for more than a week."

"Thank you, John."

"When you get to Hong Kong, Chong will send you to our fashion consultant. This is a little something, for you to put together a new wardrobe. If you're going to be running our Asia division for a while, I need you to look the part. Chong is having new business cards made for you. Your new title is 'Partner, Director, Asian Operations.'"

"Thank you, John, I'll never let you down."

John smiled that warm smile while she hugged him. "I know you won't. Now go and get ready. Your flight leaves at eleven. Franz, why don't we both take her to the airport?"

On the way there, Iris hugged John and didn't seem to want to let go. Franz noticed that John didn't mind at all.

Before going into the terminal, Iris walked over, hugged Franz, kissed his cheek, and whispered, "Please, take good care of him, Franz." She kissed him again, turned around, and walked inside.

"Chong will make sure Iris is out of harm's way. Imelda Brown, she worked for MI5 in Hong Kong, will be brought up-to-date by Chong. Imelda was Rebecca's best friend. She's smart, tough, and fearless. Chong has some surprising resources there, and we will need all the help he can give us. We have to come up with a plan as soon as we get back to the house."

They set up the office like a war room. Franz surprised John by encrypting all the computers so it would be extremely difficult to get through the firewalls he configured. Franz told John that he used FORTRAN, Cobalt and Basic, to configure the firewalls with the ability to change logarithms automatically every few minutes; if someone did get through, they would only be able to see information until it changed. "I was a cryptology expert in the SIA. That's how I was able to monitor bank accounts. I can hack into any bank in Europe."

"Great, that'll come in handy. You are a very interesting person."

They bought several transparent SMART Boards and two new laptops. After looking at Franz's list, the shopkeeper rummaged around and found several boxes of electronic gadgets. The bill came to forty-five thousand dollars.

"Franz, what the hell is this stuff?"

Franz smiled, flipped a few switches, and the entire room lit up. He picked up one of the laptops and started typing. Before he realized it, John was surrounded by information.

He played with the gadgets, per Franz's instructions. In only a few hours, he was able to segregate, merge, calculate and decipher information. Noticing the odd look on John's face, Franz explained that the encryption program he used caused an information transfer lag. Every time the logarithms changed, the computer had to store the information temporarily until the change was complete. Then it would release it to the SMART Board. John quickly got the hang of it.

They went out to dinner and then called it a night. Formulating a plan would be hard work, and they needed to be well-rested.

After a quick breakfast, John told Franz to categorize what they knew, listing the assets they had. While Franz was doing that, John went to Ivan's. He needed a clear head, and training was a good way to stay sharp.

Ivan ran him through the rigors of the hoop contraption. John was pleased; he was actually getting the hang of it. After five perfect attempts, Ivan asked John to come into the barn.

"We'll stay within the outer ring for now."

John agreed, and they began to fight.

"John, you're very ferocious today. Didn't you get any last night?" Ivan burst into his usual loud laugh.

John took the opportunity to finish him with a roundhouse kick since Ivan looked like he was tiring quickly. Ivan shot down to the floor, did a sweep-kick, followed by a cartwheel, which knocked John down; then Ivan landed him a blow to the chin. When Ivan righted himself in the middle of the cartwheel, he threw his legs out straight and came down on John's throat with his forearm. John started to gag. Ivan laughed, picked him up, and told him to breathe deeply. "You'll be all right, but never think that you have your opponent beaten until he is dead or immobilized, like you are now." Ivan laughed even louder. "You're turning green, breathe in and out, I said."

John told Ivan he had never seen that move before.

"I just made it up."

Ivan told him that practicing with the hoops allowed him to maintain his balance and sight, while flipping. "That was the purpose of teaching your body to stay balanced at any angle. The real lesson is twofold. First, never think your opponent is finished before you kill him. Second, when getting tired, overplay it. Let your opponent think you're finished, then kill him."

"Come, we drink vodka."

John thanked him but declined. He told Ivan he had a lot of paperwork to do and vodka would make him sleepy.

Back at the house, Franz told John that the data on the first SMART Board was a list of people that they knew were involved with either the Socialist Party or the Green Party, numbered one through five, the most dangerous first. The second board listed events they were aware of, categorized into first and secondhand. The third board listed their strengths and weaknesses. The fourth listed their assets, and the fifth contained possible contacts, along with assets they might have to use in an emergency.

They spent the day discussing every item on the list, adding or subtracting as needed. They developed a narrative to help pick apart the story as they knew it and try to develop an understanding of what was really happening. They took a break about three in the afternoon and bought two more SMART Boards to help them list new ideas and conclusions. When the new SMART Boards were operational, they ate dinner. After dinner, they worked until two in the morning.

John got up at six and headed directly to Ivan's.

After a brutal workout, Ivan said, "You are getting much better, but you still have a long way to go. Would you like to try some target practice?"

John climbed into the hoops. Ivan warned him not to shoot until he identified the target. He was surprised at the weight of the Russian pistol Ivan had given him, a 5.45mm PSM. As he rolled down the hill, targets started to pop up. Ivan was waiting at the bottom, examining the targets.

"Not bad, you missed three of them completely, you only wounded three others, you killed two children and an old lady… very good."

"Ivan, let's see how good you are. Go ahead."

"That wouldn't be fair. I was a professional, and it would only embarrass you more."

"Here, it's loaded eighteen rounds. Let's see what you can do."

Ivan took the pistol and got into the metal ring. "John, stay here. I don't want to shoot you."

John pushed him down the hill, and the targets started to pop up. Ivan fired once at each. When Ivan reached the top of the hill, he handed the targets to John.

"Okay, before you look, let's make a wager. For every one I missed, I'll pay you ten euros, and for every one that I hit, you pay me ten."

John said, "Now I'm really embarrassed."

"Don't worry, my friend, you'll get it. It requires practice. Pay me and let's go drink vodka."

•••••••••••••••••••••••••••

John met Franz sitting on the veranda, deep in thought. "I did some investigating, and I believe that Aristotle Saris is the primary backer of the Green Party and National Socialist Party. Look at the large amounts of money received by these major companies very shortly after they received large contracts or payments from Saris or the Liddo Group. There are some other ties between Saris and Liddo, but they're vague. It seems that the Saris Group is the majority shareholder in many companies that also have ties to Liddo. Whoever set this up is good. It would be almost impossible to prove any of this in court, but there is a common thread that runs through it all. As far as I can see, all contributions to both parties come from, or are on behalf of, these two groups."

Franz looked up, John was seething. His face was red, and the vein in his forehead seemed like it was about to burst.

"John, are you all right?"

"Those bastards, who do they think they are? They kill people for money and power. It has to stop now!"

"John, I said, are you all right?"

John composed himself. "Yes, Franz, I'm fine. But what are they doing with the Green and Socialist parties?"

"They want total control. They can control several countries with these two parties."

"Franz, maybe I'm a bit naïve, but how?"

"Controlling the Green Party allows you to control business by regulating industries, controlling natural resources and agriculture. If you could regulate what pesticides can and cannot be used in farming, you can control produce pricing. If you regulate fossil fuels, you can tax their use so high that industry would have to seek an alternative, and if you control that alternative, you can make untold profits. Let's look at the USA. ADM is the world's largest producer of soy, a meat substitute. They've been lobbying your officials for years, and it's paying off. Your government has restricted the use of vitamins and stimulants when raising cattle. Now there is less meat being produced. ADM is showing huge profits.

"The socialists openly control the unions here, and they are becoming more and more powerful with the influx of Eastern Europeans. The National Socialist Party probably has about twenty to thirty percent of the vote in Switzerland and the Green

Party has a bit more. By merging the two parties, they will win the election, so Saris and Liddo will be in control."

"Is this for real? It seems a bit far-fetched."

"This is what I was working on when I got framed. I followed the same trail, and it led me to the same place. However, before now, I never figured that Saris and Liddo were actively involved in political parties other than the massive contributions they made. Now that we've figured this out, where do we go from here? There are already people in my government who are aligned with them. Based on your catastrophe in Hong Kong, we don't know who we can trust in your government."

"Let's look at our asset board."

"We have you and I, Chong, Imelda Browne, Ivan, and Tsillman…" Franz stopped. "Not Tsillman, I changed my mind."

John said, "Why not?"

"The Liddo Group is his largest client."

"Holy shit, Franz, Tsillman got me involved in emissions credits, and I made over nine billion dollars. Do you think Liddo was behind that?"

"What did you do to earn that kind of money?"

John told him everything.

"John, I think you were the front man for the largest energy takeover in history."

"I'll kill that son of a bitch."

"John, relax, we're going to need Tsillman. They might have just given you the resources we need to fight them. We might be able to get at them with their own money, how ironic."

"Franz, I have an idea. As you know, I don't particularly like Helmut, so let's confront him. We can tell him Utsie had to go into hiding because she overheard a plot to assassinate him, and we'll see where that takes us. If these people are paying him off, one way or another, he must have inside knowledge."

"I don't know, John. We can't let them know who we are yet. We're not strong enough, nor do we have enough information to do this openly. Let me think about it."

Franz stood up and studied the boards, going back and forth, looking at the data, and then retrieving information from another board.

After about an hour, Franz stopped and said one word, "Ivan."

"What about Ivan?"

"The Russians are the only people in the world who have not been corrupted by the likes of Saris. We can use Ivan to interrogate Helmut. He can tell him that Gruber is a target of the Russian mafia. It is known that Gruber was instructed to kill Helmut. If he cooperates, he will be placed under the protection of the KGB. If he doesn't cooperate, then they will kill him. I will go to Ivan and ask him if he'll do it. Can I offer to pay him $25,000? I'm sure he'll help us."

"What if he says no?"

"He won't. He hates those people. Ivan's a good man. He would probably do this for nothing, but money will sweeten the pot."

## 26

### Jakarta, Indonesia

YK picked up the phone. "Mike, have you heard anything on your end about Saris, Gruber, or Fragge?"

"No, nothing so far, YK."

"Good. I knew the girl would be too afraid to do anything. I believe that will be the last we hear of this. Our problem now is Saris. He's gone over the top, Mike. Watch him."

He hung up and called his assistant.

"Paula, could you dig up the phone records for the last three months on Manheim's phones?"

"Yes, sir, exactly what are you looking for?"

"I want to know how many calls were made to Saris."

Although he believed Manheim was more loyal to him than anyone else, he still couldn't trust him, so hungry for power. YK knew that if Manheim had the opportunity, he would kill him. *I wish there was another way to accomplish this. All of these dangerous men might be a necessity, but they are a pain in the ass.*

There had been fifty-three calls made during the last three months. It looked normal, but then he saw one call from Saris to Manheim. His private cell number was only supposed to be used in emergencies and only between Saris and YK. There had to be a reason Saris used that number to call, and he knew he wouldn't like the answer.

"Paula, would you get these people on the phone for me, one at a time, in that order, thank you."

## GREEN TO RED

He asked everyone to come to Jakarta the following day. They all showed up, and the meeting started right away. When they were summoned by Y. K. Chen, the Shadow Emperor, they dropped everything, told no one, and came immediately.

"I'm pleased to see you all. Our plan for the global takeover of the energy producers is almost ready to implement. We are now in possession of approximately 98.9 percent of the available emissions credits worldwide. Make certain that individual companies, with no ties to us, purchase all of the coal-fired plants. Chen went over the details for several hours. After the meeting ended, he asked Wiley to join him in his office.

"What can I do for you, YK?"

"I might have a problem with Mike. Could you get rid of him for me and take over the operation if it becomes necessary?"

Wiley started to shake and thought he would vomit. "YK, Mike's been on edge for a while. Handling this new president, even though we put him into office, has been difficult. That's no reason to get rid of him."

"Your loyalty to Mike is admirable, but I have reason to believe he has struck some kind of deal with Saris."

"It's more than that, YK. Mike wouldn't do that, and he's done well for you these past years."

"Wiley, what you are saying is true, but I can't have the heads of our group making deals with my enemies."

"I thought Saris was a friend of yours?"

"He's just a partner in a large venture, and he is expendable."

"Well, YK, if that's what you want, I have no problem with it. You just surprised me. I will take care of it at your command."

"Business is business, my friend."

Chen walked him to the door.

# 27

### Washington DC

The president's chief of staff wished he had never left Chicago. He had just left a meeting with the president and couldn't believe how dense he was. Does he really believe his own hype? He must know that he is the most ineffective president in US history. *Maybe I am missing something? I wonder if he is being backed by someone else.*

Just then, something on his desk caught his eye. *That bastard is playing both sides. He is being taken care of by Saris directly. That's why he used discretionary money to fund Saris's company in South America.* He picked up the phone, called Wiley, but was told he was out of town. He left a message and hung up. *What the hell did I get myself into? I've been in this racket too long to go down in flames. How do I get this guy under my control?*

The president was interrupted by an emergency phone call. "Gentlemen, please excuse me for a minute." He took the call in private and left the oval office as soon as he hung up.

He returned later that afternoon and reconvened the meeting. "Gentlemen, I want you to drop everything and concentrate on environmental issues. We have control over Detroit, and I want to see more fuel-efficient cars coming off the assembly line now! I also want more done about foreign oil dependency, even if we have to buy foreign oil companies like we just did in South America. This is our agenda for now—our only agenda. Do you understand?"

They agreed and went back to their offices. The president called his secretary.

"I want to call a press conference before the end of the week. Make arrangements for the chief of staff to attend the conference in Europe on climate change or global warming, whatever it's called now. Do it right away."

........................................

The chief of staff jumped out of his chair and screamed, "Is he nuts?"

He stormed down the hall to the oval office. The president simply told him that the plan was not open for discussion. He wanted it done immediately. The chief of staff walked out of the office, swearing under his breath.

*Is he really going through with this? Does Saris have something on him? Or is there another force behind him that even I don't know about?* He composed himself and called the president's secretary.

"Hello, I need to see the president this evening. Please tell him that I need at least an hour alone, if possible."

He knew the president was backing Saris with all that money going to Saris's company. But it didn't make any sense. *This guy owes too many people to do this. It's political suicide, unless he's selling us all down the river. Oh my god, that's it! I knew this guy was egotistical, but does he really think he can get away with this? I better call Wiley or I'm a dead man. Hope he's there this time.*

"Hello, Wiley, I need to see you as soon as possible. Not until tomorrow? I'll come out there. You're not in the country? Okay, I'll see you tomorrow evening at your place in Washington."

*This is good. I'll have a little more time to figure this out.*

# 28

**Washington DC**

"Rob, it's good to see you, boy!"

"Don't give me any of that 'good old boy' shit. I'm not in the mood."

Wiley took him to the "bubble room," it had been debugged and was soundproof.

"What's wrong?"

"Everything, that son of a bitch is selling us down the river. I can't believe we put this moron in office and he's pulling this crap."

"Rob, slow down, tell me everything."

"He's made a deal, and he is cutting us out. I can't control him. He's listening to Saris and only to Saris. He's dropped our whole agenda and is going to set Saris up to be the only game in town. He just gave the son of a bitch two billion dollars of discretionary money. I'm not going to be there when the shit hits the fan. I'm not going down with this guy!"

"Rob, now calm down. Saris is nuttier than a fruitcake, and we let him believe he has some power, but he doesn't. You tell the president that if he doesn't change his action plan, we'll have his ass impeached. We'll leak that he has ties to Saris, and if he makes us push the fact, he'll hang for treason."

Rob started to walk in circles.

"It won't work. He's not listening to me. He won't even meet with me."

"Who is the intermediary between the president and Saris?"

"I don't know. It can't be the DNC directly. No, wait a minute. It's the Speaker. Every time they meet, he goes off on one of his tangents. It has to be her."

"Good, Rob. Do you know anyone at Justice who has a hard-on for her?"

"Just about everyone hates her for one reason or another."

"Good, get someone at Justice to start a quiet investigation. Tell them the president believes that there are some improprieties between Saris and her. We need to know how often she's meeting with him or contacting him. Tell them this is only a flyer but you need the information ASAP. Tell them to report to you only and all files will be retained by your office. If it's that googly-eyed heifer, we'll bring her down, and then we'll tell the president that he's next."

After Rob left, Wiley decided not to report this to YK just yet.

# 29

### Zurich

Helmut Fragge walked out of the bistro. It was dusk, a cool lake breeze blowing. He had overeaten, as usual, and decided to walk it off. Without hesitation, three masked men pulled up in a van, jumped out, and threw him into it.

"What's the meaning of this?"

A man slapped him hard in the face, knocking him down.

"Shut up, or we'll cut your tongue out."

"This must be a mistake." Again he was slapped.

The van pulled away, and Helmut started to protest again. The same man took a pair of pliers from his pocket, grabbed Helmut's tongue, and, with the other hand, produced a long knife. Helmut fainted.

He awoke tied to a chair. The building was empty, but the floor was oil-stained, and he smelled gas. He had not yet noticed he was naked. His arms and legs were tied, taped to the arms and legs of the heavy wooden chair. He started to yell for help as a man walked out of the shadows. Helmut began to speak. The man did not say a word; he tased Helmut's neck. Helmut convulsed violently. He was still retching and drooling when his body stopped shaking.

"You were told to be quiet. We will not tell you again."

A well-dressed man came over to him and looked him directly in the eye. The man set up a small table next to Helmut, putting what looked like surgical instruments on it. Carefully placing each instrument, the man glanced at Helmut and smiled. One of the others came in and asked in Russian, "Doctor, are you ready?"

A maniacal smile grew on the man's face.

"Yes, I'm looking forward to this."

Helmut wet himself.

"Okay, Herr Fragge, this is how it works. I will ask you a question. If you do not answer me, the doctor will persuade you. If I am not happy with the answer, he will punish you. If you continue to disobey me, he will cut off your fingers and toes, one at a time, your penis next. Do you understand me?"

Helmut's eyes went wide; he started to vomit.

"Please, we haven't even started yet and you are already making me sick."

One of the other men threw a bucket of cold water over Helmut to clean him up. The large man chuckled.

"Next time, throw warm water on him. His penis has shrunken to almost nothing. It will make it harder to cut off if we have to."

Helmut started to cry.

"Okay, let me introduce myself. I am a representative of the KGB. You are the head of the National Green Party. We have information that you are merging with the National Socialist Party. The head of that party is Gregory Gruber. We have just learned that he has gotten orders to kill you. We require some information from you. If you cooperate, we will put you under our protection and save you from being assassinated by Gruber. If you do not cooperate, we will have you delivered to Gruber cut up in little pieces."

"I'll tell you anything you want to know!" Helmut screamed.

"Who is behind the two organizations?"

"Aristotle Saris."

"Saris cannot be doing this alone. Who is he working with?"

"The Liddo Group and several major European companies."

After several hours of interrogation, Ivan had a list of organizations and the names of the "Inner Circle."

"Where is Saris now, and where is his office?"

"I don't know where he is right now. He has offices all over the world. When he's in Switzerland, he stays at hotels, rarely the same one twice."

Ivan punched the wall, and the room shook.

"You are lying to me. Doctor, persuade him to tell me the truth."

The doctor began to pant as he moved closer to Helmut.

"No, I am telling you the truth." This time he shat himself.

After another bucket of water was thrown over him, he began to weep. "Get him dressed and throw him in the street."

"Now, Helmut, do I have to tell you this is to be kept confidential? You will tell no one. If you do, you will spend a weekend with the doctor before we kill you. Is that understood?"

Helmut wept. "I won't tell anyone. I promise."

"Okay, you are under our protection. If you see anyone following you, ignore it. We will not let them kill you. If we call you, and you hear this phrase, 'It is the doctor,' hang up and go directly to the sausage stand in Limmat Platz. If you do not show up within thirty minutes, the doctor will make a house call, understood?"

"Yes, yes, I understand. Why are you doing this to me?"

"You did this to yourself Herr Fragge, the moment you took money from those people."

Later, Ivan met John and Franz at his home.

"Let's go out to the yard."

He reported everything he had learned from Fragge and gave them the list of companies and people involved.

"These people are not only powerful, they're brilliant, and no one knows about it."

John looked disgusted and angry.

"Yeah, they're psychopaths as well."

"I agree, John, but look at it. The timing is perfect. Russia is in turmoil, the liberals have taken over the United States, and Europe is totally dysfunctional due to their so-called alignment with the formation of the EU. Oil prices are up. There is almost a world currency, the euro is slaughtering the dollar, and the Chinese have become the world's bankers."

"What exactly do you hope to accomplish?"

"We don't know exactly, but I am going to bring these bastards down come hell or high water."

Ivan studied the two men and started to smile, pointing at John.

"This man is crazier than me. I am in. Now let's drink vodka!"

After several drinks, John and Franz returned to the house and began inputting the information that they received from Ivan.

"Look at this."

He hit a few keys on the computer.

"John, there is a pattern here. I'm going to hack into major banks, get some more information, and before I am through, we will be able to see the transactional flow between these companies. Once I have the pattern, I can use certain algorithms. We'll be able to forecast their business very accurately."

"Break time for me, this is a little over my head."

......................................

"Hello, Peter, is she all right?"

"She's fine. No one will be able to find her."

"Great, thanks, Peter."

He hung up.

"Chong, how's everything in Hong Kong?"

"Everything is fine here. Your girl Iris is working like a machine."

John smiled and told Chong to take good care of her.

Chong laughed. "She is taking care of me. I have never seen anyone work as hard as she does. She's happy all the time. She is a very nice girl."

"I'm glad to hear you are getting along. Chong, seriously, take very good care of her."

"Boss, you know you don't have to tell me that."

"I know, thanks, Chong. You're a good friend."

John sat back, relaxed, and tried to enjoy the view of the city, but everything he saw reminded him of how these despicable people took the love of his life away. *It's not going to happen again. This time I'm going to take everything away from them.*

"John, I figured it out, it is unbelievable."

"What the hell is this?" All the SMART Boards were lit up.

"If you follow the yellow arrows, they will clarify the transaction. The blue lines show currency, the red lines show transactions. The blinking lights are real-time transactions, the colors designate the companies."

"John, with this, we can figure out what they are going to do before they do it!"

"Franz, this is brilliant."

"No, John, it's just an effective tool."

Franz put together a program that allowed him to forecast the financial moves of all the companies on the board.

"John, as far as I can tell, these companies are owned or controlled by Liddo. These companies over here are owned or controlled by Saris. I haven't been able to identify how this group fits in yet. I have to contact a hacker. I know all banks use several programs to communicate: COBALT, FORTRAN, and BASIC. Their networks communicate using these programs, or variations of them, and firewalls protect their information. These firewalls are designed encryptions. Algorithms are used to change them quickly and simply.

"The hacker I know can get these algorithms within minutes of the changes. He designed the firewalls for several banks, but he was caught stealing and was ostracized from the banking and insurance communities."

"If he was so good, how did he get caught?"

"I knew what he was doing, I thought he would be more valuable to the SIA than to the banks, so I had him arrested. The banks didn't want the publicity, so they dropped the charges. I hired him as a consultant. By the way, I'm going to need about fifty thousand dollars to get the information I need and another fifty thousand monthly, until completion."

"Franz, here's the key to the safe. There is a million dollars in there. If the balance goes below five hundred thousand, let me know, I will add small amounts slowly. We don't want to alert the bank or Tsillman."

"John, that's a lot of money, and I don't want the responsibility…"

"Franz, only you and I have the combination. I trust you."

"Thank you, John. I will try to live up to the faith you have in me."

"You have already proved your worth to me, it is beyond measure. Can we drain the money from these accounts? That might be the way to bring them down."

"Yes, John, we could empty them all, but that would only disrupt them, not stop them. The banks would simply trace our transactions to the source and cover their depositors. We need to trace all this money to the residual accounts. We'll look for accounts that are used to pool all this money collected by the businesses. That's where the real wealth is, and that is how we can hurt them."

"Franz, simply amazing!"

"John, I was trained to do this. Back then, I would have had them arrested. Now we can use this information to destroy them."

"What are these accounts?" John said, pointing to a group that was set off to the side.

"I don't know yet. That is why we need the hacker."

"Franz, let's call it a night."

"Good idea, I'm tired. I won't be here when you get up. I'll be talking to the hacker, telling him what we need."

"I'll go over to Ivan's tomorrow and train while you're gone."

"Try to get Ivan to work with us full-time. He would be a great asset."

"Good idea, Franz. He did that thing with Fragge for free. How much do you think I should offer him?"

"John, offer him twenty thousand per month, plus expenses. That's more than fair."

When he arrived at Ivan's, he knocked on the door, no answer. He saw something out of the corner of his eye. A man he didn't know was inside. Looking through a window, he saw Ivan tied up, sitting on the floor. He entered the backyard, looked through the open kitchen window, climbed inside, and knocked something over, causing it to fall and break, making a very loud noise. He got behind the door quickly as several people ran toward the kitchen. The first man came through unseen. He punched the second man in the throat and then elbowed him in the temple. As he fell, John grabbed him and threw him over his shoulder like a shield. Running toward the first man, he threw the limp man at him and kicked him in the groin so hard that he passed out. The guy on his shoulder was coming around; John gave him a roundhouse kick that finished him. John felt a crushing blow to his head and almost went limp, but his adrenaline kept him going. *Where did this third man come from?* The man delivered another blow to the side of his head; John stumbled, caught himself, pushed off the countertop, and attacked. He delivered a powerful uppercut to the man's chin, then head-butted him, a nose bone snapped. Ivan yelled, "Stop!"

"What the hell is going on?"

"John, it was a training exercise. I didn't think you would kill anyone."

"A training exercise, are you nuts? Jesus H. Christ!"

Ivan looked at the downed men and started to laugh.

"John, I don't think I ever want to get you mad with me. John, I see you are very good in a fight. Two of my men will have to see the doctor. The other one, he was never pretty anyway."

"Ivan, you have a strange sense of humor."

They cleaned the three men up and told them to get medical attention. Ivan took John to the barn.

"John, Franz told me how kind and generous you have been to him. You're a very interesting man. You thought I was in trouble, you didn't hesitate to help me. I won't forget this, my friend."

"Good, that will make what I have to say a little easier. Ivan, I want to hire you as a consultant. I'm willing to pay you twenty thousand dollars per month, plus expenses, for your expertise."

"Are you going after those pieces of shit? I will do it for nothing."

"Ah, no, Ivan, I want to pay you. It really isn't your fight. If I lose, you will need money to hide from these people."

"What people, you mean this Gruber?"

"No, Ivan, it's much more complicated than just him and his organization."

"Now this sounds interesting. I'll go along for the ride."

John began to tell Ivan all the details, past and present.

"Ivan, I want to bring these bastards down, every last one of them."

"John, I know these bastards, I can't give you details, but I know they attempted to get into Russia. They didn't stay very long, perhaps they thought we were not worth the time. If half of what you have told me is true, this is going to be fun. This could be my last big adventure."

John looked at Ivan closely, trying to figure him out.

"Ivan, this is going to be dangerous. These people have far-reaching power. We may not be able to trust anyone."

"Great, just the way I like to work."

"Welcome to the team."

"How many people do you have?"

"You, Franz, and myself."

Ivan started to laugh.

"Three against half of the world. I like the odds. Come, let us drink vodka."

"John, I'm glad to see you. I have some bad news."

"What, Franz?"

"Every European customer you have is directly or indirectly part of Liddo. Even your distributor in China is a direct subsidiary."

"What the hell are you telling me?"

"I will say it again: all of our customers are part of the Liddo Group."

"Why would they do this? How long has it been going on?"

"John, they use legitimate businesses to launder ill-gotten money. Yachts are big ticket items. When you have to move a lot of cash, you need to justify these types of expenditures. Perhaps they targeted your company when you were in Hong Kong, and that may be why you are still alive. John, that's not all. The money you made with the emissions credits can be traced back to them."

"This is a bit too much for me to digest right now. What else have you uncovered?"

"Even though I haven't figured it all out yet, I think their two primary locations are Jakarta, Indonesia, and Memphis, Tennessee. There are more transactions in those two locations than all others combined."

Franz cleared all of the SMART Boards, and with a few keystrokes on his computer, they all streamed information.

"These companies are owned by the Liddo Group. These companies are not directly associated but have multiple transactions with Liddo companies. Here are the accounts with the hacked banks, and here are the names of the banks that are holding accounts, but I have not gotten into them yet. Here is a list of accounts holding noncurrency funds, like bearer bonds, commercial paper, property deeds, etc. I still have to identify all portfolio accounts which are not always on a bank's account systems. Once I have all this information, I have to find the black hole, the residual accounts. That's going to be difficult. Usually accounts like that are hidden in the Central Banks of third world countries. This is going to take some time. If I gather enough information, I should be able to guess where the residual funds are hidden. I will ask my friend to start hacking places I suggest. The whole process should take about two months. If I make a mistake, we could be found out, and that would be disastrous. I have covered my tracks so far, but if I'm in a bank when they are changing their encryption logarithms, it will set off an alarm, and that will be the end of the game."

"I can't believe you were able to do this much."

"Well, John, the Swiss government has been the police for the banking industry for a long time. This is the result of years and years of research. I was lucky to be trained by them."

# 30

Helmut Fragge sat at his desk staring nervously out the window. *What should I do? If I stay, they will kill me, and if I leave, they will kill me. Why does Gruber want to kill me? I've already agreed to step down. Saris must be behind this, but it doesn't make sense. I've done a good job for him. Am I really being protected by the Russians?* All of these seemingly unanswerable questions kept rolling around in his head. "What am I going to do?" he finally screamed. He had a luncheon meeting with the head of Hoffman Laroche. *Better to go there than sit here thinking about all the shit I'm in.*

Helmut tried to get his mind off his troubles during lunch. He flinched every time someone he didn't know walked into the restaurant. His guest asked if he was all right. He decided to cut his lunch short and go home.

He got home okay, but his feeling of dread became worse. He was so afraid that he began to feel nauseous. He packed a bag, went directly to the airport. *I'm off to Crete. No one will find me there.*

Helmut arrived in Crete about 11:00 p.m., and the fear left him as he looked out over the Aegean. An hour later, he decided to go out and get something to eat. He got back to his hotel and went right to sleep.

The phone rang at seven; Helmut picked it up and went pale. "Hello, Helmut, what are you doing in Crete? I thought we had a lunch date today? If you would like, we can cancel for today, but when can we reschedule? How about the same time on Friday?"

Helmut just stared at the phone, dumbstruck.

"Okay, I'll see you on Friday, and enjoy the holiday, good-bye."

Ascot Chen hung up and was very satisfied. The man couldn't even speak.

Helmut, now terrified, knew there was no place for him to go. He ran for the bathroom and vomited. He lay on the bathroom floor and cried until he was interrupted by the maid.

Helmut came to a decision. *That Russian was right. I sealed my fate when I took the money from Saris.* He decided to go back to Zurich. He went to the airport, took the next flight to Zurich, and arrived at 8:00 p.m.

He was home shortly before nine; the phone was ringing. He dropped his bags and picked up the phone. "It's the doctor," and the line went dead. He immediately went to the stand on Limmat Platz.

A man came out of the darkness and startled him.

"Herr Fragge, you look a little tired. I want copies of all the correspondence you've had with Saris and Gruber, and I want it by end of business tomorrow."

"That's impossible. It will take a lot of work to get all of it put together that quickly."

"Well then, you better start right away. I will send your friend, the doctor, to pick them up at 6:00 p.m. tomorrow. If you don't have them all, the doctor will go home with you and help you look for the rest."

Helmut vomited again.

The doctor arrived on time, and Helmut gave him boxes of correspondence. Helmut was tired and panicked. *I have to get out of here. But where can I go? They will find me anywhere I go. I better stay and accept the protection of the Russians. At least I'll stay alive.*

He went home and cried himself to sleep. Helmut woke early in the morning to the same thoughts running over and over in his head. *How did I get into this? It is not worth the wealth and power I achieved. Why are they doing this to me?* When he finally got out of bed, it was almost 10:00 a.m. He showered and dressed with no plans for the day. He milled around his flat, started to have a panic attack, and ran out, hoping the open air would help him calm down. He walked for hours. It was close to dinner with Fear as his dinner date. He didn't want to go home or to the office, so he decided to take a dinner cruise on the lake.

He was able to buy a ticket for the next cruise. He found a table, sat down, and ordered a drink. He was starting to relax when he heard an unfamiliar voice, "Herr Fragge, come with me, now."

"I'm not going anywhere, who are you?"

The man simply pointed. Helmut could feel himself becoming ill as he saw the doctor standing by the gangway. Helmut started to whimper. The man just reached down, took Helmut's arm, and lifted him up.

"Come now, don't make a scene. You will only make things worse for you."

He got up; his eyes never left the doctor.

"What does he want from me? I gave them everything."

Once again, Helmut was sitting in the middle of that same garage, hyperventilating, not tied up or beaten, just sitting there.

"Herr Fragge, how are you? Are you not feeling well? You do not look too good."

"What do you want? Why are you doing this to me?"

The man approached him with a kind look on his face.

"My dear Helmut, we are just trying to protect you. You are still alive, even though you were called back from Greece."

"How did you know I was in Greece?"

"We know every step you take. How else would we be able to protect you? You do not have to fear us. It is the people that you were involved with that are your worst fear. I want you to tell me the whole story—from the beginning. If we know everything, we really can protect you. If you leave something out, it might hurt you."

A table was brought in, food was placed on it, including a bottle of Helmut's favorite wine.

"Go ahead, my friend, eat, drink, start talking."

Helmut began talking. The more he told, the more relaxed he became. He told them how he was recruited, that his law practice had been given so much business that it became the largest firm in Switzerland. "I never believed I would ever make that much money." He told them how Saris made him believe he was doing him a favor by making him the head of the Green Party. He admitted that all of the publicity and fame was a boost to his ego and that he enjoyed it. He went into great detail about how much he admired Saris and how he thought Saris would lead the world to a new world order. He also talked about the Liddo Group, and others, and how they played into the plan, how they would rule the world and end poverty and war. His dialogue went on for hours. He talked about everyone in the inner circle and how they interacted directly with Saris and Y. K. Chen.

"Wait, who is Y. K. Chen?"

"He's the head of the Liddo Group, of course."

"But you said the head of the Liddo Group was Mike Manheim."

"Manheim is only the head of the United States division of Liddo. He is very important. He has all the politicians there on his payroll or under his control."

Ivan made a note. "Go on, please."

Helmut spilled his guts for another three hours. The more he talked, the more relieved he felt.

"Let's call it a night. If we need more information, we'll call you, Helmut. Otherwise, feel safe. You are under our protection, for now."

Little did he know that the information he had just divulged might be used against him at a later date.

Ivan arrived home to find Franz waiting for him.

"Franz, let's go to the barn."

They sat down, sipped vodka, and listened to the hours of dialogue on the tape, stopping it and copying down things that might prove important later. It was 10:45 a.m. when Franz left with the tape and went back to John's house.

"Good morning, Franz, how did it go?"

"I can't believe the stuff on this tape. We edited it and highlighted the important parts."

Franz and John listened to the entire tape, and then the edited version. Franz cleared two of the SMART Boards and noted names as John played both tapes again. They matched the names with companies, cross-matched them with known relationships, took that list, and cross-matched it again with a business contact list that they had already catalogued.

"Wait a minute, I have a profiling program. The CIA gave it to us. I can modify it."

"Franz, do your thing."

"John, go get some sleep, this is going to take a few hours."

# 31

**Washington, the White House**

The chief of staff came out of the morning briefing and went directly over to the Justice Department.

"Colin, let's take a walk. I have something to discuss with you."

"Colin, this is a sensitive, confidential matter, and if it is handled properly, it could make your career."

"Rob, you know it will. I give you my word."

"It seems the Speaker might have gone off the reservation. The president believes that there may be some improprieties on the part of the Speaker that could be detrimental to National Security. This puts the president in a difficult position. He does not want a full-scale investigation or any publicity generated. If we can get solid evidence, we will ask her to resign. Would you handle a clandestine investigation and bring me any evidence you find? The president is not to be involved or contacted."

"Do I have any cover on this one?"

"None."

"What's in it for me?"

"What do you want?"

"I want to be director, and before the president leaves office, I want an ambassadorship."

"Colin, you drive a hard bargain, but okay."

"Good, when I have the information, I want you to ask for the director's resignation. When he gives it to you, I'll give you the information. I'll trust you on the ambassadorship."

"Deal, when can I expect something?"

"Give me two weeks, a month on the outside."

When Colin got back to his office, he made one phone call. "Hello, Director, it's Young. I have to see you right now."

He played the tape. The director wasn't surprised, but he was angry.

"Who the hell do these people think they are? It's not bad enough that they screw each other, but they're willing to usurp the constitution to do it, not to mention bribing a federal officer. Colin, play it out. It shouldn't be too hard to find something on her. Let's see where they're going with this. This time they've gone too far."

# 32

### Jakarta, Indonesia

"Paula, sit down," Y. K. Chen asked his assistant.

"What is it, YK?"

"Paula, you have been a great help to me. I've made you a rich woman. You are the most mercenary woman I have ever met."

"Is there something wrong with that?"

"Oh no, my dear, on the contrary, it is a formidable attribute for a young woman. But you have no life, no normal life. You have had only one boyfriend that I am aware of, and I was paying you to spy on him."

"YK, Mike and I were seeing each other before you started paying me. I accepted the assignment because I know where my bread is buttered, and I will always be loyal to you above anyone else. Mike, as much as I love him, can be mean, and I needed your protection."

"That's why I like you. You're sensible and pragmatic. Now I want you to play a more important role in our business. I want you to head up the European section. I'll give you a salary of two million per year and an incremental bonus according to profitability. Do you want the job?"

"YK, I'm flattered. Yes, of course, I accept."

"Excellent. I want to fill you in on current business affairs. Then we can discuss the politics of the situation over dinner."

Listening to YK explain the political climate and their current business affairs in his own words gave her new insight, even though she already knew the basics. She was not allowed to take notes; her memory would have to be sufficient. They spent hours going over everything she needed to know. It was after 7:00 p.m. YK asked her if she was ready dinner.

During a sumptuous dinner, he mentioned that Saris was becoming a problem. He explained that Saris was needed, but only for a few more months. In the meantime, he wanted Paula to get close to him and come up with a plan to eradicate him. She agreed; it shouldn't be too hard to develop a feasible scenario. "Come, my dear, I have prepared something for us to enjoy and to seal our bargain, much more than a handshake."

Paula smiled, even though she was going to hate what was about to happen. YK led her to his bedroom, knocked her to the floor, and dragged her to the bed. He handcuffed her to the headboard on her stomach. She heard the snap of leather, and she winced. *For two million dollars, I can handle anything.*

YK revived her. He had only stopped when blood started to stain his floor. "My dear, I hope you enjoyed that as much as I did. We are now bound through blood. Your life belongs to me now, but you will be rich beyond your wildest dreams."

"Thank you, YK." She passed out again. YK violated her.

He carried Paula to her room and summoned a doctor. When the doctor arrived, he looked at her wounds but said nothing. He cleaned and dressed them. It was not the first time he had tended to this one.

······················

Paula was almost healed when YK called her into his office. "Paula, you look wonderful. Here are your first-class tickets and the key to your flat in London. Please visit with our businesses and subsidiaries first, get to know the players there before you visit the rest of Europe. Call this number at Wertshaft und Privat bank, use this code word to have funds transferred wherever you wish. You have up to one million dollars. If you need more, clear it with me. Call me on the scrambled line at least once a week with updates, keep that phone with you at all times, your flight leaves in three hours."

"Thank you so much, YK."

"The pleasure is all mine."

After the flight had taken off, she cried silently, remembering her sordid past. She had been seduced by a wealthy man at sixteen. He had taken her to the Orient. He abandoned her after abusing her sexually for weeks. Too embarrassed to call her family and destitute, she met Lucy Fu. Lucy took care of her, clothed and fed her, and then sold her to a club owner who beat her. He beat her and kept her in a cage, naked, without food for days. She remembered he would ask her over and over, "Are you going to be a good girl and do what I say?" She finally gave in, her spirit broken. She was reserved for special clients. After two years of extreme depravity, nothing bothered her. She was dead inside. One day, a guy came in and asked her if she wanted to get out of there. He walked her right out the front door. They got lucky, no one saw them. British Inspector Carmichael brought her to a Catholic church. The nuns took care of her until she got a decent job working at the Hong Kong exchange, then she met Ascot Chen. Within two weeks, she was in Jakarta, working for the Liddo Group. She stopped crying. I will never be taken advantage of again. I have finally made it, and now I have the power.

The plane landed in London several hours later; her chauffeur was waiting for her. Her new home, a three-story condominium on the top of the OXO building with a view of the tower of London, Parliament, and the Thames was beautiful.

Tomorrow, she would start her new life. She had made it; and no one, not even YK, would ever beat her again.

# 33

### Zurich, Switzerland

John normally bolted out of bed wide-awake. The strain he was under coupled with his need to protect Utsie was taking its toll. He felt better once he had taken a shower and was dressed.

Franz was excited. "John, I've modified the program I told you about, it works better than expected. I've already profiled each company and identified the patterns and the frequency of their transactions. It can also delete any company that doesn't have a direct relationship with the Liddo Group or Saris. That saves time."

"Franz, what do we do with this information?"

Franz went on to tell John that with the companies being profiled in this manner, he could project their moves and, if need be, screw up all the companies at once by putting false stops on any payments, or by diverting payments to the principals' accounts to cast suspicion on an individual.

"We can project their moves, put false stops on payments, and divert payments to an employee's individual account. We can really screw them up. It'll also give us a clearer picture of the entire operation and how it all works."

"Franz, that's great. I can clearly see benefits. Sorry, I can be slow on the uptake."

The program was a profiling tool; it showed a hierarchical graph of the entire Liddo Group. If you clicked on a particular company, a profile popped up showing the management structure, officers, employees, overseas affiliates, account balances, and projections for the next three years. This was a bit frightening, but it was amazing.

"Franz, can anyone with computer savvy do this?"

"No, John, these are highly classified and specialized programs. There's probably less than ten people in the world that even know these things exist. John, I have a lot more to do to get this fully functional."

"Okay, I'll get out of your hair. I'm going to Ivan's."

John arrived at the barn; Ivan was already warming up.

"Hello, John, let's spar a little to warm up, and then you can do some target practice on the hoops."

"Ivan, you're a bad man."

"I know, but if I wasn't, we would have never met."

Ivan charged at him quickly and landed a horrific blow to John's head. John went down. When he saw that Ivan was off-balance, he did a prone spin kick that landed on the back of Ivan's legs, knocking him down hard. Once he was down, John leapt to his feet and kicked Ivan in the kidney, rolled him over, and then put his foot on the man's neck.

"I'm done, you are getting too good."

"I thought we were going to spar to warm up?"

"My friend, I am older than you and slower. I needed a little advantage, so I chose to surprise you, but I was the one surprised."

Ivan led John out of the barn.

John mounted the steel rings, and Ivan handed him the pistol. He started to roll downhill, trying to remember everything he had already learned. The targets started to pop up. John carefully controlled his movements and fired the weapon. He used eight of the eighteen rounds.

"Bravo, my friend, a clean headshot in every target, without hitting any bystanders and a shoulder shot on the target with the person wielding the knife. John, this is truly impressive."

John told him it was like being on a ship in a storm, "You never know which way the boat will be thrown, so you have to keep your balance."

Next, Ivan gave John some pointers on how to evade someone who was following, how to follow someone without being detected, and basic evasion moves when being approached by multiple attackers.

"Is this a KGB crash course?"

"John, as you know, you are going up against some dangerous people. I will try to teach you everything that has kept me alive all my years in the game."

"Thanks, Ivan, the information you have given me will help me stay alive."

"Good, let's drink vodka."

Before he left, John invited Ivan to his house that evening. Ivan told him he couldn't attend.

"Why not?"

"I don't know where you live."

John gave him the address, told him he wanted to show him the program Franz had come up with and share the information they had gathered so far.

"Ivan, I think you could be a big help in the planning and development stage."

"I doubt it, John. I never used a computer to get information. I only needed a rubber hose."

John looked at Ivan, knowing the man was not kidding.

"Good then, come over around eight, and we can have dinner."

"Dinner is good, just make sure you have plenty of vodka."

John arrived home and saw Franz was sitting, having coffee.

"I'm finished. We now have the entire structure and interaction of both the Liddo Group and the Saris Group. I have found three of their major black holes—the Central Bank of Botswana, the USAID, and the DNC of the United States. I found something interesting. There have been trusts set up with only the interest being taken out, most of that goes back to the owners through a series of contributions that always seem to end up in the Green Party."

"How much do you think is in there?"

"I would say around five trillion dollars."

"Hello, Ivan, thanks for coming."

"Nice place," Ivan remarked. "The boat business must be good."

John handed Ivan a water glass of vodka. John told Franz to have a drink and then excused himself to see how dinner was going. "Come in and get it," he yelled. Dinner was simple, steak and mashed potatoes. During dinner, nothing was mentioned about the work at hand. Ivan's laughter was contagious as they talked like old friends.

Franz said, "Why don't we get to work?"

"My god, I haven't seen anything like this since we went on a tour of the FBI headquarters in Washington DC."

Ivan sat in a chair positioned so he would be able to view all the SMART Boards at once.

"Franz, explain please."

While Franz explained, Ivan said nothing. He was deep in thought.

"This is commendable. I just want to clarify a few things."

Ivan was satisfied with Franz's explanations.

"Vodka, I need vodka to talk about something this complex."

John got some glasses and two bottles of vodka, pouring a glassful for Ivan.

"Good start," Ivan said. "I think this calls for some dirty tricks. It will ultimately flush them out. The way to bring down an organization this big is to cause problems that will, without a doubt, be blamed on their managers. They will become paranoid and start fighting among themselves. This will prompt the head of the organization to call a meeting, then we can get them all at once."

"What do you mean by dirty tricks?"

Franz said, "John, remember what we talked about? It's like transferring a large amount of money from a company account to a private account and then letting someone else know about it."

Ivan said, "You can do that, Franz?"

"I was thinking more like burning down a warehouse, but I like your idea better."

John said, "We can do both, where do we start? How can we stay undercover?"

"We start with Helmut. We can get anything we want from him. I will interview him again. He knows both organizations and who is in charge."

While Ivan and Franz discussed what information they would need from Helmut, John's mind was elsewhere.

"Ascot Chen, that son of a bitch, does not show up on these SMART boards, except on the list of the Green Party advisory board. We know he's involved with the Liddo Group. Why doesn't he show up anywhere else?"

Ivan said, "If he doesn't show up anywhere, it means he is very powerful within the organization."

John replied, "During your interview with Helmut, tell him to be at the St. Gotthard for lunch on Thursday. I'll run into him there, by chance, of course."

Franz said, "Excellent idea, John, perhaps you could arrange a meeting with Chen, through Helmut, and then we could grab him."

# 34

**Schaan, Liechtenstein**

Ascot Chen sat across from Aristotle in the personal wing of Saris's castle.

"It's an honor to be here with you, Aristotle."

"I asked you here to discuss a sensitive matter, Ascot. We are very close to reaching our goal, a new world order. Looking at its structure, YK, Mike, myself, and a few others, are the kings. You and some others, like Gregory Gruber, are the princes. How would you like to be one of the kings?"

"Aristotle, I'm aware that there is some friction between you and the Liddo organization. You're too close to completion to create problems between you and my employers."

"Ascot, you always have a clear head. Your loyalty to your employers shows character. Would you like to become my second in command? Of course, I will talk to YK first."

Ascot sensed he must be very careful here.

"I would like to discuss it with YK first myself. If he doesn't have a problem with it, I would consider the proposal. It would take some time for me to make a full transition."

"Ascot, I can't ask for more than that. Will you stay for dinner?"

"I would be honored."

During dinner, they discussed what Aristotle envisioned for the future: a global society controlled by men who knew and understood wealth and power; a world free from poverty, war, and pestilence. Aristotle went over the details of the energy takeovers and how they could be used to coerce entire governments to do his bidding. They discussed the Green movement, the brilliance of merging it with the National Socialists from every country, the unions they now controlled as a result. He also mentioned that the manufacturers are regulated further under the Green laws and are weakening; therefore, they will have to capitulate with their group, or simply die.

"We will control everything and everyone, and we will forge a new world."

After listening to this for hours, Ascot couldn't wait to leave.

"Aristotle, as much as I am enjoying your company, I have to leave. I have to drive to Zurich to catch a flight early tomorrow morning." Aristotle walked Ascot to the front door.

Later, Ascot called YK and gave him a full report.

"Excellent, Ascot, I will call you back and give you my decision."

Aristotle sat alone thinking, *I know he will spy on me, and that is good. Misinformation is a useful tool, but I know that once he has tasted the wealth and power I can offer, he will become a loyal friend and trusted assistant. Nothing can corrupt a man like power. It has gotten me this far, and it will help me obtain my dream.*

# 35

## Washington DC

Colin Young left his office, carrying a small hidden sophisticated transceiver; he was on his way to meet the chief of staff at a restaurant in Alexandria.

"Hello, Rob, how are you?"

"I'm fine, Colin. Thanks for coming."

They walked into the private dining room. Both men remained quiet until they were alone.

"What did you come up with?"

"Rob, is this off the record?" A stern look was on his face.

"I'll let you know after I hear what you have to say."

"Before I tell you anything, I want to know what this information is going to be used for."

Rob's face turned a dark red, the veins in his neck bulging out.

"The information is going to be brought to the president. If there are improprieties found, the president will decide to either ask for her resignation or prosecute her. The press loves a scandal, and I don't want that to happen."

"How long will it take for him to make a decision? I don't want this information to get out before I can report it internally. Otherwise, it's my ass in a sling."

Colin could see that the chief was really getting pissed; he had him by the short hairs, just where he wanted him.

"I want something in writing, stating that I will become the director immediately after you receive this information."

"Colin, you prick, how am I going to do that? If I give you a letter now, before your boss resigns, everyone will know that we had a deal, and that's not kosher. Now, what have you found out about the Speaker?"

Colin started to get up from the table; Rob grabbed his arm tight.

"Where are you going?"

"No letter, no deal."

Rob was visibly shaken, but he picked up his cell phone and called his office.

"Cindy, Rob here. Type a letter to Colin Young, Deputy Director, Justice Department."

> Dear Colin,
>
> It has come to our attention that the Director will be stepping down within the next week. You have been selected, if you wish, to become Director of the U.S. Justice Department.

"Cindy, have the vice president sign it. Have it delivered to me at the restaurant that you made reservations for this morning. I need it within the hour."

"All right, it's done. What did you find?"

"Let's eat first. By the time we finish lunch, the letter will be here, and then I'll tell you what I found."

The letter came. Colin read it carefully and thanked the chief of staff.

"I just want to say that I took care of this investigation myself. I discovered several improprieties concerning the Secretary directly. She has awarded her husband's company several government contracts, worth millions. He is neither qualified nor capable of doing said projects. Secondly, she has had a long relationship with Aristotle Saris. Large amounts of money have been transferred into her accounts from various sources. Thirdly, she is involved in a money-laundering scheme through the DNC on behalf of Saris."

"I knew it. I'll take this right to the president and ask him to make a decision within a week. Thank you, Colin."

"Rob, there's one other thing. Her connections with Saris seem to implicate the president."

"What are you talking about, Colin?"

"The president's campaign fund received large amounts of money from the same accounts, and some of these funds were directed through the Speaker."

"Colin, thank you, I will discuss that with the president. Remember, this is between us."

Colin stared at the chief of staff. *Perfect, this is right where I want him.*

"Are you certain you want to keep this a secret?"

"Of course, I'm certain. We're talking about the president of the United States and the Speaker of the House. If this ever got out, we would all lose."

"All right then, I'll wait for you to contact me with the results of your conversation with the president."

Colin got back to his office and called in the director. They listened to the tapes. He asked the director if he wanted to call in the attorney general.

"Hell no, they're thick as thieves. We would be told to stand down. Then we'd probably disappear."

"Well, what's the next move?"

The director walked out of the office, and Colin followed him into the elevator. When the elevator reached the lobby, they headed straight for the door that led to the street.

"I've been in the bureau for a long time. I worked my way up through the ranks, and I've never seen anything like this. We're going to have to take care of this situation covertly. Colin, do you have any men you can trust?"

"No, but I know one woman. I would trust her with my life."

"There are two men I trust explicitly. They've been loyal to me for years. We have a safe house on the Baltimore–Washington expressway. Give this address to your girl, tell her to memorize it then burn it. We'll meet there at eight p.m. This is a black op. She must take all precautions, no cab or drop-off. We're all dead if anyone else finds out about this. Call the chief of staff tomorrow. Tell him you've discovered some really damaging information about the Speaker and that you have to investigate fully to make sure the president cannot be linked to it. Tell him you need a couple hundred thousand from discretionary funds because you can't use resources from here. We'll use that money to hang these bastards."

Colin watched Frank Hancock as he walked away. *I'll back this son of a bitch in whatever he wants to do.*

Colin got back to the office and called Sally Crothers. "Sally, would you come to my office? I have something I need to talk to you about."

"Yes, sir, I'll be right there."

He met her outside by the elevator. "I feel like a cup of coffee. Please, join me."

......................................

"Sally, I'm taking you off your current case." She started to say something, but he cut her off. "I need you for a black op. It's so sensitive that the director and I are running it outside of the office. No contact with anyone from the office, understood?"

"Yes, sir."

"I'll fill you in on the details tonight at eight at this address. Commit it to memory and then burn it. Come alone in your car. Don't tell anyone where you're going. Is that clear?"

"Yes, sir."

"This is an extremely sensitive dangerous assignment. You can back out now with no repercussions. You're in for the duration if you accept it, understood?"

"Yes, sir, understood, I'm in."

"I'll see you this evening. I'll tell your team at the office that you've taken emergency leave. Give me your cell phone."

"Here's my cell. How serious is this, sir?"

"It could not be more serious. No more questions. You will be fully briefed tonight."

He left her standing there, frightened and confused.

........................................

They all assembled at the safe house, it was bug-proof, the perfect choice for this operation.

The director, Colin Young, Sally Crothers, Tony Daugherty, and Pete Drake were present. The director was known for his skills in surveillance and counterterrorism. Colin Young, the deputy director, excelled in banking and international law. Sally Crothers was a field agent, specializing in communications, encryption, and computers. Tony Daugherty was a special investigator; his expertise was in organization, and he was usually the special agent in charge. Peter Drake was a bulldog, a field agent known for his tenacity and relentlessness. The director knew they were loyal to Colin and himself. They were true Americans.

The director started, "Let me thank you all for coming. This is a dangerous assignment. We'll be fighting for our lives and the preservation of our current way of life. If any of you wish to bow out, now is your chance." They all agreed to stay.

"People, we are entering into the fight of our lives. The American way of life is in jeopardy. You cannot trust anyone outside of this group. Our lives depend on that fact. If found out, we will perish. We must infiltrate our own government, discover the facts, produce evidence, and bring the perpetrators to justice, kill them if need be. Do I have your attention yet?

"Information has come to us, and Colin has verified it. Outside interests are slowly taking control of our government. Certain branches of the government have already been compromised, and it goes all the way to the top. We do not know or where the perpetrators are in the process, but we must stop it, and soon. Any questions?"

"I will ask you again, any questions?"

Sally Crothers began, "What makes you believe that someone is infiltrating our government?"

"Colin was approached by the White House chief of staff to investigate the Speaker of the House and her relationship with Aristotle Saris. The chief promised him that he would become the new director, I would be terminated. Not only is the Speaker laundering money for Saris, the president seems to be involved as well. Large amounts of money are being laundered through the DNC, community groups, and various Green organizations. Saris is also funding these organizations and developing paramilitary groups within them. Saris has been on our watch list for some time. We suspect a similar phenomenon has been transpiring in Europe. We handed some of this information over to the CIA over a year ago. They said they had already investigated and there was nothing there other than some disreputable business dealings, beyond their jurisdiction."

Tony Daugherty interrupted, "Boss, are you telling us that Saris is trying to take over the world?"

"I don't know about that, but I'm certain he's bought a lot of politicians. The chief of staff was worried enough to approach Colin. I suspect that there were promises made and it's gotten out of control. Whatever it is, a party or parties, unknown, is trying to control our government from the top down. We are certain that Saris is playing a major role. Whether or not he has others working with him is still up in the air."

This time, Peter Drake interrupted, "It appears to me that Saris and company have bought control of several of our top leaders and they've gone off the reservation. If this is true, to whom do we report?"

"I don't know. That's why this has to be a black op. We have to formulate a plan and be very careful implementing it."

Tony Daugherty said, "Sir, we have to go to ground and find out who the players are first. Then we gather information and find the root sources, Saris and/or others. A viable plan would be the next logical step, anything prior is doomed to fail."

"I agree. I will work alone. When fed information, I will consolidate and assess it. Colin and Peter, investigate within the executive branch. Tony and Sally, work both houses. Look for variations from the norm, anyone recently gotten out of debt, anyone vulnerable because of promiscuity or homosexuality. Within the houses, look at the committees. See who's chairing a committee but doesn't seem to belong there, etc. Colin, continue to appear to be investigating and working with the chief of staff. Peter, back him up. Colin will be arranging for funding from the chief of staff tomorrow, and we'll purchase computers and any equipment needed. Let's meet here each evening at eight to update and begin profiling. Once we have all the data, we'll come up with a plan to get these bastards. Do not use any of the databases at the bureau. If you need information, ask either Colin or myself, we'll get it for you. Together, we will bring these people down. Goodnight."

# 36

**London, England**

Paula Franks was a beautiful but ruthless woman. God gave her beauty, life made her ruthless. She was the head of the Liddo Group's European operation.

The day after she arrived in London, she arranged meetings with the heads of all of Liddo's operations. She called Ascot Chen and asked him to sit in on every meeting, but she also gave him strict instructions to be seen and not heard. She wanted everyone to know that Ascot answered to her.

Her first set of meetings were with the media and later with transportation and shipping company heads. Within the next few days, she met with manufacturers, sales and retail, and commodities and energy magnates. Lastly, she met with the leaders of the National Socialist Party, the Green Party, and other union leaders. The message to all was clear. She was in charge. After the last scheduled meeting, she was alone with Ascot.

"Ascot, I'd like to have a private dinner here and discuss future operations tomorrow at eight." Ascot left after agreeing.

As Paula ran a bath to unwind, she wondered how she would handle Ascot. He was loyal to no one and the most amoral man she had ever met. Paula realized that Ascot was afraid of Mike Manheim. *That might be his button to push. I'll win him over by threatening him with Mike. At the same time, I'll offer him protection.*

Ascot had arrived on time. She made him a drink and made small talk until dinner was served. She dismissed the staff immediately after coffee was served.

"Ascot, YK has told me how much he has relied on you and how talented you are at your work. I hope I can expect the same loyalty from you."

"Paula, we have always had a good relationship, what has changed?"

"I was YK's assistant before. Now, I have to rely on you. Do I have your wholehearted support?"

*She's just gotten this position. Has she already started to think of expanding her role?*

"Paula, I want you to understand that I am loyal to no one other than myself. I am a facilitator, a tool for you to use. I do not get close to anyone because I cannot afford to take sides. I'm here to do your bidding, as I am for all of the others. I need you to understand this. If you understand, we will get along wonderfully."

"Thank you, Ascot, I appreciate your honesty, but I was hoping we could have a different relationship. Manheim doesn't like you, and he's angry about you checking up on him. I'm also afraid of him. I need an ally I can count on to protect my position. In return, I will protect yours."

"It is not in my best interest to make alliances."

"I think you should reconsider. I would have never brought up the subject if I didn't know he is gunning for you. Manheim has already identified you as being loyal to YK only, and that puts you in a bad position. It's in Manheim's best interest to get rid of you, one way or the other. My only fear is that he'll try to take over my territory later…and I don't want to lose this."

"I'll think about this. We'll discuss it further on my next visit."

"Thank you, Ascot."

"I think we'll work well together," he said on his way out.

The next day, Paula made arrangements to travel to Zurich to pay a visit to Peter Tsillman and Helmut Fragge. According to YK, Fragge warranted investigation. It was best to know where all the bodies lie as part of her responsibility.

Paula arrived in Zurich midmorning; a limo was waiting for her.

"My dear Miss Franks, I am Peter Tsillman, and I am completely at your service. It is a pleasure and an honor to meet you."

"Mr. Tsillman, I would like to go to the bank and review our accounts, and then I would like to be dropped at the Bauer au Lac."

When they arrived at the bank, Paula asked for a private office, and she was accommodated quickly.

"Mr. Tsillman, I would like to have a list of all accounts and holdings, and then I would like to review each portfolio on my own. If I have any questions, I will call you."

Within minutes, he returned, followed by a line of people carrying file boxes.

"Each of the portfolios is clearly marked. If you require anything, please push the green button on the phone."

"Thank you, Mr. Tsillman."

Paula spent almost six hours going over the accounts, taking notes and reviewing expenses. She realized, after careful scrutiny, they were all stealing, but who was stealing the most?

As soon as she was finished, she rang for a car. "Mr. Tsillman, there's no need for you to escort me to the hotel. However, I do want to thank you for all of your assistance."

"Thank you, Miss Franks."

Paula got into the car and decided to call Helmut Fragge and arrange a meeting.

"Hello, Helmut, this is Paula Franks of the Liddo Group, I was wondering if we might get together later this evening for a drink. I am staying at the Bauer au Lac hotel. Nine o'clock at the bar. I'll see you then."

It was 7:15 p.m. She would be able to get into her room, take a bath, and relax a little before meeting him.

........................................

"Frauline Franks, it is an honor to meet you. I am Helmut Fragge"

"Mr. Fragge, please sit down."

After drinks were ordered, Paula continued.

"Mr. Fragge, I have taken over as the European head of the Liddo Group. You will now deal with me or Ascot Chen."

She noticed him turning red when she mentioned Chen.

"I have been briefed on your situation, and I wanted to discuss it with you further. I know you are a part of the Saris Group, but as you know, we're all working together. It would be best if you give me your opinion about what has recently transpired."

His hand was shaking, and his glass could no longer hold its contents.

"Would you rather I have Ascot present while we discuss this?"

He screamed loudly, "No!" and then tried to compose himself. "I mean, no, thank you. I will gladly discuss the matter with you directly."

He went on to tell her about the assassination attempt. "Saris ordered it, but why? I've always done a good job. I've always tried to take care of the Saris and the Liddo Group's interests. Why?"

Paula maintained her best poker face.

"I'm going to need your cooperation. If you cooperate fully, we will be able to protect you."

*Should I tell her about the Russians?* He decided against it.

"Frauline Franks, I will give you whatever cooperation you require. I can see that you are a professional and reasonable person."

Paula gently nodded her head.

"I would like to meet with you in my room at ten tomorrow morning. Once I have properly assessed the situation, after reviewing all the facts, we will put a plan together that will benefit all of us. Thank you, Mr. Fragge."

Helmut was astonished and confused about what had just taken place as she stood and left him sitting at the table.

# 37

Bewildered, Helmut left the hotel, turned onto Bahnhoff Strasse, and stopped dead in his tracks. He recognized the car. The doctor motioned for him to get in.

"Helmut, how good to see you! Who was that beautiful woman?"

"She is the new head of the European Liddo Group, her name is Paula Franks."

"What were you discussing?"

Helmut knew he couldn't lie to this man.

"They just found out that Saris tried to kill me. She was offering me protection."

Ivan had been quiet, then spoke, "I need you to meet with me tomorrow at the St. Gotthard at noon. Are you going home? I will drop you off."

Once home, Helmut ran inside and triple-locked his door.

..........................

The doorbell rang; John answered it. Franz was working on his computer. Ivan walked in and started immediately. "I have something important to report. Helmut just met the new head of the Liddo Group, a beautiful woman named Paula Franks. She just offered him protection."

Franz stopped working and jumped into the conversation.

"That means that there's a riff between Liddo and Saris, that's good news."

Ivan told John that Helmut would be at the St. Gotthard at noon.

"Good, I'll meet him there tomorrow. I will act as though I just bumped into him and ask if he can arrange a meeting with Ascot Chen."

"Good, let's have vodka."

The next day, John arranged a meeting with Tsillman at 12:30 p.m. at the St. Gotthard. John arrived at ten past twelve and saw Helmut sitting alone at a table, looking very nervous.

"What a delightful surprise!"

Helmut looked up at him with fear and confusion in his eyes.

"Helmut, are you all right?"

"John, I'm sorry, you startled me. I'm fine, and you?"

"I'm great, thank you. I'm so glad I ran into you. I have a favor to ask. Do you have a phone number for Ascot Chen?"

Fragge's face went pale.

"Why do you want his number?"

"He bought some boats from me, and there is something I want to discuss with him."

"John, I'm sorry. He asked me not to give his number to anyone, but I will call him and ask him to call you."

"Thank you. I'm having lunch with Tsillman. Care to join us?"

"Thank you, John, but I was just leaving." Helmut didn't want John or Tsillman to see him with the Russian, so he stood up and left.

John had a pleasant lunch with Tsillman. Then he took a drive and bought more equipment.

John gave everything to Franz; he started to assemble the hard drives and SMART boards immediately.

"Franz, while you do that, I'm going up to have a drink."

The phone rang. "Hello, this is John Moore."

"Hello, John, this is Ascot Chen."

He recognized the voice, the voice of the man who called him in China when Rebecca was shot. This is the bastard who killed Rebecca. John hesitated, trying to control himself.

"Helmut Fragge asked me to call you, something to do with boats."

John couldn't speak. His rage was out of control. Finally he managed, "Thank you for calling me, Ascot. Is it possible for us to meet at the Bauer au Lac, say at eight tomorrow evening?"

"I'm sorry, John, but I'm not in Switzerland at present. I'll be back on Monday, if that is all right."

"Ascot, I'll see you then. Monday evening at the Bauer at eight, thank you, good bye."

As John hung up the phone, he was imbued with overwhelming hatred. He calmed himself, went downstairs, and told Franz what had just happened.

"John, don't worry, we'll get him. Right now you have to calm down and focus. Let's go out to dinner. Don't let this ruin all the work we've done. Remember our goal, stay focused. He's just one of them. We'll get all of them."

"You're right, Franz, but this is hard for me. I finally know the person responsible for Rebecca's death."

"No, John, they are all responsible."

When they finished dinner, they went back to the house and worked. By the next afternoon, they had completed the hierarchal chart of the Liddo Group. It took all eight of the SMART Boards to accommodate it.

"Franz, can you believe this? They're in every conceivable business, the major contributors to every political party. But we don't have it all."

"What do you mean, John?"

"Ascot Chen is not here nor do we have any information on Paula Franks. How many more are lurking in the shadows?"

After discussing it, they decided that it didn't really matter. They had the books, they knew where the money was, that would be all they would need.

Monday came quickly. Everything was in place. Chen called and confirmed the meeting for eight that evening. Two cars and a van were waiting for Ascot as he drove down Bahnhoff Strasse. One pulled in front of him, the other pulled up behind while a van pulled in alongside. They stopped at a light two blocks from the hotel. Three men jumped out of the van, pulled Chen from his car, and threw him into it. It was done so quickly that none of the pedestrians nearby even knew what happened.

Once in the van, Chen started to protest, but he was Tasered. A bag was forced over his head and secured just before he recovered. He felt the pinch of an injection and quickly passed out.

When Chen awoke, he found himself sitting in a wooden chair, tied to it with wire. The more he struggled, the more he bled. Four men came out of the darkness. In a surprisingly calm voice, he said, "John, what's the meaning of this?" John lost his cool, ran over, and punched him hard in the face.

"You son of a bitch, you killed Rebecca."

"John, that was only business. That poor girl was in the wrong place at the wrong time."

John went to hit him again, and Ivan stepped in.

"Mr. Chen, we're going to ask a series of questions. You will answer or suffer dearly. If you don't answer, you're going to be dead. Do I make myself clear?"

Chen believed this man was dangerous. This thought did not make him happy.

"Good, I can see you understand. Who do you work for in the Liddo Group?"

"I work for no one. I am a facilitator. I work for myself."

"Who is the top man in the Liddo Group?"

"I don't know. I have worked for many people within the group."

The man behind Chen swung a pipe as hard as he could; it fractured Chen's left arm. Chen winced but did not scream. *This is going to be difficult.*

"I will ask you one more time. Who is the head of the Liddo Group?"

Chen looked at him. "*Do nu lo ma,*" he spat at him.

Without saying anything, Ivan walked away and returned with a blowtorch. The blue flame was at least a foot long. He stared at Chen's crotch. Chen's face contorted, but he didn't say a word. Ivan put the end of the flame to the man's genitals. Ascot began screaming. Ivan pulled it away before he passed out.

"I'm going to ask you again. Who is the head of the Liddo Group?"

"Y. K. Chen!"

"How does he interact with Saris?"

"I don't know. I'm not involved with the business aspects."

"Wrong answer."

Ivan applied the flame again. The smell of burning flesh was nauseating. Chen passed out. John was horrified.

He asked Ivan, "How far are you going to go with this?"

"As far as I have to, until we have all the information."

The doctor put smelling salts under Chen's nose; he awoke with a convulsive jump.

"Once more, how do they interact?"

He screamed, "Through intermediaries!"

"Who are they?"

Chen was hesitant, until Ivan started to walk toward him.

"He is in contact with Mike Manheim from the United States and Helmut Fragge from Zurich."

"How do they interact?"

"I cannot tell you that," then Chen slipped into unconsciousness.

"Ivan, this is over the top. This is torture."

"Yes, John, it is torture. Do you want to get the information you need? Please do not forget this piece of human garbage is responsible for killing your Rebecca."

"Yes, but—"

Ivan cut him off. "We will talk philosophy later. Right now, I will get information."

"Revive him. We will begin again."

After hours of torture, Ivan got all the information they were looking for. They now knew about all of the heads of the Liddo Group and most of those from the Saris Group. Chen eventually told them how they communicated and interacted. He also told them which ones were the core companies and which were legitimate enterprises.

"John, these are evil people. This is all they understand."

He turned toward Ascot, said good-bye, and shot a bullet directly in the center of his forehead.

"He has paid for Rebecca's death. Now we go after the rest. John, as horrible as this was, we have just prevented the torture and deaths of many good decent people. This man was evil, and he represented evil people."

When John got home, he went directly to his room and took a shower. *Ivan's right. They are evil people. Hopefully we can prevent the deaths of many others.* It was difficult for John to stomach this kind of behavior, but he realized he was dealing with amoral people. Maybe this was the way they had to be dealt with. After his shower, he went to the terrace for a drink. He heard voices downstairs, so he went to the office and found Ivan and Franz busy working.

"What are you guys doing?"

"We're trying to find Chen's bank accounts. We'll withdraw his funds and deposit them in one of Saris's accounts. If what he told us is true, this should cause some trouble between the two groups. We know that Liddo was angry about the Fragge situation and that Saris and Y. K. Chen had already had a meeting about it. We also know that Saris tried to bring Ascot Chen into his camp. We'll use this to start a war and see where it goes. The longer we can stay hidden, the better off we are."

Ivan said, "We know that Chen met with Saris in Lichtenstein last week, and we know that he reported that meeting to YK. I had the doctor bring Chen's body to one of the lakes in Lichtenstein and dump it. This will put more suspicion on Saris."

"I don't know if I can take any more of what I've just seen, but you guys definitely know what you're doing. I can't argue with the results."

John walked out, went back up to the terrace, and poured a drink.

"John, may I talk to you?" Ivan poured himself a drink and sat across from John.

"John, when I started in this business, I had much difficulty dealing with this, but I realized that the people who live their lives by the rules, normal citizens, need protection from these types of despicable people. That man spent his life destroying others and became wealthy doing it. Please don't think of me as a monster. I've learned that to stop these types of people, you have to deal with them on their level."

John looked deep into Ivan's eyes and saw a good man who was sincere.

"Ivan, how do you do it?"

"I've seen the damage people like Chen do to ordinary people. After you have seen many lives destroyed for nothing more than greed, you realize that they have to be stopped. I have tried other means, legally, and they never worked. Franz, Utsie and I have all been hurt by these people. Your Rebecca was killed because she found out information about them. It is time to stop them now, and we can do it."

"Ivan, I don't think I could ever get used to this, but I will support whatever it takes to stop them."

"Good, time to drink vodka."

# 38

### London, England

Paula, now back in London, tried to figure out how the situation with Fragge could benefit her. She decided to call YK.

"Hello, YK, Paula here."

She told him about her meeting with Fragge and asked him for further instructions.

"Paula, this is highly sensitive. You are correct, Saris is starting to get out of control. We're monitoring him. He'll be dealt with but not right now. Arrange a meeting with him, get close to him. Act as if you are ready to betray me then tell me how he responds. Mike has informed me that Saris is trying to control things in the US as well. We need him right now, so we cannot do anything permanent. I would like to find a way to bring him back into the fold."

"YK, I will arrange a meeting as soon as possible."

She hung up the phone and began planning.

The next day, while lunching with the managing director of Liddo's Media Company in Europe, she asked him what they had on Aristotle Saris. He told her that they had volumes of information, but they'd been instructed by YK not to use it.

"After Saris cornered the precious metals market, it caused all kinds of problems with the British pound. The government was up in arms, but we kept it low-priority."

Paula asked him if she could have that information.

"I can do better than that. We have a young woman who monitors Saris. I'll have her contact you."

"You are too kind. I'll only need her for a week or so."

The next day, Paula met Sara Covington, a plain-looking girl but a brilliant researcher, as she soon found out. Sara had brought stacks of computer discs containing all the information she had dug up on Saris.

"I want a complete profile, everything you have on him."

By the time she finished her review, after several days of hard work, Paula had all the information she needed, thanks to Sara. The next morning, Sara arrived at Paula's flat, per her request.

"Sara, would you care for some tea?"

"No, thank you, mum."

"I have something for you." She handed the girl an envelope. "You've done outstanding work. I might need your services from time to time, and I want us to be friends."

"Oh, mum, this extra money isn't necessary. I make a good wage."

"Nonsense, now take it, and if I need you again, I will call."

"Thank you, mum." When she was outside, Sara looked in the envelope and almost screamed. *Five thousand pounds, that's half a year's salary!* Sara began to think about where she would go on holiday. *I hope she calls me back again.*

........................................

"Paula, it's delightful to hear from you, but how did you get this number?"

"Aristotle, you know I was YK's assistant for a long time. I always dialed you."

"Yes, of course. Are you calling on behalf of YK?"

"No, I wanted to inform you myself that I've taken over all of Liddo's holdings in Europe as managing director. I thought it was appropriate as you are our largest partner. I was hoping we could meet to go over a few things to assure the events in progress go smoothly."

"A splendid idea, Paula. Where are you now?"

"I'm in London, but I could meet with you anywhere."

"How about my house in Budapest?"

"That would be lovely. Is this Friday evening good?"

"Yes, we can spend the weekend. That should give us enough time to coordinate our efforts. Call my assistant, tell her what flight you'll arrive on, and I'll send a car."

*He doesn't know what he's getting into.*

"Paula, YK here. Are you on a secure phone?"

"No, YK, let me call you back."

"YK, what can I do for you?"

"Have you heard from Ascot?"

"He was here with me almost all of last week. He left when I went to Zurich."

"See if you can locate him, get back to me."

"I'll call you as soon as I find him."

After several hours, she called YK back on her secure phone.

"YK, Paula here. I'm afraid I have bad news. I couldn't find Ascot, but I found out that all of his accounts have been emptied, as well as the European slush fund. I'm going to Zurich to meet with Peter Tsillman to see if we can track the money. I'll call you after the meeting."

Tsillman was waiting for her and took her directly to the bank. He worked feverishly for almost an hour.

"The funds have been transferred to three separate accounts belonging to Aristotle Saris."

"Oh, yes, I had forgotten about those transfers, thank you, Mr. Tsillman. Now, may I have some privacy?"

*I really do not like this woman.*

"Hello, YK, it's Paula. The funds in question were sent to Aristotle Saris."

"Paula, are you still at the bank?"

"Yes."

"Call me as soon as you're alone."

"Yes, sir."

She walked from the bank to the lake and sat on a bench with no one in sight.

"YK, do you think Saris has gone mad?"

"Yes, I do, and it is imperative that you get close to him."

"I'm spending the weekend with him in Budapest."

"I'll send a man to you. Joseph will give you a new series of electronic bugs and instruct you on their use. Try to get them into all the houses owned by Saris."

"I'll do my best, YK."

After Joseph left, Paula went out and picked up a few things that she knew would drive Saris wild. She knew she was totally prepared for her assignment after studying his profile again.

There was a warm towel and a glass of champagne waiting for her in the car. The driver told her, "The Danube River runs through the center of the city. In fact, it used to be two cities, Buda, on the right bank, and Pest, on the left. They merged with Obuda in 1873."

Aristotle's house, more like a castle, was located in the best area of the city on Andrassy Avenue, within view of Buda Castle. Aristotle was standing outside the front entrance, holding two Russian wolfhounds, one on either side of him. Paula let as much leg show as possible as she got out of the car.

"Aristotle, good to see you again."

"Likewise, you are a vision. Please come in and make yourself at home. Your suite is on the left, up the stairs, second door."

"Aristotle, I hope you didn't go to too much trouble. It is more a friendly visit rather than business."

"Even better then. Why don't you freshen up, and we will have dinner in the rose garden in a bit, such a nice view of Buda Castle."

"I'll only be a minute." She pecked his cheek.

He watched her go up the stairs, mystified by her beauty.

# 39

### Washington DC

"The president has surrounded himself with all of Saris's people, and he won't listen to anyone else. He's been on more TV shows than there are beer commercials."

Wiley asked, "Isn't there anyone who can get to him?"

The chief of staff said, "The Speaker. I think we have her, but I wish I could trust her a bit more. I had the deputy director of Justice investigate her."

"Do you mean that boy scout Colin Young?"

"Yes, and he came up with enough to have her sanctioned. We could arrest her ass if we thought it best. I met with her personally and told her she had to pass all information from Saris to us before she brought it to the president, or we'd have her husband arrested and then have her investigated, publicly. I believe she'll play ball."

"Good work, Rob. I'm going to shoot one across her bow just to get her full attention."

"What do you mean, Wiley?"

"I'll have a reliable source tell the press that her husband is under investigation. Let's see how she responds."

# 40

### Budapest, Hungary

They discussed business through dinner, and whenever she had the chance to confuse him, or at least give him the impression that she wanted him, she did. She constantly kept him off guard. Aristotle was brilliant in his own right, and he possessed a keen ability to read people, but even he was no match for Paula.

After dinner, they both drank port. Then she told him she was rather tired and wanted to retire.

"Aristotle darling, before you go to your room, could you stop by mine? I want to show you something."

"Paula, I'd be happy to, but first I have to make a few calls. Give me twenty minutes."

"Okay, see you in twenty."

When Paula got to her room, she showered quickly, covered her entire body with scented oil, and didn't bother to put anything on; she was ready. In a few minutes, he knocked on her door.

So softly, barely a whisper, "Come in, Aristotle."

She was the most beautiful woman he had ever seen. Paula walked over to him and started to undress him. He was stunned to submissiveness. When it was over, Aristotle knew that he had never experienced anything like that before, convinced that she had surrendered to his powerful masculinity. But Paula owned him now, and she knew it.

They had breakfast together. Paula gushed at him like a schoolgirl, and he loved it as she realized that his ego would be his downfall. Paula actually had a nice day touring the city from his yacht, even though she loathed Saris, aching to betray him on several levels.

Back at the castle, she mused, *This is really a beautiful place. I think I'll tell YK that I want it after we do in Aristotle.*

During dinner, Aristotle acted the charmer, and Paula could feel his desire to have her again.

"You are nothing like the crass and brutal men I work for. I wish I could work for you. Do not take all of this the wrong way. I am indebted to my benefactors for the chances and responsibility they have given me, and I will always be loyal and thankful to them. But it's so nice to be with a powerful man, a real man, one who is intellectually superior, not brutish or boring."

"My dear Paula, these men are my partners. To run a successful business empire, sometimes you have to be brutal. It's a difficult world, and that is why I'm in partnership with YK."

"Yes, Aristotle, but it's a pleasure for someone like me to spend time with you."

Paula could tell by his demeanor that he had bought into her act. In a few more days, she would control him completely.

"Aristotle, could we go to bed? I have been thinking about you all day. I never had a more pleasurable evening than I did last night, and I can't wait to relive it."

"Paula, you flatter me, and I'd love to," he replied, as he looked at her a bit skeptically.

She rolled over, facing him. The look on his face amused her as he lay there in a euphoric state.

"Aristotle, I have never experienced pleasure like this before. You truly are the greatest man in the world. Now I understand why they are so afraid of you."

"Who's afraid of me? What do you mean?"

"YK and Mike, I'm sorry, I shouldn't say any more," truly startled even though this was what she had expected.

# 41

**Zurich, Switzerland**

John, Franz, and Ivan sat comfortably studying the SMART Boards in front of them. John broke the silence.

"We know that Liddo and Saris have partnered to start some kind of a new world order, but I still can't figure out why."

Franz said, "John, that's wrong-thinking. The first thing to understand is that whatever they call it, new world order, socialism, or fascism, it is about power and wealth, nothing more. These people have money and power now, but it's somewhat restrictive. If this were to come to light, they could be stopped now. They want to control everything, to use their wealth any way they wish to without answering to anyone."

Ivan was stoic. "He's right, John. These people are maniacs, they want to control the asylum."

·············································

"Hello, John, this is Peter Tsillman. How are you?"

"I'm fine, Peter. What can I do for you?"

"I have found the perfect bank for sale. It's the Swizziferia Americano Bank in Lugano, a boutique bank with assets just under a billion US, going for about two billion. Their most valuable asset is their list of correspondent banks. It was an Italian bank that opened in Lugano, then they bought out another bank owned by Bank of America and merged the two. The original Italian bank had all the major European correspondents, and the other had the entire American listings. It has a fluid transfer system and accounts in other banks worldwide. It is a currency trader's dream."

"All right, Peter, go for it. Offer 1.665, and tell them we can close immediately, quietly and in cash. Let me know what they say."

"I think I just bought a bank."

Back to their original discussion, John said, "I got it. These people are willing to destroy governments, basically enslave everyone, simply as a power grab."

"Well, it's a little more complicated than that, but in essence, you are correct."

"Good, we all understand, now let's drink vodka."

Ivan had just started one of his famous jokes when the phone rang.

"John, it's Tsillman. They agreed to 1.765 billion."

"Great, Peter! Tell them to draw up the papers within three days. In the meantime, I'll have our attorneys work with them. The buying entity is an Asian company, the Hong Kong Financial Group. They're represented by Woo & Woo Solicitors Ltd. Hong Kong. I'll call them now and have them contact you directly. Please make all arrangements. Good job, Peter!"

"Well, guys, that's it. I'm going to own, or should I say, Hong Kong Financial Group is going to own Swizziferia Americano Bank."

"A toast, and congratulations!" They lifted their glasses and drank.

"Let's get back to work."

He asked Franz to put up the summary he'd been working on. It listed all bank accounts on one SMART board. Another had the complete list of the people who were involved. The third contained a timeline of related events.

"As I see it, these people are trying to control European and North and South American governments by using the Green

Party, the Socialist Party, and the unions, in conjunction with an energy grab. The two main players are the Saris Group and the Liddo Group. They use legitimate businesses and political parties to launder money. What do you think the energy component is?"

"I didn't see this before. Look at all of the transfers to energy companies. They're all large amounts, but not enough to be buyouts." He pointed to a group of transactions. "Note several transfers to the same companies. Can we find out what these transfers are for?"

"Franz, do you think your friendly hacker could get into these companies' databases?"

"Sure, it's a piece of cake for him. I'll call him."

"Tell him we need the information tonight, if possible."

Ivan made an observation.

"They're using the Green Party popular support, gaining control through regulation. They've already gained control of the socialists, who have control of the unions. But they still need to control the governments to make it all work."

All three said, "Money!"

"With the money they throw around, they have to be buying politicians. Without government backing, their plan fails."

"You can cause trouble for a government, but unless you control the politicians, you can't get total control."

"Let me see if I can follow any of these transfers to the American DNC, along with those to the Green and Socialist parties, and see if we can't get a better picture of who they own."

"My friend, it is time for vodka again." Ivan poured the drinks.

"John, these bastards are trying to take over the world, and no one is noticing."

"Ivan, if Franz finds out what I think he will, they are not alone. They have the cooperation of many government officials."

"Then Russian politicians are not corrupt, they are just politicians." Ivan laughed.

"These people are skilled at using human weakness to exploit officials. One man I knew in Hong Kong, basically a decent person, wound up trying to kill us for the promise of a promotion. I hope this serves as a wake-up call for a lot of people once we put an end to this."

"John, what do you mean?"

"Ivan, I hope people will try harder to make sure that our officials and police are men and women of high character and morals once we expose this to the world."

"No more politicians?

Ivan's laughter was contagious; within seconds John was laughing too. Ivan respected John, but he also realized he was naïve. He hoped John's assessment was correct.

"Besides being a professional, Ivan, you bring comic relief to this huge endeavor.

The phone rang. Peter Tsillman informed John that the deal was done. Franz was still working. John typed a letter to Janet Woo, giving her authorization to sign the documents for the purchase of the bank as a director. He told her he would be in Hong Kong the following week to sign all necessary documents and asked her to transfer the full purchase price to a Woo & Woo account to mask the transaction. He signed the letter, faxed it to Janet, and waited for a reply. With that done, he interrupted Franz.

"Can we formulate some type of game plan by next week?"

"We should have a good idea about how to go forward by then. Why?"

"We're going to Hong Kong next week."

"Why?"

"I have to sign the papers for the purchase of the bank, and I also want to see Chong and Iris. We also need to relax a bit."

"I'm very close to having everything we need, so I may not be able to get away."

"Franz, you'll have it done before we go, and we'll come up with a preliminary plan. A week or two in Hong Kong might give us a different perspective on all this."

"Ivan, would you care to join us in Hong Kong next week?"

"I'd love to, but I cannot get a visa. I am kind of persona non grata. You need me to stay here and babysit all of this equipment and information. You would not want someone to find it by mistake."

"Ivan, you're right of course. Thanks for the offer to babysit. You can stay here while we're gone."

"I'm close, but it's getting difficult, and I have to concentrate."

John and Ivan took the hint and went back to the terrace. Ivan poured more vodka.

"John, may I ask you a personal question?"

"Of course."

"Why are you doing this? You could lose everything and you may wind up dead."

"Ivan, these people hurt or killed several people I'm close to. If I don't try to stop them, I would be out of sync for the rest of my life. I don't want to live that way. I might be a little naïve, but I know that all too often, the bad prey on the good. These people are beyond bad. They're evil and have to be stopped, even if we have to kill every last one of them. I don't want another person to go through what I've been through."

"John, you're a good man, but these are evil people. Franz and I have dealt with this before. You're not used to this kind of scum."

"I've been up against them before, and I've survived."

"John, I think they let you live because they like dealing with your company."

John's face went dark, and he could barely subdue his rage.

"You've never seen me pissed off, Ivan."

"John, I know you can handle yourself well. I saw you take out three professionals. But this is different. You don't have the experience to anticipate the actions of these people."

"Ivan, that's why I asked you to join our band of merry men."

"Merry men?"

John explained himself.

"Ivan, that's why I need your expertise."

They were still on the terrace when Franz came up.

"I was able to trace the transfers to the energy companies. My friend was able to get into their computer files. Interestingly, they're all new companies or recently purchased by the Liddo Group. He was able to get account numbers from these companies. I followed those trails, and I found transactions with similar amounts, so we traced those. The Liddo Group has recently purchased over twelve hundred coal-fired energy-generation plants throughout the United States. Saris has done the same in Europe and South America. All the plants that were purchased had been shut down because they didn't meet new clean-air standards."

"What was the total value?"

"About four billion dollars. Also, the new companies purchased these plants through subsidiaries, not directly."

"What do they want with old, obsolete generators?"

Franz answered, "I don't know. The emissions are too high, so they are useless."

"I know why. They bought all those emissions credits. This is what they want them for."

"What do the emissions credits have to do with these plants?"

"Here it is—under Commodities in this old newspaper. Look, the cost of energy is $74 per megawatt if burning oil. If they burn gas, it's $60 per megawatt, coal is only $22 per megawatt."

Ivan asked, "John, what does this mean?"

"It means all of this is about money. The emissions credits are essentially a tax on greenhouse gases. Generation plants and big stack plants burn fuel to operate. This fuel gives off greenhouse gases when burned, carbon dioxide, sulfur dioxide, and nitrous oxide. A few years ago, governments insisted the owners reduce the emission of greenhouse gases by fifty percent. The capital expenditure to do something like that was huge, near impossible, so governments issued credits for five years. These credits were used to offset fines. For example, if they were emitting one hundred thousand pounds of greenhouse gases per year, they would receive credits to cover fifty thousand pounds. If they lowered their production and installed some inexpensive filters, but only reduced the emissions to seventy thousand pounds in the first year, they would have to return thirty percent of their credits. They would have reduced thirty percent of the emissions. If they used up all their credits within five years, they would have no choice but to terminate their production. Do you understand?"

"Yes, but if these plants' burning coal were already shut down, how can they be valuable?"

"Okay, they just bought 1,200 plants. Let's say each plant produces 500 megawatts of electricity. This gives them a total of 600,000 megawatts produced. I'm guessing that's 30 percent of total national production. Their cost for coal is less than a third of the existing plants using oil and gas. Because they've paid pennies on the dollar for each plant, they would probably have one-twentieth of the capital cost of their competitors. With this kind of competitive edge, they can take over the energy market. The governments have given them the ability to do it by issuing emission credits. They can burn all the coal they want just by using the emission credits to keep going."

"The government forces everyone to reduce the amount they are producing so prices go up. Then they give these credits so someone can buy them all, burn the cheapest fuel, and pollute the environment worse than ever so they can make a fortune. You don't think this is funny?" Ivan laughed.

"No, I don't."

After discussing the possibilities of the market effects, this new information was loaded into the computers and put up on the SMART Boards. "I've got it! These bastards are trying to take over the world by using energy."

"What do you mean?"

"They're going to take over the energy industry in the US, Europe, South America, and possibly Asia. If they accomplish that, they will have control."

"Control of what?"

"Everything. They could hold governments at bay by threatening to flip the switch. They could stop transportation, communications, fry databases, just about everything. They would own and control the national grids in every country. Gentlemen, we've found them out."

Ivan said, "This is a big problem. Maybe we should go to the governments, tell them everything, and let them handle it."

"No, we don't know who's involved with them. They have money in the EU, the DNC, the Green Parties, and the socialists. We know how deep their tentacles go."

"John, I don't care how big their testicles are."

"Tentacles, not testicles."

"Whatever. If governments are involved, we will have too many enemies. We cannot fight everyone."

"That's a good point, John"

"We're in a great position. No one knows we have this information. We're up against a worldwide conspiracy involving the most powerful corrupt entities known to man. The only thing we can be certain of is that powerful people will do anything to keep their power. If we use this knowledge and can manage to stay off the radar until we can set them up, one against another, we might be able to use their power to let them kill themselves off."

"John, I think you might be right. I'm in."

"I'm in too. I don't know what you are talking about, but you two are as crazy as I am. It should be fun."

"Now we have to come up with a flexible plan as things happen and before we leave for Hong Kong. When we get back, we'll refine it before we act."

They worked almost around the clock. John only left the office twice in order to buy more software and electronic equipment. After the database was complete, Franz ran it through his custom programs. They generated a complete list and profile of every company involved, a list of all the people with a hierarchal graph, a list of their accounts, and how each of them were tied directly or indirectly to either the Liddo or Saris groups. They were cataloged and grouped by industry. They could tell if there was any crossover between groups by backtracking transactions. Franz instructed John on the finer points of the system; they were ready.

"Franz, you understand the data better than we do, so why don't you start?"

Franz listed the leaders or heads of each group. "It appears that Mike Manheim is in charge in the United States and Paula Franks heads up Europe. They both answer to Y. K. Chen. Ascot Chen, who is no longer with us, seems to have been a facilitator or a consultant. Under these people, we have general managers and CEOs of various companies. For each industry, there is one person who deals directly with the heads—like a liaison. Y. K. Chen, the topman, is in Indonesia. We went through company files for plane tickets and expenses in Indonesia, and there was only one man in each group that visited Indonesia regularly. I believe those people are the second tier of the Liddo Group, covering business, media, communications, finance, manufacturing, transportation, et cetera. I'm assuming the media group is used for cover-ups and to drive business.

"We also missed one of Ascot Chen's accounts when we transferred all of his assets to Saris. It's a flow through account, but I couldn't spend too much time in it for fear of getting caught. I was able to trace some of the transactions, mostly to government officials and police, but one was to a security company in charge of all the bonded warehouses in Italy. It's owned by the Liddo Group. The Minister of Commerce gets regular payments through the account as well. This might be something to investigate further. Also, payments amounting to millions each year are being made to the head of the German Intelligence Agency. I think this would be worthwhile to investigate too."

"When you two go to Hong Kong, I will investigate these two items. Franz, give me as much information as you can, and I'll take it from there. John, I will leave the doctor here to watch everything. He is trustworthy."

"We know that the play is for the energy industry, so I've listed all energy-related companies, directly or indirectly owned by either Saris or Liddo. I have also listed the banks and organizations that we know are depositories for both groups."

"Franz, I cannot believe that you've put all of this together in a couple weeks. Now what do we do with all this information?"

"Dirty tricks to start with."

"What do you mean, Ivan?"

"Like we did with Ascot Chen. We got rid of him by making it look like Saris did it. We have to come up with a string of dirty tricks to wreak havoc and confusion. They will panic and start infighting. This won't last long, but it will rattle their boxes."

John gave him an odd look. "You mean, rattle their cages?"

"Yeah, rattle their cages."

"I have an idea. I'll get my computer friend to hack into the computer used by Liddo's media head in Europe. We'll draft an article that shows Gruber, the leader of the Socialist Party, has been linked to Saris and is under investigation by several European governments. Then I can transfer a large sum of money into Gruber's account from Chen's lost account. This way, they can't trace the money. It will appear to Saris that Liddo is responsible"

"Franz, that's pure genius. But can anyone ever find out who made the transfer?"

"Not with my software."

"Ivan, what do you think?"

"I think it's perfect as long as they can't trace it back."

"We'll do that, but not immediately. I'd like to have an overall plan before we do anything."

Once this was done, Franz had his computer guru hack into the head of the media group's computer, and they sent an article to seventeen European newspapers for their next edition. The transfer was made. They only had to wait for the results.

John and Franz were going over last-minute details, getting ready for their trip, when Ivan arrived. "This work is making me thirsty, vodka please." *It's only eight in the morning, but that's Ivan.*

"What's this?"

"You're going to investigate the situation in Italy, and I don't want you to be caught short."

"With this kind of money, you may never see me again."

"Ivan, we'll be gone for two weeks. It should be interesting to see what happens while we're gone. If you need either one of us, use one of these prepaid phones. Destroy it when you're done."

"You are getting good at this." He started laughing.

"Can you think of anything you might need?"

"John, I don't need anything. I can do whatever I have to—retire and still have enough money left over to send some to my family in Russia." He gave John a bear hug and kissed him on both cheeks. "I will drive you to airport."

# 42

### Washington DC

At about five-thirty, the director stuck his head into Colin's office. "Colin, do you want to go for a drink?"

"Sure, Frank. Give me about a half hour?"

"That'll work. I'll come back at six. Can we go together?"

"Since you are driving, mind if we go up to Camden Yards? There's a new place I'd like to try."

Colin briefed the director about the standard stuff of the day. They were both smart enough not to discuss their affairs outside of the safe house.

They arrived at the safe house, drove to Camden Yards, parked the car, took a cab to a restaurant about seven blocks away, and walked the remaining distance. When they entered, everyone was working; all the equipment was set up. Sally Crothers had put together a bug-proof communication system equipped with SAT phones. Tony Daugherty had assembled an organizational chart and a list of possibilities. Peter Drake had already chosen people and sites to investigate and asked Sally if she could bug a couple of phones without getting caught. Colin produced a list of known banks holding money for the DNC, the Speaker of the House, and a group of accounts known to be slush funds for the White House.

"We want to get these people at all costs. We want to look at bank transfers, who they see, whom they correspond with, and who they're sleeping with. I want to see all the lists you folks have compiled. We have to start somewhere. Let's get to work."

Most of the activity evolved around Sally and Pete Drake, the communications and computer specialists. The director had given Pete a "back door" to get into the FBI files. They had made good progress in such short time.

At 6:00 a.m., the director said, "Okay, what do we have?"

"We're set up to begin the investigation. We've broken it up into four categories: the secretary of state's personal affairs, her public affairs, the White House chief of staff and the president, and Saris and how he's tied to both groups."

"Okay, do any of you have any connections in the Secret Service or on the White House staff?"

"I have a good friend in the Secret Service who works on the presidential detail. He and I worked on several counterfeit cases, and I saved his life once."

"Take note of that. Anyone else have anything?"

"I dated a White House staffer. We're still on good terms. She works in the chief of staff's office."

"Good, we have the start of a list of possible assets. I want all of you to keep thinking about how we can add to it. If you can think of anyone that might assist us, let Sally know."

"All right, you all know what to do. Sally will remain here twenty-four-seven. Sally, if you need anything, let one of us know and you'll get it. Colin, I need you to keep giving bits of information to the chief of staff to keep that gambit going. Tony and Peter, I am going to announce that you are working together on a bank fraud case. Colin, go over exactly what we'll need with both of them. Colin, go over any gathered intel and make two reports—one for us and one that we can use in the office and with the chief of staff. I'm going to start profiles on the senators and congressmen who are known power brokers and have a close relationship with the Speaker. Colin, have a few more beds set up here, I expect some long nights in our future."

Colin briefed Peter and Tony. Colin asked Sally if additional traffic through the back door would draw attention to them. The director asked Colin to arrange another meeting with the chief of staff to inform him that he had found something big; it would take a week or two to verify the information. The director left.

Reviewing the complete investigation and the implications involved, Colin suddenly realized it would bring down the whole government. Sally interrupted him while he was wracking his brain trying to come up with a less invasive solution to this fiasco.

"Colin, someone just tried to breach communications. It could have been a simple accident, but I don't want to take a chance."

"Crap, if they know about us already, we're in deep shit. Can you trace it back?" "I could, but I would need some more equipment to do that without being noticed."

"What do you need?"

"I need a YF47720 modular resistor to prevent anyone from knowing I've located them."

"Where the hell do we get one of those?"

"It looks like a small computer chip with a piece of wire attached. It's back at the office in my bottom drawer, right-hand side."

"I'll be back in an hour."

Colin walked into Sally's cubicle and opened her desk drawer. Everything in every drawer looked the same to him—all electronic junk, so he looked around for a huge bag and just stuffed everything in the one he found.

Just as he was leaving, an investigator who worked in Sally's area came in. "Sally's on leave. She asked me to send her something that she needed from her desk."

The man looked at him and said, "That's nice of you. Is she all right?"

"She's fine. She needed some time off for personal reasons."

"Tell her I was asking about her."

He got back to the safe house well within the hour. Sally added the modulator and a few other gadgets to her communications array. "It was the NSA. No big deal, but I better call them and let them know it's us, before they start investigating."

"Why would the NSA be listening to us?"

"They monitor the airwaves and certain frequencies routinely. They also monitor frequencies from certain equipment, like the stuff I'm using, it throws up red flags. If they're curious, they'll investigate. I have a protocol to let them know it's the FBI, they'll back off then. I think this will take care of the problem, but if we have to, I can set up a different call system."

Colin told her to make a list of what she needed and where he could get it, just in case. Sally gave him the list. As he studied the list, Peter called out to him.

"Colin, you've got to see this."

"What do you have?"

"I went into the DNC's accounts. All of the transactions in and out from this one account were over ten million. I followed some of the transactions. Thirty million was transferred to the president's personal campaign account recently through small contributions to the Speaker's campaign fund, transferred to the DNC in a bulk amount and then into this account. It doesn't show up on any of the listed campaign accounts. I backed into it through the bank's signature data."

"Peter, can you find out where the contributions to the Speaker's campaign fund came from?"

"Colin, I think I would have to get into the bank's transfer department to do that, and that's not going to happen without a warrant."

"I'll take care of that one."

• • • • • • • • • • • • • • • • • • • • • • • • •

Harry Gold, a chief examiner at the Federal Reserve Bank, owed his job to Colin. "Hello Harry, Colin Young here. Are you free for lunch today?"

"Sure, Colin, tell me when and where."

"I'll see you at Tucker's Steak House at one o'clock."

When Colin arrived at the restaurant, Harry was already there. *Colin never changes.* Harry was the same age as Colin, but appeared at least ten years older. Harry wore his standard—an unironed white shirt, a stained tie, and red suspenders holding up gray-striped pants that hadn't seen a crease in years.

"Hello, Harry, you old dog."

"Colin, I'll be dammed. How are you?"

After reliving some old times, and a few off-color jokes, Colin got to the issue.

"Harry, I need your help. I'm working on a sensitive case involving national security. I need to get some information from a bank here in town without a subpoena. This is an extremely sensitive case, and if I had to go to a judge, the information could leak."

"Christ, Colin, I can't do that. Do you want to end up in jail? I don't."

"Harry, you owe me. All you have to do is make one of my guys a member of an audit team. I promise you nothing will be copied or physically taken from the bank."

"What kind of case is this?"

"Harry, you don't want to know."

Harry looked angry. "All right, what bank?"

The details were worked out, and they both enjoyed a fabulous meal. "I can give him ID as an outside contractor."

Colin thanked him and picked up the tab. "It was great seeing you, Harry."

"I wish I could say the same, Colin."

Back at the office, Colin observed the director being pummeled with questions from several reporters. Before he could close his office door, he was surrounded as well. "What the hell's going on here? Since when do we allow reporters in this office? Someone call security!" Within seconds, uniformed officers were herding reporters back toward the elevators.

Colin walked over to the director's office. "What the hell is going on?"

"Colin, have you started a formal investigation of the Speaker of the House?"

"No, sir." Colin's heart was racing, but he kept his cool.

"The press was asking about an investigation. Find out what this is all about."

"Yes, sir." Colin made some inquiries internally, and then he called a friend at the *Washington Herald*.

"Jim Cates, please."

"Cates here."

"Hello, Jim, it's Colin Young."

"Funny you should call me, Colin, do you know anything about an investigation of the Speaker?"

"No. Where did you get that information?"

Jim gave Colin the lowdown. "Thanks, Jim. I'll get back to you with the real story as soon as I know what it is."

• • • • • • • • • • • • • • • • • • • • • • • • • • • • • • • • • • •

"Sir, the press has informed me that the rumor was started by the chief of staff's office. Do you want me to follow up with them?"

"No, Colin, I'm going to call a press conference for five o'clock. I'll take care of it, thank you."

The director began promptly, "Neither the FBI nor anyone in the Justice Department has initiated a formal investigation of the Speaker of the House. Rumors like this can be extremely dangerous. If this rumor is politically motivated, then we, as a nation, have reached a new low. Thank you." As he walked away from the podium, all kinds of questions were being shouted out, but were unanswered as the door closed behind him.

Meanwhile, Colin was on the phone with the White House chief of staff. "Rob, what the hell did you do?"

"Colin, why don't we have dinner this evening?" Colin left immediately to meet the chief of staff at a restaurant in Crystal City.

"How are you, buddy?"

"Not well. What the hell did you do? I'm in deep shit. I had the director up my ass all day."

"Don't worry. I did this to slow down whatever is going on. The press is gunning for the entire administration. I hoped whatever it is that's going wrong would stop for a while by diverting the press until we can regroup, or at least get through the next news cycle."

"Rob, you can't hang me out to dry like that. If I go down, you're coming along with me."

"Colin, don't worry. I've already put out the word that one of my staffers overheard something out of context. I fired him to make it look good."

"Well, the director just held a press conference. He basically said it came from your office and it was politically motivated."

"Great, that'll give us a better reason to ask for his resignation so that you can take over."

*This guy is a miserable human being. He deserves everything he's going to get.*

"Rob, I'm getting close to getting you what you want. I've discovered something that could possibly have the Speaker locked up. I need some more cash. I can't use internal resources, especially now."

"All right, how much do you need?"

Colin took out his diary and a pen and appeared to be making calculations. "One hundred fifty thousand dollars."

"Holy shit! That's a lot of money."

"This kind of information doesn't come cheap."

Rob hesitated and thought about it. "Okay, I'll meet you tomorrow at the entrance to the Smithsonian. I'll have the cash."

When he exited, he signaled Tony to follow the chief of staff.

Tony followed him at a safe distance. When Rob took out his cell phone, Tony moved in closer. He put a tiny listening device in his ear. He heard Rob say, "Hello, Wiley, Rob. I need $150,000 tonight. Okay, I'll be at your apartment at nine o'clock."

He followed the chief of staff to the White House. When he saw him enter, he jumped in a cab and headed for the safe house but was dropped off nine blocks away.

"I thought you were shadowing the chief of staff."

"I was. He is going to pick up a hundred fifty grand tonight at nine. I wanted to talk to Colin right away."

"Call him at this number, it's clean."

"Colin, Tony. As he walked back to his office, I overheard him making plans to pick up a hundred fifty grand at nine tonight."

"That's great! Are you home now? I'm in a meeting right now, but it should be over in about half an hour. I'll meet you at your house in forty-five minutes."

"Tony, that's great news. We'll find out who the conduit is. I have an idea. Where's Peter?"

"Right here, boss," Peter said, walking into the room.

"This bastard is going to pick up the money I requested to continue the investigation of the Speaker, but what if he never gets the money to me?"

"What do you mean, Colin?"

"We steal it from him. That should cause him some major problems and possibly draw out some more of the bad guys."

"Boss, but that would be illegal."

"Don't be a wise guy. Do you think you can do it?"

"Perhaps we could tase him from behind, take the money, and walk away. It's doable."

"But do we know where he's going to pick it up?"

"No, but we know what time."

"Well, we better have some contingencies. What if it's in a public place?"

"We know he's meeting at someone's apartment."

"Well, that's good, probably a residential area, so it will be quiet. If not, he'll probably park in a garage. That would be good."

They discussed the possibilities and planned for each one. They asked Sally to call the chief of staff's office to ask the receptionist if the chief was available at six for a call from the attorney general. Sally routed her call through the AG's office, just in case someone tried to trace it. Pete went out since they had the time now, bought some pizza, and brought it back for dinner.

Peter and Tony sat in an official vehicle near the chief's garage. Sally waited a block away in her Honda. They followed the chief, leapfrogging back and forth; he was never more than a block away from either vehicle.

The chief parked the car and went into a building nearby. Tony walked in and watched as the elevator stopped at the fourth floor. Someone grabbed his shoulder. "May I help you, sir?"

"Oh, no, thank you. I just thought I saw the White House chief of staff, and I was hoping to get his autograph."

"I am sorry, sir, but I must ask you to leave. This is private property."

"I'm sorry. I just got a little carried away."

They parked their car halfway down the street and walked to a dark spot directly across Rob's car. An hour later, the chief walked to his car carrying a briefcase.

As Rob opened the door, they slowly walked up behind him and tased him. They shoved him into the car, picked up the case, and walked back to their car, calmly and undetected.

The director and Colin were waiting for them at the safe house. "How did it go?"

Tony answered, "Textbook."

"Who did he get the money from?"

"We know the man's name is Wiley and he lives at this address in Alexandria."

The director looked at him. "Apartment 4C?"

"Yes."

The director sat down. "Holy Crap!"

"Do you know him?"

"Colin, we all know him, Senator Wiley Pritchard. He might be retired, but he's still one of the most powerful men in Washington."

"Do you think he's behind all of this?"

"No, he always represents someone. But if he's asking Colin to investigate the Speaker and her connection to Saris, who the hell is he representing?"

"There's a possibility that the two groups have come up with the same idea, and since this administration is so weak, they both jumped at the opportunity and butted heads. The bad news is that if the chief of staff is being used, Wiley's group has already compromised the White House."

"We can't come to a conclusion until we have all the facts. Sally and Peter, plant an electronic surveillance device on Senator Pritchard.

Sally answered, "But we can only put it on his cell and his computer, and it will only be useful in Washington. We don't have long-range capability."

"Okay, do it fast. Does anyone know any outside sources that we could use to put him under total surveillance without any repercussions?"

"There's a group of call girls being used by several senators and congressmen to spy on each other. I know a few of those girls, maybe one of them could get close to him."

"That's dangerous. Wiley Pritchard has been around too long to give any information to a call girl."

"No, sir, not like that. Attractive young women go unnoticed in Washington. Why don't we hire a couple of the girls to keep tabs on him by using small listening devices."

"I can supply listening devices that will send the information back here. The person wearing it would not be able to hear what's being said."

"We also know Pritchard and his haunts. We could set a team of girls up at each location on a rotating basis."

"Peter, what do you think?"

"I think it's a great idea. The fact that we can do this by using the money we just took from the chief makes it even better."

"Get it done and keep me posted."

# 43

### London, England

Paula had returned late the previous evening and went directly to bed. She was tired from the trip and fell asleep quickly. She awoke early in the morning, sat in her den sipping coffee, thought about her weekend with Aristotle, and called YK.

YK seemed delighted with her report. "You'll be rewarded handsomely, well done."

She told him she was meeting Aristotle in Lisbon on the weekend. Within two months, she told him, all of Saris's homes would be covered. "YK, when I'm done, he won't be able to fart without you knowing about it."

"I get the point, but that is something I'd rather not think about. Again, job well done."

Paula hung up the phone and went to draw a hot bath. Her thoughts drifted; she dreamed of the day when she would be her own person, insulated by wealth, no one would harm her ever again.

*Who the hell could that be? Is there no security in this building?* She got out of the tub, wrapped a towel around herself, and answered the door.

"Sara, come in. What I can I do for you?"

"I'm sorry, mum. I didn't want to disturb you."

"It's no bother, dear. Give me a minute to get dressed. Make yourself a cup of tea and I'll be out in a minute."

"Now, Sara, what can I do for you?"

"You said that I should let you know if I found out anything new."

"And?"

"The other night I went to a club frequented by Mr. Saris. I met a young woman who confided in me that she was being kept by Mr. Saris, along with ten other girls here in London. He paid her a hundred thousand pounds per year and bought her an apartment in Swiss Cottage. He paid over a million for it and put it in her name."

"Where is that?"

"It's between St. John's Wood and Primrose Park, just down from Notting Hill. She told me that the old man was extremely kinky and perverted." Paula listened intently to Sara's graphic descriptions, then proceeded to decide what she would add to her repertoire with Aristotle. Paula thought that was some pretty gruesome stuff, but nothing close to what she had endured with Y. K. and Mike Manheim.

"Sara, this is just the kind of information I am looking for. Hey! I have the day off. Would you like to join me for lunch?"

Sara happily agreed.

"All right then, wait here for a moment."

Paula returned quickly and handed Sara a fat envelope. "Please continue to gather this sort of information, and thanks again." Sara blushed and thanked her for the gift.

# 44

### Zurich, Switzerland

Ivan dropped John and Franz off at the airport and drove back to his house. Once he was packed, he went to the barn. He retrieved a radio and some other electronic equipment, along with a ceramic 9mm Glock, from a secret compartment. It was fine for use in most areas of Europe, except Russia; ceramic became brittle in very cold weather.

Ivan got on the radio and contacted the KGB station chief in Rome. He informed him he was coming and might need assistance. Men with Ivan's experience were hard to find and were often kept on retainer. *I cannot tell my friends I am still with the KGB. What a business. I have to lie to my close friends.* With time to spare, he went back to the house, took the gun apart, and carefully fitted the parts in their designed places in his luggage. He poured himself a quick drink; it was time to go.

......................................

He checked into his room and poured himself vodka from the bottle he had purchased at the duty-free, glad that his flight had gone well. He would be meeting Vladimir in thirty minutes.

He arrived early and had time to sit on the steps and watch the tourists for a few minutes. He had just decided to go into the restaurant when he saw Vladimir.

"Vladimir, it's so good to see you. How are Luda and the kids?" "

"Ivan, you look good. Luda is good, and the kids speak Italian just like Italians."

"Svetlana must be ten by now, and little Gregory is seven?"

"You're getting old, my friend. Svetlana is nineteen, and Gregory is seventeen."

"Where does the time go?"

Inside the restaurant, seated toward the back, Vladimir started, "Ivan, what are you doing here in Rome?"

Ivan filled him in on the reason for coming to Rome, but he kept John's and Franz's identities from the KGB, along with other sensitive information. Ivan told him it involved Aristotle Saris and the people he was investigating when he retired. "Perestroika was good for you. It allowed you to get out. The new regime is back to the same shit as the old one, and it is difficult to get out now." Ivan laughed at the absurdity of it all.

"Ivan, what can I do for you?"

"I need any information you can give me on this company and the Minister of Commerce. I know they're both tied into the Liddo Group and Saris."

"Ivan, meet me at my house tomorrow for dinner about six. I'll have the information you need by then. I must report this to my superior. Is that a problem for you?"

"No, my friend, thank you for asking. But I'll share any information I find out before I bring it back to my principals."

"Good, that will make it easier for me."

"Okay, my friend. Time for vodka."

The next morning, while having coffee and rolls, Ivan's mind wandered, thinking of Francesca, the only woman he ever really cared about. She was beautiful and full of life. He smiled, thinking of the time they had spent together. He was angry for a long time when his superior transferred him to Bucharest. He was able to return to Rome several years later, but he never saw Francesca again even though he looked for her often. He decided to go for a walk. He walked for a long time and arrived at Piazza Navona.

He sat at an outdoor café he remembered there and had a cup of espresso with Sambuca. He finished his coffee and walked to the Trevi Fountain a few blocks away. Ivan felt better after lunch and a shower. Vladimir lived in the Trastevere District off of Viale di Trastevere on Via Anicia, Ivan's favorite section of Rome.

Vladimir welcomed Ivan, who was immediately attacked by Luda. She ran up to him and threw her arms around him. Within seconds, Svetlana and Gregory were hugging him as well.

I have not been back to Russia for a very long time, but it is good to see my friends. Ivan enjoyed dinner. Luda made panini and served gravlax on buttered bread with Russian caviar. They sat for hours talking about old times, laughing, while they sipped homemade vodka.

It was almost three in the morning when Luda and the kids said good-night.

"Vladimir, you're a lucky man. You have a wonderful family and a beautiful home."

"Ivan, you should have gotten married."

"Vladimir, I was a field agent, not an embassy darling like you, tied to a desk and able to come home every night."

"That's true, my old friend, but you could have tried."

"I was trained as a field agent, it came naturally to me. People like me do what we do, and it would have been unfair to marry."

"Ivan, you've gotten wiser since you got old."

They laughed and poured another vodka.

"Ivan, now, down to business. This is what we have on the Minister, and this is what we have on the companies you asked about. We've had some involvement with the bonded warehouse group. We've given them some help, and they've helped us to smuggle various items. Some of the information is classified, so I can't show it to you."

"So these people are smuggling drugs into Italy. Does the Minister of Commerce have anything to do with that?"

"I'm not at liberty to give you that information."

"Where are the drugs coming from?"

Vladimir pointed at a paragraph and said, "My friend, I'm sorry, but I'm not at liberty to say."

Ivan understood Vladimir's precautions. He knew that KGB officers are usually monitored.

"Vladimir, thank Luda for me and give the kids a big kiss. Thank you for all of your help."

As Ivan was leaving, Vladimir gave him a shopping bag full of Luda's specialty foods to take home with him.

When he got back to the hotel, he looked inside the bag. Ivan opened the envelope and found the information he really needed—names, origins of shipments, and schedules. From that, he was able to find the connection between the Minister and Liddo, including contacts, codes, and copies of payments made. Ivan went down to the lobby and put it in the safe. In the morning, he would leave for Germany.

Ivan got up early, went to the post office, and mailed the information package to his home in Zurich. He went to the airport and got on a flight to Berlin.

After checking in, he went out and purchased a camera with a telephoto lens, several listening devices, and ammo for his Glock.

He needed to check out Helmut Klug, the head of German Intelligence, a high-profile well-liked individual. Ivan didn't know what he was looking for, other than some connection to Saris or the Liddo Group, but he did know that this man received large sums of money from a Liddo account. Klug was reputed to be ruthless and very smart, so Ivan knew he had to be extremely careful.

Ivan had picked the hotel next to the Intelligence headquarters. Using a telephoto lens, he could see directly into Klug's office. He walked past the entrance of the building several times a day over the next few days; anyone watching would probably think he was a tourist.

After watching him for a few days, he was able to anticipate Klug's movements. In order to be effective, Ivan knew he had to hire a crack surveillance team. The best Ivan had ever seen just happened to be in Berlin. Ivan knew that they were loyal to only those who paid them well, and he would make certain they were very loyal to him.

........................................

"Ivan, my old friend, what's the KGB doing here? The wall is down, and everyone is friendly."

They sat opposite each other on gaudy leather couches. Gustavo offered Ivan a cigarette. "You're still smoking Russian Bellemore?"

"Yes, Ivan, remember, we stole a whole truckload of them. I still have several left."

Ivan asked for vodka, stopped laughing, and gave Gustavo a serious look.

"I need Tania, Isabella, and Sergey. I need a quiet surveillance team, able to keep their mouths shut and not ask questions."

"Who are you watching?"

"Helmut Klug."

"Ivan, my friend, this is very dangerous. If German Intelligence finds out, I am finished here in Germany."

"How much do you want?"

"Ivan, this could get me killed. I want fifteen thousand in advance, another five when the assignment is completed and expenses."

"I'll give you twenty-five thousand upfront and another ten when the job is done."

Gustavo smiled. "Ivan, you have always been more than fair. When do you want to start?"

"I will be here at seven o'clock to meet the team."

Ivan handed Gustavo an envelope. The man took the money and smiled.

Once they were all seated, Ivan told them he needed to know everything about Klug, on the job and off. They discussed the operation in depth. Within two days, they had placed listening devices and cameras in Helmut's apartment, his car, and office building. They had decided that his office was too risky to bug.

On the first evening of surveillance, he was seen meeting a well-built young man. The pictures of the sexual and physical abuse made Ivan sick. Although disturbing as they were, the pictures gave him an idea. Ivan knew that homosexuality was commonplace, but pictures like this could hurt any politician's career. Ivan concluded that Liddo had gotten to Klug via blackmail and money, used to grease the wheel, but there had to be more.

Ivan took a risk and placed a call.

"Guten Tag, Helmut Klug speaking."

"Helmut, how are you? I'm calling on behalf of Ascot Chen. He's on his way to Berlin. He wishes to meet with you for dinner at the same restaurant where you met when he was last in town."

"What time?"

"Is eight o'clock acceptable?"

"Yes, eight o'clock at the old Berliner Hotel," he said, his voice quivering.

Ivan hung up. Now he would not have to follow him.

"I want everything to be recorded." He knew they'd record everything.

•••••••••••••••••••••••••••••

Ivan was sitting in a comfortable overstuffed chair as Helmut approached him. He got up, extended his hand.

"Herr Klug, my name is Ivan. Ascot is not going to make it this evening."

"Please, Herr Klug, join me for dinner." Helmut started to decline, but Ivan insisted.

"I'll have to leave by eight thirty sharp."

"Let's have a drink, perhaps, then?"

Klug appeared angry, but he agreed.

"Herr Klug, I have some good news for you."

"Yes, what is it?"

Ivan could see that he was agitated. Ivan smiled. "Ascot Chen is dead."

"He's dead?" Helmut asked excitedly as his whole body relaxed. "That's a pity."

"There is some bad news. Before he died, he told me everything."

"What do you want? Are you also with the Liddo Group?"

"No, I'm not. If you cooperate with me, I will make you a free man." Ivan thought Helmut was going to weep.

"What assurances do I have?"

"None, only my word. I can tell you that we're going after the Liddo Group. If you help us, your secret dies with Chen."

"What do you want to know? The only thing I did was push through some currency deals with the banks by insisting it was in our national interest. I have never betrayed my country."

"You've been loyal to Germany, but there have been other things." Ivan was fishing, but he had a gut feeling that there was more than currency deals involved. "What about Saris?"

Helmut hesitated. "I did stop an investigation into the Green Party, but they're only environmentalists."

*Is he that stupid or just naïve?* "Did the currency deals have anything to do with the Green Party?"

"Yes, they were transferring monies back and forth with the US. We allowed the banks to give generous trades on several currencies. I lent several agents to Chen to work in Hong Kong on some problems that he was having there. That's all. I know nothing else. I only met with Chen a few times, no one else from Liddo."

"Would you be willing to work with us to stop Liddo for good?"

"Yes, I would be happy to help you, I despise them."

"We'll be in touch. I will be your only contact." He turned and walked out.

Ivan went back to the restaurant, smiling, and paid Gustavo the balance owed plus a bonus. *Lugano, here I come. It will be nice to take a short holiday.*

# 45

### Hong Kong

John was just starting to get back into the flow of Hong Kong when he realized he would be leaving in three days. He had just asked Franz and Chong they would like to have dinner on a junk that evening. Then John went over to Iris's office and asked her. She jumped up, ran over, and hugged John in reply.

Chong and Franz discussed how they would handle the Chinese distributor, knowing they were owned by Liddo. John told Chong he was sending Iris to the States. "It might get dangerous here, I don't want Iris involved."

Iris was excited. "I love going on junks for dinner."

The sky had just begun to darken, the harbor was picturesque. They ate and laughed; boat lights twinkled in the backdrop of the Hong Kong skyline. Small waves thumping against the boat made it sound like a soft concerto filled with intermittent shrills of bay birds. John sat back, closed his eyes, and mused, *This is like no place on Earth.*

When dinner was over, John handed Iris an envelope containing one hundred thousand dollars. He told her she should deposit it into her portfolio account. "You can't spend those bills. They can only be deposited."

She looked at him adoringly. "John, you're so kind to me. I love you."

John leaned down to kiss her forehead and said, "I want you to go to the States and work with Brad for a while. Everything is shipshape here."

She jumped on him. "You're the kindest man on Earth."

"I'll be kind as long as you continue to do a good job."

"You know I will, John."

"I do know."

Franz and Chong looked at each other and both thought the same thing, laughing hysterically. Chong took Franz's hand and said, in a feminine voice, "I love you, John, I love you."

"That's enough from the two of you."

"Yes, sir, boss man."

John broke into laughter along with his friends.

"Let's meet at six in the morning. There are a lot of loose ends we have to tie up. We also need to go over to Woo & Woo to make Chong a director of the bank."

"I'm going to be a bank director? Boss, have you lost your mind?"

"No, I trust you more than anyone I know."

The next morning, John and his group decided that it would not be prudent to fight battles on too many fronts and that Chong would have access to all information, but remain low profile. Chong was instructed to get any information about his distributors and to pass it on to Franz. Chong told them he would use his family's intelligence network with care to accomplish the task.

"Chong, we know that Y. K. Chen, the head of the Liddo Group, lives and works out of Jakarta. It might even be a better idea to stay away from him at this point, he is very dangerous."

"John, you're probably right. Jakarta is one of the most corrupt places on earth. Chen is certainly being protected by the government. I'll go there myself. I've been discussing some business opportunities with a group out of Jakarta. This might be a good time to try to close the deal."

"No, Chong, I don't want you going by yourself."

"Boss, are you getting soft? This is just business. While I'm there, I'll visit my cousin, a corrupt police detective in Jakarta, to see what he knows about Chen. Boss, don't worry, I'll be careful."

Franz joined the conversation. "How will you handle it if he's so corrupt?"

"I'll tell him that I'm going against the Liddo Group in a big business venture. If he's protecting them, he'll try to discourage me. I'll protest. He is liable to give me the information I need during our heated discussion. Otherwise, I'll drop it if I think he knows nothing."

"You're a clever man."

With that taken care of, John told Chong to meet him in two hours at Woo & Woo in the Edinburg Towers.

Janet Woo was there and had all of the paperwork ready. When Chong had signed all of the documents, Janet said, "Congratulations, Mr. Chong, you are officially the managing director of the Bank Swizzerveria Americano. You'll have to come here once a month. We will hold our first meeting now. I will have my secretary record the minutes.

"A meeting of the directors of Bank Swizzerveria Americano is now in order. Present: Mr. Chong Lee, managing director, and two nominated directors being represented by Woo & Woo Solicitors Ltd. The meeting is being held in the offices of Woo & Woo, located at suite 2417 in the Edinburg Towers, Hong Kong Central. The first course of action is to stipulate that Mr. Peter Tsillman is to be appointed general manager of the bank's European Division and will be domiciled in the existing property, headquarters of the bank in Lugano, Switzerland.

"Compensation: Mr. Chong Lee, director—Asia, will receive three million US and a bonus of three percent of net profits after shareholder distribution annually. Mr. Peter Tsillman will receive one million euros and a bonus of two percent of net profits after shareholder distribution annually. Woo & Woo will receive five hundred thousand dollars annually, to be distributed as they see fit to the nominated directors." Janet looked up and asked if there was anything else. "If there are no more issues to be discussed, I call this meeting to an end. We will reconvene on the last Friday of next month. Thank you, gentlemen."

Just as they got on the escalator to go down to the main lobby, Chong collapsed.

John picked him up. "Chong, are you all right?"

"Three million a year, boss, you've lost it."

John started to laugh. "You're worth every penny."

They went back to the office, and John decided to take them all to dinner. Iris reserved the entire restaurant to accommodate the company's sixty employees. She also hired entertainers for the evening.

The evening was spectacular, complete with great food and entertainment. John let everyone know how thankful he was for their loyalty and friendship. *I have a wonderful family.*

The next day at the airport, Chong said good-bye and Iris cried. John felt melancholic, leaving Chong and Hong Kong. Aboard the plane, his mood turned dark with anger. *The Liddo Group has taken a lot from me. I'll see to it that they become nothing but a bad fleeting memory!*

"You know, it was a little over the top for you to tell Iris to call you as soon as she lands."

"Franz, you're right. I just want what's best for her."

"Do you think of me as a son?" Franz broke out laughing.

"Screw you, Franz." Franz laughed harder.

When the plane landed after the long flight, John wasn't tired. He actually felt renewed.

# 46

### Zurich, Switzerland

After arriving home, they agreed to meet in the office in one hour. John called Ivan immediately.

"John, welcome back! I only arrived yesterday. See you in thirty minutes."

On his way to the office, he stopped in the kitchen, made a pot of coffee, and put a bottle of vodka in the freezer. Franz and Ivan were talking when John walked in.

"Ivan, it's good to see you. How did you make out?"

"It's good to see you too, John. The Italian Minister of Commerce is tied into the Liddo Group. He's given them complete protection in the customs warehouse business by letting them hire the customs agents. They're in control of everything coming into Italy, including large amounts of drugs, much more than can be consumed in Italy. They're probably distributing to all the surrounding countries. We are talking a billion a year here."

"This is unbelievable. How did they get this powerful?"

"It's all about money. They buy officials, news agencies, and police. It's understandable, not good, but understandable."

"How did you make out in Germany?"

Ivan told him everything he found out about Helmut Klug. John was amazed by all of this.

Meanwhile, Franz was entering Ivan's information into the computer. John went to get them some coffee and vodka. By the time John returned, Franz had finished entering the data.

When John saw all the information, he asked, "Do we have enough information to begin our silent war?" Franz and Ivan signaled thumbs-up.

Franz told them he had an idea. "They are using Italian customs agents to import drugs from Asia with the protection of the Minister of Commerce. It would be a large loss for them, and the minister may talk if we go after them. Let's get the Liddo name out in the open now."

"How are we going to accomplish that? It seems that they've been operating in the open, so it seems there are a lot of Italian agencies involved."

"John's right. We don't know who to trust in Italy, we would have to act independently. We don't have the manpower or political clout to pull this off."

Franz had an idea. "Wait a minute. I have a close friend in the FISA in Belgium. He's the head of counterterrorism, drug smuggling falls under his jurisdiction. John, maybe I should go to Belgium and meet with him?"

Franz made arrangements to leave, hoping to persuade his man to join them.

After introducing Chris Artts to the group, Franz brought up the information on the SMART Boards. Chris was amazed. "Gentlemen, I'm impressed. My agency doesn't have this capability. Is this CIA business?"

Franz suggested that they tell him everything, so John told him everything from Hong Kong to the present.

"We have been investigating Saris and the Green Party for some time. The information you've gathered agrees with ours, at least to the point where the socialists have tried to kill Fragge. We haven't gotten that far."

"We'll share all of our information with you, Chris."

"I'm in."

Over the next few days, Franz brought Chris up to speed on everything they had done. During that time, John and Ivan worked out at Ivan's place. Ivan shared much of the knowledge of his trade, including lists of contact numbers and names of people all over Europe to be used only in matters of life or death. "These are not people you really don't want to know. I could get into a lot of trouble for even giving you this information."

"Understood."

Upon their return, Franz had some good news for them. "John, Chris and I have come up with a plan."

Chris explained that he was aware of a drug-smuggling operation in Belgium with the drugs coming in from Italy. "We'll raid the operation and announce that we have broken up a multimillion-euro drug-trafficking group with ties to Italy. Hopefully, after that, my government will allow me to investigate further. Franz and I will work together. Maybe we will be able to bring them all down in a few weeks. John, if you and Ivan work with me on the ground in Italy, we'll get these bastards. Ivan, didn't you say that the KGB station chief is a friend of yours?"

"Yes, but he cannot do anything that has to do with the internal affairs of Italy."

"I have the same restrictions. But I'm sure he'll be able to supply information if you need it."

"Possibly."

"I am authorized to raid the group in Belgium and make arrests. It will only take me three days since I already have a file on this group. John and Ivan, can you start gathering this list of information I need from Italy to make this whole thing work?"

"We'll leave immediately. Agreed, Ivan?"

Chris continued, "I don't expect you to have it all by the time I'm ready, but anything will be helpful."

John and Ivan were on a flight to Rome three hours later.

They took a taxi to the De La Ville hotel at the top of the Spanish Steps. When they reached the room, Ivan commented, "John, this room is bigger than my house. I hope I can find my way to the WC during the night."

John told Ivan to unpack while he ordered a bottle of vodka. When the vodka was delivered, along with John's coffee, Ivan said, "Now I'm ready for work."

"The first item on the list: information on the Minister of Commerce."

"John, let me see the list."

Ivan studied it but made no notes; then he burned it in a large ashtray.

"Okay, I can do this, but let's work smart."

"What do you have in mind, Ivan?"

"I would like to have Franz draw all of the money out of this man's accounts and transfer it to the Saris account that we used before. When he knows that he has been found out, he'll run for his money. When it's not there, he'll know he was betrayed. Then he'll talk. Next, we have to identify all of the employees in the customs-bonded warehouses. We'll find one that will get us all the other documents we need. I'll use a local contact I know to approach that person. We'll need about fifty thousand dollars to procure the surveillance team I used recently."

"I brought about two hundred thousand in cash, money is no problem."

"Okay, John, I'll be back in several hours. I'll see you in the morning, and we'll start."

John woke up relaxed. John called room service, ordered breakfast, and took a shower.

"Good morning, Ivan. How did it go?"

"I'll show you the information I got."

"Ivan, have you eaten?"

"No, John." John picked up the phone, called room service, and added salmon and gravlax to his order, along with a bottle of vodka. John sat and read the information.

"Ivan, where the hell did you get all this?"

"John, your government has a policy, 'Don't ask, don't tell.' I think that's appropriate."

John nodded. "We better get this to Chris right away."

"John, personally hand it. I'm better off here. Tell Chris not to move on this until he hears from me. I need time to get to the minister and make certain he'll cooperate. I think Ascot Chen was the front man for Liddo. Once the minister learns that he's dead and that we killed him, he should be more—how do you say…pliable?"

John agreed and took the first flight to Brussels. Ivan left to meet with Gustavo.

# 47

**Washington DC**

Colin and Peter sat across from the two call girls. Peter and Tony had already had a meeting with these girls and went over the job specs at twenty-five thousand dollars per week for survcillancc.

Colin spoke, "There will be four of you, coverage twenty-four seven, report daily, and use the listening devices. This investigation is outside the bureau, you will have no protection other than what we offer you personally, and if you divulge any of the information you gather to anyone, you will be arrested and not released. Tell me if you are in or out, before we go any further."

Both were given Wiley's home address and the names and locations of places he frequented.

"Do not acknowledge the other two-girl team, understood?"

"Get as close to Wiley as possible without direct contact. The listening devices will pick up anything within one hundred-fifty feet. The information will be digitally sent directly back to us. We only need you to tell us where he goes, when and for how long. Report to Tony every day as agreed. The other team will report to Peter. Make sure you rotate your surveillance. Wear casual conservative clothing. We guarantee you two weeks' work, possibly more. Use only these prepaid cell phones to contact us, and put these numbers in your speed dial. If you need help, we will be close by."

"All right then, are we clear on the operation? I'll meet you tomorrow by St Gregory's Church on K Street."

"This is going to be a tough job. They're gorgeous."

Colin wasn't pleased. "Keep your mind on your work. Don't get friendly with these girls. Remember, no room for error here."

"Understood, sir."

The next team arrived and was given the same speech. These girls agreed to meet Peter at the entrance to the National Aquarium on Fifteenth Street. "Do not leave anything to chance. Check all equipment and have it verified by Sally before you let these girls go out. If Pritchard is so important to them, they might be watching him. We may be putting these girls in harm's way. We can't protect them all the time, so let's hope they're good."

"Don't worry, Colin, I'll tell them what to do, and I'll do my best to keep them safe."

"Listen to me, give these girls a wide berth. If you're spotted, we'll lose our cover, and then they will be in real danger. Stay away and hope for the best."

Tony and Peter knew these girls needed more tutelage before releasing them.

After a brief discussion, they left, agreeing to meet at the safe house the next evening.

Tony and Peter agreed that information gathering was the prime objective, but keeping these girls safe was also paramount. They taught the girls some breakaway techniques and showed them how to use the equipment covertly. They showed them how to operate independently as a team, to ensure a safe operation. Satisfied, they told the girls to be careful and go to work.

Peter's team were Pat and Rose; code name: PR. Tony's team were Fran and Louise; code name: Daisy. PR would work days. Daisy worked nights.

Pat went to the Hill Deli where Wiley was known to have his breakfast. Rose went to the Black Door Steakhouse, Wiley's office.

Pat was wearing a cowboy hat with her hair tucked under it and a blue windbreaker and jeans. She went into the Hill, ordered coffee, sat at a table in the corner, put the listening device in her ear. She took out a book, settled in. Wiley came in and sat down. Then a man came in and joined Wiley. *Christmas, that's the chief of staff.* She could hear everything they were saying. Pat played it cool and appeared to ignore them.

The chief of staff left quickly. Wiley dialed a number on his cell. She was amazed; she could hear the person on the other end of that call. Wiley hung up and left. She stood, took off her hat and windbreaker, shook her hair loose, and followed him. He got into a cab. She got into a cab and asked the cabbie to tail the cab in front of him. When Wiley exited his cab, she did the same, but she looked different, having donned a wig and other clothing during her cab ride. He was never out of her sight or hearing, and Wiley never knew it.

Pat followed him to the Steakhouse and then called Rose. Rose was chatting up a young man at the bar. Wiley walked in and went directly to his reserved table. Rose recorded every word exchanged between Wiley and a steady stream of Washington insiders during the course of the afternoon. It was almost seven when Wiley left. She followed him back to his apartment and alerted the next team.

Pat and Rose reported to Peter as previously arranged. "Girls, you did a great job. Tomorrow, let's switch off. Rose, you take the deli. Pat, take the Steakhouse. Wear something businesslike but not memorable. See you tomorrow." Peter went directly to the safe house; Colin was there.

"Peter, this stuff is great. Your team did an outstanding job."

"I was more than a little concerned after our meeting last night, but I don't think an experienced field agent would have done better."

"You're right. Wait until you read what they got. This information indicates a split in the administration: the president and the DNC have taken money from various parties and promised them conflicting favors. The two main groups seem to be the Liddo Group and Aristotle Saris. We've known for a long time that Saris has quite a few senators and congressmen in his pocket, including the DNC.

"The Liddo Group is more covert, but we do know that their head office is in Memphis. They seem to be in the chicken business. We don't know where their money comes from, but Wiley and the chief are on their team."

"We got all this just today?"

"Whatever they're doing, they now seem to be at odds and the administration is losing control. Wiley told the chief, and I quote, 'I don't give a shit what you do, but get him back on the reservation,' referring to the president. The president, Speaker, and her whole crew seem to be running their own agenda."

"And you think Saris is behind this?"

"No, Peter. It looks like Saris is backing the president and his group. The Liddo Group is backing another. We seem to have two outside forces interfering with the government and our way of life. Here's a copy of today's transcripts. Study them, perhaps you can come up with something different."

...........................

Sally got up to get a cup of coffee. Colin asked, "How are you doing?"

"I can't believe that a company with Pritchard in their pocket is almost nonexistent."

"Sally, they're extremely powerful. We have to find out who's in charge."

"I see chicken farmers and exporters of poultry, a private company. The CEO and other officers check out. They all have MBAs, and none of them have anything controversial on their records, solid as a rock. They have 5,356 employees with gross sales of about one billion per year. I don't see anything out of the ordinary."

"Keep looking."

"Tony, did you get your team in place?"

"Yes, but I'm not happy. That block has no cover. I positioned them at either end of the street. If he does come out, one will follow, communicating with the other, and they'll do a standard follow-and-break routine until he stops. They're not field agents, and they have no experience at this."

"Tony, don't worry. If these two are as good as Pete's team, they'll be all right."

"See what you make of today's transcript."

They regrouped in the main sitting room several hours later.

"We have identified two powerful groups, Saris and Liddo, influencing our government at top levels. Our officials are now at odds with each other. The Speaker, the president, the House Majority leader, and several of our top people in both houses have sided with the Saris group. Pritchard's crowd, including the chief of staff, has sided with this Liddo Group. We know nothing else about this division, but we do know this country is in a dangerous place in its history. Can you guys give me a read on this? Sally, you start."

"The only thing I can add is that the Liddo Group in Tennessee has ties to the Liddo Group out of Indonesia. All of their business in Asia seems to run through the Indonesian company. During Viet Nam, the CIA used the Liddo Group to smuggle drugs."

"Shit, are you telling me that this is a CIA operation?"

"No, Colin. The CIA used them because we needed them for intelligence."

Colin went into a rage. "When the hell are these CIA guys going to learn? You don't get intelligence from criminals. You get stupid from criminals. I'm sorry. Go ahead."

"Are you finished, or does that red in your face mean stop?"

"The Liddo Group in the US started in the eighties, and it has a very profitable poultry business, selling both domestically and internationally. It makes better-than-fair profits and has a diverse investment portfolio."

"What do you mean by a diverse portfolio?"

"They're heavily invested in the media, retail companies, and, most recently, energy.

A few hours later, they came to the conclusion that they did not have enough information to take action.

The next morning, Tony met with his team. The girls looked tired, but they still had plenty of info for him. He told them to get some rest. They arranged to meet again later that day.

Tony arrived at the house about an hour later. Colin and Peter were still at it.

Tony was breathless. "You aren't going to believe this. Pritchard frequents a club in town four to five nights a week. He takes home three girls, not one, but three. This could be our chance to get into his place. Tara told me that one of his girls is Pat's friend."

"Great, I'll ask her if she can find out anything about this. Perhaps we can come up with a plan to get one of our team inside."

"No, we're not going to ask any of these girls to do something like that."

"Don't worry, boss. We'll figure something out."

"Yeah, Colin, this could be the break we need."

Peter met with his team as promised. Both girls knew the three women who had gone to Wiley's apartment. "He's one freaky dude," Pat said; she had met him a year ago.

"What do you mean by that?"

"He sits in a chair and drinks himself to sleep. All he wants you to do is walk around naked, or he'll ask you to hug one of the other girls. When he goes to sleep, you get dressed and leave."

"How often does he do this?"

"He does it almost every night, but he pays, up front, $1,000 per girl."

"Can you get into his place tonight?"

Rose answered, "I'll do it. I know all the girls, and I could meet them in the club. They're friends of mine. I'll tell them I need the work."

"Okay, I'll meet you in the morning, and we'll go over the electronics and their proper placement. We'll practice tomorrow.

We will begin with his bathroom. The last time you were there, where did you undress?"

"In the study. That's where he sits."

"Did you have access to any other rooms?"

"We walked around the entire apartment as long as we were naked."

Peter knew the answer but asked, "Can you think of any way to hide something as small as a button on your person while naked."

"I think I can work that out."

Peter told her he would meet her at the Hilton Hotel across from the White House the following morning to practice the placement of the devices, as his face turned red.

While reading the daily transcripts, Peter asked Sally, "Who is this guy Manheim?"

"He seems to be in charge of the Liddo Group, but there's no record of him associated with them. He's not a nice guy. He was special ops in the military, all black bag shit. It was classified and beyond my pay-grade. He was a friend of at least one president. He pays taxes, makes lot of money, but has no known job or business. I'm still working on it. He's a tough nut to crack."

"Is Colin coming over soon? I have something I need to discuss with him."

"He should be here in a few minutes."

Peter studied the previous night's transcript. He was contemplating when he heard Colin come in. "Colin, may I see you for a minute?"

"What's up, Pete?"

"I had a meeting last evening with my team, and they know the girls who went up to Wiley's apartment. In fact, both of them had been there before. Apparently, Wiley uses girls and booze to get to sleep regularly, and he pays them a grand a piece. That's a lot of money for a retired senator. Rose wants to go in and help us plant some bugs."

"Pete, I said no before. We're not going to use these girls that way. If we want this operation to work, we have to be totally legitimate."

"Boss, I'm not asking her to sleep with the guy. He just wants them to walk around his place while he gets drunk. This could be our one chance to hear what goes on behind closed doors."

"Are you certain she wouldn't have to do anything too sleazy?"

"I'm sure of it. We won't be able to use anything we get. It's an illegal tap. However, we do it. I hope to gather enough information from this so that we can investigate further and get them cold."

Colin agreed reluctantly. "This whole affair is beyond comprehension, and I can't see a legal way to end it. I guess we have to be certain of the facts before we can come up with a viable legal outcome. Okay, do it."

Colin called a meeting to discuss the information they had collected. "Let me sum up what we have so far. Wiley is a power broker involved with private sources trying to influence high-level officials. Apparently, he represented two separate groups with the same agenda, but something went wrong. Promises were made that can't be kept to both parties. The chief of staff is on Wiley's team, but the president has gone over to the other side. Neither Wiley nor the chief have control over him. We now know that Wiley, the chief of staff, and some senators and congressmen are on the Liddo side. I believe the president and Speaker of the House and their group of senators and congressmen are on the Saris team. But what is the agenda of each side, and what are they lobbying for? That's the kicker."

"Who's this guy Manheim? He seems to be powerful and probably hooked into Liddo, but we don't know how or why."

"Sally, have you found anything else on this guy?"

"Not much other than he comes out of special ops and was involved in some clandestine secret stuff in Nam. I can't find out where he gets his money or who he's affiliated with. He does live in Little Rock. He was a friend and a very major contributor to several governors and one president. The president broke his leg in Manheim's house several years ago. Other than his military record, he has no past or present."

"That means one of two things. Either he's still working special ops and his entire existence is contrived or he is so powerful that everything's been erased."

They read over a long list of Washington insiders.

"This reads like a 'who's the most powerful person in Washington' list. We have to be very careful now. Any one of these people could stop us for good. What or who is bringing all of these people together?"

"They're probably not together in this. They're probably being used for their individual power bases. The who's, the what's, and why's could be a number of things. It is possible that their cooperation is not voluntary."

"What do you mean by that?"

"Look at Senator Fisher, fourth on the list. I discovered that he was championing casino licensing because they had pictures of him with another man. Congresswoman Howard was pushing a bill totally against her political views. The opposing side found out that, as head of a state organization, she embezzled over a million dollars from it. I would assume that many of the people on this list are in a similar fix."

"That's why Wiley is so damn powerful. He has the dirt on everybody. Let's concentrate on Pritchard, this guy Manheim, the chief of staff, and the Speaker. After tonight, we'll have ears in Wiley's apartment, so we'll only have to use the day team to monitor him. Tony, take your team to Memphis to see what you can dig up on Manheim."

Peter left the safe house and went directly to the hotel to meet Rose. Peter laid out five tiny devices, each the size of a small button. Peter gave her the devices, showed her how to use them, and asked her to practice placing them around the room.

Rose walked over to a picture and started to place a device behind the frame. Peter stopped her. He suggested she try placing one on the inside frame of the table that they were sitting at. He showed her the spot where the underside of the table connected to a leg and suggested that would be an optimum location. Even if someone reached under the table, it would be well hidden.

When he was certain she had their placement down pat, he showed her a tiny plastic sleeve and placed all five devices into it. "Rose, you have to insert this into a body cavity. You'll have to go to the bathroom, take one out, hold it between your fingers, walk out, and place the device unnoticed."

"Don't you think he'll notice frequent trips to the bathroom?"

"If he says anything, tell him you drank too much coffee. He probably won't think anything of it." Rose agreed, and Peter continued their training session.

Three days later, Rose went into action. Wiley had been to the club, and the girls left with him. As soon as they got to the apartment, the girls began to undress and hang their clothes on a rack. Wiley put a bottle of Wild Turkey and a bucket of ice on the table next to his chair. Not a word was said, but the girls knew what he wanted.

After his fourth drink, Rose wandered into the bathroom. She dislodged one of the devices and returned quickly. Wiley glanced at her, almost as if he wanted to touch her. She placed the bug behind a chair leg when he looked away. She got up and walked around the room slowly, looking for a good place to hide the next device. She stood near the door, in sight. She deftly took another device from inside herself without even removing the entire package. She walked over to the large door on the other side of the room. She ran her foot up the side of the door, provocatively. She turned facing it and raised her leg higher and higher until she had to use the hinge as a handhold to keep her balance. She moved back and forth seductively, running her hand and foot up and down the doorjamb. Wiley stared at her hard but never noticed that she had applied the bug on the bottom of the hinge. Rose was enjoying the game.

During the next several hours, she placed the remaining bugs in various parts of the apartment. *Peter will be pleased.*

He was very pleased. Peter told the girls to take the day off and went back to the safe house to see how the equipment was working.

# 48

**Rome, Italy**

John and Ivan were having dinner in an outdoor café near the Palazzo Senatorio, across the street from the Musei Capitolini. They had planned the abduction of the Minister of Commerce and made arrangements to carry it out. After ordering, Ivan said, "John, Rome has a style like no other city. I like it a lot, but I could never live here. The women have style too. They're beautiful. Don't you agree?"

"Yes, I do. There is a definite style to this city, but it's too busy and I find it a bit glitzy."

"What is *glitzy*?"

"Everyone seems a bit too dressed, a little too slick, too stylish."

"John, what is this glitzy?"

"*Glitzy* means 'too smooth, too shiny.'"

"Now I get it. Yes, too glitzy."

John paid the bill, and they went to the deserted garage they'd rented. John saw the van and realized everyone was there. They went in and saw the Minister tied up, sitting in a chair, naked. The doctor had already set up his table of horrors. Ivan walked over and took off his coat.

"Minister, we are going to proceed. I require your undivided attention."

The Minister protested loudly. Ivan calmly took the taser and put it to his neck. The Minister convulsed violently and then vomited.

# GREEN TO RED

"Now that I have your attention, let's proceed. We know that you have acquired large sums of money by assisting the Liddo Group in their business dealings in this country, including trafficking. The Liddo Group put you in the position you hold today. I suggest you answer my questions truthfully or the doctor will administer pain like you have never experienced."

The doctor stood over the minister, visibly erect, holding a surgical instrument in his hand. The Minister started to sweat, his body vibrating.

"Who is the head of the customs agency?"

The Minister answered quickly.

"Good, now I want the names of all the managers of the bonded warehouses."

"I don't know offhand. I have all that information in the office, I swear."

"Okay, who is your contact in the Liddo Group?"

"Ascot Chen."

"Anyone else?"

"No one. Wait, there is a woman. Paula something, she's American. I don't remember her last name."

"Don't lie to me!"

The doctor came forward, laughed as he picked up a pair of pliers from the table, and grabbed the man by one testicle. The Minister screamed, "She lives in London. That's all I know."

Ivan nodded, and the doctor stepped back. "We have killed Ascot Chen, but not before he told us everything we wanted to know. We know where your bank accounts are, where you live, the names of your wife and your mistress. Work with us or you will go down with the ship."

"What do you want me to do?"

"I'm happy to see you're cooperating. Tomorrow you will bring us all the information you have on all of Liddo's operations in Italy. I want trade deals, companies owned, and all the details of the customs agency and their dealings with the bonded warehouses.

I want the shipping manifests of all shipments that have gone through the bonded warehouses this year. Do you understand?"

"I can't get all of that by tomorrow."

"You will. The doctor will be at your office at seven tomorrow night. If you don't have it all, the doctor will assist you. Do I make myself clear?"

The doctor grabbed him by his testicle, and he screamed, "Okay, okay, I will have it all."

As the doctor backed away, the Minister shat himself as piss erupted from his shriveled penis.

...........................................

The doctor picked up twenty cases of documents and delivered them to Ivan and John at the garage. They went through the documents and purchased a copy machine to make two sets, one for Franz in Zurich and one for Chris Artts in Brussels.

That afternoon, John and Ivan flew back to Zurich.

"How did you get all of these Italian government documents?"

Ivan answered, "We asked, and they were given to us."

"I've entered all of the data. The information enabled me to uncover several more accounts."

John instructed Franz to hold off for the moment. "Let Chris bring them down first. Prepare some press releases. Contact your friend, the hacker, and when the time is right, we'll patch into the media head's computer and deposit some money for him from the Saris account. We can kill two birds with one stone."

"John, what do you mean 'two birds with one stone'?"

John replied with a smile, "We'll bring down their smuggling operation *and* cause them to lose faith in their own media operation at the same time and cause problems between Liddo and Saris. We're small, and they are big. We can use that against them. We're unknown, we can cause problems just by making them fight each other."

"John, are you sure you haven't done this before? You would make a good terrorist."

Ivan burst into laughter.

John smiled. "I learned this from an American movie."

"Years of training from the KGB, and I am outsmarted by something learned from watching the American *Cops and Robbers*."

"I traced all of the Liddo accounts in America. I found out that over four billion dollars have been invested in energy companies, all of it legal and binding. It seems that they're going to move soon.

"As you can see from this article in the *Economic Times*, four thousand thirty-four coal-fired energy plants in Western Europe shut down over the past ten years due to carbon emissions.

"Here's an article from the *Wall Street Journal* stating that over five thousand were closed in the US due to new requirements for emission control.

"Lastly, here's an English translation from *Pravda* showing two-thousand-plus Russian plants closed in Eastern Europe since those countries joined the EU.

"As far as we can tell, all of these plants have been purchased in the last eighteen months. They've been purchased by about 150 companies. All of the companies seem to be owned by Liddo, Saris, or one of their subsidiaries."

"Great work, Franz. How did you get all of this so quickly?"

"It's easy when you know about all of the bank accounts. When my friend gets the information on the hedge funds, we'll have to stop for a while. I don't want the bankers to get suspicious. I've gone through Wertshaft und Privat Bank because Tsillman has been busy setting up your bank."

"Franz, does Tsillman know your friend, the hacker?"

"No, why do you ask?"

"I'm not sure yet, but I know Tsillman is involved with these people. He might be able to bring those accounts with him from Wertshaft. If we introduce your friend as a computer consultant, he might be able to set it up so that we can have the information diverted from those accounts without Tsillman's knowledge."

"John, I don't think we can divert the information, but my hacker might be able to install a back door in the firewalls. He'll know for sure."

They worked until three in the morning and were back in the office at 6:00 a.m. John made coffee, and Ivan poured himself a morning vodka. They spent the morning putting together the newspaper articles they found about the raids on drug trafficking involving the Italian Customs Agency and corruption in high places tied to the Liddo Group. One article had been printed as an editorial by Nigel Palfrey, publisher. Nigel was the head of Liddo's media group in Europe. At an earlier date, Franz's friend had hacked into Palfrey's computer and inserted an article. Shortly thereafter, funds were transferred to Palfrey's account from the Saris account acquired from Ascot Chen. It looked like Saris had paid Palfrey for the article.

# 49

### Brussels

Chris Artts was ready to move. The information he had received from John proved invaluable. The team he had put together was comprised of twenty-two people he had worked with in the past. They had all the intel they needed, and he decided that the Italian authorities would not be notified. The plan was complex and needed to work like clockwork.

Once they arrived, they would meet at the Belgian Consulate and pick up the weapons waiting there for them. Ten of them would travel to Leghorn by car. Both teams would hit the warehouses and the customs offices at the same time. Chris would call the Counsel General once everything was under his control. The Consul General would call the Italian Police, informing them that a multinational drug task force had just taken over the bonded warehouses and the customs offices, with the police getting the credit.

It was crunch time. Chris gave the signal to go in. When they had overtaken the guard at the front gate, the opponents opened fire with heavy sophisticated weapons. There was heavy machine gun fire from a tower next to the main building. A sniper permanently disabled the machine gunner with two shots to the head. Chris and his men made their way forward under cover-fire. An armored car crashed through a loading dock door and sped toward them.

One of his team fired a LAW, an M72 grenade launcher. The blast knocked the armored car over and disabled its weapons.

Chris could hear heavy fire from the other side of the building and wondered how that team was doing. They all moved into the main building.

Automatic weapons were being fired in a constant staccato. The team leader in Leghorn reported equally tough resistance. Chris decided to end this now before any of his men were killed.

He told his explosives expert to put together a satchel charge that would do minimal damage and still disable the opponents. He told everyone to drop back and stand outside the building. When the smoke from the blast cleared, there was minimal damage to the building as their opponents staggered outside, hands held above their heads. The employees and customs people, guarded by six of Chris's men, were forced to sit on the ground, hands on top of their heads. Five more were found hidden inside.

Chris walked to the customs office; all the records were intact. He heard police sirens coming closer. He took out a prepaid cell phone. "It's done."

The next day, headlines read: THE LARGEST DRUG BUST IN EUROPEAN HISTORY TIED TO THE LIDDO GROUP AND ITALIAN OFFICIALS.

Several days later, other papers announced: NIGEL PALFREY, MEDIA MOGUL, FOUND DEAD IN HIS HOME—AN APPARENT SUICIDE.

# 50

### Jakarta, Indonesia

Mike Manheim arrived at the home of Y. K. Chen. Paula was already there. YK was quiet, but his rage was uncharacteristically evident. They sat quietly while YK stared as if in a trance. His face was red, almost purple, and the veins on his forehead and temples were engorged, giving him the appearance of wearing a Halloween mask.

"YK, are you all right?"

"I want him dead. I want him brought here, and I want to kill him myself, slowly."

"Saris?"

"Yes, I want him to suffer like no man has ever suffered before."

Paula said calmly, "Let me kill him, YK."

"No man has ever disrespected me like this before. I don't care if we lose this energy business. Screw the green parties, the socialists, and everyone else that he has gotten us involved with."

"YK, you told me not to let anger take over my ability to reason. I agree that this guy has to go, but let's complete the business, allow him to reach his goal and then take it away from him. That would be much sweeter than just killing him.

"Let's wait until we have control of the energy market. Then we can expose his ties to the president and other high-level officials. Then we use our allies in Congress and the Senate to go after him. They'll all be ruined. His dream of being the head of a new world order will collapse around him, along with everyone associated with him. It would be much better to watch that egomaniac go down slowly, only to end up a broken man. The message we send him will impact him where it hurts. No one can do us wrong and get away with it."

YK was silent for a long time. His face had gone back to its normal color.

"You're right, Michael. Thank you for pointing that out to me."

At this point, Mike knew that he could never trust YK again. He knew that he was correct, but it had embarrassed YK; consequences would be deadly—for him.

"Paula, how much damage was done?"

"We've lost the Italian operation completely. That'll cost us about eight billion a year. Our commercial interests in Italy are still intact, but our drug business is over. I've taken care of the media problem. Palfrey committed suicide. I've appointed a brilliant young woman to replace him. The media exposure lasted only a few days and will soon be forgotten. Sarah has assured me that the name *Liddo* will not appear in the press anywhere for the next year. The TV news does not seem concerned, a small blurb last night. I've had several teams of private investigators digging up dirt on politicians in every European country. We'll blanket the media with scandals for the next few weeks. This will soon be forgotten."

"I expect a report on my desk by the end of next week with your plan to recoup the eight billion we can expect to lose yearly."

Paula put her head down and said softly, "It will be done, YK."

"Now, Mike, how are things going in America?"

Mike replied, "It's going well. Saris controls the president, but not directly. He uses the Speaker of the House as liaison. The Deputy Director of the Justice Department is investigating the Speaker covertly. We now have enough dirt to prosecute her. She will be ours soon. We will misdirect Saris and the president in ways that will benefit us. When we take over the energy companies, we will expose Saris and have the president impeached. We will have absolute power once our man is in office."

"Very good, Michael."

YK asked them both to stay for dinner; both declined. Mike and Paula were anxious to get out as soon as possible before YK exploded again.

# 51

**Zurich, Switzerland**

John, Franz, and Ivan were having dinner at the little bistro near Bellevueplatz. Ivan stood up.

"Ivan, you just want the opportunity to toast something."

"If there is vodka nearby, there is opportunity, but I mean what I say. I've never seen a team like this, so small but so effective. You don't realize what we've accomplished here. We started a war between two huge groups, without being detected. Franz's work is abnormal."

"The word is *outstanding*."

"No, there is nothing or no one like it—that means abnormal, yes?"

Franz stood up and toasted, "To us. Ivan, my friend, you have helped me in so many ways. John, thank you for all the trust and opportunity you have given me."

Ivan said, "Wait, I want to change my panties."

*We have become so close.*

When they got back to the house, they made themselves drinks. Ivan quipped, "Good, the party continues."

When they were seated comfortably, Franz said thoughtfully, "We must be careful. If we're found out, everything will go sour. We've been successful only because they're unaware of us."

"Franz, you're right. We sucker punched them but now they'll be on guard."

"John, what is sucker punch?"

"It means they weren't looking when we hit them."

"Now they will have their guard up and it will be harder to hit them."

"Maybe now it's time to go after Saris and really heat things up."

"I'm listening."

"No, I don't think this is a good idea. If we get them in an open fight, they might call a truce and sit down to negotiate. Then they will realize that there is a third party in the game."

Franz commented, "Ivan, you're right. It's a bad idea."

"What is our next move?"

"I think we should get drunk and relax. Let's see what their next move is before we do anything."

The three of them sat, drank, and laughed for the rest of the night.

The next morning, when John got to the bank, Tsillman was busy renovating the offices.

"Peter, how are things going?"

"Wonderfully," Tsillman replied. "Renovations are moving along, and we are ahead of schedule."

John told him he wanted to have a meeting with the human resources group to discuss changes in executive staffing. "Peter, I want you to introduce me to the senior executive staff."

John and Peter decided to host an introductory cocktail party for senior executive and board members at the Baur au Lac hotel in two weeks. John would make a brief speech, then proceed with introductions, with Peter's assistance. Peter took John down to HR to meet with two of the top staff. After introductions, John took a moment to mention that he had hired a very specialized IT professional.

"I've hired him as a consultant with a compensation of 1.2 million per year, plus bonus. Please assign him an office and any additional staff he requires. I know this man, no need for a background check. I will take full responsibility for him. He will answer only to Peter or me. We've set up an office in Hong Kong. I've made arrangements to buy a communications satellite with a direct link to the Chinese, Hong Kong, and Tokyo markets. We'll be able to trade faster than any other European or American bank. If my friend's identity were to leak out, it might ruin our advantage. He is to have total access and will work separately from everyone, understood?"

"John, this will give us an enormous edge in the market."

"I know, Peter. I want you to do what you do best, trade. We should see huge profits. Once we have proven ourselves, money should pour in faster than we can count it."

"John, this is exciting news, don't worry, I'll make us a fortune."

∙∙∙∙∙∙∙∙∙∙∙∙∙∙∙∙∙∙∙∙∙∙∙∙∙∙∙∙∙∙∙∙∙∙∙∙

"Hello, Ms. Paula Franks, this is Peter Tsillman. I am now the managing director of Bank Swizzerveria Americano, and I have exciting news. May I speak to you confidentially? Thank you, this information must remain private. I have had such a long relationship with your group. I felt compelled to call you immediately. The principles of the bank have just acquired their own satellite with direct links to the Chinese, Hong Kong, and Tokyo markets. We will have ability to trade faster than any other financial institution, profits will skyrocket."

Paula knew the ramifications of this news. This would make up for the Italian losses. "Mr. Tsillman, do not call me without an appointment again. Should you wish to discuss this further, call my secretary. I expect to have some free time next week, Friday."

She told her secretary to make an appointment for Tsillman to meet her for lunch at her flat the following Friday.

# 52

## London

When Sara arrived, Paula gave her a gracious welcome. "Sara, please sit down. How is the new position?"

"Mum, I can't believe it. This promotion is unprecedented."

"Unprecedented, but deserved—you gained my trust, and that is very important. I am here to help you acclimate. If you follow my direction, you will do well. As publisher and managing editor of thirty-eight newspapers, twenty-seven magazines, and fourteen television stations throughout Europe, you have to have an equity stake in everything. I've purchased all of the stock from Nigel Palfrey's estate, valued at 7.2 billion dollars. This document turns all of the stock over to you. It is a loan from us to you. It gives us total control of the stock until the loan is paid in full. This document authorizes your compensation at 1.5 million pounds per year, and a bonus, in the form of debt reduction, equal to two percent of the stock. The net effect to you will be total ownership of two percent of the stock per year. Is this acceptable?"

Sara seemed awestruck. "Sara, are you all right?"

Sara shook her head and asked, "Why?"

Paula reached up and touched Sara's face lightly. "You shouldn't ask questions like that. Never let anyone know your thoughts until you have positioned them to your benefit. I will answer that question one time. You are thorough and trustworthy. You showed initiative and drive when you came to me with that information about Saris. This position offers you a whole new world, and there are downsides to it too. You will have to do things that you do not want to. There will be times when you do not agree with something, but you will have to do what you are instructed to do without question. I am offering you an opportunity that very few people will ever have. I have to know that you understand this and that you are willing to do what we ask without hesitation."

"May I call you Paula?"

"Of course."

"Paula, I am not as naïve as I appear. I have done a lot of research, and I understand how things work. I am ready and able to do what you wish. You have my gratitude and complete devotion for giving me this opportunity. I know my shortcomings. I am not as polished as I should be. I don't know enough to run the organization without support and direction, but I am a fast learner. Give me instructions and you can count on them being done as instructed and immediately."

"I knew you were the right person for the job. I'll give you all the assistance you need. You can work out of here for the next month. That way I'll be with you as much as possible. I will also try to give you the polish that you need to be presentable, starting today."

Paula instructed her secretary to make appointments for Sara at the hair salon and several of the best designers. "We are looking for business chic, formal and casual wardrobes, and put a stylist on retainer. Get me the prime minister when you're done with those tasks."

"Mr. Prime Minister, how are you? I need a favor. A very fine young woman, Sara Covington, has taken over for Nigel. Could you be a dear and have her titled? *Lady Covington* has such a nice ring to it, don't you agree? We would like to announce her as the new owner of the Palfrey media empire in three weeks. Oh, thank you. You're such a dear."

"That title will give you immediate credibility."

"Was that really the prime minister?"

"Yes, it was. Now, the new Lady Covington, let's get our hair done."

Paula was happy with her choice. Now she had a protégé, someone she could mold. Sara was brilliant, humble, naïve, and hungry. She had all the attributes Paula needed for this job, the perfect front.

# 53

## Zug, Switzerland

Saris's inner circle attended, about one hundred people representing some of the most wealthy and powerful business, political, and private organizations in the world. Mike Manheim was there representing Liddo, along with Wiley Pritchard and the Speaker. They were discussing upcoming legislation, an integral part of their plan.

They heard a gavel being struck, and the crowd became silent. "He's trying to look like God." Manheim was referring to Saris as he stood up front behind a podium on an elevated box surrounded by blue ethereal lighting.

"Ladies and gentlemen, let me begin by thanking you all for coming. We have traveled a long road to get here. We've almost reached the end of our journey. Shortly, we will embark on a path leading to a new world order, one devoid of hunger, war, poor health care, and archaic fragmented government control. We can look forward to a world government with a global currency, fair trade, and a productive global middle class. We, the successful brilliant all-knowing few, will protect and provide for those unfortunate souls that have worked all their lives with nothing to show for it. With media control, we can sway these masses in any direction. The masses will believe whatever we tell them. By bringing our issues to the forefront, we can make them fight for whatever we tell them to fight for.

"We control all the coal-fired energy production plants in the world now that we have acquired the world's emission credits. According to our figures, we will be able to sell energy to the global market cheaper than our competitors can produce it. Within fourteen months, we will put all of our competitors out of business and then acquire them at drastic capital cost reductions.

"In under two years, we will control the world's energy production. We have already cornered the market on alternative sources. We now control the entire 'alternative energy source' manufactures in the US and Europe through your investment portfolios. We are seeing massive profits from our battery and filter manufacturing since we had the environmental laws passed. We have enjoyed a return of over two thousand percent thanks to our affiliations with the democratic, Green, and socialist parties. Our oil fields in South America, Africa are producing enough to meet world demand. We will be able to take control of Mideast oil within three years of the boycott. No government can function without energy. They must cooperate or we will turn off the switch. Within five years, we will control the world. We will be the ruling class."

Manheim sat there listening to this crap. *This guy is completely off his rocker, but he's damn close to achieving his goal, and I was a major contributor, assisting him. I can't wait until he is dead.* He glanced at the Speaker of the House. *Yeah, lady, you're going down with him and your boss. You're all insane.*

Manheim now realized that their true goal was a world populated by nonproductive people, living in secured poverty, serving this group of self-effaced, spoiled assholes. In Saris's world, the wealthy would control everything. The rest of the population would only exist for their pleasure. Manheim knew that socialism and communism stole the one thing from people that can make them achieve: incentive. Remove incentive and need, and you kill the desire to excel. He remembered visiting the USSR. Everyone was housed, fed, and given medical care; they all looked gray. They laughed, without joy; they complained, but never suffered; housing was substandard; their medical care was lacking; and their food was below acceptable. *That was the most oppressive feeling I have ever experienced.* Manheim twitched back to the real world. Saris stood on stage and waved like a king, and everyone applauded. He glared at him knowing he wouldn't last in the new world, or any world; he knew he had to do something.

# 54

## Washington DC

Colin called a meeting. "We may have a breakthrough. The chief investigator for that big drug bust in Italy is a Belgian, Chris Artts. I called him, and he's willing to share information about Liddo's involvement. I'm flying to Belgium today. I might ask one of you to come over at a later date."

His plane arrived in Brussels at seven in the morning. Artts was waiting for him.

"Colin?"

"Yes. Chris Artts?"

"It's a pleasure to meet you. My car is right outside."

"Chris, congratulations on the drug bust. That was exemplary police work."

"Thanks, but I had a lot of help."

Chris knew he needed to be very careful. "Colin, you mentioned this was an unofficial visit. Why?"

"We have a very sensitive investigation going on in the States. It involves the Liddo Group. I did not tell my superiors I was coming here to meet with you. I hope you understand?"

"I've been there many times. I hate waiting for the go-ahead from bureaucrats."

"Chris, I think we're going to get along quite well."

"I'm going to take you directly to your hotel, and I will meet you there with the information you need. Our headquarters is not secure enough for the task."

Colin smiled to himself. Things were coming together. The ride was pleasant.

Chris dropped Colin off at the hotel and agreed to meet him later that afternoon. "You're going to need to be sharp to digest everything I have for you. Rest up a bit."

The room was perfect for the task ahead. He lay down, took a nap, and was showering when he heard someone at the door. "Chris, come in. I'm taking a shower. Make yourself comfortable."

Chris already had papers spread out on the table. Chris handed Colin the papers, one at a time, explaining each one in chronological order. Colin admired the intel this man possessed and the thoroughness of his work. "I'm impressed. You've done great work here."

Colin noticed hesitation on Chris's part, but didn't push it. "Chris, are you hungry? I'm starving, would you like something to eat? I can order room service."

"I have a better idea. I know of a good restaurant not far from here."

"Great, I'd like to see some of the city."

They had a pleasant lunch. Colin liked this man. He wished he could level with him, but there was too much at stake. Colin didn't know that Chris felt the same way about him.

Chris asked bluntly, "Does your investigation have anything to do with the Liddo Group?"

"Somewhat, they seem to be on the fringes, but we do not have much information on them. They appear legitimate on paper."

Chris decided to push the envelope. "Have you found a connection to Saris?"

Colin went pale. "Saris?"

"Colin, I'm also meeting with you without the knowledge of my superiors. We must be honest with each other now."

"Chris, what do you mean by that?"

"I have a lot more information, but I must be certain we're on the same team before I give you everything."

"Okay, I'll level with you, but if any of this comes to light, I will deny it all."

"I understand fully."

Colin took a deep breath and began. "I'm working on my own with a small group of trusted agents. We uncovered information that points to people in my government working with Liddo and Saris. We cannot investigate openly, but we are certain it goes to the highest levels."

"I already know. It goes all the way to your president. I have the same information linking Liddo and Saris to several high-level officials in your government." Chris produced several more documents.

Colin went pale. "Are you shitting me? Where did you get this?"

"Colin, I cannot divulge my sources just yet, but I know this is a serious. These people are trying to start a new world order. They seem to be close, and no one has noticed."

"Chris, please give me everything you have. I am working outside of the agency, but I still have access to powerful resources. If there is anything I can do to help you stop this, let me know. The small group I have working with me are the best in the business."

"Colin, rest easy today. Let me contact my sources to see if they'll meet with you. I'll be back tomorrow morning."

Chris called Franz. "Franz, Chris here. I have something that might be useful. The deputy director of the FBI is here, and I'm exchanging information with him. It is imperative that he meet with all of you right away. I'll explain the rest in person. You know I wouldn't do this if I didn't think it was important."

As he pulled away, Chris told Colin he couldn't say anything about their destination. Seven hours in the car gave them a better opportunity to get to know each other.

# 55

**Zurich, Switzerland**

They arrived in Zurich in midafternoon and checked into the Hotel Central.

Chris met Franz at the armory restaurant off of Bahnhoffstrasse. "Franz, it's good to see you again."

"So, who is he anyway?"

"Colin is the deputy director of the FBI. His group came across some information that led them to believe their highest levels of government have been compromised. They don't know who to trust within their own government. Franz, I know you understand this."

"Yes, I understand, but how do you know we can trust him? How do you know he hasn't been sent here to find us out?"

"Franz, just know we can trust him."

"Chris, that has always been enough for me, but let's go slow on this one. We can't afford to fail. Let me meet him first, we'll feel him out before we introduce him to the group, okay?"

"Franz, that's fine with me."

They knocked on Colin's door. When he answered it, he appeared surprised. "Franz, how are you?"

"You two know each other?"

"Yes, when I got into trouble, he tried to help me."

"Franz, that was a setup, and everyone knew it. I was sorry to see them use you as the sacrificial lamb."

"Colin, I never had a chance to thank you for trying to help me. You were one of the few."

"Colin, the people we are involved with now are the same people who destroyed me. You know how devious and well protected they are. Before we go any further, I must be certain that you're going to do what you say you will. I hate to grill you, but this situation is too important. The lives of my friends are at stake, and I will not do anything or trust anyone that might put them in jeopardy."

"Franz, I understand. I'll tell you everything. You're right. I'm in the same position. I don't know who I can trust either."

Colin told them about the chief of staff, Wiley, and all the events that brought him to this point. "Gentlemen, if this conversation was leaked, I would be tried for treason, and lose my job of course."

"Colin, I trust you, but I must be sure. Leave everything here. We'll go to the airport right now. I want to meet your people before we go any further. I cannot allow you to communicate with anyone until we're there."

"Perfect, let's go."

# 56

**Washington DC**

Franz and Colin took a taxi to an address ten blocks from the safe house. Franz asked, "Why are we walking?"

"Taxies keep records. We don't want a record floating around. It's a safe house after all."

Sally and Tony went for their guns. "Settle down, people, this is Franz. He's an old friend. He's going to be working with us. Is Peter here?"

"Right here, boss,"

"My trip was productive. Our suspicions are correct. Saris and the Liddo Group are in charge. Franz and his group have been quietly, successfully doing what we're attempting to do here. The drug bust in Italy was accomplished with information supplied by Franz and his group. I'm going to ask Franz to interview each of you. Please cooperate fully. I have to confirm certain things that I have discussed with him. Franz, start with Peter. The rest of you, get out!"

Several hours later, Franz completed his interviews. He told Colin he was convinced and apologized. Colin asked Franz to work with Sally, their communications expert. Within an hour, Franz was able to find several flaws with her system. He suggested they use prepaid phones and destroy them after every conversation. Colin took the advice seriously.

Colin called the director and told him he would be gone for at least three days. He would bring him up to speed when he got back. Then he called the chief of staff.

"Hello, Rob. Colin. I've just uncovered something about the Speaker. I'll be back to you by the end of the week."

# 57

### Zurich, Switzerland

John was waiting for them. "John, this is Colin. He's the deputy director of the FBI and a friend of mine."

"Colin, it's a pleasure to meet you. I hope you don't mind staying at my house while you're here. It will be more convenient."

"Not at all, I appreciate the hospitality."

John introduced Colin.

"Hello, nice to meet you. John, we're almost out of vodka."

John assured him that he would take care of it.

"Good, with all of these extra people around, the vodka will go fast."

When they walked to the office, Colin was amazed. "Holy shit, even the FBI doesn't have all this equipment. I'm impressed, how the hell did you put all this together?"

"Franz and Ivan did it all."

After a few days spent bringing Colin up to speed, they decided to go forward jointly and tried to plan accordingly.

"I have an idea, but first, I need vodka."

"Ivan, I'll get it. Please continue."

"We've been successful because we stayed under the radar. I've been in many operations, and the more people you have, the more complicated it gets. Eventually, someone lets the dog out of the sack."

"Colin, he means cat out of the bag."

"I think we should work separately and exchange information constantly."

Colin said, "Ivan, I agree. But how do we do that without being monitored?"

"Wait, I will show you. I brought this from my house yesterday."

"What the hell is that, Ivan?"

"This is a digital blast transmitter."

"What?"

This time, Franz answered, "It'll take either audio or print information and consolidates it into a digital blast, which can travel over the airwaves or telephone lines at amazing speed. If it's picked up by someone, other than the intended person, it'll sound like a loud scream and disappear. You have to prearrange a frequency in order to receive the information properly. The equipment unscrambles the digital signal and turns it into a printed message."

Ivan laughed and said, "I never knew all that."

Colin asked, "Ivan, where did you get this?"

"From the KGB."

Colin asked him again, "No, seriously, where did you get it?"

John answered, "Colin, drop it."

Franz went shopping to buy components needed to make modified copies of Ivan's machine. He assembled them, making them look sleeker, including computer logos to fool curious airport personnel.

"I've set all three machines to the same frequency so that they'll work over an Ethernet line or wireless. You can input four hundred pages of printed data and two hours of audio. It'll digitize the information and send a coded signal to the receiver in one-fifth of a second. It will unscramble the data in less than five seconds—and a bonus, it's hacker-proof. Ivan, this was a stroke of genius."

"Okay, good. You buy the next case of vodka." They all laughed.

"All right, Chris and Colin, I want you both to take one of these machines with you and we'll keep one here. Let's play it safe, transmit information at different times. Colin, have your group transmit on the even hours, Chris, on the odd hours. We'll consolidate all the information and send it on the half hour. Franz, is there an easy way to consolidate what we have and transmit it to these guys?"

"No, but I can reduce it to categories and transmit each category. It will probably take three days, transmitting every half hour."

"Okay, then no one will send anything to us until Franz completes that task. Chris, Colin, when you get back, buy prepaid phones. This may seem like overkill, but tough times and tough people call for tough measures."

Chris and Colin agreed.

Later that evening, Colin strolled out onto the terrace.

"Hello, John, am I disturbing you?"

"No, would you like a drink?"

"Scotch and water would be great."

"What do you think of my band of merry men?"

"John, you guys are extraordinary. I never thought private citizens would be able to undertake something like this. Franz told me about some of your escapades in Hong Kong. By the way, I'm sorry about your friend, the girl who was killed. It was big news for about a week. Nothing lasts long in the public eye."

"That's because they control the media. Those bastards think they can do anything and get away with it. I won't stop until they've been eradicated, ground to dust."

"I cannot believe no one knows what's going on other than the perps. I agree with you completely."

"Colin, we're in this together for the fight of our lives, up against opponents that have entire governments backing them. They have untold resources and near-complete invisibility. I barely survived my last battle with them. I'm going to destroy them this time."

"John, you're a good man. I'm with you to the end. We'll bring these people down. I'm not going to let our world end like this. I'm doing this outside the agency so we can do what has to be done without political interference."

John sat quietly for a long time. "I'm glad you're on my side."

John and Colin got up and headed back to the office. Chris and Franz were working on the computers; Ivan was reading data on the SMART Boards.

"Gentlemen, we'll work together in this fight. We must be at the top of our game. We have to pool our resources, but act independently. Our opponents are powerful and almost invisible. They are huge, but they have segmented themselves using commercial entities of all sizes and descriptions. They're all connected but not closely related. We know there's a problem between the two groups, and we've been using that, but it's only a matter of time before we are found out."

"John, maybe I can help with that. We know that the president and Speaker of the House are allied with Saris. Wiley Pritchard, a heavy-handed ex-senator, and the chief of staff are trying to gain control of the president. Perhaps they are linked with the Liddo Group. Now, what are they doing, what is the connection, and where does Liddo fit in?"

John asked Franz to bring up the connections they had made on the SMART Boards.

"Look at this. It appears that Saris is connected to the Green Party. The Liddo Group has the unions and is funding the socialist parties. Both groups have funded the purchases of the emissions credits. The Liddo Group owns all the energy companies. That has to be the connection."

"What are you getting at, Chris?"

Chris answered, "There seems to be a connection between these emission credits and the energy companies."

"Of course. The energy companies need the Green parties to rally around them. If Saris is trying to start a new world order, he might be using the energy companies to pull it together. He would need Liddo's muscle and their union control."

"Franz, how could they use energy and the unions?"

"Gentlemen, Liddo has money, political backing, and control of major unions—that means votes. Saris controls the European conglomerates and the Green movement, which means government regulations and control. When you put them all together, you have a very plausible scenario for global takeover."

"I still don't get it."

This time, Colin answered, "If these two groups control the unions and the Green and socialist parties, then they have enough votes to win any election in Europe. If they control the major conglomerates, they control Europe. They've gotten some control in the US by funding the DNC. They have political power over the president and other top officials. They have purchased all of the coal-fired power plants in the US, that's why they bought all of those emission credits. They're going to take control of the power. What they cannot do politically, they will do with coercion and threats."

"It is incredible that they have gotten this far without being noticed."

Colin interjected, "They're not only close, but they're doing it. They've played on the emotions of the liberals using noble ideals like 'save the planet,' only to destroy or enslave it."

Franz spoke up. They've used what Americans call "political correctness" to disarm their opponents. Their champions don't even realize they will be the slaves used to enrich and empower these few people."

John was really pissed. "They haven't taken over yet and they never will, not as long as I'm alive."

His intensity was mesmerizing, and they all knew they were with him to the bitter end.

They all decided to unwind and go up to the terrace and have a drink. They agreed to relax for now and meet in the morning to formalize an action plan.

They sat up there enjoying the camaraderie of men joined together in common conflict, a bond only appreciated by men who have faced death together. They knew they were entering a fight with little chance of survival. They were on the side of good in a battle against evil; it empowered them.

They decided that nothing would be done until all the information was exchanged, analyzed, and understood by all three groups. Once Chris and Colin were comfortable with the information and John's group had time to digest it from them, he would call on a particular prepaid phone, let it ring twice, hang up, call back, and let it ring once. Only after that would their plan be implemented.

As Franz drove Chris and Colin to the airport, they went over some last-minute details. They said their good-byes. All three were thinking the same thing. *Will I ever see these guys again?* They were in for a rough ride.

John and Ivan were at the house. Ivan looked more serious than John had ever seen him.

"John, I think the plan is good, but we will not remain invisible for long. When they know who we are, they will come at us with everything they have. Are you certain you don't want my friends at the KGB to get involved?"

"No, the more people involved, the more problems we'll have."

"Okay, I understand." Ivan said without arguing. "John, one suggestion: I think we should be prepared to go mobile. I can set up a series of safe houses across Europe, but I don't know what Franz will have to do to make all the equipment portable."

John agreed, an action plan was formulated. Franz reduced the entire computer system to two laptops and a couple of external hard drives in a custom-made suitcase. Franz encoded the information and segmented it onto three separate data sticks. He configured them so that one had to piggyback on the other two to work. That was all the redundancy he could come up with. Franz, John, and Ivan would each carry a data stick on their person. If the main system was lost or destroyed, Franz would be able to decode and reconfigure the information with a piece of software, kept by the hacker.

Ivan traveled across Europe renting criteria-specific safe houses from his contacts. Ivan installed a custom security system in each flat, with shutters on all windows. Ivan was working on a flat in Budapest when he had an idea while looking out at the Danube. He made a mental note to tell John to have a boat placed near every safe house. Before he left each location, he purchased city maps and walked the area around each house. After determining the best escape route, he marked it on the map with a black permanent pen, using other colors for alternate routes.

When Ivan returned to Zurich, he gave the information to Franz, who input it onto handheld GPSs. Franz also installed his "self-destruct" software with remote access capability.

John met with Ivan and Franz to review any new information received from Chris and Colin. The information was minimal other than transcripts of the conversation between Pritchard and the chief of staff. With that in mind, John said, "I don't think this changes anything, so I'm going to give the go-ahead to start implementing our plan. I would assume we'll get through phase one with no trouble. Be prepared for the worst after that. While you guys initiate phase one, I'm going to the States. I want to see Utsie."

"John, do you think that's a good idea?"

"Well, I don't think anyone knows about us. No one seems to be looking for Utsie. I don't think I'll put her in harm's way by seeing her, and I want to get more insight into Gruber before we implement phase two. Before I leave, I'll start phase one."

# 58

## San Francisco

John's flight to San Francisco seemed to go quickly. He thought about the plan over and over, and by the time the plane landed, he was certain they had covered everything.

Peter met him at the airport. On the ride back to Sailcraft, John gave Peter an update.

"John, are you serious? These people have gotten to the highest levels of our government?"

John responded gravely, "No, Peter. They've gotten to the highest levels of many governments."

Peter shook his head. "John, don't you think this is a little over your head?"

"Peter, this is over anyone's head. The director of the FBI and his deputy are working on this secretly. Who do you trust in a situation like this? I don't want to tell you anymore. The less you know, the better. I need Utsie's address. I'll stay here for two days, and then I'm going back to Zurich. But in reality, I'm going to visit Utsie for a few days. This will be the last time you see me until it's all over."

When Peter and John arrived at the office, Iris and Brad were waiting for them. They ran to him and flung their arms around him.

"Is this any way to treat your boss?" They stepped back quickly. John laughed and threw his arms around them. Iris spoke first, "We've planned a 'welcome home' party for you. I'm doing the cooking. We already brought everything to your house. Tonight we're having a feast."

"We have some good news for you. We'll tell you tonight."

"I think I know what it is, but I'll wait until tonight."

The four of them took a tour of the facility. John couldn't believe how it had changed. It was three to four times larger than he remembered it. Brad told him all about new manufacturing techniques and, thanks to Iris, new software. Brad showed John the new computer system and explained how it was used to achieve reductions in production time.

John smiled widely. "Brad, I'm impressed. Iris and you are doing a great job. I saw last month's sales figures. You seem to be doing very well in that department also."

Peter interrupted, "John, could I see you in my office?"

The smile left John's face as he replied, "Sure, Peter, I'll be right there. Brad, I'll see you tonight."

"What's up, Peter?"

"John, here's the location of the young lady we discussed earlier." Peter handed John a note and continued, "John, I want to hire a security firm to set up a system here. What do you think?"

"Peter, I don't think that's a good idea. If we set up security now, it might appear that everyone here is involved. I'd rather let people think I work alone. No one knows what we're doing yet, but it's only a matter of time until they do. I'll be on the run soon, that's why I want to see Utsie now. It might be a good idea to hire some bodyguards for you, Brad, and Iris. Take this card, these guys are the best. Don't say anything to Brad or Iris. I'd rather they know nothing at all."

"Whatever you think is best."

"Peter, I'm sorry about all this, but it has to be done. If anything gets out of control, call Colin Young, he'll help you. Don't ask me anything about him."

John walked into his house and was surprised by the preparations that had been made for the party. He went to his room, threw his suitcase in the corner, and went to bed.

John couldn't believe it. The entire company seemed to be there. Brad was tending bar, and Iris was busy in the kitchen preparing food, pushing out hors d'oeuvres as fast as they could be eaten. The party had been scheduled from 6:00–9:00 p.m., so they were all gone by nine-thirty; only Peter, Brad, and Iris were left.

"I hope you didn't eat too much. I've prepared a gourmet meal for just us."

John moaned, "I think I can manage a little more." As they sat at the table, John made a comment to Brad about how happy he was to see that he had continued to dress well.

"I have to look good at all times. My fiancé won't have it any other way."

John jumped up. "You two are getting married!"

"Yes, and I want you to give me away."

"Give you away? Yes, of course, I'd be honored. I'm so happy and proud of both of you." *This is not a good time for a marriage.* John said quickly, "You're both young, and I have a favor to ask of you. Could you wait one year?"

They both said at the same time, "What?"

John improvised, "This has been an exciting year for all of us. I'd like things to settle down before you make this commitment. I couldn't think of a better match, but I'm getting old and cautious."

Peter broke in, "John, I think that's a good idea. I agree, a year is not a long time, and if anything, I think it could make their relationship stronger."

Brad spoke first, "That wasn't the response we were expecting, but it makes sense."

Iris chimed in, "I agree." She jumped up and gave John a big hug.

"It's set then, a year from now. You guys start making plans. I'm paying for the wedding. Anywhere you want, just make the arrangements."

It was almost three in the morning when they left. All John could think about was their safety when the shit hit the fan.

Before John left for New York, he told Brad he had left some money with Peter for any prewedding necessities. "I'm going to be busy for the next few months, Peter will take care of anything you need. I'm going to be moving around, so you might not hear from me. I want you guys to enjoy yourselves, don't spare any expense on the wedding."

"John, you're too good to us," Iris cried.

"Nonsense, you two have done a great job, I'm only showing my appreciation."

Peter drove him to the airport. His parting words were, "I'd tell you to take care of yourself, but I know better."

# 59

**New York**

John kept thinking about the possibility of harm coming to Peter or the kids. He called Ivan.

"It's John, Ivan. Do you have any muscle here in the States?"

Ivan told him that he had a few reliable people who could handle covert protection.

"Ivan, get them on the job. Peter, Iris, and Brad are to be protected at all costs." When he finished his call, he destroyed the phone as previously planned.

It took about an hour for him to get through the airport and rent a car. Within fifteen minutes, he was at the Fire Island ferry.

John had never been to Fire Island and was surprised to see that it was not the usual beach community. The area he was going to was accessible only by foot. He found the address and walked toward the house. He bent down to tie his shoe, looking in both directions. Certain it was safe, he went to the door and rang the bell. He waited; there was no answer, so he walked around the house, onto the beach. There she was, sitting in a beach chair, reading. He approached her, heart racing.

"Utsie, what does a guy have to do to get a drink around here?"

Utsie was startled, jumped up, threw her arms around his neck, and kissed him hard. "John, it's so good to see you. I missed you terribly."

John pulled away from her gently.

"I missed you too. Let me take a look at you. The beach seems to agree with you. You're stunning."

Utsie was quivering. "I don't ever want to leave you again. Let's go inside." Once inside, she looked at him seductively, undressing.

Several hours later, Utsie asked John if he'd like to go out for dinner. "There are some good seafood restaurants just down the walk."

The restaurant was cozy, had a nice atmosphere, but was almost empty. During dinner, John told Utsie about Iris and Brad, how excited he was for them. Utsie laughed. "You really think of those two as your kids, don't you?"

"Yes, I guess I do."

The beach, at that time, was deserted and beautiful. It was a great night for a walk.

When they got back to the house, Utsie made drinks for them. They settled on the sofa.

"John, what's happening? Am I safe yet?"

"Yes, I think you are right now, but the situation may soon change for the worse."

He explained recent events and told her she would have to stay there for a while longer.

"This is a safe place. Only Peter and I know you are here." He gave Utsie several prepaid phones to be used only in an emergency. "Only use each phone once and then destroy it. The numbers I've given you will connect you with Franz, Ivan, or me. If you're in real danger, call, let it ring once, hang up, and then dial again. We'll have men nearby to protect you. They'll identify themselves by saying 'pleasant peasant.' Follow their instructions, and they'll keep you safe. They are friends of Ivan's. Now, I need some more information from you. What more can you tell me about Gruber?"

"I knew him in school as I told you. I lived with him at University. We broke up because he became sullen and mean. He was involved with the communists and the socialists. He became more and more frustrated with life as he tried to change things. I didn't keep in touch with him for over a year after we separated.

During that time, I had heard he had become an important figure in the Socialist Party. I found out later that Helmut was responsible for his success in the party."

"How was Helmut involved?"

"I'm not sure, but he told me himself that he had arranged for a group to fund Gruber."

"Why would he help Gruber if they were political opposites?"

"I don't know. I always assumed they were friends."

"Utsie, is there anything, or anyone, you can tell me about that will give me some more insight?"

Utsie thought for a while. "Yes, there's a woman, Yvette Prochard. She was involved with him politically since the beginning. She moved in with him shortly after I left. She's one of those bitter, angry people who always think they're morally superior. I never liked her. She lives in Bremen."

John called Ivan. He told John it wouldn't be hard to locate her; the doctor would be only too happy to help them. John told Ivan he should do whatever was necessary to get as much information as possible from her.

John and Utsie devoted their time to each other, putting all of the madness out of their heads. They ate, drank, and made love as if they hadn't a care in the world. Alas, John told Utsie he was leaving the next day. Utsie teared up. "John, tell me the truth. Will I ever see you again?"

"Utsie, I've been up against these people before and survived. I know who they are. Don't worry, I'll make it, and we'll be together as soon as it's over." John leaned over and kissed her. She held him very tight. They fell asleep in each other's arms.

John gave Utsie some last-minute instructions, packed his bag, and headed for the ferry. It was hard for him to leave; he really wasn't sure if he would ever see her again.

He was at the airport in minutes and on a flight back to Zurich within hours.

# 60

## Zurich

Franz and Ivan were waiting for him as he exited the terminal. On the drive back, Franz told him, "John, everything went according to plan."

John said that he wanted to discuss it further when they got back to the office.

The information was up on the SMART Boards. "John, everything went as planned with no backlash. Apparently, we're still an unknown entity. Chris was able to convince his friends in the EU Intelligence Agency to investigate the new girl in charge of Liddo's media empire. Liddo lent her the money to take over, in the form of a stock chattel. If she doesn't pay off the loan in time, the stock reverts back to them. She's bright, young, and pretty but has no prior experience. She was formally employed as a researcher. She researched Aristotle Saris almost exclusively. Her name is Sara Covington. She's very worried about the investigation."

"That's good. She'll be on her toes. Her contacts at Liddo will be leery about contacting her for a while."

"We were able to divert a large contribution from Saris, that was going to the DNC account, directly into one of the Speaker's accounts. We notified Colin, he gave the information to the FBI director, a formal investigation has been initiated. We also diverted some money from the Saris account to Wiley Pritchard, and then we had a bank executive inform Mike Manheim."

"How the hell did you do that?"

Franz told him that one of Colin's people was able to do it. He threatened to investigate the bank executive.

"Excellent. I was a little nervous about their participation. It looks like it will work."

"We were also able to put a permanent undetectable trace on all known Liddo accounts. This will help us figure out the money flow."

Franz walked to the next board. "We hacked into Saris's computer and installed a worm. Everyone in his address book was sent random information. This won't do much more than raise a lot of questions, but it will cause some problems. We had money transferred from the Socialist Party's account back into Saris's account, the one that he used to fund it originally. We instructed Helmut to notify key party delegates about the mishandling of funds by Gruber. Helmut took it one step further and tried to go public with it, but the media won't touch the story."

"Let's take a break. I want to digest this information before we continue." John went into the kitchen and made a pot of coffee.

John brought the coffee and some pastries up to the terrace.

"What's all of this going to accomplish?"

Franz answered, "It'll cause enough problems so that they'll have to come out into the open. It will give us an opportunity to get a better understanding of their operations and how they interact."

Ivan retorted, "I see this, but could it not have the opposite effect?"

"Ivan, what do you mean by that?"

"I was thinking, once they are aware of all of these problems, they might go to ground."

"No, won't happen, that's why we've done what we've done—to make it look like an internal fight. Everything we have done to Liddo appears to have been done by Saris. The things we have done to Saris look like retaliation from Liddo."

"Once they've been in bed with one another, it won't take long for them to make up. After the kissing stops, they'll realize they have been duped and start looking for the true antagonists."

"Franz, I think Ivan has a valid point. Let's suspend phase two until the dust settles."

"Okay, that's probably the prudent thing to do."

John told Franz and Ivan they had done a superb job. "I only have one question. About the information you received from Colin, what is this bit about the 457 plants condemned?"

"Sorry, John, I forgot, you weren't here for that. When we deciphered the information, we found a report from the American EPA. It was initiated by Colin through a friend of his in the EPA. They inspected, at Colin's request, all of the coal-fired plants recently purchased by Liddo subsidiaries, and they condemned 457 out of 1,200. They'll have to make enormous capital investments in order to operate them. We'll monitor any fund transfers in or out of those companies."

"That will put a crimp in their style. I like Colin more and more."

John asked Franz, "Can you summarize this? I'd like to discuss each point tomorrow. I want to get to know their operations thoroughly."

Franz agreed and went right to work.

John asked Ivan to stay with him on the terrace. John poured drinks, bourbon for himself, a large glass full of vodka for Ivan. "John, you're getting to know me too well."

"Ivan, I wanted to talk to you alone. I need to know how much danger I'm getting everyone into here? That includes Utsie, Iris, Peter, Brad, and us."

"John, honestly, we're all going to be in danger. I can keep your friends in America safe, but the rest of us are going to be in a very tough spot."

"Ivan, if you want to get out now, I'll understand. I'm going to ask Franz the same thing. This is my fight. I don't want you to think you owe me anything."

"John, what do you think I am, a woman? I would never leave. This is not just your fight. If these people are successful, the world will be hell to live in."

"I knew you'd say that, but I had to ask for my own selfish reasons."

Ivan laughed. "I know, my friend. You did not want to feel guilty if we're killed. But not to worry, I will take care of your friends in the States. They will be safe. You have my word on it."

"Thank you, Ivan."

"Thank you, nothing. You will pay. I don't know anyone else who can afford to keep me in vodka." Ivan slapped John on the back very hard. He sat back down. "We have Gruber's girlfriend. The doctor took her to Bremerhaven. He has her in a warehouse near the docks. I think he has already started the interrogation. He told me she was beautiful."

"Please, don't tell me any more."

"John, what information do you want?"

"I need to know if Gruber's involved with Liddo. We already know he's involved with Saris, but we don't know if he is involved with Liddo. If he is, we need to know what that involvement entails. I would also like to know what part the Socialist Party is going to play in this new world. Ivan, identify yourself as KGB. It will be good for them to think that the Russian government is interested in what they're doing."

"You don't want her killed?"

"Ivan, we're after the main players only. I want the least amount of casualties possible. I think it will have more effect on Gruber if he knows he is not invincible, even with his friends behind him."

"You're the boss. Now let's have more vodka."

After another round, Ivan said, "John, I'll fly to Bremerhaven in the morning. When I'm done, I'll call you on the paid-for phone."

John interrupted, "You mean prepaid phone."

"Yes, prepaid, and then I'll fly directly to the States to set up the protection myself."

"Thank you, Ivan, you are a true friend."

# 61

### Jakarta, Indonesia

Mike Manheim went straight to Chen's home office after his sixteen-hour flight. When Manheim arrived at the house, he heard Chen screaming and knew that this was not going to be a pleasant experience.

Manheim sat in the chair in front of Chen's desk, looking up at him. Chen sat there staring for almost thirty minutes. Finally he said, "Is Saris crazy? Why is he doing this to me? I want him to die a slow agonizing death right now." Manheim tried to speak, but Chen cut him off. "Do you hear me, Michael? I want him dead, and I want him dead now!"

Manheim began to sweat and spoke in a low steady voice, as Chen's neck muscles bulged and his face turned purple, "YK, you must calm down."

Chen screamed, "Don't tell me to calm down! Saris has made fools of us all. I have spent my entire life building an organization that was invincible because it was invisible. Saris has unmasked us. He is crazy, and I want him dead. I will not allow you, or anyone else, to delay this, Michael. Do you understand what I am saying to you?"

Manheim shifted nervously as he spoke, "YK, we have to be careful here. We have too much invested in this to have it fall apart now."

"Michael, do not try to talk me out of this. He's a dead man. I want that pompous ass to die miserably in lingering pain."

"YK, could we discuss this further over dinner? I haven't eaten since yesterday."

"Of course, Michael. I apologize for not being a better host, but this situation with Saris has gone too far." Chen picked up the intercom.

After several quiet minutes, Manheim said, "YK, if this goes down the tubes, we're going to lose over five trillion dollars. I don't know if we can sustain that."

Manheim could see that he was calming down. Chen looked at him, rage dissipating slowly. "Well, Michael, then what do you propose?"

"YK, I'd like to meet with Saris and try to talk some sense into him. We need his contacts in Europe and his control over the president and the DNC. Once we've taken over the energy business, we can kill him. There are some other pressing problems that I wanted to discuss with you."

"Michael, let's talk about those matters during dinner." With that, he rose and led Manheim into the dining room.

While waiting for the second course, Chen said, "Michael, you mentioned other pressing matters. What are they?"

"YK, I have some disturbing news. Just before I left, I had a message from one of my banking contacts. Wiley just received a five-million-dollar wire transfer from Saris."

Chen stiffened and ripped his napkin in half. Trying to compose himself, he asked, "Michael, do you think Wiley would betray us? He knows we have a lot on him, including the video of him with that thirteen-year-old girl."

"I don't know. I haven't had a chance to talk to him yet, but he knows I wouldn't hesitate to kill him for that."

"Wiley has his problems, but I think he knows it would be a mistake to betray us." Chen hesitated and then continued, "But he might take sides if he thought we were having serious problems."

"The Justice Department has just subpoenaed the Speaker of the House and her husband. Evidently, they traced a large transfer from Saris and linked her to several federally-funded contracts received by her husband's company. As you know, she was the conduit between Saris and the president. Saris might be going to Wiley to take over her position as his communicator."

"Michael, this is all so unfortunate. We're so close to our goal, yet our partners seem to be falling apart. When you get back, talk to Wiley. If you believe he's involved with Saris, have him killed."

"When I get back, I'll visit Wiley, and if I'm not satisfied with his story, I'll kill him myself."

After dinner, they retired to the study for some port and cigars. Chen lit his cigar and asked, "How would you handle Saris?"

"First, I would have a talk with him. If I couldn't convince him to stop what he's doing, I would kill him and try to recover our losses."

"Very good, Michael. Paula has been monitoring Saris for the past two months. Why don't you visit her first? Get her ideas on the subject. Then visit Saris. Sara Covington is in charge of our media holdings in Europe. Visit her as well. She is an expert on all things Saris. See what she knows. Then develop a plan to take over Saris's holdings, before and after his demise."

"I'll go back to the States to take care of Wiley first."

"Excellent."

Manheim felt relaxed by the time the plane lifted off. Manheim was glad that YK didn't hold him responsible for the problems they were experiencing. *I hope YK doesn't blame me for all this, or does he?*

The plane landed at Dulles airport. "Mike, are you on a secure phone?" asked Wiley. "If not, call me as soon as you can."

"That will not be necessary. I'm in Washington."

"What! Where are you?"

"I've just landed. I'm on the way to your place."

"Great, I'll see you in half an hour."

Wiley let him in. "Mike, we're in deep shit. I just received a five-million-dollar transfer from Saris."

"What for?"

Wiley panicked. "I don't know. I called him back, but he won't take my calls. I haven't seen or heard from him in months. I think it has something to do with the Speaker. She received a wire transfer too, and she's being indicted."

"Wiley, are you saying Saris set her up?"

"Mike, I don't know. That's the scary part."

Manheim thought about it for a while. "How does Saris benefit by cutting off his access to the president? If he's doing this to you too, he would have no leverage over the government. That doesn't make sense, unless he's really gone insane. I'm going to see him in a few days. Start thinking about how we can gain control. In the meantime, go to the retreat in the Dominican Republic. I'll contact you when I get back."

Manheim flew to Memphis and made arrangements to pay Paula a visit.

# 62

### Washington DC

When Colin arrived at the safe house, he asked Sally, "What's going on?"

"It worked. Manheim just left Pritchard's house. They're running scared."

"Where are the tapes? Get everyone into the meeting room."

Sally played the surveillance tape. "Who do we have in the DR?"

Tony replied, "No one, but I know a Dominican who does surveillance. We used him on a couple of drug cases. He's good."

"Good, get him down there right away. Does anyone know what this retreat is?"

Sally answered, "Yes, it's a private resort owned by Liddo. They use it to entertain clients."

"Okay, give all the information to Tony's guy and get him in there before Wiley arrives."

Colin went into his private office. "John, this is Colin. Phase one is complete, it's a success. Manheim just met with Wiley, they're scared and confused. Manheim is on his way to London to meet with Saris."

"That's great. Send a report through the blaster." Colin went back to the main part of the house and found Sally.

"Get me the flight plans for Manheim's plane."

"Tony, is there any way we can bug Manheim's plane without getting caught?"

Tony thought for a minute. "Colin, I don't know, but I do know someone who would know."

"Good. Get on it. See if you can have the plane bugged before they take off tomorrow."

About an hour later. "It's done. We can bug the plane without detection. My guy informed the pilot that they're having an FAA inspection before they take off. He'll install the device when he's doing the electronics check."

Colin had a great team, and he appreciated it. "Good work, Tony. I have to get back. I have a meeting with the chief of staff. I'll see you tonight."

Colin arrived at the restaurant before Rob and arranged for a private room. "You work fast, Colin. I didn't expect you to indict her, good job."

"I was only doing my job." Colin said humbly. *I really hate this guy.*

Rob had a big grin on his face. "This makes the Speaker powerless for the time being. When this is over, we will do some damage control and things will be back to normal. You'll be the director very soon."

Seething inside, Rob said, "Yeah, Rob, I wanted to talk to you about that. I don't want to take the position yet. If I take over now, I'd have to lock up the Speaker, and I don't want to do that. If I stay in my position for a while, I can direct things better to achieve a favorable outcome. However, if you would like to compensate me in another way, I would be amenable."

"You old dog, you are one of us. Where do you want the money sent?"

"Deliver it to me personally, in cash."

# 63

### Zurich, Switzerland

John left his meeting with Tsillman. Tsillman had brought many of his clients with him; progress was being made. Business was up almost 22 percent. Tsillman was especially excited today. He had received a call from Paula Franks; she wanted to move all of her accounts to the Bank Swizziferia Americano.

Tsillman told him this would put them in charge of over a trillion dollars. "I was surprised when she called me. I didn't think she liked me." John told Tsillman that it was probably his expertise that she was interested in. *I don't like you either.*

John thought that this would make monitoring Liddo's accounts much easier. He arrived at the house to find Franz, Ivan, and Chris present. "Chris, what are you doing here?"

"I was in the neighborhood and thought I'd drop in."

"Seriously, what are you doing here?"

"Chris came across some information, and he didn't want to send it over the airwaves."

"What could be that important?"

"I know you received the same data burst from Colin that I did, but they missed a few things. Manheim was Paula Frank's boyfriend. He's seeing her before he goes to see Saris. The reason this young girl, Sara Covington, was a researcher and the world's foremost expert on Saris. I've taken the liberty of bugging her office and her home. I'm certain that Manheim will visit her as well as Paula. I'm hoping we'll be able to find out some of Saris's flaws and exploit them."

"Chris, can we get a direct feed from those bugs?"

Franz answered, "Yes, we can. I've just set it up. We don't want a direct feed or we could get caught, so I've rigged it so the data bursts will send audio. There will be about a thirty-second delay, but it will work."

"That's great. I had some interesting news today. Chris, I'm glad you're here. Tsillman just informed me that Liddo's moving all of their accounts to our bank."

The next several hours were spent deciding how to handle the monitoring of Liddo's assets. John decided to take a break. "Good, let's have some vodka."

"We finished interrogating Gruber's girlfriend."

"Were you able to get what I was looking for?"

"Yes, we got quite a bit of information from her. The socialists are being funded by Saris. There is another low-level group of about fourteen-thousand strong directly funded by the Liddo Group. They use them for muscle mostly, but for the past six months, they've been sent in to Yemen to be trained in terrorism and military operations. In Europe, they are acting in small cells and are directed by Gruber. In the US, they are members of the Black Muslims and community action groups. Their direction comes from the White House."

"What, the White House?"

"Yes, several of the so-called czars are in full control. Gruber answers to both Liddo and Saris separately. She told us that our friend Helmut Fragge set it up. Before she died—"

John cut him off, "She's dead?"

"Yes, she died, but not before telling us that Gruber is not a socialist. He is a very wealthy man, and all of his money is in the Westminster Bank in Cyprus."

"We've already hacked in. His account is being monitored as we speak. If we can tie any of that money into an illegal operation, we have him."

Chris spoke up, "Yes, John, now that Gruber is an international political figure in Europe, my friends at the EUIA can go after him. He will probably get off, but he will no longer be of use to Saris or Liddo."

"This is good news."

"It's great news. If Saris and Liddo lose the support of the socialists, they'll have a major problem with the unions. As far as these paramilitary groups are concerned, we can start arresting them as terrorists. They'll know we're watching them even though we won't be able to hold them very long."

# 64

**London, England**

Manheim's plane landed at London's Heathrow. Paula was waiting. "Mike, it's so good to see you. I thought we'd go back to my place first for some rough sex. I really missed you."

Manheim said very little.

"Nice place. Did you decorate it yourself?"

"No, darling, I had a decorator come in."

Paula lost her clothes as they walked through the apartment and was completely naked when they reached the living room. Manheim turned to see her, slapped her in the face, and knocked her down. She started to get up, but he kicked her hard in the stomach, and she fell again. He reached down, pulled her up by her hair, and slapped her again, this time cutting her lip. Paula stood in front of him defiantly and licked the blood off her lips. Manheim stepped forward, picked her up, threw her onto the couch, and took her violently.

When it was over, he got up and walked to the bathroom to take a shower. "I really missed you."

"I missed you too."

*I missed her, she may be sick and wild, but I still don't trust her.*

She brought him into a fully equipped office. She had all of the tapes of Saris's conversations ready for him to play and in chronological order. She told him that she was going out for a while. "We can discuss them when I get back. I shouldn't be more than an hour." When she left, Mike listened to the tapes and made notes about locations and timelines.

Paula came back.

"You went to get your hair done?"

"I wanted to look beautiful for you."

*She really is sick.*

Paula walked over, opened a desk drawer, took out a file, and handed it to him. "Mike, here's the transcript of all the tapes you just listened to. I'll come back to discuss it with you after I put dinner on."

They started to discuss the tapes; the oven alarm went off. "Dinner's ready. Do you want to have it here so we can keep working?"

They worked a good portion of the night, then went to the bedroom and spent the rest of the evening having brutal, but satisfying, sex.

Mike was in the shower when the shower door opened. He almost lunged at her, but he saw the cup of coffee in her hand. He took it. "Thanks." She did not say a word; she just turned and left the room. Mike had just met Sara Covington.

·····················

Mike found Paula in the living room going over spreadsheets.

"Good morning, Mike. Did you sleep well?"

He noticed the bruise on her face, but didn't say anything, "Yes, I slept well."

The rest of the morning was spent discussing Saris.

Manheim scratched his head. "I know it doesn't add up. There's nothing in these tapes to confirm that the guy is trying to destroy us. Paula, what's your take on this?"

"I don't know. He seems reasonable, except for the fact that he that wants to be king of the world. He's either gone completely mad or someone else is pulling the strings."

"Even though YK doesn't agree with you, I do. Saris is not stupid. He knows that we would go after him and is afraid of just that." The phone rang, and Paula went to answer it. When she came back, she told Manheim that it was the attorney.

"They want to interview Sara again, what a pain in the ass."

"Why did you pick Sara for the position, rather than someone else?"

"I didn't want to deal with some self-important asshole that would try to play me all the time. This kid is hungry, tough, and I trust her."

Mike decided to tread lightly. "Do you think it would be valuable for me to speak with her? I heard she's the foremost expert on Saris."

"Sure, it would be good for you to meet with her. She knows everything about Saris. She might be able to give you some more insight." Paula picked up the phone and called her. "You can meet her at four this afternoon. She'll come here."

Sara arrived on time. Mike was surprised, she was very young, especially for the position she held: managing director of Europe Media Enterprises.

"Hello, Mr. Manheim. My name is Sara Covington; we met last evening in the shower."

"Ah, yes, Paula has told me that you know a lot about Aristotle Saris. Can you tell me more about him?"

"Why, Mr. Manheim?"

Mike was taken aback, and it showed.

"I mean, sir, what are you looking for? Are you negotiating a contract or just meeting him for the first time?"

Manheim smiled. "Good question. I've known Aristotle in a business sense for years. I have entered into a partnership with him, and it's not going well. I want to know a bit more about him before I see him tomorrow."

She described the circumstances that brought him to international prominence and gave Mike a laundry list of his idiosyncrasies. After two hours, she finished with a succinct summary. Mike tuned in on her last statement. "Saris believes he can do anything."

Mike thanked her profusely. "The least I can do is take you two ladies to dinner. Where would you like to go?"

Sara declined. "I'm sorry, Mr. Manheim, but I have a previous engagement. Perhaps, we can have dinner together another time?"

"She's young, but very smart."

Mike sat going over the notes he had taken. He told Paula that he was leaving for Monaco in the morning to meet with Saris. "Well, let's make the most out of the rest of your visit." She started to walk toward the bedroom, discarding her clothes as she walked.

"This is Manheim, wheels up at eight fifteen sharp."

They landed in Monaco before ten.

# 65

**EU Headquarters, Brussels**

Chris was trying to figure out the best way to disseminate the information he had collected. After some investigation, he discovered SITCEN, the European Union's Joint Situation Center. It was a fledgling in the intelligence community; it had been set up to work with INTDIV (the Intelligence Division) of the European Military Staff, the EUSC (the EU Satellite Center), and Europol. All of these agencies together formed the EU Intelligence Agency.

Chris called some of his friends at EU Headquarters and learned that the head of SITCEN was a woman, Raquel Fuchaurd. A meeting was set up for 10:00 a.m. two days later. Because of the situation, Chris told his boss he was taking a few days off, but not why.

Chris drove to Brussels the following day and booked into a hotel. He arrived at EU headquarters at ten sharp the next morning. Raquel walked in and introduced herself fifteen minutes later.

She was extremely attractive, well-built, and perfectly proportioned. Chris introduced himself. He was led to a small conference room down the hall.

"Monsieur Artts, what can I do for you?"

He told her guardedly, "Recently, I've uncovered some information that is detrimental to many countries throughout Europe. I want to share that information with an agency that can disseminate it quickly and efficiently."

"Monsieur Artts—"

"Please call me Chris. May I call you Raquel?"

"Certainly, we are rather informal here. Chris, may I be frank with you?"

"Please do."

She continued, "If this information is valuable, you might have just saved my job."

Chris was interested. "How is that?"

"As you may know, this agency was only set up to appease the Americans. They put a lot of pressure on the EU to centralize intelligence as part of their war on terror. After we were set up, it didn't take long before discussions started to disband us. The INTDIV and Europol are fighting to keep us around. They know there's a real need for us, but the bureaucrats in the Hague believe differently. I need a good case to change their minds."

Chris was surprised that she told him but realized it must be common knowledge there. He decided to continue. Chris told her the entire story from the drug bust in Italy to the present.

"I'm not here on behalf of my agency. I'm offering this information as a concerned European."

"Understood, I will present it to my people just that way. Chris, can you stay for the night? I'd like you to present this information to them tomorrow."

Chris thanked her for her time and candor. "Will you join me for dinner this evening? I don't know anyone here."

Raquel knew that was a lie, but decided, "Yes, I'd be delighted." She wrote the name of a restaurant on a Post-It. "I'll see you at eight."

Chris walked back to the hotel, went to his room, and jotted down information for his upcoming presentation to Raquel's group. He was awakened from his nap, took a shower, dressed, and went down to the lobby. The clerk told him the restaurant was only four short blocks away.

He arrived at the restaurant forty minutes early, so he continued to walk. The streets were lined on both sides with cafes, small bistros, and heavy pedestrian traffic. He was ready to return when he saw Raquel sitting in a bistro, having a heated conversation with the American CIA station chief from the Hague. Chris had met him several times at diplomatic functions. He watched them for a while then headed back toward the restaurant.

He was immediately shown to a table. Raquel was late. It gave him some time to think. *Is she setting me up? Did she just give my information to the CIA?* These questions were going through his mind when she arrived. Chris knew he would have to be careful.

"Chris, I'm so sorry I am late. I had a previous appointment and couldn't get away."

"Raquel, you look beautiful."

Raquel blushed. "Thank you."

"I'm sorry. I'm not usually that forward. It just came out."

Seeing his discomfort, she said, "That's quite all right, Chris. I think you're very attractive." She felt awkward as well. Just then, the waiter came and asked if they were ready to order.

"Raquel, I need your assurance that the information I'm giving you will not be given to the Americans."

"I'm sorry, but I cannot guarantee that. It is our job to disseminate information to all the security and intelligence agencies in Europe. Once we do that, you can be assured that the Americans will get the information."

"Do you give information directly to the Americans?"

"Yes, we exchange information. I just left the CIA station chief. No one gives information to the Americans without getting something back in return, but whatever you give them is always more than they give you."

Chris was relieved. "Raquel, I have my reasons. I need your assurance that you will not give the Americans this information directly."

"I can see that this is important to you. I will assure you that we will honor your wishes. We will also ask any agency that we deal with to do so, but I can't promise you they'll honor the request."

"I can't ask for more than that."

"Good, I trust them. You'll meet them tomorrow at ten o'clock."

After dessert and coffee, Chris told Raquel that he was looking forward to tomorrow's meeting.

"Do you like to dance?"

"Excuse me?"

Raquel repeated the question. "Do you like to dance? There's a great club around the corner."

"Ah, ah, yes, I do like to dance. That sounds great."

They went to several clubs; Raquel was a good dancer and easy on the eyes.

Raquel drove Chris back to the hotel about three in the morning. He told her that he'd had a great time.

"Chris, I think I am going to enjoy working with you very much."

He waited only minutes before Raquel walked in.

·····················

"Bonjour, Chris, please follow me."

He followed her down a labyrinth of narrow hallways to a conference room with an LED over the door. Raquel flipped a switch, "Room in use." All security measures and soundproofing in use. The room was comfortable and functional. There were two men already seated.

"Colonel Hugh Foster, Her Majesty's Royal Marines, formerly of the British SAS, this is Francois Dubois, formally of Interpol. Gentlemen, this is Chris Artts, of the Belgium Intelligence Agency, although he's here on his own."

Colonel Foster was the first to speak. "Chris Artts, are you the same gent who just organized and implemented the drug bust in Italy?"

"Yes, I am."

"Well done. Brilliant!"

"Gentlemen, I'm going to set up some ground rules before we start. First, Monsieur Artts is supplying this information of his own volition. We will not push him for more than he's willing to supply, no notes will be taken or recorded during this meeting. Is that understood and acceptable?"

They nodded.

"Secondly, none of this information is to be supplied directly to the Americans."

"Agreed."

"Good. Chris, the floor is all yours."

"During the drug bust, I came across some information that is so sensitive that I could not disclose it to my agency. I did discuss the matter with several field agents, friends of mine. I came to the conclusion that giving you this information will slow the overall progress of the protagonists down to a point where they can be dealt with. For this reason, I may or may not answer all of your questions."

Chris went on. "During that raid, we found evidence that there are paramilitary groups stationed in Europe. These men, over four thousand to be exact, have been highly trained in Yemen in the latest terrorist and military science techniques. They have been strategically placed around Europe in groups of one hundred. They work in four-man teams, each team works with a specialist, all controlled by Gregory Gruber of the National Socialist Party."

"Oh, that's a sticky wicket. He's the front runner in the next Swiss election."

"Yes, and the National Green Party is involved as well."

Dubois spoke, "This is very interesting. We must proceed cautiously. If the Socialist and Green parties are behind this, we can be assured that many European government officials are involved. It will be difficult to stop this."

"Gentlemen, I think we should adjourn for today, think about the possibilities, and reconvene tomorrow."

Once in the lobby, she asked, "Chris, are you free for lunch? I'll pick you up outside your hotel at one o'clock."

He left his hotel, walked to a park, and sat on an out-of-the-way bench. He pressed speed dial. "Hello, Franz? It's Chris."

After giving Franz a brief report, he destroyed the phone and walked back to the hotel.

Raquel pulled up in a brand-new Land Rover. "They must pay you people very well. I drive a Mini."

"This is from the motor pool. It's one of the perks we get." She drove out of the city for about thirty kilometers and turned down a dirt road. Chris started to feel nervous.

"Where are we going?"

"My place." They were parked in front of a nice little farmhouse.

"I wanted as much privacy as possible so that we can speak openly." She prepared some dishes of dried beef, cheese, and bread and put a bottle of wine and two glasses on the table.

"Chris, I met with Hugh and Francois after you left the office. Due to the fact that the Green and Socialist parties have joined together and have paramilitary forces in place, we are viewing this as a top-priority threat against the EU. Because of the political aspects, we have to be very careful about how we proceed. We want you to come to work for SITCEN."

Chris started to object, but Raquel said, "Hear me out. We want to borrow you from your agency on a temporary basis. This will free you up from political interference and you will have the use of cross-agency mobility."

"Let me think about it."

They finished lunch, and Raquel asked, "Are you free for dinner tonight?"

"Yes."

"Great, if I drop you at your hotel, can you check out later and find your way back here on your own? I'll cook a nice dinner for us."

Chris accepted.

"Fine, here is my cell number. If you get lost, call me. I'll be home about six."

Chris picked up his car and bought a bottle of wine. He had no trouble finding his way back. He found Raquel in the kitchen preparing dinner. As he handed her a glass of wine, she leaned forward and gave him a kiss on the cheek. He flushed. She told him to sit. He watched her scurry around the kitchen, noting how beautiful she was. He liked everything about her.

During dinner, they discussed many topics, mostly they bitched about the bureaucrats they had to deal with. After dinner, Chris helped clean up. They then went into the living room; she poured a glass of port.

"I've thought about your suggestion, and I agree—with certain conditions."

Raquel smiled. "What are the conditions?"

Chris answered, "I'll work independently with assistance only when I request it. No one will press me for more information than I offer them, and I must have full use of your agency's resources."

Raquel was quiet for several minutes. "Agreed. I will call your superiors tomorrow and make the formal request. I will tell them we have a situation involving cross-border drug dealing and we need your expertise. Is that acceptable?"

"Yes."

It was almost two in the morning when Raquel showed him the guest room. Chris said good-night. She leaned toward him and kissed him on the cheek once again.

Chris woke up around six, took a shower, dressed, and went for a walk. Raquel was still asleep. The scenery was beautiful. When he got back, Raquel was up, dressed, and had put on a pot of coffee.

"Bonjour, Chris. I have to run. Can you find your own way home?"

He smiled. "Yes, I actually live close by."

"Good, when are you going into the office?"

Chris answered, "Tomorrow."

Raquel told him that she should have everything worked out by the end of the day. "When will I see you again?"

"Monday, I have a few things to wrap up before I can join your team."

Raquel kissed him on the cheek. "I'll see you then, au revoir."

Chris arrived at his office the following morning. He cleaned up the paperwork on his desk and went in to see his boss. The head of his agency told him that he had been placed on indefinite temporary loan to SITCEN.

He reported to SITCEN early Monday morning and was shown to his office. Hugh Foster gave him a tour of the place and told him there was a team meeting at one o'clock. Chris felt good about his new job. *This is a good match, and I really like my new boss.*

# 66

## Monaco

Manheim drove up to the castle, two heavily armed guards stood at the entrance. "Mr. Manheim, you are expected. Please proceed to the portico."

Two more guards were positioned there; one of them opened his car door. Aristotle Saris stood in the open doorway.

Mike composed himself and smiled. "Aristotle, you look well."

Saris shook Manheim's hand. "Mike, I'm so glad to see you. We have much to discuss."

Saris led him to a solarium on the far side of the building. Saris was pleasant, but Manheim could see that he was uncomfortable. "Mike, care for a drink?"

Saris lost control before Mike could reply.

"Mike, what the hell are you people doing? We're so close and you're attacking me? This last incident cost me millions and I've lost some of my political connections."

"Aristotle, I was going to ask you the same thing."

"Mike, what the hell do you mean? You people have screwed this up just because I got too close to the president."

*Could he be on the level?* He decided to hit him head-on. "Why have you been attacking us? Don't you know you're putting the entire plan at risk? Furthermore—"

"Mike, what are you talking about? You've attacked me. My position with the Americans is now in jeopardy."

"Wait a minute, are you telling me you had nothing to do with current events?"

"Mike, are you insane? Why would I put everything in jeopardy when we're so close to our goal?"

Both men were confused; there was no trust between them, so neither would give credibility to the other's story.

Manheim finally spoke, "If you didn't do this, that means someone else did, but who?"

"No one else could have done these things. Only you knew how to hurt me like this."

Manheim, convinced that Saris was being genuine, said, "Hold on, Aristotle! If both of us are being manipulated, then someone else has gotten critical information. This is serious. We've been compromised. Is there anyone in your organization that might have this information? Who has the authority to transfer funds from your reserve accounts?"

"No one, I'm the only signer."

"Did you transfer money to the head of our media division?"

"Never. What are you talking about?"

Manheim was upset. "Shit, Aristotle, someone is gunning for both of us. They want us to fight amongst ourselves. I'm going back to the States to compile a list of transfers that we know came out of your accounts. I'll call you and go over them with you."

Manheim was in a plane in less than an hour. He called YK and told him the situation was more serious than they had thought. "This is serious. The damage that's already been done could only have been done by powerful people capable of amassing large amounts of covert intel. It has to have been a government agency. We're in trouble, YK."

"If it is a government agency, we should be able to squash it before it goes any further. Michael, find out who's behind this."

"I'll start as soon as I land, YK."

# 67

### Zurich, Switzerland

Ivan and John were together for three to four hours per day. Ivan wanted John to be prepared.

John was learning martial arts and spy craft from Ivan, which blew his mind, primarily evasive in nature. Ivan explained that their opponents had a lot of resources and there was no way they could fight them directly.

Ivan instructed him on the making of small explosives from household items. "They're not meant to immobilize your opponents, but very useful if escape is paramount."

Ivan also showed him how to use his problem-solving skills against his opponents.

John had just finished a training session when he received a call from Tsillman. "John, are you available to meet Paula Franks, the woman I told you about? I think you should meet her."

"Peter, what time is the meeting?"

"I'm not sure, but she did say she would be in Zurich tomorrow afternoon."

"I'll be at the bank tomorrow, call me when she arrives."

......................................

"John, do you have a minute? I have a very important client with me, and I thought you would like to meet her."

"I'll be right in."

"Hello, I'm John Moore, a senior board member here. If there's anything I can do for you, please let me know."

"You are American?"

"Yes, and I see you are too."

Paula smiled seductively. "There is something you can do for me. Accompany me to dinner this evening."

Reluctantly John said, "It would be my pleasure. Where are you staying?"

"I'm at the Baur au Lac. Pick me up around eight?"

John told her that would be fine and that he knew the perfect place to dine.

"Thank you, Peter, I will see you tomorrow to finalize the transfers. Please have someone bring me back to the hotel."

Tsillman had obviously been dismissed by this woman, his face deep red, even though he was the president of the bank. "Peter, do you think I'll make it back alive? This one looks dangerous."

"Better you than me, John." They both laughed, and Tsillman asked, "John, may I speak to you privately?"

"John, before we accept these funds, I want to be honest with you. Ms. Franks is the European head of the Liddo Group. She controls a lot of money, but I cannot guarantee where it comes from. Wertshaft made a lot of money from that account and we never had a problem, but I wanted to inform you before we continue."

"Then I see no reason to worry about it. I appreciate your honesty, Peter."

When John returned home, he asked Franz and Ivan to join him in the office. "Liddo has just put all their money into our bank. Tsillman was their account manager for fifteen years. I'm having dinner tonight with the head of the Liddo Group in Europe, Paula Franks."

Franz highlighted her name on the SMART Board. "What do we know about her?"

"Jackpot, I see she only answers to Y. K. Chen. She was Mike Manheim's girlfriend. She's at the top of the heap."

Ivan asked John, "If you go out with her, how does that benefit us?"

"Good point. I don't know, but I'm committed."

"It won't hurt to get to know her. The better you know your enemies, the better your chances are to beat them."

"Franz, that is true, but soon she will be thinking the same thing. John, you might want to play her."

"In what way, Ivan?"

"Tonight, do not act like yourself, act more like Tsillman. She'll think you're weak."

"You mean act like a pompous ass?" He laughed.

"Yes, you understand exactly, now let's have vodka."

...........................................

John arrived at eight. He left the car with the doorman and went into the lobby. Paula was sitting at a small table sipping a cup of coffee. John had decided not to act like Tsillman; he did not think he could do it.

"Good evening, John. Would you like a cup of coffee before we go to dinner?"

"Paula, thank you, but no, please finish yours."

"Would you like to walk to the restaurant? It's only a few short blocks away, and it's a nice evening." They began to stroll down the walkway along the lake, exchanging small talk. She seemed a lot more pleasant than she had been at the bank. They were given a table; John pointed out some of his favorite dishes. "Paula, I know this restaurant very well. Would you like me to order for you?"

"No, thank you, I always order my own meals."

John realized right then that this woman wanted to be in charge.

The meal was pleasant. After coffee, Paula looked John right in the eye. "John, I know who you are, and I know what the Liddo Group has done to you. I'm sorry for the loss of your friend."

For once, John was tongue-tied, he didn't know what to say, but he felt rage rising from deep within. He fought the rage and appeared to stay calm. *Is this a test, or is this a threat?* He started to say something, but Paula cut him off. "John, not here. Is there somewhere we can talk privately?"

"Yes, I have a boat tied up not too far from here."

John paid the bill, and they left. They were at the berth within minutes. This was a private pier. There were four boats tied to it. Paula realized this was John's showroom; she asked him, "Are these all your boats?"

"Yes." She followed him to the last boat, the largest of the four. They boarded, John brought her into the saloon. John walked over to the bar and started to pour a drink. "What would you like?"

"Bourbon, straight up."

John handed her the drink and sat across from her, waiting for her to begin. Paula tried to talk about trivialities, but John didn't reply. Paula looked directly at him. "John, I feel bad about what my group has done to you. I don't know if you are aware, but you're only alive because they realized how profitable your business is to them."

"Why are you telling me this?"

"I don't approve of some of their methods. Liddo has an enormous network of businesses that, if used correctly, could be even better. I was an assistant to the head of the Liddo Group, and overtime, I gained his trust and was given this position. I might not be a good person, but I want to change things for the better. Liddo has made you a wealthy man. I need your help."

"Are you kidding me? Why the hell would you think I would have anything to do with Liddo? It's been the bane of my existence."

"You knew the orders that you were receiving were from us. Don't get too moral with me. Money is money no matter where it comes from."

John was now infuriated. "That's bullshit. I didn't know Liddo was behind those orders until after the fact."

Paula knew she had pushed the wrong button. "John, I'm sorry. I'm a bit on edge. You know these people are dangerous. I have to be very careful in everything I do."

"Then why do you do it?"

"It's a long story."

"I have all night."

Paula told John her whole story from the man who abused her, to the whorehouse, Chen's rescue, the Manheim affair, and her use as a spy. "Now I can make enough money so that no one will ever be able to take advantage of me again."

"That's some story, but how does that pertain to you asking me for help?"

Paula answered him a little too quickly, "I want to change things, to do the right thing. Liddo could be a great business and use its resources to help people, rather than hurt them."

John began to laugh, and he saw a flash of anger in her eyes.

Paula said softly, "I guess it is laughable, but I can't do it alone. I need your help," looking like a little lost girl.

John pulled away as she tried to kiss him. "Look, if you want me to help you, don't play me. I'm telling you up front that I don't trust you, or anything about you. If you really want my help, you're going to have to earn my trust. You deal in a world I find deplorable. I can see how you wound up in it, but don't think I'm going to roll over because you're beautiful and have given me that 'poor, helpless girl' routine."

"I don't blame you, but the story is true. John, you're a brutally honest man. I'm sorry, I was playing you. Truthfully, you are the only person I know that has survived them. You know how dangerous they are and that they will stop at nothing to get what they want. I'm leveling with you when I say I want to change things. They've built an empire using brutal methods, but there is no real need for them now. The men in charge are ruthless and dangerous. I'm afraid that if I do try to change things, I'll be their next target. I have no one else to turn to—no allies outside of the

Liddo Group. That could be dangerous for me. I have no one to watch my back."

"I'm not convinced. I'm not going to say anything one way or the other. I might change my mind at a later date, but until then, I won't trust you. If you don't want to give our bank your business, I'll understand. It will break Tsillman's heart, but it makes no difference to me."

"John, I'm not used to dealing with honest men. If you'll work with me, I will try to earn your trust."

"Fair enough." John dropped her off at her hotel. "John, it's been a pleasure. I'm looking forward to working with you."

"Good night."

When she was out of sight, he paid the driver, got out, and waited for his car to be brought around. He knew he would have to discuss this with Ivan and Franz before he could put it all into perspective; she confused him like no one else ever had.

John called Franz and Ivan and asked them to meet him in the office. John walked into the office carrying coffee and buns on a tray. "Coffee and cake? I'd better get some vodka. This doesn't look good."

John sat down and asked Franz to bring up Paula Franks on the SMART Board. John told them every detail about what had just transpired. Ivan made the first comment.

"Don't trust her. We now have to go with the idea that they know about us. I'll arrange for security first thing tomorrow."

"But what if she's on the level?"

"John, how can you be that naïve?"

John was a little annoyed. "I'm not going to take any chances or even give her the benefit of doubt, but what if she is trying to get out? How can we use that?"

"Good point. Let's work on some scenarios, just in case, you never know."

Paula put her things away and picked up her cell phone to call YK. As she sipped a drink, she thought, *He's an honest man in this world of creeps.* She put the phone down; she decided to hold off on the call. *Perhaps I can use John if I get the chance.* Pleased with herself, she drew a bath, poured a glass of champagne, and relaxed for the rest of the evening.

# 68

### London, England

Paula entered the building; the concierge called to her, "Ms. Franks, a Mr. Manheim was here looking for you. He's staying at the Grovesnor House, room 437." Paula thanked him and gave him a tip.

*What the hell does he want now?* She called the Grovesnor House as soon as she entered her flat. "Mr. Manheim please, room 437."

"Mike, what are you doing here?"

"Paula, I have to talk to you, I'll be there in twenty minutes."

She didn't like the sound of that, so she changed her clothes and placed a gun under the cushion of her chair, just in case.

She opened the door; he pushed past her. She followed him into the living room. "Mike, what's wrong?" He walked over and made himself a drink. She said sarcastically, "Make yourself at home."

He turned, looked at her, and said with a scowl. "Don't give me any of that shit. We have a major problem."

Manheim told her what had transpired in Monaco. "Are you telling me that Saris is not behind all the shit we have been getting lately?"

"That's exactly what I'm telling you. I don't have a clue who's behind all of this."

Paula sat in her chair. "YK is not going to be happy."

"Paula, don't state the obvious. I wanted to talk to you before I talk to him. Do you have any ideas who could it be?"

"No, but it would have to be someone in Saris's organization. The money came from his accounts. I verified that myself."

"Paula, Saris told me that only he had access to those particular accounts."

"Then it has to be someone telling the bank to do it. Tsillman is corrupt enough to do something like that for the right price."

"Yeah, but it didn't come from his bank."

"Mike, the point I was trying to make is that if Tsillman could do it, why not some other banker?"

"Well, I guess that's a good place to start. Do you know where the money was transferred from?"

"Yes, from the Bank of America branch in Geneva."

"Thanks, I'll start there. Can I use your secure phone? I might as well get this over with. I'll call YK."

"Go ahead. I have some things to do." She left the room.

......................................

"Mike, how did it go?"

"How do you think it went?" he asked sarcastically. "I have to go to Geneva. Do you have any muscle there?"

She handed him a card from her Rolodex. "These guys have always been effective. They were Ascot's people."

Manheim took the card, said good-bye, and walked out the door.

Later that evening, Paula was still thinking about what had transpired when it dawned on her. *Holy shit! John Moore, could he be behind all this? He's too straight, and he doesn't have the experience to pull off something like this. Tsillman, he became the president of the bank just as all this started, and that son of a bitch has the knowledge and wherewithal to do something like this.*

By morning, she had come up with some plausible ideas. First, Tsillman was Fragge's friend, whom Saris tried to kill. Secondly, he could be easily corrupted, and finally, his new boss hated the Liddo Group.

Paula called Sara Covington and asked her if she could come over right away.

"Sara dear, I need you to do a quiet investigation of these two men: John Moore, an American yacht builder and Peter Tsillman, a Swiss banker. I need all the information you can get on them, but I don't want anyone to know I'm making queries."

Sara told Paula she would have the information by the end of the week.

"Thank you, darling. You're such a dear."

Paula walked her to the door. Sara realized she was being dismissed, smiled, and said, "Anything for you, Paula."

# 69

### Washington DC

Colin got a full report on the coal-fired energy plants that had been fined or closed down. One of his connections informed him that they were told not to cooperate with his investigation. The directive came from the top. He was infuriated.

He met with the director, who told him the EPA was told to stand down. The director also told Colin that the president and the Speaker were backing a huge environmental initiative, one that, if passed, would give a few companies unbelievable power just before cap and trade became a reality.

The director wrote this down on paper: "I'll meet you at the house tonight."

Sally met Colin at the door. "I hope that pizza is for us. I'm starving."

Tony and Peter were there. Tony got up and went into the kitchen to get some drinks. They sat at the dining room table and filled Colin in on the day's events.

Shortly before ten, the director arrived. "Those sons of bitches are destroying this country. We need to speed things up. Some congressmen have no regard for the constitution at all. Czars and community groups are writing our laws and dictating policy. That's nuts."

"Do you want some pizza? It's almost gone."

The director sat at the table, grabbed a slice, and was just about to bite into it when Colin yelled, "Holy shit! Look at this. The chief of staff met with one of the so-called community groups and was told that another four hundred soldiers were ready to be released from prison. The chief told them it wouldn't be a problem thanks to the executive order to reduce prison population by twenty thousand. Do you believe they are training these people in prison? The soldiers, once released, are being hired by community groups funded by tax dollars. Unbelievable."

The director asked Colin if he could speak with him alone. They went into the other room. "Now everything we do has to be approved by the attorney general, and we've been ordered not to give any information to Homeland Security. Colin, I think they're going to move soon. This environmental initiative, coupled with the fact that they seem to be beefing up their community organizers—everything points to a final push.

"I just got an info blast from Chris. It looks like they're getting ready in Europe as well. Chris told us that two thousand well-trained men have been scattered throughout Europe and there is double that number here in the States. I'm going to Europe to meet with Chris and his group in Zurich in two days. We just found out that there is a meeting between the chief of staff, the American socialists, the Green Party, and several union leaders tomorrow, but we don't know where it will take place."

"Colin, see what you can find out and keep me informed."

# 70

### Zurich, Switzerland

Ivan was using some of his old colleagues to put John through the paces, including evasion tactics, seizure and escape maneuvers, and some lethal arts as well. "John, I'm glad you're not older and worked for your government."

"What do you mean by that, Ivan?"

"John, if you worked for your government long ago, we would have been fighting against each other. I don't think I would have won."

That was a teacher complimenting his student. Ivan wasn't laughing.

"Thanks, Ivan. That means a lot to me."

Franz was reading some information on the SMART Board when they got back to the house.

"Hello, come in and look at this. I just decoded it."

Colin had just sent them a burst. John whistled. "It looks like they're going for it. I can't believe they're pushing this environmental bill through Congress. It's illegal."

Ivan chuckled. "Not when you control the president and the top leaders."

"Wow! Look at this. The president has taken power away from the FBI. The attorney general is running the show."

"John, what does that mean?"

"It means, my friend, that there is no longer an outside police force in the US."

Franz and Ivan both looked puzzled.

"Okay, in my government, there's supposed to be separation between the executive, judicial, and legislative branches to assure checks and balances. The AG is the head of the justice department, but he's appointed by the president. The FBI, and all of the intelligence and federal police departments, are under the jurisdiction of the justice department, but they act independently. If the president has taken away that power, then the police have to answer to, and follow, the instructions of the attorney general. That means there's no more separation. The president is calling the shots about what's legal and what isn't. This is dangerous. The US is very close to becoming a dictatorship. The fact that congressional leadership is under someone else's control tells us that my country is in deep shit."

"What can we do to stop this, anything?"

John shouted, "I got it! They've gained a lot of their power because they have the media behind them. Let's go after the media."

"John, how do we do that when they own the media?"

"What do you know about bloggers?"

"They're independent people who publish things on the Web."

"Yes, but are there well-known bloggers?"

"John, I'll ask my friend. He'd know."

"Okay, Franz, ask your friend. We'll hire private detectives and go after media people who seem to be in the White House's pocket—editors from the *Times*, CNN newscasters, and so on. We'll dig up dirt on them and force them to stop cooperating with the White House. Ivan, can you find us some investigators who could handle this kind of work?"

"John, that's what I do. I'll start immediately."

"Franz, send one of those digital things to Colin. Tell him what we're doing and see if he can help. Get in touch with your friend and get me the names of the most popular bloggers on the Web. We're going into the mass information business."

# 71

## Zurich

John decided to engineer a media blitz, and he would use that global warming nonsense to do it.

He contacted the top ten anti-global-warming scientists in the world and explained that he was offering a grant to any of the top scientists willing to write a paper dispelling the global warming theory. He invited nine scientists to Zurich for a conference, sent them airline tickets, and rented a castle on the lake to hold the event.

John and Franz interviewed bloggers and started a company: World Web Online Magazine. They hired graphic designers and developed a multitiered platform for the magazine. They hired twenty of the top bloggers in the world; together they were getting over fifteen million hits per day.

On the day of the conference, John greeted the scientists at the airport and brought them to the castle. The great room was set up with a long table for the science panelists. The rest of the room was filled with chairs for the bloggers, "the media."

Each scientist gave a talk on the real science behind global warming or climate change. All the scientists concluded that global warming was nothing more than a naturally occurring warming trend, something that happens every two hundred years and has happened for the last ten thousand years. The floor was opened to questions. The first blogger asked, "How do you know this has been a recurring trend?"

A scientist from Harvard stood up. "There's simple irrefutable proof of this. Every year for over one hundred years, several groups of scientists around the world take borings of large glaciers, which have been around since the ice age. They take these borings back to their laboratories. They measure the thickness of the pollen rings and the distances between them. This has gone on for the past hundred years, and the findings have been consistent. The thicker the pollen rings are, and the shorter the distance between them, gives an accurate record of the world's climate. We're now entering into the fiftieth year of a two-hundred-year warming trend."

The next question was, "Why is there such a clamor in the press and in the government about global warming, and does carbon dioxide really cause it?"

A professor from the Sorbonne answered, "*Mon ami*, we all breathe oxygen and expel carbon dioxide. Human beings produce more CO2 than all of the industries in the world. Even though it is important to protect our environment, global warming is not where we should be putting our efforts."

A young woman stood and asked, "Monsieur Professor, why do you think this issue has become so important?"

"My dear, I am neither a politician nor do I care about politics, but this phenomenon of global warming is political, not scientific. Ask yourself this: what new laws have been put in force since all this started, and how much more taxes do you pay? I think that will answer your question."

Another blogger asked, "Are you saying that the whole global warming phenomenon is a political hoax?"

The professor answered carefully, "Once again, I am not a student of politics, but global warming has nothing to do with science."

The room was in an uproar. The professor from Harvard stood and asked the crowd to quiet down. "May I remind you all of the history of global warming. In the sixties and seventies, a hole

## GREEN TO RED

was found in the ozone layer. A small group of scientists formed a consensus that the hole was caused by aerosol propellants, which are used in spray cans. The rest of the scientific community decided that it was premature to back that hypothesis. There just was not enough evidence to substantiate that theory. Another group of scientists blamed the phenomenon on greenhouse gases. That theory has been dispelled in the scientific community, but it has been picked up by politicians who have used their influence over the media to turn this into a political issue, taking it out of the hands of science, into the hands of politicians and documentary filmmakers."

"Professor, may we quote you on that?"

"Please do."

John was asked by Franz to leave the meeting. John read the letter Franz had in hand then told Franz to make sure it was seen by the panel. The conference emcee was asked to step out for a moment. He was given the letter and told to hand it over to the Harvard professor right away.

After he read it, he rose, saying, "Ladies and gentlemen, I have just received a piece of a correspondence that should add credence to the panel's hypothesis. Please allow me to read it. It is a letter from the United States EPA to the director of the FBI, as follows, 'Sir, this is to inform you that you must cease all investigations in relation to environmental issues. Any further investigation must be cleared by the attorney general.' It is signed by the director of the Environmental Protection Agency. I am informed that copies of this letter will be available to all in the press kits to be supplied at the end of the conference."

"Excuse me, sir, what does that letter have to do with the subject at hand?"

"Everything of course. When politicians stop others from investigating, it shows that they are happy with the status quo. That prohibits scientific development, which is, in itself, a constant questioning of facts."

— DENNIS SHEEHAN —

When the noise died down, the emcee went to the microphone, thanked the panel for their insight, and announced that there would be a seminar on search engine optimization in one hour.

John knew his idea was going to work; everyone was on fire.

# 72

## Zurich

"John, may I join you?"

"Of course, Ivan. Things went well at the conference today."

"I know, I heard. I hope you realize this is the end of our anonymity."

"Why do you say that, Ivan?"

"You spoke with all of those bloggers, and they won't keep their mouths shut. It's only a matter of time before we're found out. I'd like to take some precautions."

"Ivan, you worry too much."

"Yes, that is why I am still alive."

"What kind of precautions, Ivan?"

"I think we should have Franz download all his information to the laptops he set up, and move them to a different location. I'll take them myself. I also want to set up an LP outside the house."

"What's an LP?"

"A listening post, watchers, people who monitor movement."

John didn't like that idea, but accepted it. Ivan told him that he would get working on it right away.

Franz joined them on the terrace. "I just received word that Colin is coming and he has asked Chris to meet us here as well."

"When?"

"Tomorrow around eight in the morning."

John asked Ivan to wait until they met with Colin before he moved equipment and set up his LP.

Franz went to pick Colin up at the airport. Chris arrived just after he left. Chris told John and Ivan that he was on his way to Austria to take out one of the Socialist strike forces that had just returned from Yemen.

After exchanging greetings, they all got to work. Colin took the floor. "It looks like they're stepping up their plans, so we have to act quickly. We've discovered that they've been training militia groups in prisons. Those prisoners will be released very shortly courtesy on the USA. There have been several secret meetings between the Green Movement, the socialists, and the union leaders. We do know that Saris and Liddo have kissed and made up. I don't know how long we have. They don't know about my group yet, but they do know something is coming from my department. They've shut us out, and now we can't take a leak without clearing it through Justice. Pritchard is out of the country. We have been monitoring him, but it seems that they figured out we're on to him and have kept him out of things. I just found out that the manager of Bank of America in Geneva was tortured and killed. The papers said it was terrorists, but we're certain it was Liddo."

John asked Chris if he had anything new. "Yes, John, a group of twelve men recently arrived from Yemen. As you know, I'm now working with SITCEN. I'm leading one of three groups who are going to hit them, extract intel, and kill them. It would be too dangerous to put them in prison. Terrorists are trained to recruit prisoners."

"Do you have to kill all of them?"

Colin answered, "John, we are involved in a war against world domination. We're fighting a quiet World War III. These people have plotted, corrupted governments, and killed or ruined anyone who got in their way. We can't arrest them. It's too late for that. You must realize that the justice system in most countries is on their payroll."

Chris interjected, "John, he's right. Look at the criminals from the Liddo Group that I arrested in Italy in the drug bust. Over half of them have already been released on technicalities. Colin's right. This is war."

John asked Franz to put the new information up on the SMART Boards. Franz took the floor. "We're changing the way we communicate. As you know, it won't be long before we're all identified, so we'll have to become completely mobile. These are modified encrypted SAT phones, including special software." He handed each member of the team a set of instructions. He asked them to commit to memory and destroy them.

# 73

**Zurich**

"We've just started a Web magazine, sponsored several hundred bloggers, held a conference to dispel the global warming hoax, and we're getting results."

Colin interrupted, "John, it's been working in the States as well. There have been several demonstrations already. Several senators and congressmen are asking for a delay in the environmental initiative now in congress. Is there anything I can do to help with this?"

"Sure, Colin, anything you can find out that would slow these people down will be great. Any documents from government agencies that can be leaked that would discredit the administration would be good. We're trying to use their tools against them. I've hired agents to start investigating journalists, and we are getting some compromising information about them, including a recording and pictures of a journalist from a Washington newspaper accepting money from a congressman to squash a story. Perhaps your department should investigate these things formally. If we can discredit their information machine, maybe we can weaken them a little."

"Great, John, I'll get right to work on that."

John turned to Chris. "You're the most visible, and we've hired some people to watch your back. If there's anyone following you, confront them. They'll identify themselves by saying, 'Ivan.'"

Chris thanked John. "I'll call you with the details as soon as possible so you can get the information out to your bloggers immediately."

"Chris, be careful. Good luck. We'll see you soon."

# 74

Ivan brought the mobile computer set up to one of the safe houses right after Franz drove Colin to the airport. John made a drink and sat down just as an RPG (rocket-propelled grenade) round came through the front door and exploded in the center of the house. The blast knocked John completely off the terrace, which probably saved his life.

He was lying on the ground, deaf and disoriented; a man was standing over him. John couldn't move. The man reached down and shook him; John couldn't respond. The man whispered in his ear, "Ivan." He picked him up, threw him over his shoulder, and walked carefully down the mountain. When they were a safe distance from the house, he laid John down and tended to him.

Several minutes later. "What the hell happened?"

He told John that three of his men had been killed before the explosion occurred. He looked at John. "Can you walk? We have to get out of here now." John struggled to his feet and limped away.

The man had a car parked a few blocks down the hill. They drove to Ivan's house; they were met by several heavily-armed men. The leader told John that Ivan would return the next morning.

John slept, but was awakened by the sound of Ivan's voice. He got up, walked into the next room, and saw Ivan. "John, are you all right?"

"Yeah, I was just shaken up a little."

"You look pretty good for someone who was hit by an RPG yesterday."

"Well, Ivan, it looks like they know about us."

"Yes, but we're prepared for this. Do you need anything before we leave?"

"Yes, I need to go to the bank."

"I don't think that is a good idea, John. Let's get the hell out of here now."

"No, I have to get some cash, and I have to make sure everything is all right there."

"Okay, I'll send some men to see what's going on at the bank. Stay here until they give us an all clear."

"John, all clear. My men are stationed around the bank. I'm going to send two men in with you. I think it'll be safe, all their accounts are located here."

Nothing appeared to be out of the ordinary in his office. He had just sat down when Tsillman walked in.

"John, I heard the news. Are you all right?"

"I'm fine, Peter, just one of those things that make life more interesting."

"How can you joke about it? Do they know who was behind this?"

"No, perhaps it was a disgruntled customer?"

"John, please, this is a serious situation. We could all be in danger."

"I don't think so, Peter. Relax, you'll be fine. I need you to get some cash for me. I'm going to leave town for a while."

"Of course, that might be wise. How much do you need and in what currency?"

"I'd like two million euros in small denominations."

"John, it'll take me some time to get that for you. I'll have it in three hours."

"That will be fine, Peter, thank you."

John decided to take care of some things that needed attention when the phone rang. He had an uneasy feeling as he picked up the phone.

"Hello, John. It's Paula, meet me at six at the restaurant." She hung up before he could say anything.

Tsillman returned carrying a suitcase. "Here's the money you requested." Tsillman put the case next to John, reached into his inside jacket pocket, removed an envelope, and handed it to John. "I'm sorry, John, but this is my resignation, dated today. Under the current circumstances, I'm afraid I can no longer work here."

"I understand." John shook his hand and dismissed him. *What the hell am I going to do now?* John sat at his desk trying to figure out the next move. He decided to go back to Ivan's and talk it over.

When John arrived, Ivan had amassed a small army. After making his way through the throng, he found Ivan and Franz working hard making preparations to move. "I'm glad your both here, I have had a really bad day."

"You mean since they blew up your house?"

"Ivan, I'm not in the mood for that the comeback."

"Sorry about that, John."

"Two things happened today: Tsillman quit, and I got a call from Paula Franks."

"Why would she call you?"

"I don't know, but I have to meet her tonight at six."

"And where are you going to meet her?"

Franz stood and shouted, "Are you both crazy? Why are you going to meet her? It's probably a trap."

John didn't even acknowledge Franz. "I'm meeting her at the little bistro near Bellevueplatz."

Ivan picked up his cell phone. "Have two men posted near the bistro on Bellevueplatz. Put another man inside. Watch for anyone who might be in the business. John will be there at six tonight." He hung up.

"John, I'll have another man trail you."

"All right, thanks, Ivan. Do you have any more of those prepaid phones?"

Ivan handed John a phone and the list of their numbers. John scanned the list, found Chong's number in Hong Kong, and dialed. "Hello, Chong, it's John. Sorry to wake you, but we have a problem here in Zurich and I need you here immediately. When can you get here?"

"I'll catch a flight tomorrow."

"Good, one more thing. Call Iris and tell her to get over to Hong Kong and take over for you. You're going to be here for quite a while. When we hang up, destroy your phone. See you day after tomorrow."

"Hello, Tanya, it's John. I'm sure you know that Herr Tsillman handed in his resignation today. Mr. Chong will be taking over for him temporarily. Please make all necessary arrangements."

Ivan handed him a 9mm pistol. "It has thirteen rounds. Make sure you use it at close range. It's not very accurate at anything more than ten meters."

"Thanks, Ivan, but I hope I don't have to use it."

"Me too. Come, let's have vodka."

........................

Paula was already seated. As John approached the table, she stood up. "John, I'm glad to see you're all right."

"I'm not. They blew up my house." He spoke louder than he realized; two couples moved to a different table. "I'm sorry, but I'm pissed."

"John, I want you to know that I had nothing to do with it. It was Manheim. He's savage when he's angry. They know it was you that started the trouble between them and Saris."

"Why are you telling me this?"

"You may not believe me, but like I said last time we met, I want things to change. This is not the way I want to do business."

"What are they doing? You know. Tell me everything."

After they ordered, the waiter started to walk away, but John stopped him. "Can we get a drink first, a scotch and water for me, bourbon neat for the lady."

"Please, continue."

"You know I could get killed for telling you this."

"Now that's the level of commitment I'm looking for."

John saw a flash of pure hatred in her eyes. "I'm not someone to be played with, John."

"Neither am I. Are you with me or with them?"

"Neither, I'm on my own. I want what is best for me."

"Okay, then tell me what's going on?"

John saw a thread of truth in her last statement as she continued, "Saris is an egomaniac. He wants to start a new world order with him as the king. Liddo is pooling Saris's political contacts and money, along with theirs, to help begin this new world order. Once it happens, they'll probably kill him."

"Paula, I already know about the new world order, but how do they plan to do it?"

They paused while their meal was being served.

"John, you know that Saris is a very wealthy man. He started this many years ago. He searched for broad-based issues that angered the masses—like abortion, HIV, the gay movement. The only one that could not be fought against morally was "Save the Planet." He started to pump money into Green organizations, it gained traction. He paid off top UN officials to find scientific groups that would substantiate global warming and the dangers of greenhouse gases. He paid a few scientists, mostly through large grants, to generate the information that he wanted and then turned it into a political issue. It was not long before politicians jumped on the bandwagon, those that were looking for recognition."

"Okay, Saris made the environment a political issue, but how did Liddo get involved?"

"Saris needed publicity. We own the media. He laid out his plan to YK."

"You mean Y. K. Chen?"

"Yes. He saw potential. It was YK that came up with the idea of using emissions credits to take over the energy industry. He made a deal with Saris to give him all the media coverage that he wanted, and Liddo would take care of any problems that Saris couldn't handle."

"You mean Liddo was his muscle?"

"Correct. Over the last five years, they've been able to take control of the Socialist Parties in fifty percent of the countries in Europe, the Green Party, and the American Democratic Party. They've used coercion, bribes, and the media. Now they're going to take over everything."

"They're powerful, but not that powerful?"

"Don't kid yourself, John. They play by the golden rule. He with the gold, rules. They have control of eighty-five percent of the world's emission credits and the political clout to use them effectively."

"I know all about that, I helped them without knowing it at the time."

"Yes, Tsillman has been working with us for years. That's why I moved all of the funds into your bank. He's pliable and helpful. I don't really like him, but he gets the job done."

"He quit today. He was frightened when my house exploded."

"Oh! That's not good. If he's not there, I'll be told to move the accounts to another bank. That would put your bank in danger. I'll call him tomorrow and tell him it would be in his best interest to stay."

John wasn't sure if he was pleased with this last comment. *Does she really believe she can force him to stay? Well, I'll find out tomorrow.*

"Paula, the history lesson was fantastic, but what's the next step?

"To take over the world."

"Are you serious? How can they take over the world with emissions credits only?"

"John, you're so naïve. They've been buying up all of the coal-fired energy plants in the US and Europe, as well as Africa and South America. The emissions credits from the UN are backed up, and they can be used in third world countries. They will produce energy using the coal-fired plants at a much lower cost than the existing producers can produce it. It will only take a year or so for them to put their competition out of business. Once they've done that, they'll be the only energy producers. If you control the energy, you control the country. If the governments don't do what they want, they simply stop producing. This would stop all manufacturing and leave everyone out in the cold. "

"They wouldn't do that. The governments will nationalize them. They would lose everything."

"Do you think the politicians, who gave them this power in the first place, would try to take it away from them?"

"I guess you have a point."

"It's real, John, and it's happening soon. What you have done to date is brilliant, but all you have done is to force them to accelerate their schedule. They've already taken over every major battery company, solar energy manufacturer, even the paint companies. They've also taken over several large investment banks and hedge funds. The US government is pushing for investment in green products, thanks to their lobbies in Washington. Almost all of that money is going into the banks, funds, and companies they own."

"This is unbelievable. Wait a minute, do you have a list of those companies?"

"Yes, I do but…"

"If you really want to help me, give me that list."

"I have to think that over. That could easily get me killed. I do want to help, but I'll tell you up front that I will never do anything to jeopardize myself."

"Fair enough."

Paula was desperately trying to think of a way around this. "John, what if I give you just the list of American companies in the operation? I don't want any fallout from this."

"That would be more than satisfactory. I'll make sure that nothing is traced back to you."

"I'll go to the bank tomorrow with the list on my person. It'll be in an envelope marked 'London accounts, deliver to John Moore only,' and I'll give it to your assistant. Don't let anyone at the bank see it, John, my life depends on that."

# 75

### Gibraltar

Saris was pacing frantically. *Why haven't they called?* Two beautiful young women were just leaving, and they didn't look happy. "Yes, yes, please do hurry." And then he screamed, "Get out!"

He was about to follow them when the phone rang. He listened intently, smiled without speaking to anyone and hung up the phone.

*It's all mine. I will be the world leader directing those jackals in London, Paris, Bonn, and Washington. After all, they really do need direction. They've screwed up everything. They should thank God for my guidance.*

"Geoffrey, call everyone in the inner circle, tell them to be here two weeks from today for a very important meeting. We're going to host a historic summit, a postscript to the beginning of a new world order. Geoffrey, make certain that Manheim and Chen also attend."

# 76

### London, England

Paula went directly to her London flat. *If I get away with this, I could run all of Liddo. As much as Chen helped me and gave me all these opportunities, he has degraded me and abused me for his own pleasure. I owe him nothing.*

Her thoughts were interrupted. "Hello, Paula Franks here."

"Paula, YK, how are you?"

"YK, I've just arrived home and was going to call you."

"I understand you visited Zurich. How was your trip?"

"That's what I wanted to talk to you about, YK."

"Paula, please continue."

"YK, I just met with the banker that you tried to eliminate. I wasn't informed about that beforehand, so I moved all of our funds into his bank. I knew our relationship with Tsillman was good. Since he was hired by this bank, I thought it best for them to oversee our accounts."

"What did you learn from Moore?"

"He believes terrorists made the attempt on his life. He's frightened. I think he'll be leaving Zurich."

"Good, what else did you find out?"

"Only that Tsillman is going to run things at the bank and Moore will continue to sell yachts. Our funds are secure and will remain that way. I had a meeting with Tsillman just before I left."

"Does Moore have access to our accounts?"

"Tsillman told me that Moore doesn't involve himself in the day-to-day business."

"Can Moore gain access?"

"No, he can only get information through Tsillman. I told him to inform me immediately of any inquiries into our accounts."

"Good work, Paula."

"YK, there's one more thing. Please tell Mike not to do anything like that again. If you want something done, tell me, and I'll get it done. The whole incident was very awkward for me."

"Paula, you're right. If I request anything of that nature, you can handle it. But before you do anything, clear it with Michael. Not that I think you're not capable, but he's been trained and does have more experience."

"He failed on this one. In the future, however, I will clear everything of that nature through him."

"That's my girl!" YK hung up.

*They'll never see me as an equal. I'm just a convenience for them. They let me have this position, but will never trust me to run it entirely. I'll show them.*

Paula called Sara Covington. "Sara, I need your help. I want to visit all of the Liddo Group companies. Could you come over around seven to help me put a schedule together? I'll also need you to put together a dossier on each of the executives. Thank you, I'll see you then."

# 77

**Vienna, Austria**

Chris had located the residence where the four trained terrorists were hiding. They had just arrived in Vienna from their training in Yemen. Chris's other teams, all SITCEN people, were monitoring similar groups in different locations. One group was a crack ex-SAS team which had been sent to Budapest. The other team in Prague, however, all handpicked, had never worked as a team. Chris was concerned, but he knew they all had experience.

Chris knew how tough it was to coordinate an operation like this. All three teams had to hit at the same time to prevent the terrorist teams from communicating with each other. Chris had been monitoring his subjects for over a week to ascertain the best time; noon seemed optimal. They were all together for lunch every day. The other teams agreed with him.

Chris got the green light about eleven o'clock on the third day of surveillance. His men were in position; at twelve noon, he gave the command. His men rushed the house. When they were about thirty feet away, they were fired upon from the second floor. Chris yelled, "Get down!"

Before he hit the ground, his sniper, positioned across the street, took the shooter out. "Go, go!" His men were through the door, already shooting a second man, before he got into the house.

The other two terrorists screamed, "Don't shoot!"

When Chris arrived, the two terrorists were standing with their hands up. As he approached them, he noticed a wire going to a small red button held by one. Without saying a word, Chris fired, severing the man's hand from his arm. He called the demolitions expert to disarm the bomb.

The other teams had both been successful; however, three of their men were killed, and two were wounded. "Take those terrorists to the rendezvous point and don't give that one any medical attention, other than to stop the bleeding."

Chris stayed behind and set the explosives. When he was on his way back to the hotel, he heard the explosion.

Chris listened to a news report on his radio while driving to the rendezvous point. "A group of terrorists, now thought to be Middle Eastern, were blown up in their house today. It appears that they had a conflict amongst themselves, one of the terrorists deliberately detonated a bomb."

It took six hours of interrogation, but they got the information they were looking for. These men said Gregory Gruber had paid them directly and was responsible for their training.

He told the others to go. "I'll clean up here."

"Do you have anything else to say?"

"We're prisoners of war. We demand our rights under the Geneva Convention."

"I'm sure you abide by the Geneva Convention when you are ordered to kill innocent civilians." He raised his weapon and fired two shots, killing them instantly.

Chris called the other two team leaders to confirm that there were twelve terrorists dead. He called Raquel.

"Chris, are you all right? I watched the exercise via satellite. We lost three men."

"Yes, Raquel, but they lost twelve."

"Chris, you'll have to be debriefed, and I want you rested for the task."

"Okay, see you then."

# 78

## Washington DC

The president called the chief of staff to his office. *What does he want? He hasn't answered any of my calls in weeks. Something is wrong, very wrong.* "Mr. President, you called?"

"Rob, I apologize for not returning your calls. It's been mayhem here lately." The president walked over and turned off the recorder. "I've been getting flak from everyone. What the hell is going on?"

"Well, sir, I told you it wasn't a good idea to listen to Saris without getting a consensus from your other big supporters."

"Crap, I thought they were all in this together. They knew my agenda, and they backed it."

"Well, sir, they will back it only if it profits them. You looked like the bad guy when you ignored everyone but Saris."

The president sat down. "Rob, I need your help. This might work out great. Now that the Speaker is under investigation, I need you to liaise with Saris. Maybe you could bring both groups together."

"Mr. President, I can't do that, but the FBI is all over these people. If I'm seen meeting with Saris, it would affect you very quickly."

"The FBI can't move now without permission from the attorney general. They know they have to brief the AG, even before they fart."

"I don't know, sir. This seems dangerous."

"Rob, do you want to see my agenda come to fruition?"

"Yes, sir."

"Then do what I ask."

*This guy is a lunatic. He really believes he can do whatever he wants.* Rob got to his office, picked up his coat, and left. When he was a safe distance away, he called Wiley.

"You won't believe this. He wants me to liaise with Saris and bring him together with the Liddo Group. Wiley, I think he's out of his friggin' mind."

"But, Rob, this is great news. That means we've taken the power away from the Speaker, and the president will have to depend on you totally. I'm coming to Washington. I'll call you when I get in."

# 79

**Jakarta, Indonesia**

Mike Manheim, Wiley Pritchard, and Y. K. Chen sat in front of a small group of people who represented all of the companies involved in the new Green bonanza. Representatives from the battery, eco-fuel, paint, solar energy, coal, and windmill industries were present, as well as hedge fund managers and investment bankers.

"Gentlemen, our plans have been moved up. We now have access to the president of the United States and the prime ministers of most of the EU countries. The US government has taken over the automobile industry and the money center banks. Legislation has been put into place for us to completely take over the manufacturing of tier 2 and tier 3 supply companies of the auto industry. With the government restriction on banking, our competitors don't have a chance to fight back. We are effectively controlling hedge funds and investment banking, so we have all the credit we want at very favorable rates. Our competitors have lost or been forced to reduce their credit lines with the banks. If they come to us, we will lend to them at much higher rates. Shortly, we will be able to foreclose and pick up capital equipment for our expansions at pennies on the dollar. I will now turn the floor over to Mike Manheim."

"Good afternoon, all of this is ours for the taking, so now we have to take. You have funds available at their lowest cost to you, the inside track on government contracts, and the assistance of the media to destroy your competitors. Do not let the opportunity to drive all of your competition into the ground pass you by, strike while the iron is hot. If there are any foreign-owned companies available for takeover or demise, clear it with me first. If they're not part of our European group, they're going down. We have invested billions in this, and I won't stand for failure."

Wiley Pritchard was introduced. "As you all know, if you have any bureaucratic problems, call me. We have the president's ear, and there is almost nothing we can't get done. If any of you had any dealings with the Speaker of the House, or her group, get out now, even if you have to sustain a loss. Walk away."

"I think that covers everything. We'll reconvene in three months. Again, thank you all for coming."

YK, Mike, and Wiley walked to the house.

YK turned to Mike. "Are you sure this is the right time to start?"

"It couldn't be better, YK. Wiley has direct contact with the White House. Right, Wiley?"

"Yes, Mike. I've been asked to coordinate the efforts of Saris and Liddo with the Administration. I'm the go-between now for the White House and Saris."

"That is excellent. This puts us in total control. Wiley, please report to me before you report to the president."

Wiley was a little offended. "Of course, YK."

"Good, and, Mike, monitor Wiley so there are no errors."

"That goes without saying, YK."

"I want to thank you both for all of your efforts. I guess that's all. Would you like to stay for dinner?"

# 80

### Washington DC

The director began, "Great work, people. We have them now. The chief of staff has stepped out of bounds on behalf of the president. The taped evidence is undisputable."

Colin interrupted, "Yes, sir, we have the chief, but we still don't have a direct line to the president or the Speaker, and you know the media will be against us. We still have a long way to go."

"Colin, what do you suggest?"

Sally interjected, "Sir, why don't you gather some senate and congressional clout. Let's start feeding them some information and see what happens. After all, several were bent out of shape when they found out what the AG did to us."

"Sally, that's a good idea. We have to be careful. If the administration finds out what we're doing, they'll shut us down."

Colin broke into the conversation, "Let's feed them background only. Then give them the information we have on the Speaker. If we can just bring enough to light to cause a distraction, we could keep going until we have them cold."

"Let's continue to monitor Pritchard and the chief of staff."

"Can our friends in Zurich help us with that?"

"Not right now, they've been discovered, and an attempt was made on their lives. Someone blew up their house. They're busy reorganizing."

"How about your friend, the one who joined SITCEN?"

"His groups just killed twelve terrorists. They staged a daylight raid on three locations. He lost two men."

The director looked pensive. "I'm sorry to hear that. This is getting dangerous. If any of you want to quit now, it's okay. You've all gone way beyond what I had any right to ask of you."

"Sir, we're all in until the end. This is a war. These people are trying to take over our country, we're not going to stand for it."

"Thank you, all. Now, let's begin."

"I have something from Zurich. It's a list of all the companies involved with Liddo and Saris. Why don't you give this list to the IRS and the SEC. They can start an investigation on publicly held companies. If they have special concessions on government contracts, we might be able to slow them down."

"Sally, that's great. We can't investigate directly, but we can get information to other agencies. Perhaps this will interest some of our friendly senators and congressmen, and they can alert the press. We might have something here."

"It's perfect. I'll give the information to some of my friends and have it brought to the other agencies by people outside the department. There are several reporters who hate big business. They wouldn't know they were reporting about Green corruption, so they'll run with the story. This could slow these bastards down considerably."

Over the next few days, the director and Colin spent time on the Hill in informal meetings. The administration was using everything they had to strong-arm senators and congressmen. This new information would help them to fight back.

# 81

### Jakarta, Indonesia

Y. K. Chen sat across his desk from General Chou and Mr. Xia, the director of the China Investment and Trust Corporation. "Gentlemen, I know you have been straddled with billions in US mortgage securities. If you call them, your US Treasury Notes will be worthless. It would devalue your entire US portfolio. I would like to take them off your hands."

General Chou asked bluntly, "What will this cost us?"

"Nothing. General, I am willing to trade oil futures equal to what you paid for the securities. You'll be able to recoup your losses and make a profit. In exchange, I would like a contract to buy coal from you at $15 a ton under the world price for ten years. You will receive $0.50 per ton."

The two looked at each other. "Deal!" they both said in unison.

"That concludes our business. Do you want me to make the security transfers through the Shanghai Exchange?"

"No, put them through the Tokyo exchange. It will be safer for all of us."

"Agreed, I'll contact our broker in Tokyo this afternoon."

"Hello, Mike, call me from a secure line."

"YK, what can I do for you?"

"Nothing, I have just secured a ten-year contract for coal at $14 below world price. I've also given the Chinese 100 billion in oil contracts in return for their mortgage securities. That will drive the price of oil to over a hundred a barrel, I'm sure."

"That's great, YK. We'll have absolutely no competition then. What do you want me to do with the mortgage securities?"

"Michael, I will let you know soon. Please inform Saris of the oil and coal deal. Don't mention the mortgage securities yet."

Manheim hung up the phone. *Holy shit, this gives us almost total control of the entire world's energy supply.*

# 82

### Zurich, Switzerland

John met Chong at the airport. "Chong, how are you?"

"I'm great, boss. How are you?" Chong was looking at the man with John; he noticed a bulge under his suit jacket.

"Oh, this is Igor, your new assistant." Igor was twice Chong's size.

"Nice to meet you, Igor."

"I'll give you a rundown when we get to your new flat, it's near the bank."

"John, that girl Iris is plenty smart. She was in Hong Kong only one day, and she started to change things."

John laughed. "Did she seem happy?"

"You really like missy Iris, don't you?"

"Indeed, I do, Chong."

When they arrived at the flat, Chong looked around and said, "Boss, this is classy, but it's much too big."

"You represent my bank. I can't have you living in a tenement."

John told him everything after a quick tour.

"Boss, you're in it deep again. How can I help?"

"Just take care of the bank and watch Tsillman. I've made a list of all known Liddo representatives. Make sure that you are at every meeting with them and Tsillman. He knows banking, and he makes us a lot of money, but he blows with the financial wind. I don't want to lose him, even though I don't trust him."

"I understand, boss."

"Chong, one other thing, don't call me boss at the bank."

"Okay, boss."

"Chong, please get friendly with Igor. He'll protect you. He is well-trained, and he's tough. I need you two to work together. I don't think you're in danger, but I can't be sure with everything that's happened."

Tsillman underestimated Chong. Chong was pleasant with Tsillman, but John could tell Chong did not like him, and that's just what John hoped for. Now that he was comfortable with the situation, he could get out of Zurich.

# 83

## Milan, Italy

John, Ivan, and Franz arrived at the safe house in Milan, located near the city center in a very fashionable area. When Ivan chose that location, he knew that the lack of parking made it more difficult for an ambush.

John and Franz readied the place for work. "Nice place, Ivan."

"Yes, John, it is a good place. There's a taxi stand right outside, it's busy twenty-four hours a day, and with no parking nearby, it will be difficult to ambush us."

Franz commented, "How do we get out if we have to?"

"Franz, here are the maps, let's download the escape routes from the computer."

Franz took out the GPS and started to download the escape routes.

Ivan spread the maps out. "This will give you a better idea of the area. We're now on Villa Dell'orso, three blocks from Via Brera to the east and two kilometers from Parco Pallavicino, that's where I parked the car. If we have to escape, we'll take a taxi to the park, get the car, then drive south for 130 kilometers to Portofino. There's a boat in slip seven at the Santa Maria Marina, already programmed for the next destination."

"Ivan, you sound like you've done this before."

"I'm still around, aren't I?"

"Okay, enough. Let's get to work."

Franz looked through the files on his computer to make certain he hadn't lost anything; then he backed everything up on external hard drives.

Ivan decided to check on his people stationed around the building. John began to go over the information they had gotten on Paula Franks.

After a couple of hours, John went out to buy some more phones, practicing his spy craft along the way. He kept a close eye on the three men following him, Ivan's men.

John came back with a case of prepaid phones. "Did I not tell you that you shouldn't go out alone?"

"Ivan, relax, I saw your men following me. I identified them immediately and kept visual contact with all three."

"Three men, you say? That's good, but I only had a man and a woman following you."

"Ivan, what are you saying?"

"Not to worry, we took out the other two men that were following you. You can't go out alone anymore."

"I'm sorry, Ivan, it won't happen again."

"Franz, I need your input on this too. What if we have Fragge—now that he's number one in the Green Socialist Party again—announce publicly that he's received reliable information that the global warming scare has been a hoax. We can give the same information to the bloggers the day before. As soon as Fragge makes the announcement, the bloggers will circulate it."

"Ivan, that's a great idea, but Fragge would never go for it."

"I'll have the doctor visit him again."

John commented, "Ivan, I don't want him killed too."

"John, I can guarantee you that we will not kill him, but I can't be held responsible for what his bosses will do when he makes that announcement."

"If he does, that would stall things for a while."

"Okay, but let's contact Chris and Colin before we do it, perhaps they can use it."

"Good morning, any feedback from Chris or Colin?"

Franz replied, "We got positive feedback from Colin, but we haven't heard from Chris yet."

"Okay, I'll call him."

John dialed the next number on Chris's list. The call went through and John was about to say hello.

"Hello, hello."

John said, "Hello, who is this?"

"John, is that you?"

"Who is this?"

"It's Raquel. Chris is sleeping. He's exhausted. He had a tough go of it and hasn't slept well since Vienna."

"Is he all right?"

"Yes, but mentally, he's drained. We received your message last night, and he told me your idea was sound. Is there anything I can do from SITCEN?"

"Not right now, we'll let you know. When I hang up, destroy your phone."

"John, is everything all right?"

"I don't know, Ivan. It seems strange that she would answer that phone."

"Chris told me they were getting close, maybe he was just sleeping. I'll try him later."

Ivan gave each of them a 9 mm pistol. "I'm going to Zurich to check up on Fragge. Keep this close to you at all times, don't go out while I'm gone. If anything happens, my people will say "Ivan" to identify themselves and hold up three fingers. If they don't say "Ivan" and hold up three fingers, then shoot them immediately."

John turned to Franz and said, "I miss him already."

"Me too, he's the best in the business."

# 84

### Washington DC

Colin and the director had their last informal meeting with the congressmen and senators. The IRS, the EPA, and the Security and Exchange Commission had already gotten the details; investigations were underway.

"Colin, all we have to do now is wait. We let them come to us, just like a snowball rolling down a hill, Capitol Hill."

Two days after their last meeting, a delegation showed up: ten special investigators from the IRS and five from the SEC.

The chief auditor for the IRS piped up, "Director, we've been investigating over a hundred companies in the energy business for a few weeks based on information we received from several senators and congressmen. We have found improprieties and verifiable criminal action. We need a full investigation done, and we need your help now."

The director had his speech already prepared. "Gentlemen, you have to clear it with the AG first, per the president's order."

"Since when do we need the AG's approval to investigate any businesses?"

"Didn't you get the memo?"

"What memo? This is crazy. You have to start an investigation at our request, it's the law."

That's what he was waiting for. "Okay, I'll be happy to give you the support you need, but could you please put it in writing and mention that law?"

"Yes, I'll do that."

"I just hope they don't go to the AG with that letter."

The director said, "You and me both."

Several hours later, the delegation returned. The chief auditor handed the director the written request while he and Colin were talking. The director paused, smiled, and put the letter in his office safe. "Gentlemen, I'm sorry about that, but these days, it's CYA, as the saying goes."

The men laughed. "Now what can we do for you?"

"I don't know what to make of it, but there are over a hundred companies that we investigated that are in the energy business. All of them have received money or credits from foreign entities and have improperly reported their assets. It appears that there were several asset exchanges within each company without a paper trail. Foreign companies are impossible for us to trace. Something looks very bad here."

"How many agents do you have for this job?"

"As many as I need."

"We've been working on a similar investigation. I have a list of all the companies you are looking at and maybe more. They all lead to two sources: the Liddo Group and Aristotle Saris."

"Shit, they're the two biggest contributors to the DNC and the president. How the hell can we investigate them?"

The director stood. "Very carefully. We can start a joint operation and hit them all at once. If we coordinate this carefully, we can get all the information we need before the politicos try to stop us."

"Bullshit, I like my job. I'm not going to piss away my career for this."

The director's face turned purple. "What's wrong with you, man? We're talking about criminal activity on a national scale and you're willing to look the other way?"

"If it means losing my job, yes, I'll look the other way."

Colin interjected, "Wait! There's a way to do this so no one gets hurt."

All eyes were on Colin. "Do any of your superiors know about these investigations?"

The auditor and the rep from the SEC both replied, "No."

"Good, we can hit these people at the same time and totally disrupt them. If the administration makes us stand down, at least we'll have some evidence. The director and I will bring it to the AG. If it goes well, we'll share the credit with you. If it doesn't, we won't mention your involvement."

"We'll get back to you."

"If you drop this, and we're proven correct, we will hold you complicit for failing to report a known crime."

"Okay, we'll let you know this afternoon, before five."

"Mind if we get out of here for a while? Let's take a break."

The director agreed with a sigh.

Colin and the director returned to the office before four-thirty. Both men were waiting. "Gentlemen, what do you want to do?"

"We're ready to go."

The director's secretary broke in on the intercom, "Sorry to disturb you, sir, but it's urgent."

The director motioned to Colin. "It's for you."

"I'll take it in my office." Colin went to his office. "Colin, I don't know what's going on, but the chief of staff just got a call from the IRS. Then he called Manheim. Pritchard and Manheim are going nuts, they're calling energy companies all over the country."

"Those SOBs. Tony, I'll call you back."

Colin walked back to the director's office. He leaned near the director and whispered, "These two must have told Manheim and Pritchard about our investigation, they are alerting all the companies as we speak."

The director put on his best poker face. "All right, where are the documents that you have already reviewed?"

"We have copies at our agencies."

"Good, Colin, have some men pick up the documents at the IRS. Have our accounting team go over them while we're in the field."

"Would you call to have them ready? Our men will be there in fifteen minutes."

The director turned to the two men. "You are both under arrest for interfering with a federal investigation and conspiracy." As he read them their rights, the IRS auditor started to cry.

# 85

### Gibraltar

Saris was at his desk when he got a call. "Helmut Fragge has just announced that he received valid information from scientists around the world that global warming is a hoax, contrived to make certain people rich and powerful."

"Who told you this?"

"Fragge held a televised press conference apologizing for his participation in the scam. He said that he had been duped like everyone else. He also said he would be resigning from the Green and Socialist parties."

"Kill him, kill him now."

"I'll handle damage control, don't worry."

Paula Franks hung up the phone, smiling.

The next day, papers across Europe read, "Chairman of Socialist Green Party commits suicide." The story went on to say that Helmut had been suffering from a mental disease caused by a virus. For the past several weeks, as reported by friends and family, he had been suffering from hallucinations and acute paranoia.

# 86

**Washington DC**

"Mike, what are you doing here?"

Manheim pushed past him. "What the hell is going on, Wiley?"

"What do you mean?"

"FBI, IRS, and SEC cops are invading our companies. They came to my house, Wiley. Is this what we're paying you for?"

"All of your companies were alerted, so no harm done."

"No harm done? Are you stupid? They know the entire operation. We gave the green light, now everyone is afraid to move. Wiley, I want to know who started this, and I want it taken care of."

"I arranged for the release of both men, they told me the original information came from the Senate and Congress."

"I want to know who started this."

"All right, Mike, I'll find out right away."

"YK doesn't know anything about this yet. I want to know who was responsible before he does. I'm staying at the Capital Hilton. Call me as soon as you know anything."

After Manheim left, Wiley got on the phone. It wasn't long before he knew that the FBI director had supplied the information to the Hill.

Tony got a call from the girl monitoring Pritchard. "Get over here right away. Meet me around the corner."

She told him what she had heard and gave him the tape.

"Shit, this is serious. Thanks for the heads-up. I need to get back right away."

"Thanks, Tony, I'll meet you at the house later. I'd better get prepared now."

As soon as he hung up, the director called Larry Dewitt, his personal attorney. "Larry, I'm in trouble. I'll be in your office in an hour."

The director told his attorney the whole story. "What can we do?"

"Are you shitting me, the president is involved? You're in deep shit, my friend." Dewitt sat quietly, thinking. "He can't fire you without generating publicity. If he tries to, simply refuse, citing Hathaway versus Buchanan. If he tries to fire you, I'll call a press conference. I'll prepare a statement alleging retaliation by the administration due to your investigation of the Speaker. That will slow him down. He can't afford to push it right now."

"It's up to you, Larry. Thanks."

# 87

**Milan, Italy**

The hacker had been sending Franz updates almost every hour. Liddo and Saris were very busy, trying to move their schedule up. Everything that John's group did seemed to be causing their enemy to speed up rather than slow down. It was tedious, reading the information, matching it to accounts and processing it. John was getting weary.

"I think I have something. Here's a transfer from Saris directly to the president's personal account."

"Are you kidding me? Franz, this is the best news we've had in a long time. Get that to Colin right away."

"John, weren't the bodyguards supposed to check in with us regularly?"

"Yeah, Franz, every hour on the hour. Why do you ask?"

"We haven't heard from them in at least two hours."

John looked out the window and saw three men talking. It appeared that they were directing others who were out of sight.

"Shit, Franz, we have to go. Get everything ready. Download everything to the externals and destroy the equipment."

Franz went to work immediately. John took out his gun and looked out the window. "Here they come. Franz, I'm going upstairs. Take shelter here and don't hesitate to pull the trigger. We'll get them in a cross fire."

John went up to the next landing and saw three men coming up the stairs. They walked to the door of the flat and put some type of optical device under the door. John saw one of them make a hand signal indicating that he only saw one person. As soon as the leader kicked open the door, John heard a shot. The first man fell. John reached over the landing and fired three shots in succession. Another man fell. The third man turned and fired at John. Before John could return fire, Franz emptied his gun into the man. John ran down the stairs. "Franz, are you okay?"

"Yes, John, I'm fine. Let's get the hell out of here."

John ran back into the flat and picked up an emergency case containing money, a few phones, and a GPS.

"Franz, reload, grab your stuff."

They ran down the stairs; two of Ivan's men were dead in the lobby. John motioned for Franz to stop as he peered out the front door. As John was monitoring the street in front of the building, he turned around quickly, knocked Franz to the ground, and shot a man coming from the back hall. Another one started to come into the lobby. John fired, missing him, the man ran into an adjoining room. John waited until he heard movement and fired several shots into the wall. As he moved to get a better angle, the man fell into the lobby, dead, a hole just above his left eyebrow.

They ran out to the street. John told Franz to run to the taxi on the corner; he would cover him. As soon as Franz was in the taxi, John made his move. He'd almost reached the taxi when he heard automatic weapon fire and saw several pockmarks in the sidewalk less than one foot from him. John leaped and rolled, and while he was tumbling, he got one shot off, hitting a man in the face, one more dead.

The taxi sped off with Franz inside. He knew Franz would meet him at the car, so he decided to run, leading their attackers away from Franz and the car.

He sat on the ground next to a public toilet; it gave him temporary cover. He made a dash for the corner, hearing sirens in the distance. He jumped into a doorway, taking a minute to survey the area. John was hoping that his attackers would vacate the area; sirens were blaring.

He made his way down the street and entered a shop that looked like it might have exit to the next street. John pulled out his GPS, studying several different escape routes. John started to feel a little safer until he saw two men standing in a doorway. They did not look like frightened pedestrians. John saw another man coming across the street toward him. They had him boxed in. John was frightened, almost to the point of panic. At that moment, a police car stopped right in front of him. John ran to the police car, screaming, "It's them," as he pointed at the men he thought were the killers. "It's them, hurry!"

As the police jumped out of the car, the men scrambled. One policeman yelled, "Alto!" and then shot one of the men. During the shooting, John was able to slip back into the store and out the other exit.

He walked right through the middle of cops who were now on the street. He made his way to a taxi stand several blocks away and had the driver take him in a direction away from Franz. After walking several blocks and taking several taxis, John was certain that he wasn't being followed, so he made his way to the car.

John was almost at the car when he heard Franz, "Boy, am I glad to see you."

"Franz, it got a little hairy back there."

They both got in the car, Franz drove. John noticed that his entire body was shaking, he had started to perspire. John couldn't speak. Franz glanced over and did a double take. "John, are you all right?"

John couldn't answer him. Franz pulled the car off the road, walked around, and opened John's door. "John, can you get out?"

John just stared at him.

When Franz leaned in to help him, he saw blood. "Jesus Christ, you've been hit!" Franz laid him down on the ground. Franz noticed that John's back was covered with blood. As soon as Franz got John's shirt off, he saw a piece of wood about three inches long sticking out of his arm. Franz carefully removed it. "Thank God, it's only a flesh wound. It's not bad at all." When Franz didn't get a response, he realized that John was in shock.

Franz positioned John properly, monitoring his pulse and respiration. John began to move and regain his faculties. "John, are you well enough to make the rest of the trip?"

"I think so. Let's go. We can stop somewhere if I need to rest."

They found the boat easily. "As crazy as he appears, Ivan is a genius."

Once on board, they went below. Franz took a closer look at John's wound. "It's quite a gash, but not life-threatening."

"It felt like I had a two-by-four going through me."

"John, I'm going to have to stitch it to stop the bleeding. Are you up for it?"

"There's a bottle of scotch over there."

John took a few long swigs, and Franz began.

"There are some wood fragments in the wound, and I have to remove them, so keep still."

John winced as Franz operated. When he was done, John said, "Franz, I'm going to sleep now. Get us underway and head for our new location."

# 88

### Jakarta, Indonesia

Saris sat across from Y. K. Chen. "It's such a pleasure to see you, Aristotle. I do apologize for our recent behavior, but I'm sure you understand."

"Yes, YK, I was under the same misconception. I understand perfectly."

"Good, I've always had the utmost respect for you."

"I feel the same way, YK."

With that out of the way, YK got directly to the point. "Aristotle, we have almost reached our goal. You have weakened the economies of every major industrialized nation in the world. You have, with our help, used the media to solidify the world concerning the global warming issue, and your manipulation of the UN has been a delight to watch. The unions and the politicians are in line. We're almost ready."

"YK, what do you mean *almost ready?*"

YK chose his words with care, "Well, my friend, we have a few small problems. The FBI is investigating our energy companies, but we're taking care of that. Until that problem is rectified, we can't move forward. We also have the problem in Europe with the Green Party. Fragge was well-liked. We must replace him as soon as possible, any ideas?"

"YK, I've already taken care of that. Serge Alstead, the president of the transportation union, has agreed to take over. That kills two birds with one stone."

"Aristotle, you always amaze me. We've got one other slight problem. The EU security forces are taking out our soldiers. We believe a yacht salesman found out about our tactical movement and informed the security forces. He is being dealt with as we speak."

"Let's give the EU information on all of the soldiers."

"What?"

"YK, they were recruited by Gregory, and he's dead. We can contact our Saudi friend in Afghanistan and get a new crop of soldiers, better soldiers. If they're captured, they can say they're fighting a Jihad."

"Aristotle, that's brilliant. I'll have my London contact start a media investigation and turn the information over to the EU before we publish it."

"YK, one more thing, I need three billion dollars."

"That's a lot of money. Why do you need it?"

"I'm going to put up three billion, and I need you to match it. China and India are not going to sign the Climate Change Agreement. I arranged to have the US promise them one hundred billion a year, and they won't agree. We have to take over the energy industry in those two countries as well. I have the plans. It will cost approximately six hundred billion. I have arranged some financing with the World Bank."

"I don't know how you accomplished that, Aristotle. The Americans owe billions to the Chinese, and you got them to agree to give them billions for climate change. Dealing with these fools only proves the need for our world government."

"Yes, but we must move fast. The American people are starting to raise questions."

"Aristotle, I'm surprised at you. They're like sheep—if they hear something on TV, they'll believe it, and we control the television media."

The two men laughed, full of their own brilliance.

# 89

**Washington DC**

The director arrived at the safe house. "I'm sorry, it looks like I'm going to be out of this. Colin, you were promised my spot and you have to make sure they give it to you."

"Aren't you going to refuse termination?"

"Yes, I am, but they still have the power. I don't know how long I can fight them. I'm going home to prepare. In the meantime, I'd like you guys to begin working on a contingency plan."

"Okay, sir. We'll start running scenarios and see what we can come up with."

His notice came at 5:00 a.m. "Sir, the president would like to see you at seven fifteen." The director smiled. *They're not wasting any time.* He showered and dressed and was at the White House at 7:00 a.m.

"Director, I'm not going to beat around the bush. I want your resignation on my desk, effective immediately."

Expecting this, the director replied, "No, sir. With all due respect, Mr. President, I will not resign."

"I'm not asking you, I'm ordering you."

"Well, Mr. President, if you force the issue, I'll take you to court. Before the case is settled, you'll be out of office." The president looked at the chief of staff.

Rob was now obviously upset. "Who do you think you are? If the president asks for your resignation, you have to give it to him."

"No, I don't. I cannot be fired without just cause, I'm staying. I have a press conference right after this meeting. If you try to frame me, I'll tell the press everything." The director put on a good poker face, but he was trembling inside.

The president sat back to reflect. After a short time, he smiled. "Director, you are a persuasive man. I appreciate your feelings. Maybe you are the right man for the job. I won't ask for your resignation under one condition."

"What's that, sir?"

"I want you to promise me that you will clear everything with the AG. There are many complex situations going on right now. I just want to know that all of my people are behind me."

"Sir, I'll agree to notify the AG before anyone in the department, including myself, starts any major investigation."

"Okay, then we agree, and thank you for your time."

He walked out of the oval office and realized he was in terrible danger. He went to his office and found a gaggle of reporters waiting.

"I'm going to make a statement, but I will not answer any questions at this time. The president has asked for my resignation due to differences in political ideology. We have just had a meeting, and he has withdrawn his request. I'm going to continue to serve as the director." He went to his office, closed the door, sat down, and shook with anger.

The next day, there was no mention of the press conference. He was now a target.

# 90

### Somewhere in France

Franz tied up the boat and went to the parking lot in the marina to find the car Ivan had left them.

He went back to the boat and used the GPS to find the location of the next safe house, only five kilometers away. When Franz came back to the boat, after loading the gear into the car, he found John making a cup of coffee.

"John, how are you feeling?"

"Like I was hit by a truck."

"It took ten stitches to close the gash. I'll take a look at it and change the dressing before we leave."

"How long was I out?"

"About six hours."

"It looks fine. You're a tough man."

"I don't feel very tough right now."

"You evaded several killers and the police. Then you made it to the car without falling out, that's tough."

They left for the safe house, a farmhouse about three kilometers from Mentone, a town not far from Monaco. Ivan had picked this location for its accessibility by water and its proximity to the A8, the main highway into the Cote d'Azur.

The small house was warm, comfortable, and positioned on a small rise, giving the occupants complete visibility. While Franz was unloading the gear, John told him that he was going into town to get some groceries.

"John, look at this. While I was setting up, Brad's locator program popped up. It looks like there are over eighty boats in Monaco."

"What? Let me see. Can you pull up the owners of those boats?"

Franz brought up the list.

"Franz, they're meeting with Saris."

"How do you know that?"

"Franz, don't you think it's odd that all of the boats bought that night at the Green Party dinner are all in the same place at the same time?"

"Good point."

"Get a message to Chris, see if he can get a satellite view of Saris's place in Monaco. Ask him to get his team there to see what he can find out."

Within seconds, Franz had sent a digital blast to Chris; in five minutes, they had their reply. "Have satellite contact. You were right. Team on the way to site. Will contact you with results."

John turned to Franz. "Let's see what's going on with Colin." Before Franz could respond, one of the phones rang.

"John, it's Ivan. Are you all right?"

"Yes, Ivan, I'm fine. I got a splinter in my back, but Franz took care of it."

"I heard. Are you at location two?"

"Yes, we just arrived, and we're setting up."

"I'm on my way. Keep a low profile until I arrive."

"Okay, Ivan, we'll see you soon."

John and Franz spent the rest of the day going over the files, monitoring the Liddo and Saris accounts. Franz received a digital blast from Colin. "Franz, this is not good. If the president is willing to take the power away from the FBI, he must believe Saris and Liddo are very close to their goal."

"We need to do something immediately, but what?"

"Franz, the bloggers."

"What do you mean?"

"Ask Colin to send us any documentation he has that shows proof of presidential interference. We'll put some heat on the White House."

"Is that wise?"

"It's too late to be smart, we have to be bold."

Five minutes later, they had what they needed.

"Franz, look at this stuff!"

Franz e-mailed the information to several prolific bloggers; the story was online within the hour: "High-Level White House officials under investigation. President threatens to fire FBI Director."

•••••••••••••••••••••••••••••••••••

"It's Colin, John. You caused a shit storm, one like I've never seen. This ought to slow them down a little."

John smiled and went back to sleep.

# 91

### Washington DC

The director was already at the safe house. "Colin, can you believe this shit? The White House switchboard is overloaded. The media is in a frenzy, they're denying everything, but the documents are out there. I called a few of my friends in the Senate and the IRS, I gave them an earful. They are going to continue to investigate the energy companies. The SEC has backed off. They're afraid of repercussions from the oval office."

"What do we do now?"

"I'm going to resign."

"What?"

"Just listen, Colin. Get in touch with the chief of staff. Tell him you can get me to resign once you are assured the position. This will free me up to lobby Congress and the Senate. I can't do that if I'm still the director."

"Sir, if you quit now, they'll discredit you, you won't be effective."

"You're probably right, but we don't have an alternative. We have to keep the heat on if we're going to stop them. Once you take over, make an announcement that you're investigating your predecessor. It will make the administration comfortable with you and keep them busy trying to come up with something on me. As soon as I contact you, hold a press conference, announce that your investigation of me is complete and you have found no problems with my work but you have found damaging information on others in Justice. If we time this just right, I will be able to turn over more information to our friends on the Hill. That will translate to more heat on the president."

"That's brilliant, sir."

"Colin, get to work and ask Peter and Dan to come in."

"Rob, it's Colin. I have to see you now."

"Colin, we're real busy up here—"

Colin cut him off. "Now. The entrance to the Smithsonian. Thirty minutes." He smiled. He knew Rob would be there.

## 92

**Monaco**

Chris and his team were positioned around Saris's compound, using sensitive listening devices and infrared heat-sensitive scopes to transcribe everything that was said.

Chris reported the situation to Raquel.

"Chris, can you record any of this?"

"Yes, but it's not clear enough to use because I can't identify the speakers."

"Get as much as you can. Stay on site and photograph everyone present. I have an idea. I'll fill you in when you get back."

After the meeting broke up, all of the participants were photographed on their way out. Chris had another team in place, monitoring them as they readied to sail back to their home ports.

Three of his team were left behind to watch Saris.

He arrived at the office; Raquel was waiting for him. "Chris, that was great work. We identified everyone in the photos, and we're going to act on this tomorrow."

"What are we going to do?"

"We're not going to do anything. I've passed the information upstairs. Interpol and the EU are going after every company that was represented at that meeting."

"Going after them for what?"

"For the improper trading of euro dollars and UN commercial paper."

Chris was angry. "That's crazy, it won't work."

"We know that, it's just a pretense to look into their companies. It will also alert them to the fact that they're being investigated."

"Well, Raquel, I guess it will slow them down."

"I wish we could get media coverage. That would really slow them down. But they own the media."

"We can use the bloggers!"

"Chris, what do you mean *bloggers*?"

"John Moore has started an Internet magazine comprised of about two hundred bloggers in Europe and the US. He's gotten good results. He got the story out about the bogus climate figures and scientists fudging the numbers."

"Chris, this is very interesting."

"I'll call Franz." Chris called Franz and was told it would be no problem to spread the information.

"Chris, send me the information you want disseminated, we'll flood the Net within an hour."

"Thanks, Franz, I'll blast you in two hours."

All of the information was sent via blast, entitled, "Unscrupulous dealings lead to an investigation by the EU and Interpol."

The next morning, as investigators charged into each of the company headquarters, the news hit the Web: "MAJOR EUROPEAN FIRMS BEING PROBED BY THE EU FOR ILLEGAL CURRENCY TRADING AND MONEY LAUNDERING—CONVICTIONS IMMINENT."

# 93

## London

Paula sat at the table of a small restaurant in SoHo, waiting for the man she had called earlier that day.

"Ms. Franks?"

"Yes, please sit down, Mr. Barlow, you were recommended to me by the late Ascot Chen. He told me you were efficient and discreet. This transaction must remain between us, understood?"

"Perfectly, Ms. Franks."

"The men you select must carry Indonesian passports. Under no circumstances do I want the job completed, but it has to look like a valid attempt on his life."

"You wish to make it look like a real hit, but you do not want the person killed, correct?"

"Yes, Mr. Barlow, that is correct."

"Who is the target?"

Paula slid a picture across the table. "Michael Manheim."

"The price just tripled, Ms. Franks. Do you know that I work for him as well?"

"I'm willing to double the original price, no more. Mr. Barlow, you are not the only person Ascot introduced me to. Just by taking part in this conversation, your life may be in jeopardy."

"I heard you were tough, I'll accept your offer to double the original price. It's a pleasure doing business with you."

Paula went back to her flat and sat in a hot tub for most of the evening. She called Manheim several hours later.

"Mike, please call me back on a clean phone."

"Paula, what can I do for you?"

"Mike, be careful. Have you heard what went on here today?"

"Yes. I've been having similar problems here."

"I talked to YK earlier. He blames you and me for these problems. I'm going to get out of town for a few days. I suggest you do the same. I did not like his tone."

"Have you spoken to Saris?"

"No, I was told that he is traveling."

"Paula, take care of yourself." He hung up.

Manheim thought about the conversation; he picked up the phone and called Wiley.

"Wiley, it's Mike."

"Mike, we're losing it, buddy. What do you want me to do?"

"Contact the chief of staff and tell him to suggest to the president that he hold a press conference. When the president asks why, the chief should mention that perhaps he could tell the press that he's been trying to get too much done at once, causing confusion on several levels of government and that everything will be put on hold to give everyone a chance to regroup. Tell him to make sure the president stresses that the climate-control issue is paramount, it will not be tabled. He should also let the press know that nothing will be done from now on without his approval. Wiley, that should calm things down and give us a chance to regroup."

"Good idea, Mike, I'll get a hold of Rob right away."

Mike hung up and started to walk to his office when he heard a single shot, the bullet dug into the floor near him. He dove over a piece of furniture and crawled toward the door. He heard five more shots and saw five bullet holes patterned near the door before he got there, so he ran across the room and dove behind his desk. He opened a panel, allowing him access to the MAC 10 and the M79 grenade launcher that he had hidden there. He rolled across the room and turned off the light. Seeing one assailant, he moved silently toward the window, and with lightning speed and precision, he broke the window, grabbed the man, and pulled him through. With one fast motion, he broke the man's neck and dropped him to the floor.

He sat in the corner of the room and remained motionless, waiting. Another man, a professional, came into the room only a few minutes later. He waited until the man was visible and fired the MAC 10; the man's head disintegrated.

Manheim waited for several more minutes; when he was sure there were no other assailants, he searched the bodies. Looking at their passports, he said, "Holy shit, it was YK." While waiting for the police, he called Paula.

"Paula, it's Mike. Someone just tried to take me out. Be careful."

Paula replied tersely, smiled to herself, and called YK. "YK, it's Paula. I just got off the phone with Mike. He thinks you're disappointed with him, so be careful. You never know what he might do." She went to have a late dinner.

# 94

### Washington DC

Colin motioned to the chief of staff, signifying that he sit on a bench away from normal traffic flow.

"Rob, would you like the director to resign?"

"Yeah, but he refused in front of the president and myself."

"If I am assured the position, I can get him to resign by tomorrow."

"How?"

"Make a public announcement first thing tomorrow that he has resigned and I have been appointed. When I hear that, I will bring his resignation to your office and you will swear me in."

"But, Colin, how are you going to do it?"

"Rob, he's already agreed, as long as I succeed him."

"It couldn't have come at a better time, consider it done." They shook on the deal.

Colin went directly to the safe house; the director was given the details and left for the night. Colin and the group started planning for the days ahead. Sally showed him several listening devices and how they worked.

The plan now, they decided, was to engage as many members of the administration as possible to see what information could be gleaned. Colin had gotten a ticket into the enemy camp, and they knew they had to capitalize on it.

The announcement was made on every major radio and TV station in the country: FBI DIRECTOR RESIGNS. THE DEPUTY

## GREEN TO RED

Director, Colin Young, has been appointed as the new Director.

"Good morning, Colin. Do you have it?"

"Right here in my pocket. Do you have the official appointment in writing?"

"The president wants to give it to you himself."

..........................................

"Colin, congratulations, welcome aboard. I'm sure you're aware that the last director and I did not see eye-to-eye on many things. I hope we will have a better relationship."

"I didn't see eye-to-eye with him on everything either. I don't think he really understood the changes you're trying to make. I will do everything in my power to help you reach your goals."

The president smiled. "Colin, that's what I wanted to hear. It's a complicated world out there, and we have to stay ahead of it."

"I agree wholeheartedly, Mr. President." *I think I'm going to puke.*

"Colin, before we go to the press room, I want to talk to you privately." The president motioned to the chief of staff, walked to his desk, and flipped a switch. "Colin, the world is changing rapidly, and we have to change with it. The US is no longer a major superpower, and we have to adapt. We can still be the shining light of the world, but in a different way. I've taken steps to bring us into a new world. I need to know that you are behind me, helping me to bring this concept to fruition."

"I'm with you, Mr. President."

The president watched Colin closely.

"Mr. President, may I speak frankly as well?"

"Go ahead."

"Well, sir, we've lost our manufacturing base. We have no true allies left. We can't be the world's policemen. The only alternative is to become part of the global village. We can still be leaders, but we must embrace the world economy and social systems."

"Colin, I'm so glad you joined my administration. We might have to bend the rules a little, but we're moving into new territory, and we can't let old rules stifle us."

"I'm with you one hundred percent."

"Colin, if you play your cards right, you will retire a very rich man."

"Thank you, Mr. President."

Colin was officially appointed as director in a press conference held right after their confidences were exchanged.

# 95

### Zurich, Switzerland

Paula walked into the bank and asked to see Tsillman.

"Fraulein Franks, I would have met you at the airport had I known you were coming here."

"I thought I would come in and meet the new director on the spur of the moment."

"Fraulein Franks, he is only here on loan from our Hong Kong office. There's really no need for you to meet him."

"Are you telling me I cannot meet him?"

"Fraulein Franks, I will get him immediately."

Tsillman brought Chong to her. "Mr. Tsillman, may I have a moment with Mr. Chong. I would like to get to know him."

"Yes, of course. Chong, take Fraulein Franks to the client lounge."

When Tsillman left, Paula asked, "Mr. Chong, could we go somewhere for coffee or something?"

"Of course, Ms. Franks."

"Call me Paula."

They left the bank; while walking, she said, "I have to get something to your boss immediately, some very sensitive information."

"Today might be difficult, but certainly tomorrow is possible."

"I guess that will have to do. Can you come to my hotel in an hour or so?"

"Yes, where are you staying?"

"I'm sorry, the Baur Lac, room 213."

Chong was excited. "I'll see you there in one hour."

"Mr. Chong, no need for coffee now. I'll see you in one hour."

Chong arrived a little early just to play it safe. Satisfied, he went to Paula's room and knocked on the door. She ushered him in quickly.

"I'm sorry, but I have to be careful. The information I'm giving you could get me killed. Tell John that Liddo and Saris are in turmoil but not to underestimate them." She handed him a portfolio. "Here is enough information to bring down Liddo's operations in America, well, at least Mike Manheim."

"It's none of my business, but why are you doing this?"

"It's a long story, this is my chance to make things right. Deliver this to John personally. Don't tell anyone, especially Tsillman. He has a long history with Liddo."

Chong called John from the deck of a sightseeing boat. "Hello, John. It's Chong. I have to see you right away."

"Why?"

"I can't tell you on the phone, but it's important."

"Chong, get to Monaco."

"Okay, I'll take the train."

"When you arrive, take a taxi to the Grand Square."

"I'll call you when I'm leaving the station."

"Ivan, or one of his people, will pick you up at the Square."

Chong arrived in Monaco three hours later.

Chong was approached by a large man with a Russian accent. "Are you Chong? Ivan sent me to pick you up."

Chong followed him. In his peripheral vision, he saw Ivan approaching. Ivan walked past the man, turned quickly, and jabbed him with a large needle. Chong and Ivan grabbed him by the arms and carefully lowered him to a bench. "Let's hurry, they obviously know you're here."

The car sped off, taking evasive action. "Chong, it's good to see you. How do you like Zurich?"

Chong knew that Ivan was a professional, so he relaxed a little.

Ivan pulled off the road about twelve kilometers off the Square. They walked over a hill, through a pasture, to a dirt road and a parked car. Ivan drove to the farmhouse where he knew John was waiting.

After they spent a little time catching up, Chong told John about Paula.

"Chong, hold on, I need everyone to hear this."

Halfway through the story, Ivan said, "Hold on, I need vodka. No offense, Chong, but I barely understand you. A little vodka will make it better." He poured himself a water glass full of vodka. "Please continue."

Chong handed the portfolio to John after he finished relaying the events. John opened it. "Holy shit! This is everything—all of Liddo's illegal operations in the States, everything from drug trafficking to murder and then some!"

"But can we trust her, John?"

"I don't know yet, but get this off to Colin immediately and be sure to mention the source. If half of this is true, he should be able to shut Liddo down forever."

# 96

**Jakarta, Indonesia**

Y. K. Chen got the call from his man in airport security. Manheim had arrived and had left the airport. Chen arranged for maximum security in the house. Chen could not believe his most trusted partner would try to harm him.

Mike realized security had been heightened. *How did this son of a bitch know I was coming?* Two guards stopped him at the front door.

"Mr. Manheim, could you please raise your hands? I must frisk you."

"Of course, are you expecting some kind of trouble?"

"No, sir, just precautions."

"YK, what's with all the security?"

"Michael, we're living in dangerous times. Everything is in flux. I'm taking extra care."

"Good idea, YK, someone has just made an attempt on my life." Manheim studied YK's reaction.

"Michael, who do you think did it?"

"I'm not sure, YK."

"Perhaps Saris, I've heard he is not happy with the way things are going in America. Truthfully, Michael, I'm not happy either."

"YK, the situation in the States is a little erratic, but we have it under control. The head of the FBI has been forced out. His replacement will work with us, I'm told."

YK seemed satisfied, but Manheim didn't like the fact that he remained so calm. YK was most dangerous when he was calm.

"Michael, do you think I tried to kill you?"

"No, YK, why would I think that?"

"Michael, don't lie to me."

Manheim stood up; the two guards cocked their weapons. "YK, do you think I came here to hurt you?"

"Michael, why would you come unannounced when things are so bad in America?"

Manheim was certain that he was in trouble. He started to pace the floor. "YK, we have been through a lot together. I thought you trusted me." Manheim lunged at one of the men and, with one swift motion, took his weapon and shot the other one. He gun-butted the man that he had just disarmed, who went down unconscious.

"YK, I would never harm you. You have been like a—"

Before he could finish his sentence, YK stood with a gun pointed at Mike. Manheim didn't hesitate. The shot hit YK in the center of his forehead. Manheim heard footsteps running toward the room. He got behind the door. Manheim took out the three men before they even knew where he was. He killed four others on his way out.

He called Paula from the plane. "Get on a secure phone."

Paula called him back within seconds. "Mike, is everything all right?"

"Paula, you were right. YK is dead. I had to kill him."

"Mike, but are you all right?"

"I'm talking to you, right? Contact our attorneys in Hong Kong, have them turn over YK's stock and the deed of trust to us. Then go to your banker in Zurich, have all of YK's private holdings transferred into Liddo's four holding accounts. Do not put any of it into the central banks in Africa or South America. Do it now, before anyone finds out he's dead.

"Friday, I'm going to have a meeting in the US with all of Liddo's managers. Be there. You should have everything done by then."

"I'm on it, Mike. See you Friday in Memphis."

Paula smiled. *One down, one to go.*

# 97

### Washington DC

"Colin, it's Rob, we're going to have briefing tomorrow at ten fifteen, conference room six on the fifth sublevel. Pick up your new security ID card today, you'll need it to get in. The president wants you to find out what the previous director was working on before he stepped down. I know this is short notice, but we're on a tight schedule here."

"Damn, I don't even have access to the computers yet."

"Welcome to my world. I'll see you tomorrow."

Colin started to compile a list of everything that he was going to need for tomorrow's meeting—no real important information, just enough to appear to be on their side.

Colin was still working when the phone rang. "Colin Young here."

"Mr. Director, it's Sally Crothers. Congratulations, I just heard. I'm sorry to bother you, sir, but I've been on leave. I have to see you as soon as possible?"

"Well, Sally, call me back at the beginning of next week, okay?"

"Yes, sir, I'll do that."

Colin cleaned up his desk and pressed the intercom button. "Mary, I'm taking a break, going to dinner. I'll be back in about two hours. I've left a list on my desk, I'll need everything by the time I get back. Thank you."

He went home, walked through the building and out the back door. He hailed a cab, after taking precautions, and gave the driver the address of a restaurant eight blocks from the safe house. He walked the rest of the way making sure he wasn't followed, before walking in.

"Sally, what's going on?"

The director came into the room. "Colin, this is unbelievable."

"What's going on, sir?"

"We just got this from your friends in Zurich."

Colin began to read it and jumped. "This is just what we need. This will put all these bastards behind bars."

"Colin, correct, it should put them behind bars, but how do we do it?"

"What do you mean, sir? This is irrefutable evidence."

"Yes, but it goes all the way to the top. Do you think they'll let you use this?"

"They wouldn't dare to try and stop this."

"Colin, calm down. They can squash this. If you presented it, you'd be gone too."

"What are we going to do?"

"Colin, that's a good question. First, I am going to have Pete and Dan check out this information. If we can put some solid evidence together, we can act on it. Right now, we need to make sure this information is bulletproof. If we have hard evidence, we can make an end run through the oversight committee. The AG will not be able to suppress it."

"Can we trust them?"

"Colin, are you getting cynical in your old age?"

"No, sir, just being careful. I still want to think it through a little better before we take it to the Hill."

The director looked at him proudly. "Agreed, you're right, Colin."

"I have an idea."

"What do you have in mind?"

"Sir, I've been asked by the president to give him a briefing tomorrow morning. I was also asked by Rob to see if I could find out about anything you were working on. Why not jot down some notes about Manheim and Liddo? I could tell them I found it in your desk. It should be enough to get a rise out of them."

"That's a great idea. We can't monitor the president, but we can monitor Rob, Pritchard, and Manheim. This might be just what we need to put the icing on the cake."

The director took out a yellow legal pad and wrote down,

> Manheim
> Liddo
> money transfers
> Pritchard
> the Speaker
> the President

He then drew arrows, linked them, wrote something else, then blacked it out. "Here you go, Colin, this ought to frazzle their nerves."

"Sir, I'm going back to the office to finish up. It won't be safe for you after tomorrow, please stay here. I'll contact you as soon as I can."

Colin was still preparing for the meeting several hours later. A communications specialist knocked on his door.

"Come in."

"Director, we just got this, I thought you might want to see it."

The man handed Colin a notice from the Indonesian Police. "Mr. Michael Manheim is wanted for questioning in the murders of Y. K. Chen and eight others at Mr. Chen's home. We do not have jurisdiction, but we ask for the cooperation of the FBI." Trying not to look too overjoyed, Colin thanked the man and dismissed him.

Before the briefing was over, Colin asked if he might see Rob and the president alone. The president agreed; everyone else left the room.

"What is it, Colin?" asked the chief of staff.

"Something has come up that I thought should be dealt with privately." He pulled the folded piece of paper out of his pocket and handed it to Rob. "Do you know these names: Manheim or Liddo?"

Rob replied, "No, do you, Mr. President?"

The president just shook his head.

"I found that in the director's desk. I received this very early this morning." Rob read it and handed it to the president. The two men looked very uneasy.

"Mr. President, if you know anything about this, please let me know now so I can deflect any further inquiries."

The president went to answer, but Rob interrupted.

"Well, Colin, this is a little sensitive. I just remembered something. Liddo is a major contributor to both the DNC and the president's campaign fund. The press would have a field day if they found out."

Colin had gotten the response he'd hoped for. "Gentlemen, what do you want me to do?"

"Nothing. Send a message back to Indonesia telling them that you'll give them all the cooperation that you are able to. However, you'll have to conduct your own investigation since an American citizen is involved."

"Anything else, do you want me to bring this Manheim person in?"

Rob, clearly agitated, said, "No! Don't go near him. We'll handle this ourselves. Is that clear?"

"Crystal."

The president got up. "Gentlemen, if that's all, I will let Rob handle this thing with Manheim, let me know what happens."

"Yes, Mr. President."

As the president was leaving, he said, "Colin, you are doing a great job so far. Keep it up."

"Yes, sir."

# 98

## The Hague

Raquel woke up. "Good morning, my darling."

Chris leaned over and kissed her. Raquel threw her arms around him. Chris couldn't believe how wonderful it felt. "Raquel, I love you."

"Of course, you love me. Do you think you'd be in my bed if I thought you didn't?" She started to laugh. "Chris, for a tough man, you're so easy to fool." Chris grabbed her around the waist, and she laughed even louder. After their wrestling match, they fell comfortably into each other's arms and lay silently for a time. He felt warm and secure, as the horror he'd seen recently drained slowly from him.

"Chris, what's next on the agenda?"

"I'm not sure. Our raids were successful, but the rest of the terrorists have probably scattered. With Gruber out of the way, they probably have no central contact. Let's give their names and last known locations to all governments in the EU and let them handle it."

"Good idea, I'll give the information to our friend in the CIA as well. It will give me some collateral for the future."

"Raquel, let me tell my friends from Zurich before you tell the CIA. I haven't talked with them lately."

"Okay, I'll hold off until I hear from you."

The rest of breakfast was spent talking about their future plans. They showered and dressed. Raquel asked, "Do you want to drive in with me?"

"No, I think I'll locate my friends and visit them. I'd like to give them a rundown from here and get brought up to speed on their efforts."

"All right, is there anything you need done while you're gone?"

"Yes, why don't you start surveillance on Gruber's replacement. He'll be contacting Saris, it could prove interesting."

"Consider it done. Have a safe trip. I'm missing you already." Raquel leaned toward him and kissed him on the check. He grabbed her, pulled her close, and gave her a warm passionate kiss in return.

"Now I'm really missing you, but let me go or I'll never get to work."

Chris called Franz, found out his location from him, packed, and got ready for the trip. As instructed, he stopped in town, bought some red duct tape, and put three stripes on his rear window to identify him as a friendly.

# 99

### France

Chris had no trouble finding the small farmhouse. As he drove up the narrow road, he noticed two men; he assumed they were part of Ivan's team.

"Chris, how are you?"

"Franz, I'm doing well. I saw two bodyguards on the road."

"You only saw two? Good, there are over twenty out there."

"Please, we better go in. They're getting good at finding us."

Chris was greeted by Ivan and John. "Chris, you look well."

"Thank you, Ivan. I feel great. You don't look any the worse for wear."

"I think this calls for vodka."

While Ivan was pouring drinks, John told Chris, "I'm glad you're all right. These people are tougher than the ones I've seen in Asia."

Chris told them the details of the mission and everything that had transpired since.

"How do you like working with SITCEN?"

"It's a fledgling organization, but it's well-equipped and well-funded. The team leaders are good, one is from Interpol and the other is an SAS officer. They're great to work with."

"Who is Raquel?"

"She's the head of SITCEN." Chris didn't offer any other information.

"Is she a bitch? Most women in this field are."

Chris looked a bit taken aback. "No, she's a wonderful person."

Ivan laughed. "So you've fallen for her."

Chris, visibly embarrassed, admitted, "Well yes, I think I'm going to ask her to marry me."

All three chimed in, "Congratulations, Chris!"

"Yes, thank you. She is smart, tough, and beautiful."

"Then how did you get her?" They all laughed.

"Okay, guys, let's get back to work."

"Work, work, work, that's all we do. Our friend has found love, and all you can think of is work."

"Ivan, you're right. We can use a break, and this news calls for a celebration."

Ivan started to make drinks. Franz went to the kitchen to begin cooking, and Chris and John sat in the small living room.

"Chris, do you think we're making any headway?"

"Yes, John, I think we have them running. Our only weak spot is that we've put all of our efforts into stopping Liddo. We have not put pressure on Saris yet."

"Good point, do you have other ideas? You know we've slowed him down a little by disrupting the Green Party and by you taking out Gruber."

"They have a replacement for him already, and the loss of Fragge didn't seem to bother Saris at all."

"You're right. The European press is already behind him. We've started using bloggers, they're effective but no competition for the papers and TV."

"John, you're barking up the wrong tree."

"What do you mean?"

"Saris has all his eggs in America. His power is now with the American president."

"Yes, I know, but what are you proposing?"

"Perhaps we can discredit them financially. Hire some well-known financial advisors and have them show proof that the Green movement will cause an economic disaster in America.

Maybe your bloggers might have enough clout to spread the word."

Franz called them to dinner. "I've prepared a celebration feast."

The food was great and the conversation was animated. They continued to discuss Chris's idea, and by the end of the night, they had a plan. They discussed it well into the morning.

John was the first one to hear something after sleeping for a few hours. He bolted out of bed, armed himself, and woke the others. They counted at least ten people moving outside the house. Ivan saw a shadow pass the window; he fired. The man dropped. Ivan moved close to the window, but he was too close. It gave one intruder the chance to grab him and pull him through. Several more shots were fired. John was worried that Ivan had bit the bullet. Someone dove through the window, bringing John back to the moment. John fired and missed. It was Ivan. "Thank God you're a lousy shot!"

Chris moved to the door; just as he positioned himself, it flew open, and a hand grenade rolled in. Chris dove, picked it up, and tossed it back. After the explosion, two men came through the door firing automatic weapons. Chris dropped one of them. Franz took out the other.

Then they heard footsteps on the roof. Ivan grabbed a pump shotgun and ran up the stairs. He fired through the roof and heard someone fall as another one swung through the window on a rope. Ivan fired at such close range, obliterating his attacker. He moved to the other side of the loft and waited. He could hear nothing above him, other than the gunfire downstairs.

As he started down the stairs, he saw another guy near the banister; the man's head exploded like a ripe watermelon as he was shot between the eyes. He decided to go back up and reload. This time, as he made his way down the stairs, he saw another man pointing his weapon at him. Ivan rolled and tumbled down the stairs. At the bottom, he was on his feet, and he fired. The round almost cut the man in half while he was running down the stairs.

Ivan noticed that John and Franz were pinned down by automatic weapon fire. Chris was trying to get into position. Ivan ran into the room, fired one way, and then the other. Neither of his shots connected, but it gave Chris enough time to take out the man who had Franz pinned down. Franz was then able to get a clear shot at John's attacker.

John motioned for them to follow him. They entered through a small door under the stairs and found themselves in a tunnel. It came out into a field about thirty meters from the house. John looked out carefully and made a hand gesture; he saw six more. He rolled behind a cluster of bushes as the others followed. Chris noticed a shallow ditch that they could crawl into and get within a few feet of the house. They positioned themselves within five feet of the attackers and fired, killing all six in seconds. Chris and Franz ran through the house and out the back to check for additional assailants. They took a body count, not bad odds, four against nineteen.

Ivan was happily surprised. The attackers had used tranquilizers to subdue his men. Three hours later, Ivan instructed them to get rid of the bodies and do the usual clean up.

Chris searched the bodies; two of them had cigarettes from Yemen on them. "These are probably the same men we've been hunting."

"But now they're hunting you."

"I have to report in. Raquel could be in danger."

Franz and John packed up. "Thank God, none of the equipment was damaged."

"I think I might have lost two of the hard drives. They're drenched in blood." He cleaned them with alcohol and hoped for the best.

Ivan sent two of his best men to the boat. "Do some long-distance surveillance, do not engage."

Chris left first. John, Franz, and Ivan drove to the boat. When they arrived, Ivan's men motioned for them to hurry.

Ivan yelled, "Get out of here now!"

Franz spun the car around and sped away. John started to ask, "What are you doing?" A car pulled out of a hidden drive and blocked them. Franz started to back up, but another car pulled out behind them. Ivan reached into his bag, pulled out a hand grenade, opened the door, and rolled out. He screamed, "Get down," as he lobbed the grenade under the car behind them. There was a horrific explosion, Then Ivan jumped back into the car. "Drive, drive backward."

Franz put the car into reverse and pushed the pedal to the floor. The car lurched backward, pushing the wreckage off the road. The windshield exploded, and the interior filled with glass shards. Ivan reached under the seat and took out a pump shotgun. "John, take this." He handed it over the seat. "Franz, hit the brakes when I tell you to. John, as soon as I tell you, blast them with the shotgun—keep pumping and firing."

Ivan yelled, "Franz, now!" Franz slowed down slightly and then hit the brake hard. The car in front almost hit them. Ivan yelled, "Shoot, John, shoot."

John fired three times. The first round pulverized the head of the driver. The second pulped the shoulder of the man in the passenger seat, and the third round killed the man in the rear seat.

Ivan yelled, "Good shooting, John!"

John was shaking, pure adrenaline.

Ivan told Franz to stop the car. "John, give me the shotgun."

He gave John a 9mm. "Stay here. Franz, take John and hide behind those bushes. I want to rescue my men. I won't be long, I hope." Ivan drove back to the pier area; John and Franz heard the shotgun, four quick shots. It was quiet for a minute, then another volley of three shots. They heard the rapid fire of a machine gun, followed by one more shotgun blast. It was only a few minutes, but it seemed much longer; Ivan returned with his men. "These people are well-trained and well-equipped. We have to change our strategy."

"Ivan, whatever you want, you got it."

The team, along with Ivan's two men, crammed into the car and drove back to the pier. They boarded the boat and left. "John, where are we headed?"

# 100

**The Hague**

"Chris, it's so good to have you back. Are you all right?"

"Raquel, I couldn't tell you over the phone, I'm certain we're being targeted."

"What makes you think that, Chris? They were after your friends from Zurich, not us."

"Raquel, I didn't tell them, but I found this on one of the bodies." Chris held out a piece of paper.

"Chris, my god. Where could they have gotten this?"

"From any of the bureaucrats that work here." It was a diagram of their building, both Raquel's and Chris's offices were highlighted.

Raquel called an emergency meeting of her inner circle. She outlined events of the past several days. "Do we have enough evidence to pick up Saris?"

"No, we have nothing that can tie him directly to any of this."

"Can we go after the new head of the Socialist Party?"

"No, we have nothing on him either."

Francoise continued, "If he's taken over for Gruber, then he's directing this activity. Let's put him under surveillance. The minute he meets or corresponds with any of these terrorists, we'll grab him."

"How long will it take to set up a surveillance team?"

"We can have one in place by tomorrow."

"Do it."

"I'd like to make a suggestion. Let's buy ten prepaid phones for each of us, exchange numbers, and communicate in that manner. We'll destroy each phone after using it once. We'll separate and work on the move, pay cash for everything. We'll try to uncover as many of their cells as possible and call in strikes as soon as we find them. I'll contact my Swiss friends. Raquel, I suggest that you work with them. They have sophisticated communications equipment and Ivan is a security genius. Hugh, can you organize ten SAS strike teams?"

"Yes, but it will take a few days to get proper clearances."

"Okay, order strikes through Hugh. Give your contacts to Raquel. Make certain she has the authority to order strikes directly just in case you cannot. Francoise, communicate with Hugh or Raquel only. The people at Interpol have too much political interference."

"All right then, we all know what has to be done. Be careful and don't go home. We'll meet here the day after tomorrow at ten a.m. Remember, we all go underground. Chris, could you stay for a moment? I want to speak to you."

"Do you think I should contact my friend from the CIA?"

"Raquel, the fewer people that know what we're doing, the better. Why don't you feed him the information we discussed. If we need him, at least he'll owe you something."

"Good, Chris. That was my feeling exactly."

# 101

### Washington DC

"Director, can you come out to Langley? This is a priority one directive. We will meet at 1500 hours in the CIA director's office."

Colin drove to CIA headquarters in Langley. The deputy director met him at the door. "Colin, good to see you. Please come this way."

The CIA director, Tom Lindy, offered a hand. "Thanks for coming. What I'm about to tell you is classified, it's so sensitive that I didn't want to get Homeland Security involved."

"I understand. What do you have?"

"We just got this in from our station chief in the Hague."

"This is serious. Do you have any idea who these people are?"

"We only know that they are being trained by and represent the National Socialist and the Green parties."

Colin thought that this might be his best opportunity. "This confirms information we've gotten from an investigation we're doing. There seems to be some paramilitary training going on in our prisons. It's tied into community organizers and it has something to do with the Green movement."

"Do you have any intel on this?"

"Not much, we're still looking into it, but we keep getting blocked as soon as we get too close to any of these community organizations. As you know, they're tied into the Hill with a lot of friends up there."

The CIA director asked everyone to leave the room, except Colin.

"Colin, I don't like this. It has all the earmarks of a takeover. What do you think?"

"I don't know, but it looks bad. We're still trying to recover from our recent agency upheaval, but our hands are tied with the AG in control. That all leads to the big man himself, and it's not good."

"Are you saying what I think you're saying?"

"Like you said, Director, it doesn't look good. I still have some investigating to do, but can I count on your cooperation if I need it?"

"The security of this country is our job. You can count on my cooperation."

"Colin, are you available for dinner this evening?"

"Yes, Director, just tell me where and when?"

"Meet me at my house at seven, Shirley will give you my address."

"Sally, call the director. I need to see him right now."

"He's here, in his office."

"Great!"

Colin walked into the director's office. "The shit has just hit the fan."

"What do you mean, Colin?"

"I've just come from Langley. The CIA director asked me to participate in a discussion concerning information he had just received from the Hague." Colin handed him the file.

The director looked it over. "Colin, you're right, the shit has hit the fan."

"Tom Lindy asked me to his house for dinner tonight."

"Colin, that's a good thing. If he didn't have some suspicion about what was going on, he wouldn't have asked you to dinner. He must have a feeling that this is more than just terrorism, keeping the intel so close to the vest. What time are you going to dinner?"

"Seven o'clock."

"Good, that gives us a few hours, but we have to be careful, this could be a setup. The CIA director is a good man, but he is an ass-kissing politician."

Colin arrived at Lindy's house at seven o'clock sharp.

"Colin, please come in."

"Thank you, Director."

"Colin, please call me Tom."

"Would you care for a drink?"

"Yeah, I could use one, scotch over ice."

"I asked you here because I know this place is secure. I have it swept for bugs three times a day."

"Who's your exterminator?"

"This is serious. I need to know your thoughts on it."

"Tom, our investigation leads right to the top."

"What kind of an investigation?"

"Outside forces, economic, not military, are using the Green movement to take control and change our way of life. They're calling it the New World Order. But every time we seem to be getting a handle on it, some politician stops us. An enormous amount of money has gone into the DNC, and that's why our previous director left."

"I know, he was a good man. It's too bad he left."

Colin shook his head.

"I have a very bad feeling about this. Our European intel shows that a new world order is in the making there as well, but we are having the same problems that you are—half of the politicians are behind it."

Colin asked, "Do you know who might be behind the whole thing?"

"Aristotle Saris has a hand in it. But I don't think he's powerful enough to pull it off alone."

"He wouldn't have to if he has half the politicians in his pocket."

"Good point!"

They ate dinner.

"We need to exchange intelligence under the radar. Let's meet tomorrow in the garden at the Center for the Arts and exchange information directly. We can meet in our offices later."

"Okay, but let's keep this between ourselves for now."

As soon as Colin sat down at his desk, the phone rang.

"Colin, the president would like to see you now."

"Sure, Rob, I'll be right over."

Rob was waiting at the door for him. "Rob, what's up?"

"That's what we want to know, Colin."

Rob led Colin to a secure conference room. "This room is secure. The president will be here shortly."

"Who's attending the meeting?"

It'll be just the three of us."

"Mr. President."

"Colin, it's good to see you. Listen, I heard you were called over to Langley, why?" "Well, sir, Tom Lindy has just received some sensitive information about a terrorist network in Europe, and he was wondering if we had heard anything about it here."

"Why didn't he go through normal channels?"

"You would have to ask him about that, sir."

"Colin, I need a straight answer. Those bastards at the CIA have been against me from the beginning. I'm not going to sit here and be blindsided."

"Mr. President, I have your back. They can't act on US soil. I agreed to see him so that I could deal with it personally. That way there are no leaks of any kind possible. The only thing that was alarming was the fact that Aristotle Saris was mentioned. They're looking into his involvement with the terrorists. I would diffuse that situation by simply going to the press first since he is one of your major contributors. Schedule a press conference and tell them that you've received information that some contributors to the DNC and the Speaker are under investigation. I'll stand next to you so the press believes that the FBI is conducting the investigation."

"Rob, what do you think?"

"Mr. President, I think Colin has a good point. The CIA can't really investigate here, so no matter what they say, we will say we are already working on it. It's brilliant!"

The president smiled. "By mentioning the DNC and the Speaker, that keeps prying eyes away from the administration."

"Mr. President, may I suggest that you call the press conference tomorrow."

"Rob, set it up. Thank you, Colin. It's good to know I have a strong team behind me."

The president left.

"That was good. You're going to be a shining star in this administration. One more thing, was Saris the only one mentioned?"

Colin thought for a minute. "Yes."

Colin went to the safe house after using heavy evasive tactics.

"Colin, how are you?"

"Not good. Tom Lindy received intel from SITCEN. He has information on Saris, but I didn't see anything about Liddo. I told him we would share information, and I'm supposed to meet him tomorrow. They're watching me, so I don't think that's a good idea."

"Do you think he's on the level?"

"Yes, when I left his house, I had a strange feeling, so I went back to the office. Before I could even sit down, I was called to the White House. The president and his stooge grilled me about the meeting. They seemed relieved when I told them I covered their asses. I suggested they schedule a press conference tomorrow to dispel any information that Lindy might come out with."

"Good work, Colin. I'll meet with Lindy and fill him in on what's really going on. We can use all the help we can get. I've met with a small group of congressmen and senators, and they have reviewed the information. They think it's enough to go to the floor with. But last thing we want is for this to go political, especially with the press in the opposition's pocket. I want to talk to Lindy. Perhaps we can use some of his unique talents."

Colin went to talk to Sally. "Did we get anything interesting today?"

"I think this is pretty interesting."

"Director, did you see this?"

"Yeah, your friends in Europe are having a tough time."

"*Tough* is not the word for it. This means that we are getting to them but we still don't have enough to stop them."

The director had a grave look on his face. "Colin, that's what I'm going to discuss with Lindy tomorrow."

# 102

"Hello, Mr. Chong, this is Paula Franks. I've just arrived in Zurich and have some urgent business I must discuss with you."

"I'm at your service, Ms. Franks."

"I'm staying in the Bauer Lac Hotel, room 332. Could you join me here in an hour?"

"I'll see you then."

"Thank you, Mr. Chong."

When Chong arrived, she greeted him at the door. "Mr. Chong, thank you for coming on such short notice."

"It's my pleasure, Ms. Franks. What can I do for you?"

"I want all of the funds in these accounts transferred to Liddo's accounts, in euros and in the amounts shown here."

"That might be difficult. Some of these accounts are in Central Banks. Are you a legal signer?"

"No, Mr. Chong, I'm not, but here's my corporate authority and power of attorney."

"Everything seems to be in order, but it might take some time to have the funds released from the Central Banks."

"Thank you, Mr. Chong."

"You're welcome, it will be done."

Chong was about to leave when she passed a note to him.

"Ms. Franks, I apologize, may I use your restroom before I go?"

"Of course, Mr. Chong."

Chong went into the bathroom and read the note:

I must contact John immediately. He's in danger.

Chong threw it in the toilet and flushed. He ran the water and wrote a note to her:

> I'm giving you a prepaid phone. I will leave it on the vanity in the restroom. Call John at this number: 49-266-2347. Call him after 5, that way I can prepare him. After the call, destroy the phone.

On his way out, Chong extended his hand. When Paula shook it, she palmed the note and said, "Thank you again, Mr. Chong."

"Thank you, Ms. Franks. I assure you everything will be done to your satisfaction."

•••••••••••••••••••••••••••

"Boss, it's Chong. Ms. Franks is going to call you after five. She says it's urgent. I gave her a prepaid phone and the next number on the list."

"What does she want?"

"I don't know, but she said you were in serious trouble."

"Okay, Chong." Chong dropped the phone, stepped on it, picked up the pieces, and threw them in the lake.

•••••••••••••••••••••••••••

"Peter, your friend from London was just here. Please process these transfers for her."

"She was here? Why didn't she call me?"

"I don't think she likes you."

John received the call shortly after five. "Hello."

"John, Paula here. You're in serious danger."

"I know. I've just been shot at in two countries."

"You don't understand, it's Manheim. He found out about you, He's gone into a rage. He killed YK."

"He killed him?"

"Yes."

"Paula, do you know who's controlling the terrorists?"

"Manheim. He used Gruber as a front, but I don't think he trusts the new guy, that union leader."

"Paula, are you sure?"

"Yes, John, I'm certain."

"How does he contact them?"

"Manheim calls a man named Gottfried, and he gets the word out by using a series of restaurants and reservation schemes."

"Paula, do you know his address?"

"No, I just know he lives in Vienna."

"Thanks, Paula."

"John, I just remembered, Manheim always meets him in a bar, Pete's Place."

"I owe you one."

"Be careful. He's very dangerous."

"Franz, can your equipment work out here on the water?"

"Yes, John, but it's dangerous."

"How so?"

Franz started to explain.

"Never mind, you're over my head already. What do we have to do to send out a secure message?"

Franz thought about it. "We should get closer to land, otherwise we could be picked up by a ship's radio."

"How close do we have to get?"

"Within four hundred yards of shore."

"All right, Franz, bring us in."

John told them about his conversation with Paula.

"Contact our FBI friends. If Manheim killed this YK guy, they can arrest him."

"Not true, if a high-level official is involved, he would be released right away."

Ivan nodded. "Good point, but if you tell them and he finds out, that could slow him down."

"We have to tell Chris as well."

"Franz, be sure to tell Chris about this guy Gottfried in Vienna. Chris will take care of him. Let's see how tough it is to set up new communications with the terrorists once Gottfried is dead."

They pulled into shore. John told Franz, "Get the messages off quick, let's get out of here." It only took Franz a few minutes to send a blast to Colin and Chris. They sailed back out without being noticed by anyone, or so they thought.

# 103

**Vienna, Austria**

Chris had his Gottfried surveillance team in place. "Team one, it's a go."

Two men jumped out of a van, and before Gottfried could scream, he was thrown inside. He protested, "What are you doing to me?"

He got a pistol across the head and was told to shut up, but he refused. A masked face came close to his. "I told you to shut up. I will not tell you again."

Gottfried sat quietly, pants now wet. The van pulled into an empty warehouse and stopped. "Get out now." When Gottfried didn't move fast enough, he was thrown out. He landed on his face, bleeding and crying.

They picked him up, put him in a chair, and taped his arms and legs to it with duct tape. They dragged the chair into the only lighted area; daylight shone through the only window.

Chris walked out of the shadows. "Mr. Gottfried, you are going to answer some questions. If you do not answer them correctly, you will suffer the consequences." Another man was holding a bolt cutter. "How do you get your instructions from Manheim?"

Gottfried's voice quavered. "I don't know any Manheim."

"Wrong answer."

The man put one of Gottfried's fingers between the blades. Gottfried screamed, "Okay, I'll tell you!"

The man snapped the blades shut. Gottfried's finger fell to the floor.

Gottfried had to be revived. Chris said, "No wrong answers allowed."

"I'm sorry, it won't happen again."

"Answer the question now."

"He calls me on a secure cell."

"Where's the phone?"

"In my jacket pocket."

"Do you speak to him?"

"No, he just gives me instructions and I…" Gottfried passed out.

Chris used smelling salts to revive him. "Continue."

"He calls me with instructions and he hangs up."

"What kind of instructions?"

"He just gives me a name and location."

"Then what?"

Gottfried hesitated; the man stepped forward.

"I call a restaurant near that location. Then I leave a message for a Mr. Kane."

"Then what?"

"I wait for a callback number and give the name of the target and the location. That's all, I swear it."

Chris motioned his team outside. "Move the van. I'll meet you back at the hotel."

"How did you meet Manheim?"

"I was introduced to him by Herr Gruber."

Chris revived him the third time. "Are there any other go-betweens like you?"

Gottfried answered haltingly, "Yes, only one that I know of, Hans Schroeder from Bremerhaven, he's the party secretary."

Chris took out his pistol and shot the man in the forehead. Chris, repulsed by his own actions, checked the man's pulse. On his way back to the hotel, he called Raquel, gave her a report, and informed her that he and his team were on their way to Bremerhaven.

# 104

**Bremerhaven, Germany**

Chris and the team located the home of Hans Schroeder. They knocked on the door. When Schroeder answered, they subdued him. Chris simply took out a Ka-Bar knife and thrust it into the man's chest. He was dead in seconds. They did a quick search and found several cell phones.

The following day, one of the phones rang and Chris picked it up. A voice said, "Raquel Fuchaurd, the American Hotel in Paris." Chris turned pale, body shaking. He controlled himself and called Raquel, "It's Chris. Leave immediately, there's a hit on you. Take all precautions and call me when you relocate."

Chris mobilized his team. "We're going to Paris." They went to the intra-city airport, bought tickets with cash, and used false ID.

# 105

### Paris, France

Within two hours, they were positioned around the restaurant. One of their men was inside when Chris made the call, "I would like to leave a message for Mr. Kane. I was supposed to meet him, but I am running late. Could you please ask him to call this number?" He had walked to the curb to get as close to traffic as possible. He used the background noise in case the person on the other end knew Schroeder's voice. The call was returned quickly. Chris said, "Raquel Fuchaurd at the American Hotel." He hung up and saw the man leave the restaurant.

They used a standard technique to follow the man to a flat on Rue de Temple. Chris's team was linked to another team at the American Hotel. Chris observed; he saw the man leave the flat with four others. "Five hostiles, three in a black Citron and two in a green Ford, their ETA is twelve minutes."

"We're in position."

Chris got into his car and arrived at the hotel just as the shooting started. Chris walked closer slowly when he had a clean shot; he took it, one down. The other four were inside the office behind a desk; they had taken a hostage. Chris pulled the pin on a stun grenade and tossed it. As soon as it exploded, Chris charged in and picked them off one by one. He carried the hostage out and laid him on the lobby floor. Chris heard his name, spun around, and shot a man aiming at him.

Next, he heard automatic weapons being fired outside. He motioned to his team to go out the back and circle the block. They flanked their attackers and killed all twelve. "That's it. Let's get out of here."

As they drove away, Chris heard sirens coming from all directions. He told his team to keep going while he and three others stayed behind. When the police arrived, they surrounded them. He quickly showed them his identification, asked them if they needed assistance, was told no, and was asked to leave the area at once.

While he was slowly driving away, he commented, "That was better than having them chase us and getting into issues with the police."

# 106

### Gibraltar

Aristotle Saris sat across the table from Mike Manheim. "I was devastated to learn of YK's demise."

"It was unfortunate, but it had to be done. He was getting ready to back out."

"Mike, I am so happy to have you on my side. You have the strength and vision to achieve our goal."

"Aristotle, you're a great man. I would have never believed that a small group of people could take over the world, but you're doing it."

"Mike, it appears that you've overcome all of the political difficulties in your country and we're ready to proceed. You have proven to all of us that the media can shape the will of the people. Your brilliant use of information utilization has been a work of art. I am delighted that your president believed us and ignored all opposition to push through the bills that benefited us in our endeavors. I will guarantee him a place in the new world order."

"Aristotle, we still have a few minor problems to work out, but we're very close now."

"Mike, what do you mean by close? I'm ready to begin. Europe is already embracing our philosophy. The UN is already in motion. You've been able to complete the work of Saul Alinsky by bringing about the demise of individual liberty and the acceptance of the authoritarianism of socialism in the USA. The media has gotten a president elected, brought about an economic downturn, showed the banks and Wall Street for what they really are, and maintained order throughout the process. You are a great man. You will have a place in history, right next to me."

"Aristotle, remember one thing, I'm only in it for the money."

# 107

## Washington DC

Sally transcribed the tape she had just received from the SITCEN agent who was monitoring Saris in Gibraltar. When she was done, she composed herself and brought it to the director. "Sir, I think you should see this."

The director's face turned darker shades of purple as he read further into the transcript.

"Sally, get Tom Lindy on the phone. Tell him to be at the side entrance to the Black History Museum in one hour. Call these senators and congressmen and tell them to meet me at the Capital Steak House at ten a.m., and arrange for a private dining area."

••••••••••••••••••••••••••••••

The director walked up to the museum. "Tom, thanks for coming."

As Tom read through the transcript, he said, "Are you shitting me? The president is involved?"

"Tom, it's time to act. Can you take out Manheim?"

"That would be illegal."

"Tom, this is war. That son of a bitch has been killing people without sanction and with the highest protection."

"What about Saris?"

"Not yet. If we do that, he'll become a martyr and we'll lose our cooperation with the Europeans. I'm trying to discredit him and have him tried in absentia."

"Where did you get the intel, is it reliable?"

"We got it from the horse's mouth. We have them cold."

Their meeting finished, Tom went back to the office and called Fred Thompson, head of covert ops. "Fred, it's Tom. Meet me in the bubble room in five."

"What do you have, boss?"

Tom slid a file across the table. When Fred opened it, he saw a picture of Michael Manheim with ELIMINATE stamped across it. He read the file, said nothing, incinerated the file, and headed for Memphis.

Fred arrived in Memphis two hours later. Fred checked a map, finding every possible route from the airport to Manheim's home. At one point, there was a sharp turn in the road to Manheim's house that hid the view from both sides.

Two female operatives were dressed in very short shorts and revealing tops. They set everything up and dug in, waiting for Manheim's plane to arrive.

The women positioned their red Miata at an angle almost totally blocking one lane. Fred positioned himself in a tree directly across from them, cradling his Howa 1500 rifle using a .308 load—a lot of weapon for this job, but he could not afford to miss.

Manheim's car made the turn. The driver jammed on the brakes. A woman approached the car, and the driver rolled his window down. "Are you crazy, girl? I almost hit you."

"I'm sorry. Our car broke down, we don't have a phone."

Manheim was agitated; he rolled down his window to tell the girl that he would call for assistance. He just started to roll the window up when he heard a shot being fired, the last thing he heard in his life.

The woman next to the driver's window pulled a gun and shot the driver between the eyes. The women got into Manheim's car and drove it to a tractor/trailer waiting to take the car and the bodies very far away.

Fred climbed out of the tree, sauntered over to the Miata, and dismantled his weapon. He drove to the airport and took an agency plane back to Langley. When he arrived, Lindy came in and thanked him for taking care of the problem. "It never happened."

# 108

**London, England**

Get to your office. Call me on a clean line.

Paula finished her lunch, smiling. She said good-bye to her client and made her way slowly back to her office. "Hello, Wiley, I just got your message, what's up?"

"Paula, Mike is missing."

Paula responded in an excited tone, "What! What do you mean he's missing?"

"Paula, he went to Europe to meet with Saris. His plane landed, he was picked up at the airport, but he never made it home."

"Wiley, that's disturbing. Let me try to contact him. I'll call you back."

Paula put the phone down and sat back. A few minutes later, she went to her computer and started to go over all of the Liddo America accounts. She made a copy of accounts that she knew were Manheim's personal funds, and then she deleted them from her list, eight billion dollars' worth.

"Wiley, I can't find him anywhere. Saris confirmed that Mike left and was going to Memphis."

"Paula, I don't like this. There's a lot happening here I can't explain. The administration is behind us one hundred percent. They even got rid of the FBI director, but there seems to be somebody else coming after us."

"Wiley, I think you're paranoid. This has been difficult for everyone."

"Maybe you're right, but I'm getting out of here for a while."

"Wiley, you can't do that. You have to run things until we get this straightened out. I'll contact Saris and tell him that you'll be handling things between him and the president for now. If Saris knows Mike is missing, there's no telling what he'll do. He's not the most stable person on earth."

"Paula, you're right about that. Okay, I'll keep things going. It is better to buffer his demands before they get to the White House."

When she finished her conversation with Wiley, Paula dialed Saris. "Aristotle, darling, how are you?"

"Paula, to what do I owe this pleasure?"

"Darling, I am sorry to say it's business. I'm calling you from my secure phone, are you on one?"

"No, my pet, let me call you back."

"Aristotle, it's nice of you to get back to me so quickly."

"My dear, every moment away from you is like an eternity."

"Aristotle, you flatter me. I'm calling on behalf of Mike. He is very concerned about some investigation in the States, he has made himself scarce. He asked me to call you and tell you that Wiley will handle everything in his stead."

"Paula, is anything wrong?"

"No, Aristotle. Mike wants everything to go as smoothly as possible. He thought it would be better if he absented himself for a while. Aristotle, I need a real man. I've been so lonely. When can I see you again?"

"Paula, be patient, my dear. Good things come to those who wait."

"Aristotle, how can you be so mean to me?"

"Anticipation is often sweeter. I'm doing you a great service. I guarantee I will see you soon."

Saris hung up the phone. *I wonder why Paula really called me.* He started to dial Manheim's number; his assistant came in and handed him a note from the new head of the Green Socialist Party.

> Aristotle, thirty of our best men have been eliminated. I cannot find out who is responsible. If there is a similar event, I will resign.

Saris cursed. "Call our precious head of the party. Tell him I want to see him tonight."

# 109

### The Celtic Sea

By John's estimation, they were somewhere between Wicklow and Wexford, off the Irish coast. John set a course for Calais. The safe house Ivan had set up there was very close to the marina, the best place for a quicker getaway.

John instructed Franz to set the autopilot for Calais. About twenty minutes later, Franz came back on deck after checking the computers.

"John, Chris sent us a message, they've left SITCEN temporarily, but everyone is fine. They also eliminated the go-between and one other. We also received a message from Colin, Manheim was taken out.

"How?"

"He didn't say, but it was confirmed."

"When we get out to sea, let's all go below and sort this out. Franz, pull up the organizational charts and the financials for the Liddo and the Saris Groups. We'll go over it all when I come below."

"Franz, put the dead ones in a different color."

Franz said it might be easier to put the live ones in a different color.

John came below and, after making coffee, settled in with Franz and Ivan. They discussed possibilities; their consensus was that they were winning. "As far as I can see, Liddo is now controlled by Paula Franks." After the words came out of his mouth, he realized, "She is using me."

Ivan laughed. "You thought she liked you so much that she gave up her organization?"

"No, Ivan, I didn't think that, but this never occurred to me."

"You're a naïve American. How do you say it, you think everyone is on the smooth?"

"What? You mean 'on the level.'"

"Yes, on the level. She is using you to take over the Liddo Group, but that's not a problem because we know who she is."

"Ivan, you're right. She is using me and I've used her, but I'll get what I want and she won't."

They continued to study the computer charts. "Looking at this information, we have to focus on Saris now."

"John, we can't take our eyes off of Liddo. That woman is aggressive, she is in with Saris."

"She might be a snake, but maybe we can use that to our advantage."

"John, you might be coming around, let's have some vodka."

They broke for dinner. John went up on deck, took GPS readings and manual sextant readings. Comfortable that they were on course, he sat, relaxed, and looked up at the night sky. John had almost fallen asleep when the first round hit. The explosion knocked him off his seat. He looked around and saw the boat about a half mile directly behind them. He instinctively brought the boat around hard to starboard. It was the right tact; the boat lunged forward, and the mast swung over to the other side. Ivan had an M79 grenade launcher armed and ready, fired a round, but it landed short. "John, slow down. I don't have the range they do. I need to get closer."

John spun the wheel. "Duck!" He instructed as the mast flew over their heads. Their boat was now heading directly at the attackers. Another round hit almost a hundred yards behind them.

"John, can you make this thing go any faster? We'll only get two more attempts before they have a direct bead on us."

John knew that turning on the engines would only boost their speed marginally, but it might be enough. "How close do you have to be?"

"Close enough to hit them."

Franz ran below and came up with an RPG. "Where did you get that from?"

Franz put the RPG over his shoulder and climbed up the mast, but the sail was in front of him. Franz yelled down for John to turn hard to port. John spun the wheel hard to port. When the boat righted itself, he took aim and fired. There was a small explosion on the attack ship; a split second later, there was a much larger one. John and Ivan cheered just as another round landed nearby, too close for comfort. "How are they still firing at us?" Then they saw it; another attack boat came through the smoke.

"I got his one." Ivan had five grenades in the air before the first one splashed down. The third made contact with the boat. "John, see if there are survivors. Let's try to find out who sent them."

John headed toward the two attack boats. Franz ran below and came back with three machine guns. "Just in case we need them."

There didn't appear to be any survivors. Ivan said, "I hear something."

John and Franz looked at each other. Ivan ran to the bow. "Over there."

To their amazement, Ivan had heard and spotted two survivors. "It must be the vodka." They all laughed.

Franz pulled the men into the boat. Franz checked them for weapons while Ivan covered him. The two men lay on the deck like fish caught on a sport boat while Franz went below to fetch duct tape.

Franz came up on deck. Ivan looked at him for a second. One of the men jumped at Ivan with catlike speed. Ivan fired his weapon; the man's head flew across the deck.

Ivan kicked the body over the side and looked at the remaining interloper. "Well, my friend, it's just the two of us. I'm going to enjoy this." He kicked the man hard and hit him in the head with the barrel of his weapon.

"Who are you working for? I'm not going to ask you again." The man remained silent. Ivan put the barrel to the man's knee. "I didn't hear you." The man glared at him, and Ivan pulled the trigger. "I will ask you only one more time. Who sent you?"

The man screamed, "I'm a member of the Socialist Party."

"But who sent you?"

"I don't know."

Ivan put his weapon to the man's other knee. "No, please, no. I follow the orders of my group leader. I'm just one member of an elite military unit."

"Were you recently trained in Yemen?" He pushed the barrel into the man's knee and got the response he was looking for.

"Yes!"

"Where in Yemen?"

"A camp…ten kilometers from Al Hazm."

Ivan shot the man in the head and threw him overboard.

"Ivan, how could you do that? That's over the top. We're not animals."

"That man was a trained terrorist. I don't get any pleasure out of doing it, John, but if I didn't, the entire world might pay."

"I understand, but it's still wrong."

"John, that's between me and God. Franz, send a message to Chris. Tell him the terrorists are being trained at a camp ten kilometers from Al Hazm in Yemen."

John looked at Ivan and started to say something, but changed his mind.

"I'm going to have some vodka now." Ivan went below.

The following day, a group of SAS raided the camp in Al Hazm. Over a hundred terrorists-in-training were killed. The camp was obliterated.

# 110

### Gibraltar

"Serge, how good of you to come." Aristotle Saris greeted him. "Please, come in."

Alstead, the new head of the European Socialist Green Party, could not believe the opulence of this man's house. *He must be a very powerful man.*

"Serge, I understand how you feel, but you must understand that we are forging a new world order, and the capitalists will do anything to stop us."

"But, Mr. Saris, another one hundred of my best people have been killed since you got my note. I'm a union man, not a soldier."

"Ah, my friend, we're all soldiers fighting against the horrors of capitalism and imperialism."

"But, Mr. Saris…"

Saris stopped him. "Please, call me Aristotle. We're all brothers, no one man is subservient to the next."

"Ah. Aristotle, I'm a politician and a union organizer, I'm not keen on this. I have no choice but to resign immediately."

"You cannot do that. Could a father resign from his children, or could a man resign from his destiny? I think not."

Saris could sense that he was losing the argument. "Serge, we all have to do what we must. This is for you." Saris handed him an envelope. "Perhaps this will change your mind."

"Aristotle, I don't know what to say, ten million euros!"

"Say nothing, my friend. Sometimes we all need a little comfort in these troubled dangerous times." Saris walked him to the door. "Serge, I know you will make the right choice. If you need my assistance, do not hesitate to call."

When the door closed, Saris's body twitched with anger and his face turned dark red. *That coward does not deserve to be in a position of authority in my new world. He will die at my hand when the time is right.*

# 111

### Calais, France

Franz was setting up the computer and communication systems. John and Ivan were at the kitchen table. "Ivan, I can't get used to the brutality."

"John, I have had to realize that there are many evil people in the world, the likes of Liddo and Saris. When the government can't take care of problems through normal means, the intelligence community is the first and last line of defense protecting society. John, think of it like this: Your neighbor has a viscous dog. Every day when you walk by, he tries to bite you. What do you do? You go out, get a meaner dog, and let it solve your problem for you."

John was about to respond when Franz came over. "I just picked up an interesting piece of information. Serge Alstead just deposited ten million euros into his account."

"Franz, do you know where it came from?"

"Yes, I do. While the check was being deposited, ten million was withdrawn from a Saris account."

"Get that information to Chris right away. Tell him to act on it immediately. Contact Bob at the Web magazine and tell him to write an article on 'influence buying,' with Alstead as a prime example. Check the Saris accounts for funds transferred to scientific or environmental groups, give him that information. Tell him to release on my approval only. I'm going to London. See you tonight."

Ivan jumped up. "John, let me go with you."

"Ivan, I need you here to help Franz, just in case."

"Hello, Paula. It's John Moore. I need to see you right away."

"John, I don't think it's safe."

"I'll pick you up in front of your flat in one hour." John hung up. *I hope I'm doing the right thing.*

Paula was standing by the curb.

"Get in."

"John, it's good to see you, but I'm being watched by Saris's people. I'm not sure this was a good idea."

"Paula, I need exact details on illegal transactions between Saris and Liddo in the US."

"John, I told you from the beginning that I wouldn't do that."

"It'll all be blamed on Manheim, and he's dead."

"Are you sure?"

"Yes, Paula, I'm sure. You told me you wanted to do the right thing. Here is your chance."

⋯⋯⋯⋯⋯⋯⋯⋯⋯⋯

The next day, Igor walked up to the doorman at Paula's flat. "I am Igor. You have package for me?" The doorman handed a package to him, and he drove directly to Calais.

⋯⋯⋯⋯⋯⋯⋯⋯⋯⋯

"Son of a bitch, this is just what we needed. Franz, use your magic fingers and confirm these transactions with the banks."

"I'll try my best."

"They're confirmed. Here is the transfer information."

"Great work, Franz. Get this information to Colin, tell him I'll call him at ten tonight. Call Bob and tell him to release the story about Saris and Alstead, and be ready for another story. We have to get out of here, so pack up as soon as you're done. Igor or myself could have been followed."

Ivan agreed. "Good thinking, John."

John and Ivan were having a drink when Franz came up. "I sent out an article from Bob, it hit the Internet about five minutes ago." The headline reads, "Widespread Corruption and Influence-Peddling has Hit Europe."

"That should keep the bastard busy for a while."

"Ivan, the sad thing is there are so many politicians in his pocket, very little will come of this."

"John, you're right, but with the bloggers, you have gone to the people. The politicians might be afraid to do too much on behalf of Saris if enough people are angry."

"Ivan, that's a very good point."

John looked at his watch. "I have to call Colin."

"Colin, it's John. Did you get the message?"

"Yes, we're working on it. I have a slight problem, the AG is preventing me from handing out indictments."

John said, "That's why I called. I can have my Web magazine run the entire story, along with the evidence."

"John, that's fantastic, just what we need to get around these bastards."

"All right, Colin, let me know when you're ready and I'll pull the trigger."

"Sally will let you know."

# 112

**Washington DC**

Colin brought the news to ex-director Hancock.

While reading it, Hancock interjected, "Colin, if you bring this information to the AG's office, it will be covered up."

"I know that, but John Moore told me he would use his Web magazine to get the information out if necessary. Let's censure what we need to and then put together bullet points that they can develop into an article. Once it's been approved, you can go back to your congressional and senatorial teams and give them the hard evidence. The administration wouldn't dare cover it up at that point."

"Colin, as soon as I do that, you're going to be the scapegoat."

"I know, that's why I carry this." Colin took out a small recorder and played it. "This is my 'get out of jail' free card."

"Colin, I'm really glad you're on my side."

"Sir, I'm going to go home and get some sleep. Tomorrow's going to be a big day."

The ex-director chuckled. "Colin, thank you. You have done an exemplary job. No one but our little group will ever know it."

"That's why I get the big bucks, sir."

# 113

### Gibraltar

"I told you to hold all my calls."

"Sir, I hate to interrupt, but I think you should take this."

"Excuse me, gentlemen."

Saris followed his assistant. "Hello, Aristotle Saris here."

"Aristotle, it's Fabio, the inspector general. I've gotten requests from three countries, they want us to turn you over for questioning."

"Fabio, what's this about?"

"I'm not sure, but it might have something to do with the articles on the Web."

"What articles?"

"You haven't seen them? They mention details concerning payoffs to certain union leaders."

Saris had to sit down. "This is preposterous. I've never paid off anyone."

"Aristotle, I'm not your accuser. I told them all that you have broken no law here in Gibraltar that I am aware of, but there's nothing I can do. This is just a courtesy call."

"Thank you, Fabio, I won't forget this."

Fabio hung up the phone. *I hate that egotistical maniac. I'll be happy to see him go to prison.*

Visibly flustered, Saris went back to his guests and told them that something urgent had come up. As soon as the last guest left, he ran to his computer. His eyes bulged as he read the articles. He yelled, "I'll kill that bastard, that moron, I'll kill him!"

After he calmed down, he called Paula Franks. "Paula, it's Aristotle. Have you seen the lies on the Internet?"

"Yes, Aristotle, I have. Sarah's working on something to counteract these ridiculous fabrications, but we need a little time."

"Thank you, my dear. I will not forget this."

*I'm sure you won't, you disgusting little man.*

# 114

### Somewhere in the North Atlantic

John had just finished reading the bullet points from Colin. "Franz, get this to Bob at the magazine. Tell him to write the article but not to publish it until we see it. Colin will want to see it before it hits the Web."

"I contacted Bob. I received this from your girlfriend." He handed John the headlines from six European newspapers, postdated, "Aristotle Saris Wanted for Questioning in the Largest Racketeering Scandal to Hit Europe in Decades." Another read, "Aristotle Saris is Being Investigated for Murder in Connection with the Union Scandals." The last read, "Saris, There is Nowhere to Hide"

"Franz, maybe we've misread the woman."

"Don't count on that."

"Franz, send this to Colin, I'm sure he can use these."

"John, maybe you should wait, and send everything at once. It's only a matter of time before someone locates us."

"Ivan, good point. Franz, wait."

When the information was sent to Colin three hours later, they were unaware that the transmission had helped to locate them.

"Franz, what's the depth here?"

"Six fathoms."

"Okay, let's anchor here, relax, and have a drink."

"Ivan, what are you doing?"

"I need some exercise. I'm going for a row."

"All right, but take a light and a horn. It's dark out there."

They were laughing when the first explosion almost knocked them to the deck. "Get the weapons!"

Before they could get below, there were two more explosions. The boat almost flipped over. As the boat righted itself, they were all armed. "Port side!" Ivan used the grenade launcher; he hit it with the first shot. They heard another explosion; it covered their boat with debris.

"Listen, I hear something, two boats, they're circling. They're going to come at us from opposite directions, so be ready."

In a few seconds, they saw them: high-speed attack boats—one coming from starboard, the other from port. Both boats exploded, almost at the same time.

Floodlights were turned on, shining them on the surrounding area.

"What the hell was that?"

Ivan started to laugh.

"Ivan, I don't see anything funny here."

"John, when you were making drinks, I surrounded us with mines."

"I should've known you wouldn't go rowing just for exercise."

"I get enough exercise just raising glasses of vodka. They know where we are, so we better move fast. We have less than one hour to find a place to go ashore. By that time, they will know their people are dead—and by our hand."

"Where do you think we should go?"

Ivan looked at the charts. "We're going to Iceland."

# 115

**Washington DC**

The director called the meeting to order. "We have asked you here due to a grave situation within our government. We are in the midst of insurrection. Our country, and our way of life, is being taken over by several groups for their own gain. This is a covert takeover, it will end capitalism and the way we live as we know it.

"The scheme is near completion, we have to act now. All of our investigations have been foiled by political clout. The AG has been blocking us every step of the way. That's why I resigned and Colin took over in my stead. I want you all to know that he has put his life in danger by doing this."

Colin flashed *The Saris Group* and *The Liddo Group* up on a screen. "These are the main elements behind the takeover. They have used the Green and the Socialist movements to further their agenda."

A senator from North Carolina asked, "How did they do that?"

"As you all know, the Saris Group has funded environmental groups all over the world, regulations have changed, laws have been implemented, and businesses have been restricted. The Liddo Group has funded union politics and the socialist left by manipulating the unions and organizing large voting blocks. This has forced politicians to make grievous concessions to them. The Liddo Group has purchased or started 'green' businesses in every market. Using political capital, they have forced their competitors out of business or crippled them severely.

"These groups"—he flashed their names on the screen—"were all initially funded by Saris and Liddo. They have swung elections and been positioned to act as an enforcement group. Several days ago, the British SAS raided a terrorist camp in Yemen. Of the over one hundred killed, forty were Americans with known alliances to these groups."

One of the congressmen spoke up, "I didn't think those people were on the level. They're being run by criminals and terrorists. We are funding them, giving them massive contracts."

"This, the Emissions Control Act, is the arrow that found the heart. I know several of you voted for it, but you were unaware of the reasons behind it. You all know about the scientific debunking of the information that was originally supplied to you. The renowned scientists who supplied the original data were on the Saris or Liddo payrolls. Saris and Liddo have purchased, through intermediaries, all of the existing emissions credits offered here and through the UN."

"What the hell can they do with those?"

"The Liddo Group, fronting for Saris, has purchased all of the decommissioned coal-fired plants in the US and elsewhere. They plan to operate them at approximately half of the operating expense of gas or oil-fired plants. By the time their emissions credits would have been used up, they would have effectively put all of the other energy companies out of business. They plan to control our nation's energy. Control our energy, and you control the nation."

"That's crazy! If we nationalized the energy industry, we could stop that."

"Senator, two words: *cap* and *trade*."

The director put his hands up to quell some minor outbursts. "The control goes right to the top." After hearing the taped conversation between Colin and the chief of staff and then the conversations between the chief of staff and Wiley Pritchard, they all started to shout even louder.

After everyone quieted down, the director continued, "They're close to taking over. They have the unions, the Green Party, the liberals, and our top officials. We have to stop this now."

"What are you proposing?"

A plan was discussed.

"The plan could work, but do we really have enough power to pull it off? We need to have the backing of a lot more folks in Congress and the Senate."

"How do we do that?"

"You've been asked to come here because we know you're all above reproach. If the wrong people intercept this information before we act, we may lose."

"Director, do you know who is in on this up on the Hill?"

"Not everyone."

"If we had evidence that key figures were part of it, we could approach them quietly, tell them that if they don't play ball, we're going public. Most of them would protect themselves before they protect anyone else, especially when we have the goods on them."

"Yes, that's true. Let's reconvene in three days. Do not discuss this meeting with anyone, and return the information packages we gave you."

"Sir, I think I can accomplish the information gathering in two days. The quicker we act, the better."

"Okay, listen up, everyone. We'll reconvene in two days at ten."

When they left, Colin asked, "What do you think?"

"I hope we had it right, thinking these people are beyond reproach."

Colin went directly to the safe house. After he watched Sally send a message to John, he went to his office.

# 116

### Grindavik, Iceland

They had set up in a small guest cottage in Grindavik, a bleak little strip of land. Franz had set up the computers. Ivan was on his constant quest for vodka.

"John, here's an urgent message from Colin. He needs evidence on every senator or congressman who has taken money from Saris or Liddo. He wants us to run the story tomorrow, the one about Saris being investigated."

"I can get the story out tomorrow, but can you get the financial records in two days?"

"I can't on my own, but if I can get my friendly hacker to help…maybe."

"Call him now. Let's get this show on the road."

John called Bob and told him to run the story "as is" the following morning; then he called Paula Franks.

"Paula, I have some good news for you, the Americans are going to indict Saris."

"That's interesting news. Thank you very much, John."

He knew she would use this opportunity to put a final nail in Saris's coffin.

Franz called his friend in Zurich; they were working frantically, progress was slow. It took him almost an hour to investigate each person.

"Franz, I have a suggestion. Do you have that list of those who have been contacted by Pritchard?"

Franz responded positively.

"Look at the people on that list only, it will save you time."

"Ivan, that's a very good idea."

He pulled up the list and divided it in half. He took one half, his friend took the other.

Morning newspaper headlines and blogs throughout Europe and the United States exposed the corruption of the Saris Group.

In the meantime, Franz and his friend had compiled evidence on over one hundred senators and congressmen who had accepted contributions from Saris or the Liddo Group.

"Franz, you did a great job. It saddens me to see that the leaders of my country are so corrupt."

"They are politicians, not priests, John."

The information was sent to Colin. "Ivan, how long do you think we have until they find us again?"

"Perhaps a few days, they are probably looking for us in the UK."

# 117

**Washington DC**

The director called the meeting to order.

"You now have the updated information package. Note the one-hundred-plus people who have taken contributions from Saris or Liddo, look closely, some of your names are included."

The assembly erupted. "Hold on. We are targeting the second list of twenty. They have accepted funds into their personal accounts. I want you to form four-man teams. Each team will approach five congressmen or senators. Show them the information about themselves only, tell them that you received the information from the Justice Department. Tell them you have the authority to offer them a deal." Holding up a document, he continued, "If they sign this document, they will be granted immunity." He held up another document. "When they sign it, you will give them this document, it is signed by Colin, director of the FBI. If everyone signs it, you will represent twenty of our most senior senators and congressmen when we implement our plan. We must accomplish this task today."

Colin handed everyone a list containing the names of their group members and their assigned targets.

"We will meet in the Capitol Building rotunda at nine this evening."

When everyone assembled at the Capitol, all the documents were signed, except two. Reporters noticed the group and were curious. They were told that they would be given exclusives the following morning. The director asked Colin to call the chief of staff and arrange for an immediate meeting with the president.

"Rob, it's Colin. I have to meet with the president."

"Colin, where have you been? The president is pissed. Get over here right now."

Colin, the ex-director, and the four most senior senators arrived at the White House. The guard told Colin they were expected, called the chief of staff, and announced him.

Rob walked into the reception area; he paled. "What are all of you doing here?"

"Don't give us any shit, Rob. We're going to see the president."

"Everyone can't see him."

"We've called an emergency meeting of the Senate and we have invited the media. If we don't see him right now, he'll see us on television very soon."

"All right, but he's going to be angry."

"What's the meaning of this? I didn't schedule a meeting."

"Mr. President, we're here to offer you a deal. You will do as we suggest or you will be impeached and probably tried for treason."

"You're overstepping your bounds. I'll have you removed from the Senate."

"Sir, read this."

The president read through it; he seemed a bit uncertain. "You would never go after the presidency with this."

"Mr. President, twenty sworn affidavits calling for your impeachment. We will have two hundred by tomorrow, in the wake of recent headlines."

"Mr. President, may I present your personal and campaign account figures along with copies of transfers from the Saris and Liddo organizations. I also have documents showing ownership and monetary transfers of organizations that you were employed by before you became president. Sir, I am sorry, but if you do not cooperate, we will make this information public."

"What do you want me to say?"

The chief of staff screamed, "Don't say anything!"

Colin turned to Rob. "You're under arrest. You have the right to remain silent—"

The chief of staff ran out the door, calling for security. The president waved security away; he knew that it would be futile not to agree. "What do you want me to do?"

# 118

### Gibraltar

Saris knew it was the end for him. "Fabio, I'm so glad you're here. I want you to arrest every newspaper manager printing all those lies about me. Who do they think they are?"

"Aristotle Saris, I am placing you under arrest. I have been instructed by the World Court to detain you, come with me."

Saris smiled. "Dear Fabio, I will accompany you, but first let me get a few things from my desk." He pulled the trigger and was dead before he hit the ground.

"I will call the coroner." He shook his head and walked out.

# 119

### Washington DC

The next day, the president held a press conference. "I have decided that I will not run for reelection for personal reasons. Please, do not ask me any questions. Thank you."

An emergency meeting was held. It was decided that the president would not be impeached. But he would be stripped of his powers; a committee of four, representing both parties, would assist with the decision-making process for the remainder of the term.

Frank Hancock resumed the directorship of the FBI. Colin was installed as attorney general; the current AG resigned. A new chief of staff was appointed. Washington began to operate as usual after the recent political upheaval. Several indictments were handed down; ten senators and congressmen resigned.

Colin requested an investigation into the energy business. More indictments were issued. All of Saris's US funds were confiscated and used to dismantle coal-fired energy plants. The property would be turned over to the Federal Parks Commission.

Colin received an invitation.

> We would appreciate your presence at a dinner at the Fischstube Zurichorn, Bellerivestrasse, 160 Zurich CH 8008 on July 18th. 8 p.m.

# 120

### Zurich, Switzerland

Franz was waiting at the berth when John and Utsie arrived. "How was your holiday?"

"It was like a dream."

"Franz, how are you. Well rested?"

"I slept for days. If it wasn't for Ivan waking me up to have someone to drink with, I'd still be sleeping."

"Have our guests arrived?"

"Everyone's at the Bauer Lac except Colin, he'll arrive tomorrow. I had the things you bought taken to your suite."

"Thanks, Franz, what would I do without you?"

As John and Utsie walked into the lobby, Iris jumped on John, throwing her arms around him. He hugged her; he couldn't believe how good it felt seeing her. "Iris, you look beautiful. Did you enjoy Asia?"

"I loved it until I found out you were out saving the world without me."

John took her hand. "What's this?" A large engagement ring was on her finger.

"Brad and I are getting married. We were waiting for you to get back to give me away."

Brad walked up to them. John hugged them. "I'm so proud of you both."

"Well, if it isn't the mighty warrior."

Peter joined the group hug.

## GREEN TO RED

"Let's get cleaned up. Meet you at the Vodka Bar in two hours."

"Of all the fine restaurants in Zurich, why did you pick the Vodka Bar?"

"Because that's where I met you."

John was surrounded by the people he loved. "I never saw a bartender look like that after seeing Ivan put away the vodka. The more he drank, the sharper he got. He's still a mystery to me."

Everyone sat at a big table; they were drinking when Colin arrived.

"Sorry I'm late. I hope I didn't delay anything?"

"Not at all, we're glad to see you."

"I was waiting at the hotel for these to arrive." The plaques he handed John read,

> On behalf of the United States of America, we thank you.

They were also awarded the Medal of Honor for their role in preventing a disaster that could have affected the American way of life beyond reparation.

"Colin, this wasn't necessary but thank you."

Ivan said, "Can't a hero get a drink around here?"

"I have spent the last two years fighting, I've grown accustomed to it. I don't think building boats is going to keep my attention. I've just established a new company: SAFE."

"What the hell is that?"

"It stands for *S*trategic *A*lliance *f*or *E*veryone. I want to use our unique talents to help people who find themselves in desperate situations with no way out."

"If there's vodka involved, I'm in."

"Good, Ivan, but can I call on the rest of you if needed?"

They agreed.

"I hope I won't need your help any time soon. We've just beaten some of the most ruthless people on earth. I hope we can enjoy some peace for a while."

# 121

### London, England

Paula Franks walked onto the stage.

"I have asked you here to assure you that even though my predecessors overstepped their bounds, nothing has changed. The Liddo Group will continue to operate as before. We've enjoyed wealth and stability for our companies, it will only get better. We are too strong to be controlled. We will continue to grow without being hampered.

"One of my representatives will meet with each of you to explain the new rules. This is a new world for us, and we are in control of it."